I0637985

ARCHIVES

THE THRILLING LIBRARY:

ARCHIVES

VOLUME 1

BY

NORMAN A. DANIELS

INTRODUCTION BY

TOM JOHNSON

THRILLING PUBLICATIONS

2017

TABLE OF
CONTENTS

INTRODUCTION

TOM JOHNSON

REX PARKER was one of those late arrival masked crime fighters from Ned Pines' Standard pulp house, beginning in Fall 1940 with his own magazine, *The Masked Detective*, under the byline of C.K.M. Scanlon. This was the period when someone at Standard, probably Leo Margulies, the man in charge of the single character line for Pines at the time, was trying to revive their super hero pulps. The Phantom Detective and Dan Fowler (over at *G-Men Detective*) were also suddenly seeing some changes. Perhaps there was a slump somewhere. Sales were possibly dropping, and Leo may have been looking for some new characters. Whatever the situation, suddenly the Black Bat appeared in *Black Book Detective* in July 1939 and The Ghost popped up in January 1940. The Crimson Mask showed up in *Detective Novels* in August 1940, The Eagle appeared in *Thrilling Spy Stories* in Fall 1939, and the Purple Scar appeared in *Exciting Detective* in Fall 1941.

All of the new characters seemed a little off the beaten path, except for maybe the Black Bat and The Eagle. The Crimson Mask was a pharmacist by day, and crime fighter by night. The Ghost was a magician turned crime fighter, and the Purple Scar was, of all things, a plastic surgeon who turns to fighting crime after his brother is brutally murdered. The Masked Detective, more commonly referred to as the Mask, is uncommon in the fact that he isn't a young millionaire playboy. In fact, he isn't rich at all, holding down a low-wage job as a reporter for a second rate newspaper. But that doesn't stop him from wearing a domino mask and busting up gangs of criminals and uncovering murderers! In fact, I kind of liked the guy.

Pulpster Norman Daniels, while knocking out the Black Bat, also kicked off the Crimson Mask, The Eagle and the Masked Detective—along with some other new characters along the way. Daniels had already been churning out Phantom Detective yarns, and probably some of the

Dan Fowler tales that we're not aware of. He had started out slow in the mid 1930s, but by the 1940s was very prolific. Mr. Daniels was ideal as the scribe for the Mask, unfortunately he was busy with the Black Bat and other chores, so only turned out a handful of the first novels, then the series was handed off to other authors, among them Sam Merwin, Jr., G.T. Fleming-Roberts, W.T. Ballard, and Lawrence Donovan—that we've been able to identify. Four stories remain unidentified.

Of the late-comers, only the Black Bat was long-lasting, continuing until 1952 and 61 issues. The Ghost (later changed to the Green Ghost) lasted only 14 stories. The Purple Scar had a worse record with only four stories and The Eagle followed with five stories. The Crimson Mask made it for 16 stories. Sadly, The Masked Detective could survive for only 12 issues in his own magazine, then he was relegated to the pages of *Thrilling Mystery* for a thirteenth entry, and then vanished.

Rex Parker has a lazy appearance, but is actually an expert at *la savate*, the French fighting technique of boxing with the feet, making him one of the first martial artist long before Bruce Lee's Kato. Although, the World's Greatest Detective, the Phantom often used this technique in his own battles with crimedom. However, after Daniels leaves the series, the Mask also eventually drops the use of *la savate* in the stories, making him just another masked vigilante. In fact, Donovan's later entry, "Candles of Murder" (Spring 1943), is merely a reworking of one of his Phantom Detective yarns, barely resembles Rex Parker. Finally, in the *Thrilling Mystery* story, "Monarchs of Murder" (Fall 1944), he doesn't even wear a mask, and at one point uses jujutsu instead of *la savate*, and we're told that he was taught judo by Winnie Bligh, the love interest in the series. "Monarchs of Murder" may have started out as a novel length entry, but ended up in a drawer when the decision was made to cancel the magazine title. An editor probably cut the wordage to novelette length to fit in Thrilling Mystery. A shame.

The characters involved in the stories are, of course, the formula for all such series: Rex Parker, the title's hero, Winnie Bligh, the love interest, and the ever-present bumbling police officer, Det.-Sgt. Dan Gleason of Homicide. The plots were regular run-of-the-mill murder mysteries for the most part, with the occasional Fifth Column Nazi stuff. All of it very typical fair for the 1940s pulp detective/super hero stories appearing in all of the titles.

Unfortunately, with the war starting in Europe and the paper shortage, it was a bad time for the pulp magazines, especially the new, untried single character titles that had recently hit the stands. Plus, it's likely that many of the writers were joining the war effort in some capacity.

All of this resulted in fewer and thinner magazines. Perhaps, if Norman Daniels could have remained with the series, the Masked Detective could have survived as a companion title to Standard's other popular heroes.

Alas, it wasn't to be.

Happy Reading!

Tom Johnson
Seymour, Texas

I

ALIAS THE MASKED DETECTIVE

CHAPTER I

CRIME STRIKES HOME

DR. JAMES TRENT, young curator of Egyptology, laid down his newspaper and sighed deeply. He removed his glasses and looked over toward where his wife sat knitting and softly humming to herself.

"Double headlines these days, my dear," he said. "War scareheads and some sort of a local war we have right here in our own city. In a way the one we have to fight is much like that which is ravaging Europe."

"Local war, James?" His wife frowned, wrinkling her pretty forehead.

"Yes," he answered. "In Europe certain belligerent powers act exactly like gangsters—hoodlums. If there is something they want, they simply move in and take it. If it's someone they dislike—there's a brick wall and a grave of lye. But mark you—they don't pick on strong and powerful victims. No, that would be too dangerous."

"I can't understand how you compare them with something going on right here, James," Mrs. Trent said.

Dr. Trent held up the newspaper, pointing to the bold headlines.

"This is what I mean. Two more men murdered in cold blood by gangsters. Shot in the back without a chance to fight for their lives. The reporter who wrote this article knows his business. Some chap named Rex Parker. He relates how these two killings bring the total up to the astounding figure of twenty-nine. Nervy fellow too—says the police can't do a thing even though they suspect who is behind the murders. No evidence. But, this Rex Parker goes on to say that if the police can't do something, there ought to be another agency, outside the law if necessary, to handle these murderers. Sound psychology too. Gangsters only hold the upper hand because they carry guns and are not squeamish about committing murders."

Dr. Trent glanced at the clock over has mantelpiece. He arose and removed his smoking jacket.

The two thugs blasted Dr. Trent down without the slightest signs of regret.

"Almost eight o'clock. I'll have to hurry or I'll miss the lecture tonight—and I'm the principal speaker."

His wife held his coat and vest, adjusted his tie and fussed with the handkerchief sticking out of his breast pocket. She handed him a gray fedora and helped him on with his topcoat. She kissed him lightly, patted his cheek and with a smile watched him walk down the apartment corridor.

DR. TRENT nodded to the doorman, and walked with a springy step along the quiet street. Abstractedly he saw a car parked half a block away and he noticed that the exhaust was emitting white vapor showing the engine was running. Mentally rehearsing the lecture he was to give. An interesting lecture, for he was going to demonstrate it by removing the shrouds from a mummy.

He was so engrossed in his own thoughts that he wandered to the wrong portion of the sidewalk. Suddenly he was almost hurled off his

feet by a collision with a bulky man who came out of an alley. Dr. Trent murmured a routine apology, then a smile crossed his face.

"Well, Officer Casey—it's good to see you back from your vacation. Wife and children all right?"

Casey's red face broke into a broad grin. "Fine and dandy, Doctor. I understand my beat has been nice and quiet since I've been away. Maybe the crooks are just waiting for me to come back. The murdering rats. Well—good night, sir."

Dr. Trent bowed. Good old Casey. If there were a few hundred more like him on the force, those murdering, thieving gangsters wouldn't flourish quite so well.

Trent was about twenty steps from the corner when two men stepped out of the shadows of a doorway. They hurried up, separating as they neared him. At the same moment the car parked down the street a bit, began rolling slowly along, keeping close to the curb.

Someone seized Dr. Trent's arm and whirled the startled man about. A cruising taxi slowed and the driver gaped.

"So you decided to show your lousy face after all, eh, Joiner? Don't start putting on the weeps. You know what's been coming to you and it comes—right now."

"But—but there's some mistake," Trent started to say. "I—I'm sure you have the wrong...."

A gun was rammed into his stomach. Before Trent could finish, the gun blasted. Six times—until every chamber was empty. Trent jerked as each slug smashed through his body. He stood swaying like a drunken man. His lips moved, trying to utter words. No sound came; only a trickle of blood. Then he slowly buckled up, pitched forward and lay very still on the pavement.

The second thug stepped over him, deliberately aimed his gun and pumped two more slugs—through the back of Dr. Trent's skull.

"That," the killer yelled, "is for rats like you, Joiner!"

The other man grabbed his companion's arm and pulled him to the car. Patrolman Casey was running toward them, yanking his gun free. The thug with four bullets remaining in his gun, scowled and raised the weapon. Casey's gun blazed and the bullet hit the back of the car. Then Casey was dead—instantly—with the murderer's slug through his heart.

Both killers leaped into the back seat of the car and it streaked away with a nerve shattering clash of gears. The taxi driver hastily wrote down the marker plate numbers, then began yelling frantically for the police. He didn't start in pursuit. The manner in which those men had committed two murders impressed him far too much.

WITHIN FIVE minutes radio cars blocked the street while others were on the alert for a maroon sedan with certain marker numbers. An official sedan pulled up and two men emerged. One was Chief Inspector Mullane, a dour, gray-haired man whose appointment to this high office had been political.

But Mullane had taken his job seriously and handled it well. His face was grim as he looked down at the sprawled-out figure. It grew even more solemn as he looked toward Patrolman Casey, crumpled in a heap on the sidewalk.

The second man was shorter, stockier and wore a hat with a turned-up brim which made his fat face seem even wider. A cold cigar bobbed up and down between his teeth—the only sign of emotion that he betrayed.

"Another one," Inspector Mullane groaned. "Sergeant Gleason, you're on the Homicide Squad. This case is in your hands. Find the men who did this. Don't rest until they are in a cell."

A uniformed lieutenant stepped up and saluted.

"Looks like another of those gang killings, sir. Several bullets fired through the man's stomach and then two more through the back of his head. I picked up the slugs."

He rolled two chunks of lead in the palm of his hand.

"Just another crook, I suppose," he went on. "A cruising taxi driver saw it all. He said that there were two killers and one man in a getaway car. They acted swiftly, but he did hear both of them mention the name of the victim. They called him 'Joiner.'"

"Joiner Seddon," Sergeant Dan Gleason muttered. "He used to work for a phony union and they nicknamed him Joiner because he used to walk up to a prospective worker and just tell him to join. If he refused— brass knuckles. I…. Wait a minute. Inspector, look at the dead man's feet. He's wearing button shoes. They're as old-fashioned as a horse-drawn patrol wagon. Joiner wouldn't be caught dead wearing a pair of shoes like that."

Sergeant Gleason dropped to his knees beside the body and gently raised the dead man's head. He lowered it even more gently and his eyes were narrow and cold. He slipped a hand into the pockets of the corpse, extracted several pieces of paper, a letter and a notebook. He arose slowly.

"This time it isn't just another gangster killing," he said between his teeth. "This dead man is Dr. James Trent—something to do with the museum. The mugs who were planted to rub out Joiner Seddon made a mistake. A bad mistake, Inspector. Trent's address is on this envelope. Somebody has to go there."

A long, slender arm reached above the shoulders of several policemen gathered in a circle around the corpse. Tapering and strong looking fingers lifted the papers from Sergeant Gleason's hand. Gleason didn't even turn around.

"So you're here, Parker. I'll bet you can smell blood ten miles away."

The man with the long arm elbowed his way to Gleason's side. He touched a finger to a rather battered hat in due respect to the chief inspector. He was a little taller than average and if he had only shaved in the last thirty-six hours and had worn clothes that fitted better, he might have been mistaken for a romantic movie star.

REX PARKER, ace crime reporter for the New York *Comet,* was not an ambitious man. In fact such aspirations never entered his head. He collected a hundred and ten dollars every week for reporting crime news and he was satisfied. He took a piece of folded paper from his pocket and made a few notes.

"So they finally got the wrong man, eh?" he said. "Too bad. I knew this Dr. Trent. Nice guy, too. I fell asleep a couple of times listening to his lectures on mummies, but I don't hold that against him."

Sergeant Gleason hurled his cigar into the gutter, shoved a fresh one into his mouth, but didn't light it. Gleason never lit a cigar until his nerves were ripped to shreds. Rex Parker stepped over beside him.

"Sarge, we ought to go tell the poor guy's wife, eh? He's got no kids. I know where he lives."

Gleason fell into step with his taller companion. They stopped beside the body of Patrolman Casey. Gleason thrust his hat to the back of his head.

"Rex," he said slowly, "Mullane gave me the assignment to run these killers straight into the electric chair. You know just as well as I do, how impossible that is. What'll I do? See Joiner Seddon? He won't know a thing. Check up on the mugs who don't like him? So what? They'll have alibis tighter than a snare-drum. Then I'm a monkey again. I stand on the carpet and catch merry Hades because I couldn't do what no man on the force has been able to do—crack this wave of murders."

Rex Parker didn't answer right away. He seemed lost in thought and when he did speak, his voice was so low that he seemed simply to be thinking aloud.

"Thirty-one murders in less than eight months. Something should be done. If it can't be handled with the law, then to the devil with law. These killers don't abide by any rules."

They turned into the apartment where Dr. James Trent had lived.

CHAPTER II

ENTER CAPTAIN BLIGH

REX PARKER maintained what he called bachelor quarters in Greenwich Village. Anyone who peered through his windows would have agreed with his description. It looked as though no woman's hand had touched anything in those two rooms for years, though a discouraged housekeeper did clean up daily.

Parker's coat hung on one chair, his vest was flung across another. His hat lay on the floor where it had fallen after missing a hook. His shoes were lying just as they had dropped off his feet. His tie lay in a crumpled ball.

In the adjoining room, with the curtains carefully pulled down, was a different Rex Parker, a man whom his colleagues in the press rooms at Police Headquarters would have given a week's pay to see. Rex Parker still wore his shirt, open at the throat now. His trousers were of black silk and fitted the calves of his legs tightly. A pair of soft, flat-heeled shoes were on his feet. He looked much like a dancing master.

Suddenly the buzzer at his front door startled him. He forgot how he was dressed and ambled flat-footedly to the door. He threw it open and stared at a girl who gaped back at him in turn.

She was an amazing bit of femininity, this girl. About as tall as Parker, with raven-black hair worn rather short and a supple, graceful form. Her eyes were clear blue, her lips exactly right. In fact Rex Parker thought no other person in the world could be so just right. Even if he never betrayed this to the girl.

Winnie Bligh stepped into the room, pushed the saucy little hat she wore to the back of her head and began walking around Parker slowly, looking down at the close-fitting silk pants. She placed a smooth white finger against her nose and nodded.

"If you learn to bow properly, I've no doubt they'll present you to the king next year. You have the legs of someone the king might want to meet. Very nice legs. Why haven't you shown me them before?"

Rex Parker gulped, turned red and hastily kicked the door shut. He ran a finger around his collar, which was wide open.

"Well, you see, Winnie, I—I…. Oh, what the devil! Come in the other room and I'll show you what's up."

He preceded her, walking with long, angry paces. There was a dummy in the middle of the floor. A life-size model with its base rounded so it could be knocked over and bounce right back into a vertical position again.

Rex stepped close to it. His right foot came up in a flash which the eye could hardly follow. The dummy went careening to one side. As it bounced back, Rex's foot moved again. This time the toe caught the dummy full in the face and sent it rocketing backward. As it rebounded, his foot caught the dummy's head again in a lightning blow.

"But what on earth?" Winnie Bligh asked.

Rex Parker faced her. "This is what they call *la savate.* It's a French way of dirty fighting. Saw a guy do it one day and got interested. Say do you know it's possible to tackle two or three men at once with this stuff? You kick their faces in—that's how it goes."

WINNIE BLIGH seized Parker's arm and piloted him into the next room. She plopped him into a chair and pulled another directly opposite.

"So that's how you kill spare time," she said hotly. "I read your story about the murder of Dr. James Trent and that poor policeman, Casey. It was a good story, Rex. It makes you want to get up and find those gangsters. Kick their faces in just like you did to that—that dummy. Oh, Rex, why won't you do something about all this murder and violence? You got it in you. I know you have because you helped Gleason solve a few involved cases."

Rex Parker closed his eyes wearily and sighed.

"Again we have to go through this. Why don't you cut it out, Winnie? Always getting behind me to kick me in the pants. If I let you push me around, I—I'd be like a—a…. Listen, I got a name for you. Winnie Bligh doesn't suit your type. It's Captain Bligh to me and I don't know of a more piratical, dictatorial, pusher-around than he was. I'll lay five to one he's related to you.

"Why don't I go and round up those human vultures who think no more of a man's life than they do of a cigarette butt? Look—I get a week's pay to write for my so-called public. I do it the best I know how. I'm not paid to go around shoving out my neck for some ratty-faced gangster to shoot off. Why don't you stick to your beauty and heart throb column? Nobody is asking you to go after those lugs."

Winnie leaned forward.

Rex Parker, the Masked Detective

"Listen to me, Rex Parker. Nobody paid Dr. Trent to take eight bullets through his body either. Patrolman Casey got fifty-five dollars a week to risk his life, and he did it without a murmur. Every policeman, in or out of uniform, is constantly on the spot. Do they complain? But they're handicapped—by things known as laws. They can't break them any more than ordinary citizens can. If this gang of killers is to be wiped out, it must be done by someone who will fight them with their own weapons. Someone who won't care any more about laws than they do. And you're the man, Rex. I've always thought so."

Rex groaned.

"Look, Captain Bligh—"

"Stop calling me Captain Bligh," Winnie snapped. "I don't like it."

Rex grinned. "As I was saying, Cap'n, only a few hours ago I helped Sarge Gleason break the news to Dr. Trent's widow. She took it like a soldier, but I know how she suffered. Right then, if I'd had one of those killers by my side, I swear I'd have committed murder too. But I cooled off. It's none of my business. Suppose I go out, as you suggest, and throw laws overboard—fight those rats with their own kind of claws. What will it get me? A nice cell with a wooden pallet to sleep on until they throw me in a death cell at Sing Sing. Oh no, baby, I don't like that kind of life. It's too short."

"Rex," Winnie said slowly, "what if they didn't know you were Rex Parker. I've got it all figured out. You know how seriously I take my work—especially that side of it which has to do with helps to beauty. Well, I've studied every angle of makeup. I've watched plastic surgeons do their stuff and learned a lot from them. I could change that long face of yours so you'd start to shake hands with yourself if you saw your own reflection in the mirror.

"No one has to know you're this new kind of gang buster. Think of the stories you'll get out of it! Think how you'll feel when those rotten, mealy-mouthed crooks run from you! Think how it would seem if you'd adopted this work yesterday and today saved Mrs. Trent that heartache—and Mrs. Casey and her children."

REX PARKER was staring off into space. Every word that Winnie uttered struck home. Every since he had been a police reporter he had studied the lay-outs, looked for clues, offered theories and enjoyed every minute of it all.

When, through his efforts, some sniveling killer reached the end of his rope, the satisfaction in his soul may have been grim, but it was also completely full. He was just as much a detective as Gleason or any of his associates. Scientific backgrounds were simple for him. He'd majored in science and attended all the post mortems he could worm his way in to see.

Then he shrugged. This was too much like a dream.

"No soap, Cap'n. It just can't be done."

"Rex Parker," Winnie said sternly, "you'll either listen to me until I'm through or I—I'll put you in my beauty column tomorrow. I'll even run your picture and tell how you keep your slender shape by exercising with a dummy."

Rex Parker sat up straight. "Holy smoke, Winnie, you wouldn't do that?"

"I'll make a series out of it," Winnie said flatly. "I'll tell how you've trained yourself in rough-and-tumble fighting and you're too scared to go out and kick a few gangsters in the teeth. Will I do it? Huh! Read tomorrow's paper."

She half arose and Parker seized her arm.

"I'd rather be crucified, Winnie. Listen—I'll do this much. I'll let you see if I can take makeup. Ill give it a whirl to that extent."

Winnie threw both arms around him and kissed him full on the lips. Then she sped to the door.

"Come to my apartment as soon as you're dressed. I'll get things ready. And don't keep me waiting. I might get inspiration for a beauty item about a man who wears silk pants."

Parker lit a cigarette and rubbed the back of his neck as he resumed his chair. Now he really had let himself in for something. With Winnie always behind him, encouraging, taunting, pushing, he was sunk. She'd force him to go through with it. Then a queer light came into Parker's eyes. Was it necessary to push him into this thing? Did he really need a Captain Bligh to chide him into seeing what was right?

He ground out the cigarette and began peeling off his clothes. When he was fully dressed he opened a drawer in his bureau and extracted a .45 automatic. He examined the clip, saw that it was full and then pumped a slug into the firing chamber. He'd have to do something about this gun though. He had a permit but the serial numbers of the weapon were listed on that permit and filed at Police Headquarters.

He slid the weapon into his back pocket, buttoned his coat and jammed on the battered fedora. Then he walked out and took an uptown subway express for Winnie's apartment.

CHAPTER III

JOINER LAUGHS—ONCE

SERGEANT DAN GLEASON stood near the door of "Joiner" Seddon's apartment, in the same building where Dr. Trent had lived. Seddon looked worried but defiant too.

"I'm telling you, Sarge, there ain't nobody who would want to gun me out. Sure I know maybe this Trent was mistook for me, but I still say I don't know nothing about it. Don't you think I'd sing when maybe them bozos will try to get me next?"

"No," Gleason growled. "You wouldn't sing because you've got some damned fool code of ethics which says a squealer is the lowest of the low. And you're scared. Sure they'll knock you off, too. I'm sorry that they didn't land you instead of Dr. Trent, who was of some use to the world. You're about as much value to humanity as a louse on a monkey's tail. All right, you won't talk. I could put the cuffs on you right now, hold you as a suspicious person and the courts would back me up because I'd be trying to save your life. But why should I? You're not interested in trying to protect your own skin."

Seddon grinned.

"Aw, have a heart, Sarge," Joiner protested. "Look—maybe you oughta put a guard around me, huh? Cops are supposed to see that murders ain't committed. How about a couple of flatfeet to stand outside my door and go with me when I travel around on business?"

"The only thing I'd throw around you is a cell," Gleason snapped, and walked to the door. "You had a chance to talk and you won't. Well, if you want protection, you can amble down to Headquarters and ask to be locked up. If I put the pinch on you, there'd be a shyster at the booking sergeant's desk before I dragged you in. You can come with me if you like."

Joiner's eyes showed the terror that raged within him, but he had reasons for not wanting to enter a police station, even voluntarily. They might take his prints. So far he had no record, but if they printed him, there'd be one—headed by murder.

He was distinctly between two fires. If he went with Gleason, perhaps he'd eventually land in a death cell. If he stayed here, it was possible that death might come sneaking into the apartment at any time of the day or night.

"I'll stick here," he told Gleason. "I ain't scared. Nobody is after me, see? Never mind the guards. That Trent guy musta been mistaken for some other mug—not me."

Gleason shrugged and walked out. Joiner Seddon wiped sweat off his face and shivered. Of course Gleason had been right. They had mistaken Dr. Trent for him. Joiner was sure of that because almost all of his friends were dead. Not being a prominent or influential member of the mob, he'd be at the bottom of the list, but the bottom was being scraped now and his time had come.

Joiner arose, poured himself a tumbler half full of whiskey and drank it in three gulps. He felt a little better after the alcohol stiffened his courage a bit. Walking into an adjoining room, he took two big suitcases out of the closet and began filling them. He couldn't go to the police for protection and every second he spent in this apartment building was dangerous. If the killers had mistaken Trent for him, then certainly they knew he was hiding out here. It was time to lam, and the more distance he put between himself and New York, the safer he would be.

JOINER DIDN'T put on one of his expensive suits. He donned a cheap, threadbare suit, fished a pair of smoked glasses out of his trunk and put them on. He would take the back way out of this apartment, reach a cab and run for the nearest airport. Joiner had money enough. His pocket bulged with bills of large denominations.

Winnie Bligh

He picked up his two bags and hurried into the next room. Then he let both suitcases bang to the floor. Behind the dark glasses his eyes grew round and terror-stricken. Someone was in the room, someone who sat in a high-backed chair. Joiner couldn't see the intruder, but he watched a spiral of cigarette smoke curl upward.

"Come over here, Joiner," a calm voice urged. "I want to talk to you."

Joiner licked his lips. One hand stole toward his hip pocket and extracted a gun. Suddenly he lunged forward, faced the man in the chair and gaped, open-mouthed. His visitor was dressed in a neat black suit. He wore a gray shirt and a dark bow tie. A sleek black hat was tilted at a perfect angle—and his visitor wore a velvet mask which covered his eyes, forehead and nose.

"What—what—?" Joiner stammered.

"Put the gun away and sit down," the masked man said. "If you possess any brains at all, perhaps I can help save your worthless life."

Joiner's jaw snapped shut with a click and the corners of his mouth drew down. He leveled the pistol and stepped back a pace.

"No, you don't. Just because you're wearing a mask don't mean you ain't one of Cal Carson's boys. You came here to knock me off. Well, you're going to get it instead! Stand up so I can frisk you."

The masked man arose and his mouth twisted into a strange smile. He raised both arm and shoulder high.

"Joiner," he said stonily, "I said, 'Put the gun away.'"

Joiner made a derisive sound in his throat and then gave a nasty laugh.

"Turn around, sucker, while I see if you're heeled."

The masked man moved slowly. Something flashed upward and Joiner found that his gun was sailing toward the ceiling and his whole arm had gone completely numb. The masked man's right foot had traveled so fast that Joiner didn't even know how he had been unarmed so efficiently. The masked man sat down again.

"Relax, Joiner," he said. "Stop playing the fool. I said I was here to help you. I'm aware that another man was mistaken for you a few hours ago and he died because of that error. Those rats meant to kill you, which means you must know who they are. Talk, Joiner. Wag that tongue of yours."

Joiner scowled. "I don't know nothing about it."

Half a second later Joiner sat in a chair, but not of his own volition. He shook his head and tried to figure out what had happened. Then a strong hand grabbed him by the collar and shook him until his teeth rattled.

"Sing, Joiner," the masked man urged quietly. "Sing or I'll knock your stupid head off. When Gleason was here, you had a choice of accepting his protection or taking your own chances. Now you no longer have that opportunity. You can only choose between death at the hands of those killers—or death right here!"

JOINER GULPED and licked his lips.

"You're nuts," he wheezed. "That mask don't kid me none. You're just a copper like Gleason and you wear the mask to scare me. But I don't scare. No masked detective can make me rat."

"Masked detective." The visitor nodded in satisfaction. "You've christened me, Joiner, but in a way you're wrong because I don't own a badge. Gleason couldn't bang you around because he's handicapped by law. I'm not, so would you like another punch on the nose or will you talk?"

Joiner was a coward, but he was also big and brawny. Fifty men had gone down under his savage onslaughts. Two or three of them had never awakened. This masked man was no giant in size, nor in strength, so far as he could see. He was a fool, too, or he'd have picked up the gun and held it.

Joiner suddenly shot out of his chair, made a lunge straight for the masked man and bounced back, hit the wall, and sat down on the floor ungracefully. He tried to puzzle things out. The masked man's hands hadn't moved. What had delivered that terrific wallop which lifted him completely off his feet?

The Masked Detective hauled Joiner back on his feet, held him at arm's length and poised a right fist that loomed up like the side of a mountain in the crook's eyes.

"I'll ask you once more, Joiner. Only once. Who sent those men to kill you? Who is responsible for all the murders that have been committed during the last eight months? I'll wait exactly half a minute."

Joiner knew when he was licked. He would rather have felt a bullet smash through him than that menacing fist full in the face. Joiner wasn't used to this kind of treatment. Usually he was the man who held the upper hand in everything.

"I—I'll talk if you promise to put me in a safe place. I'll tell everything I know. Just protect me, that's all I ask."

"I'll put you where those killers can never get you," the Masked Detective promised. "But I want the truth. If you lie, I'll know it."

Joiner indicated the flask of whiskey by jerking his head. The Masked Detective let him take a huge jolt. Then Joiner talked—so fast that sometimes he lost the thread of his story.

"It's Cal Carson. He's a hot shot from the West. Came to town a year ago and started taking over. Them who stood in his way got blasted. I was one of Charley Morelli's boys and Charley was on the spot. Carson just began wiping us out. So I lammed and hid. Then I read about other boys being chopped down.

"Y'see, some of the important mugs joined Carson's mob. Little guys like me knew too much so we were slated for the executioner. Maybe I know a few other things, too, but I ain't talking any more until I know I'm safe. You're right—I don't owe Carson nothing. When I really sing, you'll hear plenty. Now, how do I get protected?"

"Sit down at the desk, Joiner," the Masked Detective said. "Put in writing all you have told me. Sign it and then I'll take care of you."

Joiner Seddon was in a mood to do anything. His terror had reached the stage of frenzy. He wondered if this masked man could even get him out of the building without being riddled with bullets. Joiner wrote his confession and almost eagerly affixed his signature. Somehow he found that he trusted this masked man. There was something about those steady eyes that peered from behind the velvet mask to reassure his warped little soul.

The Masked Detective stuffed the confession in his pocket and walked toward the door. Joiner rushed after him.

"You ain't gonna give me the double cross?" he pleaded. "You ain't running out on me?"

"Stay here," Joiner was told. "I've got a car around the corner. I'll bring it directly in front of the apartment and then come back for you. Stay away from any windows facing the court. Let no one in."

CHAPTER IV

A GIFT FOR GLEASON

THE MASKED man closed the door and peered around the corridor for a moment. Then he walked nonchalantly toward the elevators and stripped off his mask on the way. The face which was revealed looked nothing like that of Rex Parker, ace crime reporter on the *Comet*. It was rounder, somewhat darker of complexion and the nicely shaped nose of Rex Parker had become flatter. His voice was different, also, for he had practiced a long time on gruff, husky tones. He must remember that, he told himself, whenever he took his masked man identity.

The Masked Detective rode to the lobby, walked leisurely out of the building and betrayed no interest in a car parked across the street, nor in the man who lounged against the side of the apartment building not far from the entrance. This time there were only two killers. Evidently they felt sure of themselves.

Walking across the street the Masked Detective fumbled in his pocket and found a cigarette. He stopped beside the parked car and searched his pockets. Then he apparently noticed for the first time that a man sat behind the wheel of the car.

"Mind giving me a light?" he asked and stuck his head in the window of the automobile.

The driver eyed him suspiciously but with a shrug, handed over a pack of matches. The Masked Detective lit one, puffed a couple of times and handed them back. But the same fist gripped a gun.

"Just call to your pal and tell him to come over here," the Masked Detective said stonily. "That is, unless you'd like to die."

The thug took one look at the face of this stranger and decided it would be healthy to obey. He yelled to his partner and the second thug hurried across the street. Before he could reach for his gun, the Masked Detective had him covered.

"Get inside the back seat, gentlemen," he urged the two killers. "If you want to shoot it out, reach for your guns. I don't mind killing off rats. If you think it unwise to shoot it out, then remove your neckties instead."

Five minutes later both thugs were trussed up and disarmed. The Masked Detective pushed them to the floor and threw a blanket over them. Then he got behind the wheel, turned the car around and parked it directly in front of the apartment entrance.

It was almost two in the morning and there was no doorman. He made sure his two guests could not get loose, then he hurried back to Joiner's apartment. The frightened crook's voice came in a quavering reply to his knock and the door opened a crack.

"Never mind your suitcases," the Masked Detective said. "You won't need 'em where I'm taking you. Let's go!"

Joiner came out, started back when he noticed his visitor was no longer wearing a mask, then he sighed. He might as well see it through. They rode to the lobby. The Masked Detective walked ahead, wandered out to the sidewalk and made certain no other killers were posted in the neighborhood. Then he signaled Joiner and the crook came dashing out. He jumped into the front seat of the car and shivered violently.

"Hurry, will you?" he begged. "Carson's boys may be hiding around the next corner."

"Look in back—pull up that blanket," the Masked Detective chuckled. "Carson's boys are hiding all right, but I don't think they like it very much."

Joiner looked and heaved a great sigh of relief as he let the blanket drop back on the two trussed-up killers.

"Say, brother," he told the Masked Detective, "you don't fool around, do you? I'm beginning to think I used my head by going with you."

The Masked Detective stepped on the starter and the motor purred smoothly. He grinned at Joiner. "For the first time in your life you've told the truth. Now if you want to see something else, bend down and have a look near your feet."

JOINER BENT over and the Masked Detective's fist came down to crack against the back of the crook's neck. Joiner felt no pain, for the blow was scientifically placed. The various autopsies which Rex Parker had witnessed had provided some excellent lessons in anatomy and he had forgotten none of it.

He drove the car straight toward Police Headquarters, parked it only a short distance away from the entrance and waited while a squad of patrolmen filed out. Then he took a square piece of paper from his pocket and hastily scribbled a message. He got out of the car, laid Joiner across the seat and made a slit in the message he had written so that it could be fastened to one of Joiner's vest buttons. He placed Joiner's confession beside it.

Then he took a match from his pocket, shoved it down between the horn button and the driving shaft. When it was well wedged into place, he gave the horn a hard push. It roared and the bit of match held it down.

The Masked Detective sprinted away into the night. As he rounded the corner, another car started moving slowly and the door opened. He leaped into the back seat. Winnie Bligh was at the wheel.

"How did it go, Rex?"

"Neat—very neat. I tossed Joiner around a bit to make him talk and he spilled plenty. He's in a car where Sergeant Gleason is bound to find him. Now keep your eyes on the road. I'm changing back to Rex Parker's pants."

After he had changed clothes, Parker removed the disguise.

"Captain Bligh," he said in an apologetic voice, "I withdraw all the harsh statements I made about your idea. It's grand fun and I've accomplished something too. What a story I have for the next edition! Also I have a name. From now on I'm the Masked Detective. Joiner's puny little brain thought that one up."

"It's good," Winnie said as she swung around a corner. "Are you Rex Parker again—completely? You've got to get back to Headquarters fast. If a man ever needed alibis, that man will be you. From now on you have two identities. And Rex—how can you write these stories up without giving yourself away?"

He laughed. "Easy. The Masked Detective is a personal friend of mine and he gives me the lowdown on everything. You don't think I'm going through with all this and not write it up? Now a little quiet from you while I talk into this recording machine. You know exactly what to do with the record."

Winnie brought the car to a stop three minutes later. Parker jumped out, ran around and stood beside the driver's window.

"See you later. Got to establish an alibi now. Lucky I used one of the old storerooms to sleep in. I can reach it without anyone seeing me. And thanks—Captain Bligh—for putting me wise to myself...."

Sergeant Dan Gleason was half asleep, exhausted by hours of intense work on the murders of Dr. Trent and Patrolman Casey. Someone shook him hard and he awoke to find his office crammed with reporters.

"Sarge—hey, Sarge, wake up! There's another job out front. Somebody knocked off Joiner Seddon."

GLEASON JUMPED to his feet and rushed outside. A Headquarters doorman tried to explain as they raced toward the car around which a score of patrolmen were gathered.

"We heard this horn blowing steady. We looked out and spotted this buggy. So we opened the door and inside is Joiner—deader'n a salt mackerel. Somebody put a note on his chest and pinned it there—with a knife. Then there's a lot of cut ropes in the back seat like somebody had been held prisoner."

Gleason pushed his way to the car, two men held flashlights, spraying the grisly object slumped on the front seat, with light. Gleason gingerly maneuvered the piece of paper, which had once been white and was now a horrible crimson. He managed to read what was inscribed on it.

Dear Sergeant Gleason:

Here is Joiner wrapped up for you and ready to sing any note you desire.

The Masked Detective.

" 'Masked Detective,'" Gleason grunted. "Haven't I got troubles enough of my own without some halfwit running around calling himself a masked detective and delivering a dead man on my doorstep?"

Reporters were streaming out of Headquarters. Someone thought of Rex Parker and a cub was sent to rout him out of bed. Rex Parker was fast asleep when the cub shook him. He stretched, yawned and listened to the youngster's excited story. Then Parker came close to giving himself away.

"Joiner is dead?" He jumped to his feet. "I can't—Oh, thanks, kid, for calling me. I'd have slept through a riot. Let's go!"

CHAPTER V

HEARTACHE

PARKER FOUND Sergeant Gleason walking slowly back toward Headquarters, holding a bloody piece of paper in his hand. He fell into step with Gleason and saw that this bit of paper was the note he had written and fastened to Joiner's vest along with the crook's confession.

"How about the lowdown, Dan?" he asked. "Did they finally get Joiner without making a new mistake?"

"He's dead," Gleason answered. "I found this note pinned over his heart with a knife. No fingerprints, of course, but what gets me down is the signature. The Masked Detective! Maybe those hoods are getting funny. Anyhow it's one swell yarn for you and a sweller headache for me."

Rex Parker thought fast. He took Gleason's arm and piloted him back to the privacy of a Homicide Bureau office. He closed and locked the door, dropped into a chair and looked at Gleason steadily for a moment.

"I'm going to trust you, Dan," he said quietly. "I've got to. That note—it was written by a man who calls himself the Masked Detective. How do I know? Because a masked man paid me a visit around midnight, shortly after the Trent and Casey kills. He had a gun, but he didn't even draw it. The man is okay, Sarge. He told me that he was going to see Joiner and make him talk. I think he did, and brought Joiner here as a prisoner. He either tied him up or knocked him cold and left him in front of Headquarters for you."

Sergeant Gleason made a wry face.

"Rex, I'm surprised. Listen—this man who calls himself the Masked Detective—he's nothing more than a cold-blooded killer. Chances are he works for the mob behind these murders. If he came to see you, it was only to get as much information out of you as possible. What did he look like?"

The phone on Gleason's desk buzzed. He answered it, then passed the instrument over to Parker. Rex Parker gave a visible start, then held the receiver far enough away from his ear so that Gleason could hear also. From his actions no one could ever have guessed that Parker himself, in his rôle of Masked Detective had himself dictated the words he was hearing into a recording machine, and that Winnie Bligh was now playing that record over the telephone.

"Rex Parker!" the voice was saying. "This is the Masked Detective. I have delivered Joiner Seddon into the hands of the police. He made a full confession and signed it. This is attached to one of his vest buttons. In the back seat of the car are two men who were assigned to murder Joiner. With the proper influence they will talk—or the Masked Detective will pay them a visit even if they are in cells. You haven't heard the last of me, Parker. You may publicize anything I tell you. Good night!"

A click indicated that the connection was cut off. Gleason yelled orders to have the call traced, but it had come from a dial phone and its origin could not be determined.

Gleason whirled on Parker. "I want everything you know about this Masked Detective. His description first."

Parker grinned. "Just look for a man who wears a mask. That's him!"

Gleason almost bit his cigar in half in his anger. "Damn it, Rex, you've got to cooperate! This Masked Detective murdered Joiner. He's no different than the mugs who have started this murder wave—if he isn't one of them."

"Wait a minute," Parker objected. "If the Masked Detective killed Joiner, would he phone and give that story? I believe him. I think he did force a confession out of Joiner, that he drove him to the street out front and left him there for you. He was trying to help."

A sharp knock on the door interrupted Gleason's sarcastic answer. A medical examiner's assistant entered.

"I think you ought to know about this," he said. "Medical evidence shows that the dead man didn't struggle at all, indicating that he was unconscious at the time the knife was driven into his heart. I found bruises at the back of his neck, proving that he was given a scientifically placed blow. Upon opening his vest I discovered a torn scrap of paper lodged beneath a button. Here it is."

Gleason took the corner of paper. Only a few words were left on it, but they brought a puzzled frown to his face.

......and they mistook... for me.

Joiner Seddon.

"See?" Rex broke in excitedly. "There is Joiner's signature and that is certainly a part of his confession—the same one the Masked Detective indicated that he pinned to Joiner's vest. It ties up, Sarge."

"Yeah—yeah, I guess you're right. If this handwriting compares to Joiner's, then the Masked Detective must have done exactly as he said, but someone beat him to the gun. All of which adds up to zero. If this phony detective is innocent, he's got to come forward and reveal himself. If he doesn't—well, I'll still think he's guilty. At least I have a sample of his handwriting. Some day I may happen to run across him and then...."

Rex Parker arose and headed for the door. "My dough is on the Masked Detective, Sarge. I think he's straight, trying to help you—and me. I'm writing this yarn just as I promised him I would. See you later."

But when Rex Parker left Headquarters, he didn't rush to his newspaper offices. It had taken every ounce of will power he possessed to keep his emotions hidden. He knew exactly what had occurred. Some devilishly clever man had watched him deliver Joiner to Police Headquarters, waited until he vanished and then murdered Joiner and freed the two men who were supposed to murder him. That didn't bother Parker so much, but what if that unknown man had spotted Winnie's car and taken the marker numbers? Had her plans resulted in some deadly peril for herself?

Parker's heart pumped madly as he paid off a taxi driver two blocks from Winnie's apartment. He assumed an easy pace and ambled by the apartment house. There seemed to be no spotters in the neighborhood. He turned abruptly, walked through the lobby, brought the self service elevator to the bottom floor and rode up to Winnie's apartment on the twelfth. He was tense with excitement.

His hand was shaking badly as he pressed her doorbell. If anything had happened to her, he was licked. Not only was he worried for her, but there wasn't a clue to indicate the identity of the two hoodlums assigned to kill Joiner, nor a single lead to the mysterious individual who had turned the Masked Detective's little plan into a murder jamboree.

He heard the bell ring, but no one came to answer it. He didn't wait long. He pulled a bunch of keys from his pocket—keys that would have made any burglar envious. He had picked them up, over a period of years, at Police Headquarters. They represented the art of an assorted number of sneak thieves. He had the door open in one second and wished that he clutched the gun which was part of the Masked Detective's makeup.

HE DIDN'T turn on any lights, but scratched matches and shielded their glow from the windows as he moved around. In the room Winnie used as a combination home office and workshop, he discovered her hat and coat thrown over the back of a chair. There was a piece of paper in her portable and he read it with bated breath. Nothing there—just the usual formula stuff she handled in her column.

His right foot stepped on something hard and round. He knelt and saw a number of small pearls—simulated ones, for Winnie's income didn't run to the real thing. Rex Parker's spirits sank as low as they had ever been in his life. The killers must have slipped into the apartment, surprised her, and she had retained wits enough to break the necklace and let it drop to the floor as a silent clue to her abduction. He was certain of that.

Sex Parker sat down weakly and cursed. He should never have permitted her to begin this foolish adventure with the Masked Detective. He should have known it would eventually lead to a situation just like this. Those crooks might even know that Rex Parker was the Masked Detective. It was highly possible that they had watched him jump out of Winnie's car. The whole thing was a fiasco right from the beginning.

He began to beat the arms of the chair he occupied until his fists hurt. He had known Winnie for nearly two years and she was his best friend.

It suddenly occurred to him that the despair in his heart was too intense to be developed from just friendship. He was in love with her! He knew it now, for the first time. In love with her, and because of his stupidity she was in the hands of a gang of merciless killers!

He threw caution to the wind then, turned on every light and ransacked the apartment for some clue which might lead him to her. There was none. He groaned, raced out of the building and yelled frantically for a cab. If she was able, by some miracle, to send word she would forward it to his office. Or if this gang knew that Rex Parker and the Masked Detective were one and the same, they might contact him holding her as hostage to enforce any orders they would give.

His face was grim as he thought of the peril she was in.

CHAPTER VI

THE MASKED DETECTIVE TRIES ACTION

NOT PARTICULARLY surprised was the skeleton staff on the *Comet* when they saw Rex Parker dash between the desks and head for his cubby-hole of an office. He called the operator and hung up slowly. No one had phoned him. There were no messages on his desk.

It was growing light outside and the great city was bustling into activity. Parker smoked a pack and a half of cigarettes in less than ninety minutes, flung the last crumpled pack into the basket and yelled for a boy.

One came, too promptly to be just answering his summons. He had a white-wing in tow—one of the city's street cleaners. The man held something clutched in his hand.

"Guy says he wants to see you, Rex," the boy reported. "Did you yell for me?"

"Scram!" Parker yelled. He advanced toward the street cleaner so swiftly that the man backed away. "Well, what do you want me for?"

The street cleaner opened his clenched fist and displayed a crumpled ten-dollar bill.

"I was cleaning up on Amity Street and I finds this ten spot in the gutter. I looked at it close to see if I was dreaming and there's something written on it with red stuff. Says if I bring it to you I get this one back and another like it. Or am I a sap?"

Parker grabbed the bill, smoothed it out on his desk and read the words written rather crudely across the surface in lipstick.

Finder bring to Rex Parker, N.Y. Comet and get another like it. 2Y39801.

Rex fumbled in his pocket, found two ten-dollar bills and thrust them into the street cleaner's hand.

"Boy, you earned it!" he howled.

Then he pushed the street cleaner out of the office, sat down behind his desk and picked up the phone. He called the State Motor Vehicle Bureau and identified himself.

"Check on the owner of Two-y-three-nine-eight-o-one. Mixed up in an accident and took a powder. I'm writing the story and want to play up the rat who didn't stop to see how badly the kid was hurt."

He knew from experience that the Motor Vehicle Department was only too glad to cooperate. The report came promptly. Rex wrote down the owner of that marker plate.

WALTER ORTH

VARIETY HARDWARE STORE

He memorized the name and the accompanying address, tore the paper into shreds and swept papers off the desks as he rushed for the elevators. He hailed a cab and had himself driven to the garage where Winnie stored her car. It was there, and the garage attendants knew him well enough to turn the sedan over to him.

He merely drove it around the corner, got into the back seat and found the clothing he had worn as the Masked Detective, intact. The .45 automatic felt better in his hand than a diamond of the same weight. He left the recording machine where it was, covering it with a blanket. Then he drove to another garage and parked the car. With his Masked Detective regalia stuffed under his coat, he headed for Winnie's apartment, reached it unobserved and went in.

He hastily removed his clothes, donned the black suit worn by the Masked Detective, then sat down at Winnie's triple-mirrored vanity table. The creams and putty she had used on his face were in one of the drawers. He had never applied makeup himself, but he performed a reasonably good job of it. Once more he became the rather flat-nosed, round-cheeked man who had visited Joiner Seddon. He concealed his own suit, patted the gun in his back pocket and went to the street.

CAB FARES were making a terrific hole in his bankroll, but the address of Walter Orth's hardware store was many blocks away. It turned out to be a frowsy looking place with dirty windows and a bunch of rusted andirons in the window. There was no time to fool around observing the place. First of all, he had to find out whether or not this Walter Orth was just an innocent victim—if the car registered in his name had been used with his permission or whether it had been stolen or the marker plates forged.

Parker thought he knew a good way to find out. He entered the place, assuming a slouching walk and when he spoke to the stout, bald man behind the counter, he talked out of the corner of his mouth.

"You Orth?" he asked and received a cold nod. "Certain parties tell me you're a right guy. I need dough and I pack a rod. No numbers on it—never have been. Paid thirty bucks for it. Sell for a sawbuck. A deal, pal?"

Orth glanced out of the window, made no reply, but merely walked toward a curtained doorway. Rex Parker followed him into another room, apparently Orth's sleeping quarters.

"Let's see the hardware." Orth stuck out a flabby hand.

Parker drew the gun, but instead of exhibiting it for sale, he pushed the muzzle squarely against Orth's fat neck.

"Sit down," he said in a frosty voice. "If you have any ideas about yelling for help or trying to reach one of the guns you peddle to gangsters, forget it. You can't make a squeak faster than this rod can shoot."

"What do you want?" Orth's eyes were narrowed in hate. "Who sent you here?"

Parker dragged a chair over and put one foot on it. The gun never moved an inch.

"You haven't heard much about me yet, Orth. I'm the Masked Detective—minus the mask at the present moment. I'm looking for someone. A girl."

Orth moved his massive shoulders. "Why ask me?"

"Last night," Parker went on, "I had a talk with Joiner Seddon. You know he's not the type to sing. The cops never made him open his mouth, but I did. You know that too. Perhaps I'd better show you just how I go about these things."

Orth sneered at him. The hardware dealer was big, but not all fat. Huge muscles bulged from beneath his tight fitting clothes. Rex Parker, the Masked Detective, backed up to the door and closed it. He slid the bolt, walked over to a table and snapped the ammunition clip out of his automatic. He stuffed this into his pocket and sauntered toward Orth.

"My methods." he said, "are peculiar. I don't go in for torture, but when I want to make a man talk, I let him try to beat me up. I'm waiting, Mr. Walter Orth."

The big man arose and on his coarse features was a cruel smile.

"Why, you half-witted fool, I can tear you into half a dozen pieces and I'm going to do it! I quit the wrestling ring because I killed a man. I wrenched his neck so hard he died. They found out I hated the mug,

Rex Parker's fist cracked Carson squarely on the jaw.

but they didn't have enough evidence to pin a rap on me. So you want me to try and snap your neck too, huh? It's a pleasure."

The huge man ripped off his shirt and exposed a chest that looked like a gorilla's. He spread his big arms wide and started forward slowly. If the Masked Detective had ever seen murder mirrored in a man's eyes, he saw it now, but he never moved a muscle.

Orth gave a savage shout and lunged for him. Then Orth suddenly discovered that the ceiling flashed by his range of vision. Then the further wall. He landed hard enough to knock all the wind out of his lungs.

BUT THIS strange man didn't move in to attack. He merely stood there, just as he had been standing before. Orth was no fool and he was wise to all methods of dirty fighting. He knew that his opponent had met his attack, with a well placed kick.

Orth got up, crouched and went into another animal-like lunge. He flew backward and a wave of intense agony shot through his squat, powerful body. That kick had caught him full in the stomach and his abdominal muscles had grown soft since his retirement. He looked around wildly as he arose again. He streaked forward once more, but on his way he scooped up a chair and hurled it straight toward the Masked Detective.

Orth handled this bit of business so fast that Parker had no opportunity to move. The chair struck him on the chest and sent him reeling. He tripped and fell heavily. In a flash Orth was upon him. Thick fingers fastened against Parker's face. Fat thumbs sought his eyes. Orth was a type to stop at nothing to overpower anyone he fought. Once those thumbs found the eye sockets, Parker would be blind and he knew it.

His arms were long and held plenty of strength. He brought his fist down hard against the back of Orth's neck. The big man grunted and winced in pain. His fingers slipped off his victim's face. With a violent push, Parker shoved his opponent up, doubled his legs and kicked out.

Orth went sailing backward. This time he didn't arise quite so fast and when he did, the Masked Detective was close by. A foot came up. Orth tried to duck, but the toe clipped his chin and threw him down again. Each time he struggled to reach the Masked Detective's legs, he received the same treatment.

"I—I give up," he said thickly.

The maskless Masked Detective moved a little closer and drew back one foot.

"Now you know why Joiner talked. You may also know that one well placed kick can break your neck quicker than you could twist somebody else. Last night your car was used to kidnap a girl. She doesn't know what this is all about, but I do. The hoods who took her made a bad mistake because she happens to be engaged to Rex Parker, a friend of mine. Where is she, you rat? I wouldn't kick a man when he's down, but you're no man. Which is it—talk, or a kick that will hurl you into eternity?"

Orth looked at the poised foot, then up into the face of this man who called himself the Masked Detective. He shuddered.

"All I know is two guys asked to borrow my car, see? They're right guys so I let 'em have it, but honest I didn't know it was gonna be used in no snatch. If you kicked my face in, I couldn't tell you anything more."

"Then I'll see."

The Masked Detective's voice was cold and brittle. His foot moved forward and Orth cowered.

"The guys were a couple of Cal Carson's boys. They—they took the dame to a flophouse about six blocks from here. Murphy's place. But I didn't have nothin' to do with it. I didn't—honest. Now Cal will know I ratted. He'll send a couple of his boys around to blast me."

THE MASKED DETECTIVE walked over to a pile of scrap iron and debris. He picked out a strong rope and bound Orth until the man was unable to move a muscle. Then he casually searched the back of the hardware store, opening cupboards and digging out their contents.

He spotted an iron ring near one corner of the room and lifted a small trap-door. Under it were several boxes. He opened them and revealed new automatic rifles and pistols.

"Wh-what you gonna do?" Orth asked fearfully.

"Protect you from Cal Carson's bunch of executioners," the Masked Detective said.

He picked up a telephone and dialed Police Headquarters. Sergeant Gleason answered in a sleepy voice that cleared the instant he heard his caller speak.

"Sergeant, this is the Masked Detective. First of all, I want you to know that I did not murder Joiner. I don't know who did it, but I'm well on my way to finding out. No—don't interrupt. Trace the call if you like. I'll be gone in ten seconds. Now get this. Come to Walter Orth's Variety Hardware Store. You know where it is. You'll find Orth tied up and ready to tell you all about the profession of furnishing guns to killers. Look him up and be careful that none of Cal Carson's men reach him. Good-by, Sergeant."

CHAPTER VII

THE MASKED DETECTIVE'S TRICK

FEELING SECURE in his disguise, Rex Parker hurried out of the place. He didn't wait to watch the arrival of Gleason and a squad, nor to see Orth whisked out of the place and a patrol wagon loaded with guns and ammunition.

Parker made his way to the flophouse which turned out to be a cheap, dirty-looking hotel. It contained, possibly, thirty rooms listed at seventy-five cents a night and up. He knew that by a direct invasion of the place he would risk not only his life, but Winnie's as well.

Effecting her rescue must be done with stealth and dispatch.

He hurried around the block, saw that he could reach the rear of the hotel through an alley and used that means of approaching the back door. It was going to be difficult, for he had no idea to which room

Winnie had been taken. She might even have been transferred from this place to another and safer hideout.

A colored houseman emerged with a sack full of papers. He approached an incinerator, dumped them into it and applied a match. As he started away, Parker stepped out from behind the incinerator and called to him. The houseman turned quickly and surveyed Parker in astonishment.

"Listen," Parker said softly. "Want to make five bucks for yourself? I'm on the lam and I need dough. I got a rock worth about two grand and I'll sell it for a couple of hundred bucks. I been told there's certain parties in the hotel who will take a bargain like that."

The houseman's eyes lighted up. They grew even wider when Parker showed him a ring. It was his own and worth about thirty dollars, but his sales talk made the simulated ruby look real in his eyes.

"You might even make a little extra dough on it," Parker said. "All I get over two hundred I'll split with you. Only I can't wait long."

"I dunno much about them things," the houseman muttered. "But I'll see what I can do. You wait here."

Rex Parker didn't wait long. The moment the houseman disappeared through the back door, he was after him. As he stepped into the hotel, he slipped on the velvet mask, transferred his automatic to a side pocket and kept his fingers curled around the trigger.

Parker had seen all manner of violence in his career as a newspaper reporter, but he had never shot a man in his life. Yet if it meant Winnie's freedom, he was ready to empty the whole clip of slugs into anyone who might oppose him.

The houseman dropped the empty refuse sack and ran up the stairs to the fourth floor. Parker knew dumps like this. Frequently well organized gangs, like Cal Carson's, took over the entire place. The various mob connections could come and go without arousing any suspicion. It would serve as a perfect meeting place and even a hideaway for some of the men who were in danger of being picked up. Police raids on joints like this were much too infrequent.

The houseman proceeded straight to a door at the end of the corridor. He knocked on it and was instantly admitted. As the door closed the Masked Detective went into action. He tried the door of the room adjoining the one into which the houseman had disappeared. The door was locked, but the lock was ancient and easy to open.

Gun in hand, the Masked Detective stepped into the room. The cheap, brass bed had been slept in, but the occupant was out somewhere now. The Masked Detective opened the window gently and stuck his head out. The window of the room into which the houseman had gone was about six or seven feet to the left.

WINNIE, IF she were still in the building, would be well guarded. He might reach her, but getting out of the place was something more difficult. Therefore, the Masked Detective formulated a more dangerous, yet highly efficient plan. He moved over to the door and pressed an ear against the flimsy panels. Voices reached him. The houseman's was the only familiar one.

"Yeah, man," he heard the houseman state positively, "I saw the rock and it was bigger'n my thumb. I never saw the guy before, but he's on the lam all right on account of he's scared stiff. Boss, you gimme two hundred. I'll get the rock and shoo him away."

A cold, calculating voice ventured a better idea.

"Look—if the guy is on the lam, why should we pay him good dough for the rock? You beat it back and bring the sucker up here. I got four boys in the room and we'll take good care of him. There's fifty in it for you if the rock is worth anything, so scram and get the sap."

The houseman's flat feet padded along the corridor. The Masked Detective held his breath now. Everything depended on what psychological reactions these crooks would show. The houseman returned after four or five minutes, running, and panting for breath. He banged on the door.

"Mr. Carson, the guy is gone! Ain't no sign of him no more."

"You fool!" Carson was the man who spoke in that monotone. "Why didn't you knock him stiff? That must have been a plant. It might even have been this nutty Masked Detective." Carson raised his voice. "Mac—Joe—both of you beat it to the dame's room and tell the boys guarding her to get ready for trouble! Stay there yourself and keep your guns handy. The rest of you mugs cover the front and back entrances. Wake up the rest of the mob. I want this dump searched—every room, every closet. Get going!"

The Masked Detective smiled complacently, moved toward the window and slipped out. He stood up on the sill, hung onto the window frame and reached for the ledge outside Carson's room. He couldn't spend much time negotiating the transfer because Carson's men were bound to take up posts outside the building and if they spotted him, he would be brought down like a clay pigeon in a shooting gallery.

His foot reached the sill and his hand clung to the window frame. With a prayer on his lips, he swung out into space, nearly lost his footing, and then managed to perch safely outside the window of Carson's room. The curtain was drawn—a definite break for him. He saw that the

"Two men with guns came in and threatened me,"
Winnie told the Masked Detective.

window catch was not fastened. He placed both thumbs against the window frame and pushed gently. The window slid up about an inch.

Nothing moved within the room. The Masked Detective slid the window up slowly, and as silently as possible. He knelt on the sill, drew his gun and took a long breath. His fingers found the curtain pull and he jerked it. The shade snapped up its full length and he leveled the gun.

No one was in the room. But he heard footsteps in the corridor outside, for the door was wide open. Carson had apparently stepped out to direct the search, but the noise of the spinning shade brought him back to the room.

THE MASKED DETECTIVE jumped lightly to the floor, took time to lower the window again, then darted softly across the room until he was flat against the wall just inside the door.

A slender, foppishly dressed man of about thirty barged into the room. His right hand held a revolver. He saw the window shade rolled all the way up, cursed, and went over to pull it down again. The thud of a closing door brought him around in a flash. He started to raise his gun, but instead he let it drop from his hand and raised both arms high.

"I see you are possessed of a few brains." The masked man stepped forward. "You were closer to death a second ago than you might realize. Well, Carson—it's very unpleasant knowing you."

"The Masked Detective," Carson said through his teeth. "Of all the stupid crackpots you take the cake. Listen, sap, I got twenty of my boys in this joint. How do you expect to get away alive?"

"Perhaps I won't," the Masked Detective said lightly, "but you'll die before I do. I've already locked the door to this room. If any of your men knock, send them away immediately, do you understand?"

Carson scowled and didn't answer. The Masked Detective stepped close to him, placed the muzzle of his automatic directly over Carson's heart and searched him deftly. He stepped back a pace.

"Carson, you've taken over this town pretty well in the past eight months. I give you credit for your organizing ability although your methods are not particularly creditable. If anyone opposes you, he dies. Of course you don't do the killings yourself, but those lily-white hands of yours aren't free of blood. Now you've stooped to the lowest racket of all—kidnaping. You snatched a girl, a woman incapable of defending herself.

"You took her because you believe she knows me. She doesn't! She happens to be a friend of Rex Parker, and I have selected him as my only contact with the world. He has agreed to help me by publishing stories which will publicly announce just what kind of a rat you and your kind can be. But the girl does not know me and never will. Since she is a friend of the man I have chosen as my representative, I feel obligated to protect her."

Carson sneered. "And all I'm to do is turn the dame over to you, huh? Try and make me."

"It would be a pleasure," the Masked Detective said. "I worked on Joiner and he talked. I worked on Walter Orth and he spilled the beans in no uncertain way too. How do you think I located this place? However, I won't take the time to bat your ears down. I'll simply say this. Summon one of your men by yelling for him. Order him to bring the girl out of this hotel. From the window I can see the street. She is to be allowed her freedom."

"And if I don't?" Carson asked.

He was getting a little worried. Orth must have talked and if this masked man could punish Orth enough to make him open up, Carson wondered if he wanted to stand up against him.

"If you don't," the Masked Detective said almost casually, "I shall put a bullet through you. It's just another way for society to avenge itself against the wrongs you have committed. You have about fifteen seconds to make up your mind, Carson."

CARSON LOOKED steadily at the eyes gleaming through the slits in the velvet mask. They were uncompromising, without the slightest iota of mercy. Followed by the Masked Detective's gun, he stepped closer to the door.

"Chappie," he called loudly. "Hey, Chappie!"

Someone came running down the corridor and the knob twisted violently.

"Never mind coming in," Carson called. "Go get that dame. Take her to the street and let her go."

"But, Boss—" the thug called "Chappie" protested.

"You heard me!" Carson bellowed. "Do like I say."

The Masted Detective sidestepped to the window, always keeping Carson in front of his gun. He gestured and the crook grimaced as he obeyed. The masked man was able to glance out the window and watch Carson at the same time. He saw Winnie emerge from the hotel entrance, a look of incredulous surprise on her face. Once she turned and stared back at the building. Then she ran into the street and hailed a taxi. When she was out of sight, the Masked Detective calmly stowed his gun in his pocket, and for the moment deliberately removed the mask so that Carson could see the face was not that of Rex Parker.

"You kept your word, Carson, which shows just how dangerous a man you can be," he said. "You accept defeat wisely. Now I suppose you wonder just how I'm going to get out of here. By that smug expression on your face I can see you're quite satisfied in losing the girl to get me."

"Right," Carson barked. "All we snatched her for was to get you on the spot. We were going to tell this Rex Parker guy to come and get the dame because I figured you and Parker are one and the same. Now I know you ain't. And even if I hadn't seen your face, I don't savvy a lazy snooper like Parker sticking his nose into a mess of trouble like you did. So now the dame is gone and you're here."

The Masked Detective grinned. "Also I no longer have a gun in my hand. You're a brave man, Carson, with a dozen of your hoods to back you up, but I don't think you have the guts to attack me bare-handed. Or am I wrong?"

Carson suddenly came forward with fists flying. One blow glanced off the Masked Detective's cheek. Then Carson was seized around the throat and spun around. A fist cracked him squarely on the jaw.

"Sorry I couldn't give you a few more lessons," the Masked Detective said, with a soft laugh, "but it would have made too much noise."

He eased Carson to the floor, stepped over by the door and listened. He turned the key, opened the door a crack and took a quick look along the corridor. Apparently Carson's men were still searching the place. He picked up the unconscious gang leader, draped him over one shoulder and stepped into the hall.

Approaching the door of the room across from Carson's, he unlocked it and went inside. He stowed Carson in a closet, then closed the door, locked it and beat a hasty retreat down the corridor. There was a dark nook just behind the staircase landing and he sought refuge in it.

CHAPTER VIII

THE MAN'S A WHIZ

ONE MINUTE later a terrific din came from down the hall. It was Carson, yelling and banging on the locked closet door. Four men came rushing up the stairs and the banging drew them like a magnet. They held guns ready as they approached the room. Two more men hurried to help. The Masked Detective looked over the railing to the third floor. No one seemed to be on guard. He walked down the stairs, and had reached the second floor when the front door closed with a bang.

"The boss must be nuts," someone said. "Letting the dame go like that. I tried to trail her, but she gave me the slip."

"Better go upstairs," another man warned. "Looks like Carson didn't give them orders because he wanted to. Somebody is yelling up there. I'll stay by the door."

The Masked Detective moved back into the protection of a dark corner. Two more men raced up the stairs. Then the Masked Detective extracted the gun from his hip pocket and walked boldly down to the foyer.

One man leaned against the door. Another was behind the small desk in a corner of the small lobby. The Masked Detective's gun leveled and he ran the toe of his shoe against the balustrade supports.

The guard at the door looked up, startled. One hand reached toward his left armpit, but stopped halfway and froze there. The Masked Detective walked serenely down the rest of the stairs, keeping the guard covered every moment. The man at the desk looked up, saw nothing out of the ordinary, for the Masked Detective's back was toward him and the gun he held was carefully concealed.

"We'll take a little walk," the Masked Detective said.

The guard gulped and bobbed his head. He offered no resistance when the masked man took his arm, opened the door and strolled out into the broad daylight. The Masked Detective faced the guard, pushed him back with his left hand and drove a right to the jaw. Then he whipped off the mask, stepped onto the sidewalk and kept close to the building until he was far enough away to risk a quick dash. Carson and his men caught a glimpse of him as he leaped aboard a taxi. Carson stuffed a gun into his holster, kicked a chair out of the way and cursed his men roundly.

"Enough of you to land six guys and this one slips through your fingers! I kept yelling for you to get him, and not mind me."

"Yeah, Boss," one of the men protested, "but you was in the closet and we didn't know it was you. We figured it might be some other guy."

Carson demanded a cigarette, chose one from the several packs hastily proffered him, and lit it. He blew a column of smoke toward the ceiling.

"This Masked Detective is no dream," he said. "And no joke either. He won the first round, but from now on I want every man to watch for him. No matter where or when you spot the rat—give it to him. In the back, in the face. I don't care just as long as he's damned good and dead. Those are orders. Now get your stuff. We got to blow. That guy may work with the cops and send a raiding squad here…."

REX PARKER dismissed the taxi at a safe distance from his apartment and hurried there. He removed his disguise, changed clothes and went to the offices of the *Comet*. He stopped beside a door labeled with Winnie Bligh's name, tapped on it and Winnie answered. He stepped in. She arose impulsively and reached out both hands. Parker kicked the door shut, took her hands and smiled at her.

"Smart of you coming back here so they couldn't grab you again, Captain Bligh."

"Then—then you really were in that—that awful place?" Winnie asked. "You were responsible for their untying me and letting me go?"

He parked himself on the edge of her desk.

"I was there, sweet, but Carson gave the orders to let you go. He had a sudden change of mind. Of course, my gun may have had something to do with it."

Winnie sat down and her hand shook slightly as she strove for nonchalance and powdered her nose.

"Now do you see how right I've been, Rex? About running down those men, I mean?"

"I see only how wrong you were," Rex answered. "One of them trailed you, but got lost in the shuffle. They won't hesitate repeating that little performance. They know you're a friend of the Masked Detective—or of Rex Parker who is the Masked Detective's contact. From now on you're in danger. Tell me what happened after you left me?"

"I put the car away, went back to my apartment and played that recording over the phone. Luckily, I hid the playback machine. Then I started to write tomorrow's column, and the next thing I knew, two men were in the room—with guns. I managed to break my necklace and drop it. I hoped you'd guess I hadn't left of my own accord.

"They took me out to a car, but on the way down in the elevator I powdered my nose and put on some lipstick. They couldn't do much to prevent me because I didn't give them a chance. I palmed a ten dollar bill—which reminds me, you owe me ten bucks. I also palmed the lipstick.

"When I saw the car they were taking me to, I wrote down the marker numbers. After we started away, I wrote down the message on it and managed to drop the bill out of the car window without being seen. They took me to that terrible hotel, tied me up and—well, that's all there is."

"Did they at any time indicate that they actually saw the Masked Detective get into your car and Rex Parker emerge later on?"

"No, Rex. They asked me who the Masked Detective was and I denied knowing anything about such a person. I was warned that a masked man was seen getting into my car, but I insisted that it was all a mistake, that it must have been another car like mine. They asked me if I knew you and of course I admitted it. Rex, they're suspicious that you really are the Masked Detective. We've got to do something to change their minds."

Rex Parker got up.

"All you'll do is answer that flock of mail on your desk. Tell the doting grandmothers how they can achieve the complexion of a twelve-year-old kid. You won't have to convince Carson that Rex Parker isn't the Masked Detective, because from now on the Masked Detective goes into retirement."

Winnie looked up at him in amazement.

"You mean you're going to quit? Now? When you've got them on the run?"

"When I got who on the run?" Parker asked acidly. "Look, I don't mind getting shot up myself, but when they involve you, it's time to call it off. Oh, no, lady, the cops can handle Carson and all others like him."

Winnie leaned back in her chair.

"Rex, I would never have believed you were a coward. Still, I suppose there's a certain test that reveals all men in their true light. But don't make the mistake of thinking that the Masked Detective is dead. Oh, no! I brought him to life and he'll continue to flourish even if I have to wear a man's suit and velvet mask myself. I could get away with it, and I will."

REX PARKER blinked in amazement. Then the full force of her threat struck him. He leaned across the desk.

"Okay, okay. It's just another way of pushing me around. You know I can't let you risk such a thing. So I'm still the Masked Detective. I'll find Carson, kick his teeth in and turn him over to Gleason. But then I'm done. Washed up, hear me? You—you—you Captain Bligh!"

Parker slammed the door and stalked to his own office. He spent half an hour writing the story of Orth's capture and the adventure at the flophouse. He wrote as though the Masked Detective had personally told him every detail. He used the Masked Detective's name freely and gave an account of a spurious meeting with him, and the result of their conversation which made Rex Parker the only contact which the Masked Detective had.

He presented this story to the city editor and watched the emotions on his face as he read it.

"Rex, you know who this Masked Detective is? You can contact him? Why, it's marvelous. That man's a whiz. In one night he did what police have been trying to accomplish for months. He broke up Carson's armament connection. All the other papers are playing up a story about the Masked Detective being nothing but a murderer. Get back at your typewriter and pound out a yarn saying this is a lie. Give the public what they're entitled to know—the truth. I don't think the Masked Detective killed Joiner Seddon, and neither do you. We've got to make everyone else think the same thing. Now get busy."

At two in the afternoon Rex Parker wandered into Police Headquarters, waved to the desk lieutenant and the various men around the main office, then made his way to the big room where the ace crime reporters gathered. They swarmed around him, asking questions, demanding answers. He made only one brief statement.

"Yes, there is a Masked Detective. He contacted me and appointed me as his outside man. That's all I know about him except a certain method by which I can reach him. Nobody can make me tell that secret, so save your breath. If you want to know what happens—read the *Comet*."

He pushed his way to the door and went immediately to Sergeant Gleason's office. Gleason looked tired, but there was nothing weak is his handclasp.

"You were right, Rex. Nobody can convince me that the Masked Detective knifed Joiner. Not after what happened last night."

"The Masked Detective gave me the lowdown," Parker said with a smile. "He also mentioned that until Carson was dead or driven away, he wouldn't stop."

"So I can reach this man through you, eh?" Gleason pondered. "Remember not so many hours ago when you and I were walking over to Dr. Trent's home? You were muttering something about the need for a man who'd go after these gangsters with weapons they'd fear more than they do a badge. I'm mentioning this because it seems just a little odd that the Masked Detective should suddenly come to life so soon after that."

PARKER SAT down and guffawed. "In other words you think I'm the Masked Detective. Look, Sarge, you've known me for years. Did I ever have the habit of shoving my face in front of a machine-gun? No, sir, I've seen too many of those mugs dead. I know what happens to people who go around looking for that kind of trouble. And you forget the Masked Detective phoned me while I was in your office."

"Maybe I was just hoping, Rex," Gleason admitted. "I know what you can do. For a long time now, I've given you lessons in how to solve crimes. You've learned a lot from district attorneys and coroners. If there was ever a man suited to become a detective, that man is you. Instead, you're the contact between someone we don't know. Someone who will think nothing of breaking the laws if he finds it necessary. Well—let him. I'll not go after a man who tries to help me. Furthermore, I'm convinced that he did not murder Joiner. If I mentioned that before, it's worth repeating."

"Nothing new on the Joiner murder, eh?" Parker asked. "Or the killing of Dr. Trent and Patrolman Casey?"

Gleason's cigar wagged.

"The only new thing is a fresh batch of violence. Four mugs stuck up an express office and got away with thirty thousand dollars in new bills. They murdered one watchman and got clear. We rounded up a couple of Cal Carson's boys, put 'em in a lineup and another watchman was pretty sure they might have been members of the mob that did it. He wouldn't swear to it—and the mugs had alibis we couldn't hope to break."

"Why didn't you sweat 'em?" Parker asked.

"Because we didn't have a chance. Before the desk sergeant's ink was dry after booking them, they were out on a *habeas corpus*. If that hadn't worked, it would have been bail. Rex, our greatest problem in fighting Carson is his bail bondsmen. They stand ready, day or night, to furnish any amount of cash to free Carson's men. They know that unless we got 'em cold, we can't hold 'em. The twenty-four hour law? Sure—we've tried it. Held 'em without bail, but they wouldn't talk. It takes three or four days to make those ten minute eggs open up. If I—"

Gleason's phone interrupted him. When he hung up, he scowled blackly.

"It's happened. Inspector Mullane wants me in his office. There's a delegation of worthy citizens waiting on him and demanding to know why the murderers of Dr. Trent haven't been locked up. You can come along if you promise to keep everything off the record."

CHAPTER IX

COMMITTEE OF FIVE

GLEASON WAS followed into the chief inspector's big office by Rex Parker. In a row of chairs before the inspector's desk, sat five men. Mullane himself was red-faced and nervous. Parker walked over to the other side of the room and said nothing. He knew these men, and he was also aware of just how much trouble they could make for Gleason and the whole police force. Take Leonard Adams, for instance. The portly, gray-haired banker possessed a lot of power behind his financial transactions. His demand, alone, would probably cost Gleason his job.

Then there was Elijah Squires, a thin-faced, crabbed-looking man who had piled up a fortune out of a phony patent medicine and who now headed the Civic Aid Society. Squires was a professional grouch and looked it.

Ingerman, a city official in charge of all public buildings was different. As nice a man as existed. Open-minded, tolerant and understanding. Parker knew why he was present. Ingerman and Dr. Trent had been fast friends.

The member of the committee who spoke first was Pritchard, a shrewd attorney and present head of the Bar Association. He spoke as though Gleason and Mullane were a twelve-man jury.

"We have come to demand faster and more concrete action on the part of the police. We can no longer tolerate crime and violence. The murder of Dr. Trent was a distinct loss to this city. As an expert on Egyptology he stood far above anyone else here. As a man and a citizen he was a credit to our community. He was murdered wantonly. Simply because his death was a mistake on the part of gangsters, makes no difference."

Gleason stepped forward.

"You know we've done all we could, gentlemen. And don't forget, another man died with Dr. Trent. Patrolman Casey, who sacrificed his life in trying to save Trent. Casey was just as much a man as Trent. We are exerting every effort to uncover the killers. Our major clue—Joiner

Seddon—was killed so he couldn't talk. No matter what you or anyone else believes, Joiner was not murdered by this new crime fighter who calls himself the Masked Detective. That man, whoever he may be, is trying desperately to help us. A few hours ago he wrecked a business dealing in unregistered guns and handed us the man behind it."

Elijah Squires got up and looked directly at Rex Parker. He pointed a thin, wagging finger.

"I'm no fool. This man Parker—the reporter for the *Comet*—I think he is our Masked Detective. I demand that he be arrested for the murder of Joiner Seddon."

Parker stated in amazement, then he forced a wide grin. Elijah Squires was simply trying to get in a few low blows because he hated Parker, hated him for the condemning stories he'd printed about the Civic Aid Society. In Parker's eyes the society was merely a method of publicizing wealthy people who knew nothing about the subject they tried to handle.

The fifth member of the committee began laughing. He was a small man, conservatively dressed and distinguished by a white, neatly trimmed beard. Hamilton Weaver, one of the biggest importers of *objets d'art,* was a mild-mannered person who seemed out of place with this belligerent committee.

"Now, Elijah," he managed between laughs, "you're being foolish. You have no more idea who this Masked Detective is than I have. Perhaps he is Rex Parker, but I wouldn't say so. After all, the Masked Detective is suspected of murder. Your accusations are libelous."

"Libelous, are they?" Squirts shrieked. "I'll show you how libelous they are! There was a note pinned with the murder knife to Joiner Seddon's corpse. And it's hand written. Let Inspector Mullane produce that note and then make Rex Parker show us a sample of his hand. Bah! The police—all of you—are fools! If you'd listen to the advice of my society, you'd learn how to handle crime." He was getting angrier by the second.

REX PARKER'S throat was suddenly dry. He realized that there were many things in this business of fighting crime and avoiding contact with the police that he still had to learn. In his haste to dispose of Joiner he had made no attempt to disguise his handwriting. Now crafty Squires wanted it checked. The reporter began visioning what the interior of a cell looked like after it had been lived in for several years.

"How about it, Parker?" Mullane challenged. "You don't have to go through with this."

Rex Parker stepped forward.

"If I don't, you'll all be sure I'm the Masked Detective. Certainly, I'll agree. I only want to venture this much—I know the Masked Detective, but not his identity, for he refuses to reveal that to anyone. I know how to reach him. If that's abetting a criminal, then make the most of it. Now bring on your handwriting specimens."

Gleason got up and disappeared. Rex Parker wondered if anyone else in the room could hear his heart beating. Inspector Mullane and Sergeant Gleason were bound to jump at conclusions if he refused to submit. They would shadow every move he made. How could he operate as the Masked Detective then? One thing sure—if he got out of this mess, he would blow Squire's society wide open; show it up for what it was.

Gleason returned, holding the bloodstained piece of paper in one hand. Parker walked up to Mullane's desk, seized a pen and asked for a piece of paper. Mullane provided one promptly. The others pressed close. Squires kept talking.

"Of course Parker is the Masked Detective. How else does he write those stories about the masked man's activities? Because the Masked Detective tells him all about his adventures? Poppycock! Would a man deliberately go out of his way to create a crime file against himself?"

Parker felt sweat break out all over his body. He wished that Winnie was here to observe what her lunatic suggestion had finally accomplished. He glanced at the blood-stained paper and his eyes flickered once. What prevented him from showing any emotion was something he never did understand. The blood-stained message was not in his handwriting! Not the slightest similarity existed. The words were there—the blood, the slit made by the murder knife, but the writing had changed.

Parker copied the words on another piece of paper, and everyone in the room scrambled for a good look at it. Mullane leaned back and curled his under lip.

"I'm satisfied," he stated. "That certainly is not Rex Parker's writing."

Elijah Squires fumbled with the narrow black tie he habitually wore. He didn't look up at Parker.

"Well it was a good idea. Maybe there was some funny business. I still think I was right."

Hamilton Weaver walked up to Parker and extended his hand.

"This is in the form of an abject apology, Mr. Parker. I speak for the entire committee. We're sorry. Whatever action you wish to take against Squires is none of our business."

Parker's grin spread all over his face. He couldn't even feel sore at Squires. A miracle had happened. How, he had no idea, but he was safe.

"I think," he said, "it makes a good story for my paper. An exclusive too. Will you mind the publicity?"

SQUIRES MADE a violent protest which was overriden by the others. Then Attorney Pritchard went into his song and dance again. But the committee was more or less mollified. Mullane made his usual pat promises.

Parker walked out with Pritchard and stood in the hallway with the attorney.

"Don't be too hard on Squires," Pritchard said. "He meant well enough. All of us are under a terrific strain these days. I suppose you wonder how a committee of so many prominent men was formed so quickly. I'll tell you the truth. We had formed weeks ago. Our main object is to provide, for the various museums, libraries and art institutions, new and exemplary forms of art. We represent a number of wealthy men—of course we donate also—to locate and buy up certain ancient relics and art of a more modern school. It's a fascinating job."

"*Hm,*" Rex Parker said, "that's a darned good story. How about breaking it, Mr. Pritchard?"

Pritchard smiled and shook his head.

"Suppose we wait until things are ready. I promise you a scoop then. Until I give the word however, I'm depending on you to keep all this dark."

They shook hands and Rex Parker forgot all about such things as ancient relics, museums and *objets d'art.* The only thing on his mind was Sergeant Gleason's suggestion that the Masked Detective break up the collusion between bail bondsmen and Carson's racketeers. An idea had slowly developed, only to be broken into a million pieces when Squires demanded a sample of Parker's writing. Now it was coming back.

Rex walked over to the records department and studied files on some of Carson's known thugs. He made a list of the bondsmen who had jumped from nowhere at the instant these crooks were dragged in. If he could break up that combination, he would deliver a telling blow against Carson and men of his kind. As hard a blow as the capture of Orth. He whistled gayly as he headed back to the offices of the *Comet.* Then he stopped whistling as he recalled the substitution of notes. Who was responsible?

CHAPTER X

MURDER MONEY

IT WAS shortly after dinner when Rex Parker approached his Greenwich Village apartment and turned abruptly into a tobacco store two doors away. He bought two packs of cigarettes and glanced idly out of the window as he waited for his change. Something moved in the doorway of an old church directly across the street. His eyes narrowed. That church was ready to be torn down. Nobody should have been lurking in that doorway. He went to the phone booths, selected a coin out of the handful he received in change and called Winnie.

"Have to make this fast. I think I'm spotted—Carson's men of course. Perhaps they've even tapped my phone. Soon as I get in, I'll call you again. When I hang up, hurry over here and bring along your kit of disguise material. Drive your car right down the alley to the back of the place and use the service entrance."

He heard Winnie excitedly agree, then he strolled out of the store, entered the apartment building and went to his own floor. He let himself in cautiously, prepared to resist any possible attack if men were planted there to trap him.

But nothing happened. He turned on all the lights, walked over to a window and looked down at the street. If he was under observation, then let the spies see him.

He grinned widely at all the attention he was receiving.

He phoned Winnie and told her he was tired and would be staying in all night. Winnie arrived half an hour later and Parker told her what had happened while she attacked his face with putty and dye. This time she prepared an entirely new countenance—that of a man who might easily be a Mexican. She made his lips thinner, his nose pointed and slender. Parker looked at his new identity with amazement.

"Captain Bligh," he said, "you're good! If anybody can recognize Rex Parker under this face, he's good too. Now I've got orders for you and I mean orders. You are to put on my smoking jacket, comb your hair back and sit down near that window. I'll pull the curtain so your silhouette will be plain. There's a new pipe in the humidor—see if you can use it like a man. Never mind going in for realism. I don't want to find you unconscious when I get back. The idea is—"

"That you have all the fun and I have all the work," Winnie pouted. "I don't like your ideas, Rex."

He pushed her gently into a chair and stood looking down at her.

"I have an idea that Carson still thinks Rex Parker may be the Masked Detective in spite of his run-in with his masked enemy," he said seriously. "That association of ideas must be broken up and this is the one way it can be done. With this disguise on my face I can walk out of here and those spotters outside will never recognize me. I can work as the Masked Detective and they'll swear Rex Parker was in his apartment all night. Can't you see how important that is?"

"I suppose so," Winnie sighed. "All right. What are you going to do tonight?"

"Give Cal Carson a yen for some aspirin tablets. Good night, Captain Bligh, and don't prowl around my personal stuff."

He shoved his gun into his pocket, folded the velvet mask and stowed that away too. He bowed ironically to Winnie and closed the door.

Then he finally sauntered out to the street. In his disguise he knew that Carson's men would show no interest in him, so he took time enough to study the lay-out. The man in the shadows of the church doorway wasn't the only lookout. There were two more, carefully posted up and down the street. Parker walked within two feet of one, paused and lit a cigarette, letting the flare of the match illuminate his features. The man merely glanced at him and turned away.

AT THE corner, Parker hailed a taxi. He went uptown for several blocks, changed to a subway and finally crossed town on a trolley, heading for the East Side. Both the bail bondsmen he wanted to thwart and the actual instigators of the express office robbery, had headquarters only a few blocks apart. He went first to a cheap cafe. Two of Carson's men were there, drinking beer.

Rex Parker knew that the money taken from the express office would be hidden somewhere until the hold-up men were certain the currency couldn't be traced. Gleason had carefully kept from all newspapers the fact that the bills were new and their numbers listed. Parker wanted that money for a particular purpose.

He selected a booth, ordered drinks and poured all but one on the floor. An hour and a half passed by before the two crooks got up. Parker sauntered out after them and derived some profitable experience in shadowing men.

This happened to be easy for neither of the two crooks were suspicious. After all, what had they to worry about? They'd been arrested and Cal Carson's wonderful system for taking care of his men went into quick operation. They'd walked out of Police Headquarters as freely as the cops who scowled at them.

They turned into a boarding house, unlocked the door and vanished. Parker waited ten minutes before he stealthily examined the lock and let himself in with the use of those keys he carried.

A faint night light illuminated the corridor and the staircase. There were mail slots at the foot of the steps and he studied them. Carson's four men were all listed as occupants of the fourth and top floor of the house.

When Parker reached the top floor, he saw that there were only two doors, and apparently the four burglars occupied the rooms as a suite. That suited his plans nicely. He crouched beside one door and listened. He heard nothing so he went to the second door. Faint voices came to his ears, but he was unable to distinguish the words.

However, he did place four distinct voices and he smiled. Two of the crooks had gone out to enjoy themselves. The other pair had remained home, and men of this kind didn't stay in nights unless it was important. They had been guarding the express office loot.

Parker returned to the first door, knelt and examined the keyhole. There was no key on the other side of the lock. He had that door open in less than thirty seconds and discovered that it led into a bedroom. Off this was a second bed chamber, then what seemed to be a dining room. From this led the last portion of the suite and the door to that room was open. Light streamed through and the voices of the quartette were plainly audible.

"Pretty nice of Carton to let us keep all but fifty percent of the dough," one said, "seeing how he had the job cased for us and when we were picked up he made sure that watchman wouldn't be too positive we were the guys. Got us out of jail too—so quick the cops don't know what happened."

"Yeah," another said, "but there's a string attached that I don't like so much. I used to know Tony Desher in the old days before Carson took over. Tony ain't such a bad guy. Wonder why he wants him knocked off?"

"Aw, Desher knows too much," the first thug growled. "That's why he's gotta be taken. If we don't do it, somebody else will and we might as well get the dough for the job."

REX PARKER carefully drew on his velvet mask, took the automatic from his pocket and moved in. One of the thugs saw him, gasped and couldn't find his voice. The others turned swiftly.

"The Masked Detective!" two of them chorused.

"Line up," the masked man ordered sharply. "Turn your faces to the wall."

They obeyed promptly. The manner in which the Masked Detective worked had been passed around in the underworld already. Neither of these four crooks wanted to tangle with him. The Masked Detective searched them, accumulated an assortment of weapons, and then marched the men into the bathroom.

"Just let me hear one yelp out of you," he warned, "and I'll shoot."

He locked the door and then systematically tore the place apart, making as little noise as possible. He slit the cushions of the furniture, dumped out the contents of drawers, tore pillows and mattresses apart and even rolled up the carpet in the living room. Finally he examined the various windows. There was a fire escape outside one of them and he slid the window open, then returned to the bathroom door.

"You birds are not as clever as you think," he said. "But this is a warning. Next time you take part in any stick-up or any other violation of the law, I'll look you up again—and start shooting the moment I see you. Give my unkind regards to Carson."

The Masked Detective walked to the door, opened it, then closed it again. But he didn't go out. Instead he cut across the room, climbed out onto the fire escape and lowered the window shade. He also slid the window itself down to within half an inch of its casing, crouched low so he'd present no telltale silhouette, and waited.

It took the four crooks only a couple of minutes to force the lock of their temporary prison. They streamed out and howled at the destruction of their living quarters.

"He must have got it," one groaned. "How could he miss?"

Another man gave a yelp of triumph. "No, he didn't! None of the pictures were taken down!"

He hurried over to a large, cheaply framed picture, removed it from the hook and turned it around. The back of it bulged in a comforting manner.

"We better take the dough and get over to Carson," one of the men suggested.

"And do just what the Masked Detective maybe hopes we'll do?" another protested shrilly. "I'm betting that guy will stick us up again. He didn't find the dough and he'll figure we'll scram with it. I say leave the dough right here. What if he nails us—or the cops decide to haul us in? If they find all that new dough on us, they'll have a good idea we knocked off the watchman."

His arguments seemed to have won. Five minutes later the four crooks hurried out of the rooms and the Masked Detective moved in. There hadn't been time to search the rooms completely for this loot so he had permitted the crooks to locate it for him. He took down the picture, ripped off the backing and removed a wad of bills. He thrust them into his pocket, smiled complacently, and left the house without being seen.

He removed the velvet mask and, in his disguise, walked the streets safely. In a drug store, he dialed Police Headquarters and got Sergeant Gleason on the wire.

"THIS IS the Masked Detective," he said. "Before you start sending radio cars to corner me, listen to what I have to say. The four thugs who held up the express office and murdered a guard are heading for Carson's new hideout. I don't know where it is, but if you flash a pick-up signal to all officers, they may be able to arrest those men. Hold them and wait for developments. Incidentally the other watchman who wasn't killed listened to some effective persuasion from Carson's men. He can identify your murderers. See that you make him do it. And have the bail for those four men set at a high figure. That's important."

"I'll send out an alarm immediately," Gleason said. "And don't worry about my trying to pick you up. If you can deliver those hoods into my hands and give me time enough to break their stories, I guarantee you'll have no trouble from me. How do you figure I can keep those mugs?"

"Tell your bail bond clerk to keep his eyes open," the Masked Detective chuckled. "You might hang around his office too. Good luck, Sergeant."

Parker hung up and walked briskly along the street until he reached a shabby section of the city where a Magistrate's Court was located. The court was closed at this hour of the night, but in the section were all manner of offices calculated to help crooks. A sign indicated that Simmis and Carfano, Bail Bondsmen were ready to help twenty-four hours a day. Parker grinned, rang the bell and waited.

A hawk-faced man let him in. The reporter looked over his shoulder as if he were afraid of being trailed. Then he reached into his pocket, drew out the loot from the express office robbery and spoke in a low voice.

"Carson sent me, see? Some of his boys are gonna be picked up any minute. They'll be booked at Headquarters. Scram over there and get 'em out. The bail may be high, so Carson says use this dough."

He handed over the thick wad of bills. The bail bondsman took the money and nodded. He didn't know this dark, Latin-looking man, but that wasn't out of the ordinary. Carson frequently sent messengers who were not well known.

"You tell Carson," the hawk-faced man said, "that we'll have his men out ten minutes after they're booked. If there's no bail set, we'll get a *habeas corpus* writ."

Parker nodded, and hurried away.

CHAPTER XI

MURDER MISTAKE

WHEN SERGEANT GLEASON'S radio alarm was sent out, it bore fruit. Twenty minutes after the Masked Detective phoned, a squad car brought in the four crooks. Gleason had them searched and booked them on suspicion. The four men were singularly cool and unworried.

"Wasn't I right?" one whispered to his companion. "The Masked Detective figured we'd take that dough and scram. He works with the cops, that's what. They were set to grab us, find the dough and maybe we get the chair, huh? Did you see how disappointed Gleason looked when we didn't have the coin?"

Gleason parked himself in the bail clerk's office, chewed on a cigar and kept watching the clock. Usually Carson's bondsmen appeared within thirty minutes after his men were booked. This time they arrived three minutes ahead of their usual schedule.

The hawk-faced one smiled at Gleason.

"I understand you ain't satisfied yet—about that express office job. You got four men locked up again. Can't you learn, Sergeant, when you're licked? Those boys are innocent and you have no right to keep 'em locked up. Did that watchman identify them last time? No—he did not. What's the bail?"

"Ten grand apiece," Gleason barked, "and let's see you pony up with dough of that color."

The bondsman laughed derisively, consulted his partner and they took sheafs of currency from their pockets. The clerk began to make out the necessary papers. The bondsmen signed them, handed over the money and sat down to wait for the release of the prisoners.

Gleason walked behind the clerk's desk and picked up the money. He almost swallowed his cigar when he saw the new, crisp currency. He picked up the phone and called the records division. Then he casually walked over to where the bail providers sat.

"Somebody," he said happily, "gave you the double cross. So those four mugs didn't rob the express office, eh? Then maybe you can tell me how come half of that dough you just gut up for their bail happens to be the money stolen from the express office. The numbers are on file here. Simmis, I didn't think you or your partner, Carfano, were such damn fools. Possession of this dough marks you as accomplices to robbery and murder. Where did you get it?"

The hawk-faced Simmis turned ghastly pale. His companion seemed to shrink into his dirty collar.

"This ain't no stall?" Simmis quavered. "That dough is hot—honest?"

"As hot as the electrodes on the electric chair," Gleason said. "Boys, this is one time you'll have to look for a bondsman for yourself and even then I don't think it will do you much good. Murder raps have no bail. I don't think you robbed that express office or bumped the watchman, but somebody wants me to think so. You've got one chance—tell me where you got this money."

"Tell him!" Carfano urged frantically. "We been made saps of. Not even a big shot like Carson can do that to us."

Simmis clamped his jaws together for a moment. Then he talked and with each word Gleason's grin grew wider. He sent the pair to a cell, hurried back to the Homicide office, and asked to have the watchman at the express office brought in. The man arrived, shaken and nervous. He listened to Gleason, then sank weakly into a chair.

"Sure, I know I did wrong," he admitted. "But a couple of guys came to see me. They said if I fingered those mugs, I'd be tied to a pole with a stick of dynamite in my mouth. What was I going to do?"

"Are you married?" Gleason asked. "Is there anyone those thugs could harm, to keep you quiet?"

The watchman shook his head. Gleason's hand slapped the desk.

"Then what have you got to worry about? You're under arrest. We'll put you where those mugs can never reach you. Now will you identify them and make a statement why you refused to do so before?"

"If—if you're sure I—I won't be killed."

Gleason turned the man over to a patrolman, hurried to Inspector Mullane's office and told him what had happened.

"Now can't you see how this Masked Detective is helping us? Listen— Simmis and Carfano are ready to sing to high heaven. They think Carson framed them. If they testify that Carson provided that stolen money, we've got him, too. I'm issuing orders that he's to be picked up on sight."

Inspector Mullane gave a shout of pleasure.

"Now we can tell that committee where to go! This may not solve the murder of Trent, Casey or Joiner, but it shows we're working. Whatever I've said about the Masked Detective, I retract here and now. Get busy, Sergeant."

SHORTLY BEFORE midnight, Rex Parker, still disguised, but without the mask he wore when he was the Masked Detective, applied some of the knowledge imparted to him by his newspaper connections. He knew Tony Desher, the next apparent victim of Carson's ruthless purge. Desher was not wanted by the police, but they kept their eyes on him and Parker knew where the man lived under an assumed name.

This turned out to be a fairly swanky apartment hotel with an ornate lobby and a desk clerk and switchboard operator. Parker bought a newspaper at the stand and casually mentioned that he was waiting for a friend. Without arousing the slightest suspicion he sat down where he could watch the switchboard and see if Desher received any phone calls.

Parker knew that if Carson had Desher slated as his next victim, he would put his murderous plans into effect before Desher got wind of it and ran out. By now Carson would know about the arrest of his four men and would have assigned others to take care of Desher.

At exactly twelve-fifty the sleepy operator plugged in the connection to Desher's rooms. Five minutes later Desher himself stepped out of the elevator, looked around suspiciously, then headed for the revolving door.

Desher looked as though he'd just emerged from a smart tailoring establishment in his two-hundred-dollar gray suit, topcoat and expensive gray hat. He turned left on the sidewalk and began walking rapidly.

Parker followed him—very closely this time—because if things happened, he wanted to reach Desher first. Once the crook realized that Carson was intent on silencing him, he might become sore enough to talk. It had occurred to Parker several times, though, that neither Desher nor Joiner Seddon were important crooks and couldn't possibly know so much that their being alive menaced Carson enough for him to commit murder. Desher, especially, was a weak-brained thug, but if he did know something, Parker wanted to find out what it was.

Desher seemed to have a definite destination in mind and was in a hurry to get there. Parker found him easy to follow. That in itself seemed odd, because Desher must know that Carson's men might be looking for him.

The crook turned into a fairly busy street, deliberately crossed to the other side and slowed up considerably. Parker got himself primed for trouble. If his theories were right, Desher had been tricked into leaving his apartment and exposing himself to the wrath of Carson's killers. Parker kept looking over his shoulder every few steps. Death might come from any direction and so swiftly that Desher could be dead before he could be reached.

Then it came—just as suddenly as Rex Parker had feared. Desher passed by a cross street. A car suddenly pulled out. Guns gleamed and Parker went into action.

He sprinted toward Desher. The startled crook heard him coming, gave a cry of terror and started to run. Parker gained on him, went into a lunging tackle and wrapped both arms around the thug. He brought him down and hauled him into the protection of a doorway.

The guns spoke their venomous pieces. Parker, expecting to hear slugs smash all around him, saw instead, a man across the street suddenly curl up and drop to the sidewalk. The killers' car slowed, turned toward the curb and a submachine-gun was thrust out of the back window.

"So long, Desher," someone called out raucously, and the gun spat.

The body jerked as the bullets hammered into it. Then the murder car darted away, and was gone.

"You stay here," Rex Parker told Desher, "unless you want me to break your jaw. Those slugs were meant for you, understand?"

Parker raced across the street. Pedestrians had promptly scattered for whatever shelter they could find. Kneeling beside the victim, Parker raised the man's head.

"Buck Neal!" he gasped. "What a mess this will make!"

For the dead man was one of the better known citizens of the great metropolis. Neal had served on the Council, been secretary to three different mayors and served two terms in the State Assembly. He was as well liked as he was well known. Now he lay dead—riddled with thirty or forty machine-gun bullets. And the killers had called out Desher's name. They had mistaken Buck Neal for the scurvy rat who was hardly worth saving.

PARKER AROSE slowly, looking down at the dead man. He was dressed in gray, as Desher was garbed. Parker frowned. Was this a form of coincidence too strong for belief?

For the first time doubt assailed his mind. Was this a mistake, after all? Were those slugs actually meant for Buck Neal? It seemed hardly possible. Neal didn't have an enemy in the world, no more than had Dr.

James Trent. Both had lived exemplary lives and were noted for their kindness.

A radio car screeched up and Rex Parker quietly faded into the background. When the opportunity arose, he returned to the doorway where he had left Desher. The man was gone!

Parker swore softly. He should have knocked the rat stiff and made sure he'd be available later on. He made his way to the nearest subway station. He wanted time to think—to mull over these strange murders that were so obviously the result of mistaken identity. He wanted to hear what Winnie thought of them. The substitution of that note kept worrying him, too. Someone must know he was the Masked Detective.

CHAPTER XII

A CROOK ON THE LAM

C AL CARSON sat primly erect in a straight-backed chair and listened to his lawyer give him facts about what had taken place. Carson grew paler and paler.

The attorney, McKenna, was almost a counterpart of Simmis, the bail bondsman. He wore round-rimmed glasses and the eyes behind them were shrewd and sly. His mouth was a thin line, perfectly formed for the sneering comments he made to juries. McKenna was smart as they came—and crooked through and through.

"So Simmis and Carfano got possession of that hot money. Don't ask me how, because they won't let me talk to either of those two rats or the four boys locked up for murder. The watchman you handled so well has ratted too, and they've got him put away in a safe place. Those four boys haven't a chance, Carson. As soon as they realize that, they'll dicker for a life rap instead of the chair. You know what that means."

"Yeah," Carson said stonily. "They'll bust this mob wide open. I ain't fooled either. The Masked Detective is responsible for all of this. He must have tricked the boys and those lousy bondsmen, too. Looks like I'd better lam. But not far, McKenna. Not far. I got some business to clean up and anyhow I ain't finished with this town. Before I'm done, the cops will pay right through the nose. I took over some of the rackets, but now I'm taking 'em all and if anybody tries to get in my way—*blooey*—they get it in the neck.

"You see what you can do for the boys. Buck 'em up. Tell them I've got things fixed. That's your job—to convince 'em it won't be healthy to sing. I'm breezing for the country place. Contact me there, but only if something important turns up. That louse, Gleason, may have you tailed. Now beat it. I've got to think."

McKenna departed and Carson called in several of his men. Two of them had watched Rex Parker's apartment since early evening.

"You mugs are positive Parker didn't go out all night?" he asked.

"Sure, Boss. We saw him movin' around. We could watch his shadow on the curtains. We left Limpy back there to keep watchin'. So help me, that guy never even went out for a minute."

"Then he can't be the Masked Detective," Carson snapped. "But Parker knows how to reach that guy and Parker is going to tell us. That masked bozo is no push-over, understand? He's smarter than the cops and twice as nervy. If this keeps on, I won't have a gang left. They'll all be in the cooler and that includes you bunch of lunkheads."

"So we nab Parker, make him tell us who the Masked Detective is and rub both of 'em out, huh, Boss?" one of the men suggested.

Carson lit a cigarette and puffed on it thoughtfully.

"Yeah, that's the angle. Nobody crosses Cal Carson and gets away with it. I'll bust that nosey reporter's face in until he sings. Then we'll take the Masked Detective and when I finish with that guy, he won't need a mask no more because his own relatives won't know him.

"Three of you guys go up and get Parker. Bring him to the hideout across the city line. He can holler all he wants there because nobody can hear him. And no slip-ups, understand? That reporter is smart, and maybe he'll be tough to handle. If you slug him, don't bust his skull. I take care of that part."

WHILE REX Parker's doom was being concocted by Carson, the reporter himself talked to Winnie as he removed the disguise.

"I put a crimp in Carson's mob tonight, Winnie. He'll have to round up some new bail bondsmen, and I have an idea the others in that business won't want to monkey with Carson. I put him on the lam too. Here—see if you can wash this dye off the back of my neck."

Winnie's eyes were gleaming. Rex Parker hadn't only delivered a severe blow to Carson and his mob, but he also talked as though he enjoyed it. Now perhaps the Masked Detective would go on existing, threatening every crook and killer. Someone like him was desperately needed. Rex's elation was no less than Winnie's.

"However," he went on, after she finished removing the last traces of the disguise, "there's an angle that puzzles me. Buck Neal was killed tonight. Every bit of evidence points to the fact that he was mistaken for Desher. But that's what happened to Dr. Trent. Joiner Seddon was dressed almost exactly as Trent was. The same thing with Desher and Buck Neal. If that's coincidence, it's a little too strong for my blood. I'm beginning to suspect there's something bigger than any of us have realized in these murders."

"But, Rex," Winnie argued, "Dr. Trent and Buck Neal didn't have an enemy in the world. I don't think there were two more well liked men in the city. They were honest, conscientious and fair in everything. Poor Dr. Trent—an expert in Egyptology. Why should anyone want to murder a man like that? And Buck Neal—politician and a good one, too. I wrote an article about him not so long ago. He was taking an active part in refurbishing our art galleries. Buck was a connoisseur of medieval art. And I've always maintained myself that if you want to be beautiful, you should look at beauty now and then."

Parker sat up straight. "No kidding, Winnie. Say—take a good look at me. I'm a good-looking guy. I must be if your theory is right. I've been looking at you for the last half hour and as you say—look at beauty...."

Winnie colored and got up.

"I'd better get out of here before you start proposing to me."

She walked into the next room for her hat and coat.

"You know I've been thinking of that for a long time," Parker said distinctly. "This joint needs a feminine hand and.... Oh, oh, someone at the door. Must be Gleason coming to pat the Masked Detective on the back through me. Stay in there, will you? This is no time of the night for a gal to be visiting a guy without a chaperone. Next thing you know well have to get married to protect our fair names in the community."

Winnie quietly closed the door between the two rooms. She stood in front of the dresser adjusting her hat. There was a song in her heart and it would have been on her lips if Parker hadn't had a caller. He had actually proposed to her. In that nonchalant way of his, yes, but she knew he could be serious when he pretended flippancy.

Then her heart stopped beating and the breath froze in her lungs.

"Hello, pal," a harsh voice came from the next room. "A certain party wants to have a little talk with you. Do you come nice and quiet or do I put the bee on you?"

Rex Parker, his arms partly raised in due respect to the gun that prodded his stomach, never thought of his own safety. Winnie was in the next room. He had to get these men out of the apartment before they discovered her presence there.

"CARSON, EH?" Parker asked very quietly. "Why not? I wouldn't mind talking to him. In fact, I'd give a lot for the privilege. You can put the gun away, brother. I'll come willingly."

"You'll come with the gat on you," the crook rasped.

He signaled the other man who also held a drawn weapon. Parker was searched. He put on his hat, picked up a pack of cigarettes and walked out ahead of his two captors.

There was a sedan parked at the curb and the driver opened the back door as the three men approached. Parker climbed in. Now the guns were exposed and pushed firmly against his ribs. Yet he felt more relief than fear. Winnie was safe.

They headed uptown and each time the car stopped for a traffic light, the guns were hard against him. They left the city, rolled along a highway for about eight miles, then turned abruptly onto a dirt road over which the car bounced crazily.

"Carson seems to like country air," Parker said lightly. "He might as well get his fill of it, too. Sing Sing may not exactly be located in a big city, but I doubt the air smells like new-mown hay. Or do you boys know more about that than I do?"

"Shut up," one of the men snarled. "You're too damned wise. But believe me, pal, that'll be taken out of you."

CHAPTER XIII

IN A SPOT

HASTILY REX PARKER steadied himself.

This was no mere interview with Carson. The gang leader had resorted to kidnaping and the *Comet* reporter had a good idea of what was in store for him. Carson knew that the Masked Detective could be reached through Rex Parker and he would go to any extreme to trap the masked man.

Parker was in a bad spot. No matter how excruciating the torture, he couldn't tell anything at all about the Masked Detective because he'd simply be placing his own neck in a noose. Things looked darker than the pitch darkness rolling by the windows.

Then a faint light gleamed ahead of them and the car turned into a driveway and rumbled across a bridge of loose boards. One of the thugs got out, held his gun ready and Parker slid out too. He raised his arms and marched ahead of the two men, walking straight into the bloody face of gruesome death.

A door opened to admit them and reveal Carson in the light. There was an ugly slant to his mouth. Parker nodded pleasantly to the crook, walked into a room equipped with old-fashioned furniture and sat down in an overstuffed chair.

He was alert for the first chance to fight his way clear. Fighting with his feet, which might prove effective, was out entirely. Once he pulled that, they would connect him with the Masked Detective and guns would blaze. They must have learned that the masked man had a peculiar and effective manner of defending himself.

Carson pulled up a chair and sat down.

"Parker," he said acidly, "you know why I had you brought here. The Masked Detective has been busting up my racket. Until that guy is dead, I'm sunk. All I have to do is mention his name and the boys turn white. So he's a clever bozo, see! But me, I'm smart too. You know who this guy is. Spill it, or so help me, I'll have every bone in your body busted."

Rex Parker crossed his legs and leaned back.

"Sorry, Carson, but you've made a slight mistake. I don't know who the Masked Detective is. He never offered to tell me and I never asked him."

"Maybe," Carson admitted grudgingly, "but you know how to contact him. Every story you wrote says that. So you'll contact him for me and we'll set a nice little trap for him. How about it?"

Parker shook his head.

"Nothing you or your gang of pirates can think up will make me do that. Not even if I die—and let me warn you the Masked Detective protects and avenges those he trusts. Whatever happens to me will boomerang on you—two or three times as hard. You're done, Carson. You're on the lam. Every cop in the country is looking for you with orders to shoot if you show the slightest sign of resistance. Say—I've got a suggestion that'll get you out of all your difficulties. Take a gun and let some of that foul air out of your skull."

Carson jumped up and struck Parker across the mouth.

"Yeah? Wise, ain't you? Listen, sucker, before I finish with you, that tongue of yours will be yelling for that same thing—a bullet through the head. Only I'll let you keep on yelling until you tell me how to reach the Masked Detective. Take him, boys!"

Parker made a flying leap for Carson, landed a short, hard blow to the face and saw Carson's features become bloody. Then the butt of a pistol landed on his head. Things went black and he slumped to the floor....

SOMEONE THREW half a pail full of water in his face and it brought him back to his senses. First of all he thought that blow had deranged him. When his eyes opened, everything seemed to be upside down. Then he discovered that he was hanging by his feet. The blood rushed down into his head, made his senses reel again.

Carson knelt and laughed at him. He pushed over a piece of scrap iron—what seemed to be part of an old anvil. He had this lashed with rope and now he tied the other end of the rope around Parker's neck. Two of the men lifted the anvil until Carson had the rope in place. Then they dropped the heavy article and Rex Parker thought his body had split in two.

This lasted for fifteen minutes while he grew weaker and weaker. He could no longer see anything and Carson's voice, droning over and over a demand that he talk, sounded miles away. He hoped he wouldn't pass into a semi-oblivion from which he'd say anything to get rid of this ghastly torture.

When he believed only a matter of minutes spelled life or death for him, Carson ordered the ropes cut. Parker dropped like a sack of flour and lay on the floor, unable to move a muscle. Carson kicked him in the ribs.

"Talk, damn you! It's your last chance."

Somehow Parker managed to get, "No" past his lips, then he fainted.

This time they brought him back to consciousness by slapping his face. He was on the verge of a complete collapse. His head ached until he thought the top of it had been hacked off. The muscles in his neck were protesting violently against the harsh treatment they'd suffered. As he opened his eyes, the entire room spun crazily, but his lips parted and that same stubborn word came forth.

"No."

Carson cursed luridly. "This guy will never talk and we ain't got time to fool around with him. So his lights go out. There's an old well in back of this dump. Well throw him in and drop rocks down to cover him up. He can keep the other sap company!"

"Hey, Boss," one of the men objected with a short laugh. "We ain't scared, understand. But if we knock this guy off and even hide his body, the Masked Detective will know who did it. He'll start gunnin' us out, one at a time. Honest, Boss, I know this bozo has gotta be bumped, but can't we do it some way so nobody will be sure we did it?"

"Cowards—all of you," Carson rasped, but he saw the significance of the man's reasoning.

Carson didn't want to be facing the wrong end of a gun held by the Masked Detective. Not when that Nemesis of crime knew Carson had murdered Rex Parker.

"All right," he snapped. "We'll make it look like an accident. The old way. It worked before, so it'll work again. Tie him up, hands and feet. First roll some gauze around his skin so the ropes won't leave any marks. Gag him, dump him into the bus and we'll go over to the highway and let him have it."

Rex Parker could offer no resistance at all when they wound gauze around his ankles and wrists. Then ropes pinned his limbs until he couldn't move. Last of all, his mouth was wadded with a chunk of gauze and a gag wound around his head. Two men picked him up and carried him out to the car. Carson slid behind the wheel and two men got in beside Parker.

"THE REST of you yellow bellies stay here," Carson told his men. "Afraid of the Masked Detective! If I could lay my hands on the louse, I'd take him apart for you."

He started the car and rolled back of the house to turn around. He switched on headlights and the ride which would end in Rex Parker's death, began. One minute later it stopped abruptly. Carson braked the car, got out and looked down at the little bridge which had covered the stream. Only the bridge was no longer there. The loose boards which formed a passageway had been picked up and flung to one side.

"Hey, Boss!" one of the men in the back seat mumbled. "Boss, you don't think the Masked Detective did that?"

"Aw—I'm a sucker to take on a bunch of sniveling babies like you guys. What if he did? All I got to do is put the boards back. Watch that mug in the back seat."

Carson peered around in the darkness and hoped his men could not see his face. The Masked Detective might be lurking anywhere out there in the gloom. A gun might explode almost in his face. Carson put the boards back on the bridge, but his whole body trembled with fright. He cursed the loneliness of the place, cursed the police, but most of all the Masked Detective.

When he had finished, he walked back to the car, grabbed Parker and pulled his bowed head erect. Rex Parker wasn't pretending weakness that made even the ropes around his limbs unnecessary.

"A cinch," Carson grunted. "You guys take care of this rat. Do it right, too. I'm staying here."

"But Boss—" one man protested.

"Will you do like I say?" Carson roared. "I suppose you think I'm scared—like you are. Well, that ain't it at all. I think maybe the Masked Detective is around here some place. When he shows his face I want to be here to drill him. Now beat it and make sure you take the ropes and gag off that reporter when he's finished."

One of the men got out and manned the wheel. The car rolled over the loose boards, hit the dirt road and headed for the highway. Carson watched it disappear, then he bolted for the house. His own men had never looked so comforting to him even though he greeted them with a scowl of contempt.

In the back seat of the car Rex Parker fought to recover his strength. It surged into his limbs slowly but surely, yet it could do him no good. The ropes were tight and even with his usual strength, he would have been unable to break them. He wondered what manner of death Carson had prescribed for him. It would be horrible, no doubt about that.

One comforting thought remained with him. Winnie was safe. But he regretted the finish of the Masked Detective even more than he did the finish of his own life. There was so much to do and the case had taken such interesting angles. But when he waded into this mess, he had realized what it meant.

Yet he had not believed the end for him would come quite so soon.

The car rolled off the highway. It was about four in the morning, Parker reasoned. There was no traffic along the road at all. The two men hauled him out, dragged him down the road about two hundred yards and straightened him up.

"You just stand here, pally," one of them said, and laughed harshly. "Just stand and watch the headlights of the car get bigger and bigger. Then boom—you don't see no lights no more. We'll be doing about forty when we smash into you, so it won't hurt—much."

They left Parker standing there in the middle of the highway. He couldn't move. By hopping he might reach the shoulders but what good would that do him? They'd only set him up again like a tenpin. The car would crush him.

He saw the two men climb into the car, heard the motor roar, and then the headlights came toward him. He braced himself for the terrific impact.

CHAPTER XIV

THE MASKED DETECTIVE'S DOUBLE

A S REX PARKER was led out of his apartment by the two thugs, Winnie had hardly dared to breathe. If they found her his one chance of getting free was gone. It never occurred to her that if she tried to save him, her own life might be forfeit. She made a bundle of the clothes he wore as the Masked Detective. Into this she shoved his automatic. Should the crooks return to search the apartment, she didn't want any trace of the Masked Detective around. Then she rang for the elevator, reached the street just in time to see a car start off. Her own sedan was around the corner and she raced toward it. Speed was essential now. She had to keep that car in sight. The bundle of clothing and the gun went into the back seat. She got behind the wheel, stepped on the starter and then, suddenly, the other front door opened. A thin, dirty man peered in at her and there was a gun in his hand.

"Goin' some place, baby?" he asked with a leer. "Maybe you want to play tag with that bus you saw rolling away, huh? Okay, we play tag—only you don't have to be in a rush because I know just where they're taking Rex Parker and I'll take you there, too."

Winnie decided to keep quiet. Perhaps with some break of luck, she might overpower this man. He wasn't as tall as she and a good deal skinnier.

"Just drive like I tell you, baby," he jibed. "They left me behind to be sure the Masked Detective wasn't casing Parker's joint. You ain't him, are you? What a laugh! Come on, get this crate started. Carson don't like waitin'."

Winnie tightened her lips and obeyed. Under her captor's instructions, frequently backed up by gun jabs in the ribs, she sent the car toward the city's outskirts. She kept looking for a policeman, but never had known such a dearth of blue uniforms.

They rolled across the city line and the highway was masked with darkness. Winnie brought the hand throttle out, removed her foot from the gas pedal and slipped out of one shoe.

Dirty Neck made no protests about this curious way of driving. Apparently he knew little about driving. In fact, Winnie decided after a quick look at his ugly face, he probably knew little about anything. Except, perhaps, how to kidnap a girl. She deliberately reached down and yanked the choke halfway out. The motor began sputtering and she turned the car over to the road shoulder.

"No matter what you intend doing to me," she said icily, "I can't make a choked car go. Someone has to get out and fool around with some wires under the hood."

"You ain't kiddin' me, babe?" Dirty Neck asked. "I might put a nice piece of lead through your face if you were."

"Would I kid at a time like this?" Winnie demanded. "Either you get the motor working again or we stay here all night. I'll tell you what to do."

Dirty Neck gave her a fishy stare, but there was no doubt in that feeble mind of his that the car was stalled. Maybe she was right. Cars acted funny sometimes. He kept his gun leveled, climbed out and ran around to her side of the car. Winnie moved fast during those several seconds. She picked up the hard-heeled walking shoe and thrust it under one arm, covering it with her hand.

"Come on out, babe," Dirty Neck invited. "Show me what I gotta do to get this crate rollin'."

"Raise the hood," Winnie ordered. "I'll show you the wires you have to work around. It won't take a minute."

THE THUG was still suspicious, but he raised the hood. She pointed to a maze of wires. He bent over the motor and then Winnie's Cuban heeled shoe came down with every ounce of strength she could muster—square on the crown of his head. It was enough, for Dirty Neck collapsed over the fender and then rolled quietly onto the road shoulder.

She slipped her shoe on again, picked up the gun and then wondered what to do next. Perhaps she'd only stymied herself by knocking this man out. Now he'd never tell her where Rex Parker had been taken.

Then an idea took shape in her mind. She whirled, opened the back of the car and got it. For a few moments there was no sound, then Dirty Neck groaned and opened his eyes. From mere slits, they grew round as quarters. They saw two things simultaneously—the wrong end of a gun, and a man in a velvet mask.

"D-don't shoot!" Dirty Neck yelped. "D-don't kill me! I'll talk! I'll tell everything! Carson sent us to get Parker. They took him to a farmhouse up the road. Honest I didn't wanta do this. He made me! Don't shoot!"

The masked man gestured with the gun. Dirty Neck got up, trembling so that he could barely maintain his balance. He got into the car under the silent orders of that gun. The masked man climbed in beside him and gestured again.

"R-right up the road," Dirty Neck said hoarsely. "I'll show you where to turn. Only don't shoot me. Let me live!"

The masked man sent the car racing north on the highway. Dirty Neck had no chance to open the door and jump, for the masked man operated the car with one hand and kept the gun trained on him with the other.

"Y-you turn right here," he quavered. "It's the first house. You gotta cross a little bridge. You can't miss it. There ain't no other houses."

The car turned into the lane, proceeded along it for several hundred feet, then the masked man turned off into a pasture lot and parked behind the protecting branches of a big tree. Dirty Neck was breathing like a hunting dog at the end of a long chase. His eyes were dilated by terror. Suddenly the masked man raised the gun. It crashed down and Dirty Neck passed out.

The sigh that came from the lips of the masked man wasn't masculine. Winnie made sure her recent captor was cold, then began running in the direction he had indicated. Would she be too late? Had they already shot Rex Parker?

Winnie had never fired a gun in her life, but savage determination was burning in her soul. She would shoot this gun, and pray that Carson would somehow get in the way of at least one bullet.

She crossed the rickety bridge, made sure no one was on guard outside and crept up to the house. She risked a quick look into a window and had to get a grip on her nerves to keep from fainting. Parker was in there, suspended by his ankles from a rafter.

She could hear Carson's monotonous voice giving orders. Then Rex Parker was cut down. Tears welled into her eyes. To her he seemed very close to death. Then she forgot tears, and hatred gleamed instead as she witnessed Carson kick Parker several times. At that moment she raised her gun, and Carson never knew how close to death he was.

SHE HEARD him give the orders for Rex Parker to be taken out to a car. Hope surged through her heart once more. Then she realized that her own car was far down the road. Before she could reach it, they would probably have killed Rex.

She thought of the rickety bridge and raced back to it. Working frantically, she raised the boards and hurled them aside. Then she was racing down the road, stumbling at times, but keeping on with a strength she had never realized that she possessed.

She reached her car long before the murder sedan came bumping down the road. She let it pass her and disappear before she maneuvered her own car to take up the chase. She didn't dare turn on her headlights and frequently hit ruts that sent her head banging up against the top of the sedan. Grimly she clung to the wheel until the highway loomed up. She caught sight of the other car roaring south and streaked in pursuit.

When the car slowed, she applied the brakes too, and pulled over to be out of sight. She saw, in the gleam of the murder car's headlights, how the two men dragged Parker up the road and propped him there. Instantly Winnie guessed the manner of the intended murder. As the two men hurried back to their car, she sent her sedan hurtling forward. When she sideswiped the crooks' machine, she was doing forty-five, and the impact was terrific. But it served. Both cars missed Rex Parker by yards.

They came to a stop and the two crooks jumped out. So did another figure, with a mask over the eyes.

"Masked Detective!" one crook howled.

They turned and raced away into the night. Winnie lifted the gun and tried to pull the trigger. There was no explosion. She tried again and without result. Then she thrust the gun into her pocket and rushed over to where Parker had fallen. She got him loose in a few minutes, cradled his head in her lap and gently stroked his lopsided face as she ripped away the gag and he spat out the gauze.

"For the love of Pete," he said, weakly, "if you hadn't spoken to me, I'd have thought I was dead and in—ah—heaven. Winnie, help me up. We've got to get away from here. Did you see those mugs run? They were afraid of you—afraid of a girl! Wow, what a laugh! Why didn't you put a bullet over their heads?"

She helped him up and she was not smiling.

"That was the Masked Detective they were afraid of," she snapped. "And I couldn't shoot the gun. Somethin's wrong with the darned—"

Then she moved into the protection of Parker's arms and wept unashamedly. He was still badly shaken, but he got her back to the car.

"Oh Rex, I called myself every kind of a name I could think of. I sent you into this mess. You—you were almost killed. Rex, what would I have done?"

"Chin up, darling—" He grinned crookedly. His face felt as though a steam roller had flattened it. Carson had been anything but gentle. "I'm not forgetting what you did tonight. From now on I take my orders from you—Captain Bligh."

She clung to his arm as he backed her sedan away, untangling it from the wreckage of the other car. Luckily no tires had blown, and except for a crumpled fender and a smashed running board, the sedan had survived surprisingly well.

"THEN YOU won't give up being the Masked Detective?" she asked.

"Give up?" he said between his teeth. "Not until Carson is where he belongs. Maybe not even then. This stuff gets in your blood after a while. Sure—I know a car very nearly got in my blood too, but that's over with. Still, I figured you had enough. And, oh yes—about the gun. Always pull the safety off before you try to yank the trigger. And another thing—if you go around impersonating the Masked Detective—well, I've got only one suggestion."

"Didn't I do it right?" she asked, and all her terror had left her.

"Yes," he answered slowly. "You certainly scared the daylights out of those two mugs, but if they had a closer look at you—well, I mean you ought to wear a girdle or something."

Winnie's laugh was the nicest thing Parker had heard in hours. Then suddenly, he jerked erect. A low moan came from the back seat. He stopped the car fast, pushed Winnie away and got the gun out of her pocket.

"Oh, I forgot," she said. "That man in the back seat. I—I slugged him. He captured me and I let him have it. How's that for lingo from a beauty and heart throb column editor?"

"Swell," Parker admitted, "if he hasn't heard us talking about the Masked Detective. No, he's still out. What'll we do with him?"

"You're sitting on his gun," Winnie said. "I took it away from him. Isn't it a crime to carry a gun?"

"Uh-huh. We're all guilty, I guess, but this little rat should be taken care of. We're inside the city limits now. Write a note and I'll pin it on him. I'd do it myself except that I had one experience with handwriting that still lingers. Print the words in big block letters. I'll tell you what to say."

Winnie found a piece of crumpled paper, and printed the Masked Detective's message in big letters. Parker hauled Dirty Neck out, held him against a small tree near the sidewalks of the suburbs and fastened him there, using his prisoner's belt and ragged tie. Then he hooked him under the chin, pinned the note on his clothing and started away.

Winnie's message was terse. It read:

ONE OF CARSON'S PETS FOR SERG'T GLEASON. TAKE HIM AND WELCOME.

CHAPTER XV

THE BODY IN THE WELL

J UST AN hour and a half later Rex Parker and Sergeant Gleason pulled up beside the farmhouse to which the *Comet* reporter had been taken as Carson's prisoner. There were state police there. The lieutenant in charge made a terse report to Gleason.

"They were gone before we reached the place," he said. "Stripped the house of practically all personal possessions. We came as soon as we could."

"I figured this would happen," Parker said. "The two killers who were set to run me down fled like deer when the Masked Detective showed. I suppose they reached this farmhouse in time to warn Carson. Suppose we have a look around, Sarge."

"Why not?" Gleason agreed. "We won't find anything, but there's no use taking chances. That little crook the Masked Detective tied to a tree was hauled in just before we left. He's known as Limpy—and a rat if there ever was one. Found a gun in his pocket, and he was so scared that the Masked Detective would get at him again that he confessed the gun was his and that he bought it from Walter Orth. If this keeps on, Rex, your friend the Masked Detective will have all of Carson's mob cleaned out."

They started a careful search of the entire house. Apparently some of the gangsters had lived in the place for weeks. One of the smallest rooms on the second floor hadn't been stripped. There was a soiled suit of clothes in the closet and a pair of worn shoes, one of them built up.

"Limpy's room, without a doubt," Gleason said. "He wears exactly that type of shoe to offset his short leg. Ties Limpy up pretty well."

Rex Parker walked over to the cot occupying one side of the little room. He pulled up the blankets, prodded the pillow and heard something drop to the floor. He pulled the cot away from the wall and picked up a round, enameled object. It had a small spring and he pressed it. The lid flew open.

"A snuff box." Parker looked bewildered. "Valuable one too—must be very old. Now what would Limpy be doing with this? Snuff isn't used much any more and certainly not by a lug like him. He wouldn't bother with an expensive case like this anyway."

Gleason shrugged. "I learn things about crooks every day I live, Rex. However, I'll find out if Limpy owned this. Looks as though we might as well get going too. Carson's too smart to have left anything important here."

"Just one more thing," Parker said. "When I was half conscious I heard Carson say something about knocking me off and dumping the remains in an old well behind the house. Said I could keep another sap company. Let's have a look."

They hurried out to the well, and found that it had been boarded over and the well house long since removed. Parker raised the wooden platform which covered the well and Gleason shot the ray of his flashlight into the bottom of the well. It showed the body of a man dressed in gray.

State police brought ropes and one of the men went down to retrieve the body. It was hauled up. Gleason shook his head slowly.

"If they killed Buck Neal by mistaking him for Desher, they certainly rectified their error quickly," he commentated. "It's Desher all right—knifed through the heart."

PARKER SAT down on a huge rock, lit a cigarette and suddenly remembered that he hadn't eaten for hours. He looked at what was left of Desher and shivered. He had come dangerously close to sharing an identical fate. He called Gleason over.

"Sarge," he said, "I've been thinking. I heard how Buck Neal was dressed and Desher is wearing the exact duplicate of Neal's suit and hat. As I recall it, Dr. Trent was also finicky about his clothes—and usually wore a certain color. And Joiner Seddon was dressed like Trent, wasn't he?"

Gleason frowned. "Why, yes, he was. What are you driving at, Rex?"

"Just suppose, Sarge, that Trent and Neal were not killed because of mistaken identity. Suppose their deaths were necessary to some plan of Carson's—or even someone higher up than Carson? Remember how the killers called out the name of their supposed victim in each case, and there were witnesses to testify to this? I'm beginning to smell something rotten. Perhaps this whole affair has ramifications so big we've missed them by their very size."

"Now why," Gleason asked patiently, "would Carson want to knock off Neal and Dr. Trent? They never did him any harm. In fact, I doubt either of them ever heard of Carson."

"If I only knew the answer to that one," Parker said. "You know this isn't my idea alone. The Masked Detective hinted around about just such a thing when he drove me back to town a few hours ago."

"Does he think there's someone higher up?" Gleason asked quickly.

"He does—and so do I. Look, Sarge, Carson is just a mug. He came here a comparative stranger and took over the various rackets. He kicked the other crooks out, or killed them when they resisted. He methodically wiped out every man who might oppose him or give away the secrets of the rackets he chiseled from them. All this takes a lot of cash—and some solid brain matter which Carson doesn't possess. Is there anything in Carson's history to indicate he's capable of such splendid organization? No, he was nothing but a plain punk and he still is."

"Whew!" Gleason said. "I never considered that angle before, but the way you present it makes a man think twice. If it is true—if Carson has a boss and the murders of Trent and Neal were deliberately staged to make us think they were accidental, then what in thunder is this higher-up after? It can't be blackmail or any other form of extortion, because both Neal and Trent would have notified us immediately if such a demand was made. What profit was there in killing those two men?"

"I don't know," Rex Parker said, "but I'm going to contact the Masked Detective as soon as I'm able and put this entire business up to him. Let's go back to Headquarters and see if Limpy wants to sing. He may know what rathole Carson and his hoods ran to this time."

Parker and Gleason ate a hearty breakfast in a lunchroom close by Headquarters. When they returned to Gleason's office, he sent for "Limpy." A turnkey appeared after a couple of minutes.

"Limpy's got a visitor, Sergeant. Guy named Elijah Squires—he looks like one of them posters denouncing prohibition snoopers."

Gleason looked at Parker with considerable surprise.

"Never mind Limpy for the moment. Ask Mr. Squires to step into my office. If he seems a little reluctant, bring him in."

Squires came after a few moments, very defiant and showing his anger by crabby threats.

"You've no right to have me dragged in here," he exploded. "Just because I visited one of my friends. Don't snicker. I class Limpy as a friend. My society and myself have worked on Limpy for months and we straightened him out. He is an innocent man and I shall see to his release immediately."

"Limpy," Gleason said, "was born a punk and he'll die one. His father and mother were both out-and-out crooks. His only brother was electrocuted for murder. Limpy has a record as long as your nose, Squires. What are you trying to hand me?"

Squires glared at Rex Parker out of baleful eyes.

"I refuse to talk in front of this reporter. He'll write a story about this conversation and pack it full of lies—make a fool of me. I won't stand for it."

SQUIRES PACED the floor. Then he slowed up and his eyes opened wide. He walked over to a table beside Parker and picked up the enameled snuff box.

"Humph!" he grunted. "I must have left it here yesterday. First time I ever saw a spark of honesty in a police department. This container happens to be worth more than a hundred dollars."

"Yes," Parker said smoothly, "I noticed your teeth were badly stained from chewing snuff—even smelled the stuff when you came in here chewing it. But are you certain you left this box in here yesterday? As I recall it, you were in Inspector Mullane's office, not Sergeant Gleason's."

"What matter?" Squires barked. "It's mine, isn't it? I'm warning you, Parker, if what you heard in this room goes into the paper and one word is misconstrued, I'll sue."

He turned on his heel and stalked out. Gleason growled something decidedly uncomplimentary and his swivel chair creaked as he leaned back in it and faced Rex Parker.

"So old Blue Law Squires owns that snuff box. Smart of you to put it out as bait, Rex. That's a trick I'd hope for from the Masked Detective. Now what do we do? Should we lock Squires up?"

"There's been no crime committed, Sarge. Yet we certainly have something to mull over. Squires operates the Civic Aid Society. It's composed of smug, righteous and parsimonious people exactly like him. I gave the whole set-up a going over in a special article a few months back. They claim to reform criminals and ex-convicts by showering them with kindness. They're just a bunch of self-centered saps, because the mugs they work on simply take them for every cent they can get."

"Sure," Gleason agreed. "But doesn't that give Squires a beautiful contact with the underworld? Couldn't he be fooling his own associates by using them as a front, and the Civic Aid really be a hotbed of crime? I'm going to look into this, Rex. Maybe you are right—that someone is bossing Carson. Everything has been handled too competently. Carson's not capable of such strategy. We'll let Squires go ahead and show his hand. I won't even question Limpy at present."

Parker got up. "A good idea, Sarge. Well, I can't hang around here forgetting I get paid to write up news. I'll be in the press rooms if anything breaks."

The sergeant nodded.

"Okay," Gleason said and then, almost as an afterthought, "Say, you certainly must have contacted the Masked Detective quickly after I suggested it would be nice to break up those bail bondsmen. We've got those birds on ice for good. Now if your friend could only see that McKenna, the shyster, wouldn't start fifty nice court actions to get them free, I'd appreciate it."

Rex Parker just grinned and went out.

CHAPTER XVI

SIXTEEN MILLION DOLLARS

LOUNGING OVER to the big press room, Parker took his expected kidding good-naturedly.

"Rex Parker, hero of the day," Blane, ace reporter for the *Globe*, shouted. "Snatched by the bad mans and all he does is whistle and out pops the Masked Detective. Some story!"

Parker laughed. "Wouldn't you birds give both arms to be able to write it under my by-line, though? You mugs know the big points, I know the details. Let it be a lesson to you, boys. When you want the real news first, read the *Comet*—especially Rex Parker's stuff."

Blane chuckled. "All kidding aside, Rex, you must have had a tough time. Boy, is your puss banged up! What did they use on it—a sledge-hammer?"

"Just a pair of old-fashioned shoes," Parker admitted. "Now stop asking questions. I refuse the interview and if you has-beens will move out of the way, I'll write my little yarn and make the city editor think I'm worth the salary he pays me. Scram, mugs."

He pounded the typewriter for an hour, then sealing his story in an envelope, he called for a messenger, and leaned back. He wondered how Winnie was taking it—without any sleep the night before. He yawned, parked his legs on the edge of the desk and pulled his battered hat down over his eyes. In one minute flat he was asleep.

The confusion, the jangle of telephone bells and the coming and going of reporters never registered on his brain. But when he heard one reporter gasp in astonishment, his feet slid off the desk and was instantly alert.

"Flash from a West Side precinct," the reporter said. "They just found Arnold Marquod dead along an express highway. Struck by a hit-and-run driver."

The prominence of Arnold Marquod aroused Rex Parker's interest. Like Trent and Buck Neal, he was well known and respected. Wealthy, charitable and clever, he was most of all known for his forays into China and Indo-China in search of ancient relics.

Parker had one break. Sergeant Gleason was going out to the scene of the accident and the *Comet* reporter piled into the detective cruiser. Moments later he studied the place of death. Marquod's car was parked beside the road with a rear tire flat. His body lay close by, smashed almost beyond recognition.

"Poor guy," Gleason ventured. "He got out to have a look at the flat and some drunken fool must have clipped him—good. Well, I've got to make measurements and look for something that may have fallen off the hit-and-run car."

Rex Parker went over to the limousine and knelt beside the flattened tire. He saw what had caused the blowout. A shiny nail was imbedded in the rubber. He used his penknife to pry it loose.

He sat down on the running board and studied the nail. It was the kind usually dropped from the shoes of farm horses. The shank was rusted badly, but the surface of the head was fairly bright and streaked, as though it had been pounded by some uneven article.

He got up, went over to where Marquod's corpse lay on the pavement and lifted the blanket which an emergency squad had thrown over the remains. Gently turning up the sleeves of the dead man's coat he picked off a few strands of white thread. Then he took Gleason's arm and led him away from the crowd.

"Arnold Marquod wasn't killed by a hit-and-run driver," he said quietly. "Nor did he get out of his car to look at that flat tire. I'm betting the tire was deliberately punctured. Look at this nail I took out of it. It's from a horseshoe and since when did they allow horses to proceed over this speedway? It's against all regulations. This nail came from a farm and it seems to me Carson and his boys were living on a farm not so long ago."

"Too circumstantial," Gleason disagreed. "Suspicious, maybe, but I haven't a thing to go on except supposition."

Parker opened his right hand and revealed the strands of white thread.

"And is this circumstantial, too? Those threads came from a piece of gauze. They murdered Marquod exactly as they planned to kill me. They wound gauze around his wrists so the ropes wouldn't mark his flesh. They removed the ropes and gauze after Marquod was dead. I can't be wrong, Sarge. This is murder—and it's Carson's own pet way of disposing of people he doesn't like, or whose death may be profitable to him."

Gleason took the threads and carefully placed them in an envelope. The nail went into another container.

"Keep this under your hat," he warned Parker. "I'm making a public statement that Marquod is the victim of a hit-and-run driver. Let Carson believe his little plan worked. Give him rope and sooner or later he'll spring his own gallows trap. Incidentally I might add that having you around is almost as good as having the Masked Detective to work with. You must be learning a lot from him. Now break down and tell me just why Carson would want to murder Marquod?"

Rex Parker smiled. "Maybe before the day is over, I'll find out. Will you have a radio car take me back to town, Sarge? Work to do."

The radio car deposited Parker in front of a building where Attorney Pritchard, Bar Association president, maintained his elaborate offices. Pritchard was out, attending some kind of a meeting at the Gaylord Art Gallery. The reporter went there by cab and found Pritchard elated and quite willing to grant an interview.

The attorney took the news of Arnold Marquod's death with genuine sorrow. Either that or he was an accomplished actor.

"It's horrible," he told Parker. "You may say for publication, that we of the group planning to augment our museums, miss his guidance tremendously."

Parker made a few notes. "Tell me, Mr. Pritchard, just what this augmenting of museums amounts to. I promise to keep it off the record, but I'm intrigued and you did say I could have the beat on it."

Pritchard nodded. "Very well. Just don't release the story until early next week. You see, our various museums and art galleries have suffered to a great extent during the past ten or twelve years. With business conditions so poor and so much public funds necessary for relief, no money has been granted the institutions for the purchase of new material.

"As a lover of art, I called upon certain people for help. We formed a committee—the men you met at Inspector Mullane's office. A score of the wealthiest people in the state agreed to donate substantially. We were to use the money to buy certain art treasures from abroad. Such things can be acquired now at a great discount because of the war. So, we have purchased sixteen million dollars worth of these articles."

"Sixteen million!" Parker gasped.

PRITCHARD SMILED.

"The sum is staggering, isn't it? But these various *objets d'art* are to be displayed in special rooms, each named after the men who donated the money for them. We perpetuate the names of these wealthy people and at the same time provide something substantial for our citizens."

Rex Parker whistled in surprise. "Do you know this will be one of the biggest yarns of the year, Mr. Pritchard? But I'll keep it strictly quiet until you give the word. When does this stuff arrive?"

"It's already here. I'm having our various experts study the authenticity of the goods. Each man is an expert in his own line. One handles the Renaissance paintings and tapestries. Another knows everything about such things as perfume jars from ancient Egypt, stone tablets that have made history, and various trinkets buried with the mummies of renowned Pharaohs.

"Lastly, we have a collection of pottery and jade as far back as the Chinese Ming and Sung Dynasties. It has taken us a year's hard work rounding up these articles. We of the committee have given all of our spare time to the task. That's why we wish to spring the news suddenly. We feel that by so doing, we can arouse the interest of all our citizens."

Parker shook hands with Pritchard as he left.

"I hope," he added, "that you keep those treasures well guarded. Crooks like Carson would go to any extreme to get their hands on the stuff."

Pritchard laughed. "After investing such sums don't you think we've taken the necessary steps? We have armed guards everywhere, and when no one knows about the arrival of the articles, how can a burglary be planned? No, Mr. Parker, don't worry about that."

But Rex Parker did worry. He discussed it with Winnie over dinner.

"See how it adds up?" he said. "Pritchard has bought Renaissance art, with which Buck Neal was familiar. The Chinese stuff was right up Arnold Marquod's alley. The Egyptian art was Dr. Trent's forte. They're all dead. Why?"

Winnie wound spaghetti around her fork and most of it fell off. She picked up her knife to attack the slippery strands.

"Maybe Carson and his men plan to steal the stuff and sell it, Rex. Perhaps fix it up so it would look like something else just as valuable. If Trent, Marquod and Neal were alive, they'd be able to tell the difference."

"Maybe." Parker dumped three spoons full of sugar into his coffee and stirred it energetically. "I've been thinking that maybe the stuff might be phony—duplicates of the real stuff. But Pritchard has experts passing on the stuff."

Winnie sniffed. "Pritchard. The high and mighty. He's so self-centered I'll bet his name will lead all the others who get credit for supplying that art work. What if Pritchard is a crook and is in league with Carson?"

Rex wrinkled his nose.

"Be reasonable," he said. "Pritchard works hand in glove with four other men. They're not all crooks. However, there may be something in what you say. Remember what I told you about Elijah Squires? He certainly acts suspicious. So, Captain Bligh, I think the Masked Detective will have to see Squires and have a little chat with him. I don't believe he'd act quite so cocky if a gun was poked under his long nose.... Here, for the luvamike, let me show you how to eat that stuff."

CHAPTER XVII

BANNED

EIGHT O'CLOCK saw Parker back at Police Headquarters. The Masked Detective would be in action before the night was over, but it was too early to tackle the prospects the reporter had in mind. He waved to the desk lieutenant and wondered why he received no answering welcome. A detective-sergeant brushed by without speaking. Then, as he entered the press room, Gleason took his arm and led him to the corridor outside.

"Some bad news, Rex. Mystifying news too. Mullane gave orders about an hour ago that you were no longer permitted to enter Headquarters on newspaper business. He phoned your editor and asked to have you removed. Don't ask me why. I just work here."

"Has he gone crazy?" Parker demanded hotly. "Why should I be barred? What's Mullane got against me except for some of the kidding I hand him now and then?"

Gleason shrugged. "Figure it out for yourself. He just went on record as saying the Masked Detective is not authorized to investigate crime and that he has deliberately broken the law several times. Mullane's orders are that the Masked Detective is not to be aided in any way and if he is contacted, a gun must be used on him if he refuses to surrender. I suppose that you, being the Masked Detective's mouthpiece, automatically fall under Mullane's ban. I'm sorry, Rex, but you know there isn't a thing I can do."

Parker looked just as angry as he felt.

"Tell Mullane to jump in the lake and tell him to watch the *Comet*, too. I'll make a dummy out of that guy. What is he but a politician and a cheap one at that, who wormed his way into the chief inspectorship? Before he came, that job was only given to men who rose from the ranks. I…. Say, Sarge, I'm getting an idea. Could be that Mullane knows more about this business than he's letting on?"

Gleason's face was serious.

"Could be, Rex. I thought of the same thing. Now beat it, will you, before I'm called on the carpet for not shooing you off fast enough."

Parker walked out of Headquarters and wondered how all this would end. Mullane giving orders like that, when every member of the force realized that the Masked Detective worked with the police. After all the danger he'd gone through to nail Orth and the two bail bondsmen to the wall, after putting Carson on the lam—this was his reward.

Parker returned to his apartment and planned a course of action. Finally he shoved his gun into his pocket, thrust the velvet mask where he could reach it quickly and went out. He didn't waste time putting on a disguise. What he intended to do should entail no danger of being unmasked. But before the night was over, Rex Parker hoped to have instilled some twinges of terror into the hearts of three men.

McKenna, the shyster, retained on a permanent basis by Carson and his men, needed to be told the error of his ways. Gleason wanted that.

Then Elijah Squires might give an interesting interview. After he finished there, Parker meant to pay Inspector Mullane a visit and learn what was behind those strange orders.

He proceeded to McKenna's home first. It was a spacious house, giving eloquent evidence that McKenna didn't handle gangsters' troubles for nothing. Parker vaulted a hedge and crouched behind a lilac bush, shrouded by darkness. He slipped on the mask, ran lightly toward the rear of McKenna's home and stepped softly onto the back porch.

THE KITCHEN was dark and so were all the upstairs rooms. Apparently McKenna hired servants who worked by the day so that he'd be quite free to have his criminal clientele contact him at night.

The Masked Detective forced the key out of the other side of the lock and held his breath as he heard it clang to the floor. No one came to see what had happened. He opened the door, stepped in and closed it again. On tiptoe he approached the butler's pantry, passed through it and emerged into the dining room.

Now he could hear voices and had to stifle a grunt of surprise. There was no mistaking that whining, high-noted voice of Elijah Squires. What was he doing here, talking to a man of McKenna's reputation? Parker crept closer until he could hear every word.

"...and I come to you as a representative of the Civic Aid Society," Squires was saying. "Limpy has been wrongfully incarcerated. We feel that he is quite innocent of the charges against him. With your skill as a trial lawyer we are certain any judge or jury will agree."

McKenna must have been enjoying a secret laugh. It was almost evident when he escorted Squires to the door. And when the door closed, McKenna gave vent to a derisive howl of laughter as he returned to the living room.

The Masked Detective wasn't laughing. If there was a higher-up—the brains behind Carson—that man would permit none but those he could absolutely trust to know of his existence. Certainly McKenna wouldn't be among those favored few, and it might be that Squires was putting on a splendid little act. In this bizarre case anything was possible. Parker drew his gun, made sure the mask covered his features well, and started toward the living room.

He ducked back suddenly for someone with a heavy tread stamped across the porch and a moment later the doorbell buzzed. McKenna, grumbling, arose to let his visitor in. Then the Masked Detective had a real shock. Inspector Mullane walked in. The masked man had never seen the man look so haggard. Mullane dropped heavily in to a chair.

"Don't bother with any formalities," Mullane told McKenna. "I'm not here because I enjoy it. My opinion of you and your methods corresponds with what I think of a snake. But I'm forced to come here and beg your help."

"Beg my help?" McKenna asked in a puzzled voice "Now don't tell me you've committed a crime."

"McKenna, my wife has been kidnaped. Carson is responsible for it and you know how to reach that rat. I heard from one of his men. They don't want money. I was told to get the Masked Detective and get him good. Also to deny Rex Parker, who is the Masked Detective's outside man, admission to Police Headquarters. It's all calculated to stymie the Masked Detective, and I'm the goat.

"Well, I gave those orders. Parker was thrown out and every man on the force is looking for the Masked Detective. I can't reach Carson and I want him to know this. I don't want them to lay a finger on my wife. Perhaps I'm no criterion of exemplary living or behavior. I've made mistakes and taken advantage of my fellow men more often than I like to think about—but I happen to love my wife. I'd do anything they ask, but I must be sure she isn't harmed."

THE MASKED DETECTIVE didn't wait to hear any more. He peered around in the semi-darkness and saw a small desk and telephone at the further end of the hall. He moved cautiously, climbed the stairs and sought the bathroom. He took a can of powder from the medicine cabinet, dumped some of it into his handkerchief and made a pouch of it.

Then he slipped back to the hall and gently dusted the telephone dial with the powder. He carefully removed all traces of the powder except for a fine film which covered each finger slot. And every moment that he worked, his ears were absorbing Mullane's almost frantic pleas for McKenna's intercession. The man was on the verge of panic.

As the man in the black, velvet mask ducked back into the dining room, McKenna walked to the door with Mullane.

"Inspector, I'll do everything I can," the lawyer was promising. "I don't know where Carson is, but I'll try to find out and the moment I know anything definite, I'll call you."

McKenna stood in the doorway until Mullane got into his car and drove off. Then McKenna closed the door hurriedly, and rushed over to the phone. He dialed a number.

"Carson? It's working like a charm. Mullane has done everything you ordered even to kicking that fool Parker out of Headquarters. From now on the Masked Detective won't have such an easy time of it. We'll keep the pressure on Mullane and that won't be hard because he hates Parker anyway and the Masked Detective has stolen too much of Mullane's thunder to suit him. Everything is okay, I hope? Good—and watch your step!"

McKenna hung up and rubbed his hands gleefully. Then his lower jaw dropped a notch and his eyes bulged. A gun muzzle was resting gently against his right cheek and McKenna had no doubt about who held the gun.

"You should watch your own step, McKenna," the Masked Detective said. "Get up and keep your hands high." He searched the attorney and took a small, pearl-handled revolver out of a pocket holster. "Now walk into the dining room where it's dark. I detest shooting people in too much light. The sight of blood nauseates me."

"You can't get away with this!" McKenna snapped. "I'll have the law on you."

"The law! You've twisted it around to suit your own ends, but this time you twisted it just a bit too far, my friend. So Mullane's wife has been kidnaped and you knew it all the time—just as you knew Mullane would have to come to you for advice. That makes you guilty. Or is your knowledge of the law so poor you didn't figure that out?

"Kidnaping is a peculiar crime. Those who aid in it even without actual contact with the victim, pay the same penalty as the actual snatchers. Wasn't there a law passed in this state not so long ago that makes kidnaping a capital crime—the electric chair, you know."

"What do you want?" McKenna snarled. "You're no better than I am. You're a crook, or you'd show your face and come out from behind that mask. If you're looking for a cut, perhaps I can arrange it. Certainly you can't turn me over to the police. I'd like to see you get on the witness stand with that mask on your face. I'm not afraid of you."

THE MASKED DETECTIVE laughed gayly.

"But you are," he accused. "Or have you some nervous disorder that makes you shake that way? Listen to me, you money grabbing shyster. Because of your trickery men have gone free to kill, to rob and maim. If I were one of their kind, I'd send a bullet crashing through your skull. However, I believe in letting the law take its natural course. In your case that means more years behind bars than you'll live. Reach in your pocket, McKenna. Take out a piece of paper and your fountain pen. Then write me a nice little confession about the kidnaping of Inspector Mullane's wife."

"Try and make me," McKenna snarled.

"If you wish it that way," the Masked Detective said. "Perhaps I'll start by breaking your nose. Did you see Walter Orth after I finished with him? I worked on his jaw and I rather think he doesn't enjoy eating any more. You forget, my sharp legal minded friend, I'm not a policeman and regulations do not affect me. I can be as ruthless as any of Carson's men. Now will you write that confession?"

McKenna did not have to look up at the Masked Detective. There was menace enough in that calm voice. Above all things McKenna hated violence when he happened to be on the receiving end of it. There were no doubts in his mind but that any confession he wrote for the Masked Detective wouldn't be worth the paper it was written on, and certainly this masked man couldn't go to the police with it. McKenna wrote as the Masked Detective dictated.

"Now stand up," McKenna was told. "Put your hands by your sides. I'm going to tie you up, then I'll pay our mutual friend, Cal Carson, a visit."

CHAPTER XVIII

FIRE TRAP

Mc**KENNA OFFERED** no protest as the Masked Detective trussed him with cord taken from the drapes. He was positive now that this masked man bluffed his way along. How could he know where Carson was hiding?

Or did he? Why hadn't he demanded that information? McKenna made up his mind to supply a wrong address to his Nemesis.

But the Masked Detective asked no further questions. He merely tripped McKenna and proceeded to tie him to a radiator. Next the masked man turned on the hall lights, sat down at the telephone table and examined the finger holes in the dial. When McKenna had made his call, he had also left a clear mark in the thin film of powder. It required no more than a minute to determine the number McKenna had called.

"So now we'll see to Carson," the Masked Detective remarked and looked down at McKenna. "I hope you'll be quite uncomfortable. If the ropes don't bother you enough, roll close to the radiator and perhaps you'll get burned. Good night, Barrister."

The Masked Detective bowed ironically, let himself out the front door and disappeared into the grounds around the attorney's house. He whipped off the mask and headed for the nearest telephone.

But if Rex Parker had been just a few moments later in leaving McKenna, he might have saved himself one of the narrowest escapes he would ever experience. As the darkness swallowed the Masked Detective up, a car rolled to a stop in front of McKenna's and one of Carson's hoodlums climbed out. He sauntered up to the front door, rang the bell and when he became impatient, he looked inside and saw McKenna trussed up and lying on the hall floor.

The crook smashed a window, reached the attorney and hastily cut him loose. McKenna reached for the telephone and called Carson as quickly as he could.

"The Masked Detective heard me talking to you and he has the number of the phone where you are. He's on his way over, so prepare a welcome. This time don't fail. None of your funny business trying to capture him. Kill him! Make damned sure he doesn't get away. Mullane's wife? I don't give a damn what you do to her. She might be an easy way of trapping the Masked Detective. Just don't miss, Carson. That man can send both of us to the chair."

As the attorney talked, the Masked Detective was also doing some talking on the phone. He had stepped into a store and called Gleason.

"Would the estimable chief inspector mind if the Masked Detective phoned you, Sergeant?" he asked. "He would, eh? Yes, I understand. Now I'll repay him, but not in kind. Go to Attorney McKenna's place. You'll find that great lawyer tied up in the corridor. Hold him, without bail. The charge will be kidnaping. Never mind who has been snatched. Now use another phone and find out where a phone number I'll give you is located. Work fast—and I'm trusting you, Sergeant, not to send a radio car to grab me."

Gleason closed his office door before he made the call to the telephone supervisor. Then he relayed the information to the Masked Detective. Rex Parker hung up, hurried to the street and hailed a cab. The address Gleason had given him was in one of the modest sections of the city. Parker knew the neighborhood as being inhabited by mechanics and clerks of moderate income. Carson selected his hideouts carefully.

THE HOUSE turned out to be a two-story, one-family dwelling. There was a wide vacant lot on either side of it and then other houses of a similar pattern. The house was darkened and Parker noticed a peculiar thing from his hiding place across the street. The front door was slightly ajar.

Immediately he sensed a trap, but decided McKenna couldn't possibly have slipped out of his ropes to warn Carson. One thing he did not notice was the fact that the windows of the second floor, and some of those on the first were boarded up.

He made certain that he was unobserved, donned his mask and cut cross the street half a block away. He crouched, seeking shelter in the darkness and tall grass of the vacant lot to the south of the house. Slowly and cautiously he approached and drew his gun as he lay flat on the ground near the front porch, listening for any signs of life. He wondered if it were possible that Carson had another hideout somewhere nearby and used this apparently vacant place merely as a telephone station.

As the Masked Detective he had to take chances. It was all part of the game of life and death into which he had entered. Inspector Mullane's wife: might be a prisoner inside or, if she wasn't, some clue might be present to give ham the necessary lead.

He climbed noiselessly onto the porch, tiptoed across it, bending double to avoid passing the window. The partly opened door both intrigued and alarmed him. He gave it a gentle push and ducked back in case he was to be greeted by a salvo of gunfire. Nothing happened. He opened the door wider, and stepped into the dark hallway. Not a sound was to be heard.

Directly ahead he saw a staircase leading to the second floor, but, decided to examine the first floor rooms before he let himself in too deeply. He headed for a doorway, and then froze in his tracks. From upstairs came a single, agonizing scream. It filled the house and re-echoed through the rooms.

The Masked Detective hesitated no longer. That scream could have come from no one but Inspector Mullane's wife!

He went up the stairs two at a time, gun ready for instant action. At the top he paused to peer through the darkness and listen for more sounds. He heard a banging noise, like someone might make if strapped down in a chair. It came from the right wing and he followed this sound. A closed door barred his way. He put an ear against the panels and heard the banging again. He set his shoulder against the door and shoved.

Now he could hear the muffled sound of a woman's voice. Mrs. Mullane must be gagged, but how, then, had she screamed? More and more he sensed a trap, but he could do nothing about it now. He had to try everything in his power to save this woman.

He drew back and splintered the door with a savage attack. But he didn't see a shadowy form slip out of another room, duck down the hallway and vanish at the head of the staircase.

When this man reached the first floor, five men emerged from hiding places in other rooms. Each held a pail and then promptly sloshed the contents around. Liquid from two of the buckets was thrown all over the staircase.

Then the men retreated to the porch. One took a match from his pocket, grinned evilly and lit it. He flipped the tiny torch into the hallway and instantly the combustible fluid they had sprinkled around, caught fire. It spread so fast that there was a miniature explosion and the entire staircase became a mass of roaring flame. The arsonist slammed the front door, turned the key in the lock and all five men sprinted away into the night.

THE MASKED rescuer, unaware of the flaming trap, had broken the door down and rushed over to the side of a gray-haired woman, who was cruelly roped to a chair. He got the gag loose and as he worked on her bonds, he asked questions.

"How did you scream with that gag in your mouth?"

"There was—a man here," she panted. "Only a minute before—you came. He removed the gag and twisted my wrist until I screamed. Then he put the gag back and ran out. Who—are you?"

"One of your husband's favorite playmates—the Masked Detective. We're not out of this mess yet. I didn't see or hear anyone when I came in, so they must be waiting for us. I want you to remain well behind me. If those crooks are downstairs, I'll start shooting. No matter what happens to me, you must get out and then run—run as fast as you can. I'll be all right I…. Listen! That crackling! I smell smoke! Wait here!"

The Masked Detective ran out into the hall and let out a shout. The fire was already eating at the top steps and spreading fast. The house was old and dry. The gasoline-induced flames gained headway with each passing second.

He rushed back into the room, put an arm around the woman he had untied and tried to buck up her courage.

"They've set fire to the place," he said quickly. "It looks rather bad, but since when did a bunch of hoodlums get the best of good upright citizens like you and me?"

"Even if one of us wears a mask," Mrs. Mullane appended, and tried to smile bravely in the light from the flames.

The Masked Detective led her into the hallway. He saw instantly that it would be nothing short of suicide to try a descent down the staircase. He turned and darted back into the room, looking for a window. He found one—and also discovered that it was boarded up and well nailed. He grabbed the chair, the only article of furniture in the room, wielded it as hard and fast as he could. The boards held.

"We've got to hurry!" Mrs. Mullane called. "The fire is almost at my feet now."

"The attic!" the Masked Detective cried. "There must be an attic. It's our one and only chance."

He found the attic door, opened it and both of them rushed up the narrow, steep flight of stairs. The Masked Detective slammed the door to check the fire as much as possible. Then they were in darkness.

He lit a match and held it high, looking vainly for some kind of trap-door which might lead to the roof. All he saw was an old shovel leaning in a corner, and that the attic apparently had once been used as an indoor laundry for there were clothes line ropes strung from end to the other.

"Looks like we'll have to become acrobats," he said, and grinned at the woman. "Mind very much?"

She had courage which amazed the Masked Detective.

"No indeed. Still I can't understand just what you're up to, Young-Man-With-a-Mask."

THE MASKED DETECTIVE grabbed the shovel, threw his head back and studied the underside of the roof shingles until he found a section that was cracked. He inserted the sharp edge of the shovel and pried. Some of the shingles flew off.

He attacked the spot vigorously, for he could already hear the rapid advance of the flames below. In about five minutes the whole house would be gutted, attic and all. Unless they were out of it, they'd either roast there or when the floor fell in, would land among flaming embers. Neither idea appealed to the Masked Detective.

"Can't I help?" the woman asked excitedly.

"You can. Take some matches out of my pocket and find where that clothes line is hooked up. Get it free—and hurry. We haven't much time left."

The shovel continued to bite small bits out of the shingles. Then, with a savage determination, the Masked Detective ripped several shingles away and cool air filtered down. Mrs. Mullane returned to his side, holding the coiled piece of rope. He studied the hole he had punched in the roof, then seized her around the waist.

"Up you go. Wiggle through the hole and hang onto the shingles for all you are worth. Never mind slivers or torn clothing!"

CHAPTER XIX

UNMASKED

DECIDEDLY MRS. MULLANE was no young woman, but she was agile and slim. She worried her way through the hole and disappeared from sight.

The Masked Detective heard an ominous crackling, looked around and saw a tongue of flame shoot through the floor. It spread with amazing speed. He gave a leap, hauled himself through the hole and Mrs. Mullane was ready to help as much as she could.

When the Masked Detective finally reached the roof, he worked fast. Judging by the way the flames had spread in less than six or seven minutes, the whole roof would be afire in three more. He braced his feet against the edge of the hole he had created, while Mrs. Mullane clung to the shingles and waited for orders. He slipped one end of the clothes line under her arms, knotted it firmly and then spoke in a soothing voice.

"We're as good as saved. I'll let you down slowly. Roll over the edge and when you reach the ground, yell. Untie the rope and I'll wind my end around the chimney and slide down myself. Ready?"

Mrs. Mullane nodded and smiled. "Happy landing, Mr. Mask."

She slid down the roof, went over the edge and the Masked Detective braced himself against the rope. It tightened and he slowly let it out. He winced as flame shot out of the hole in the roof and singed his legs. Then, unexpectedly, he found that there was no more rope.

In the distance he could hear sirens and someone yelled from one of the nearby houses. He had to get away from here fast. There would be police along with the firemen and now police meant arrest and exposure.

"How near the ground are you?" he yelled.

"Just below the second story window," Mrs. Mullane called back.

"I'm going to let you drop," the Masked Detective told her. "Get set! Don't brace yourself, and roll away from the house if you get hurt."

He released the rope and hastily moved his legs out of the path of flame. Half a minute later Mrs. Mullane called that she was unhurt and safe. Then the Masked Detective tried to figure out his own predicament. The roof was blazing in spots already. If he let himself slide down the roof, off the edge to plunge to the ground, he would be lucky if he broke nothing more than a leg. Which spelled instant capture for him.

THEN A man's voice, strident with excitement, called out directions.

"Crawl up and go down the other side! There's a big tree. You can grab a branch. Hurry—the whole place is ready to cave in!"

The Masked Detective clawed at the shingles and pulled himself slowly to the peak of the slanted roof. There was a tree, almost touching the roof. It was huge and thickly branched. The Masked Detective took a long breath, gave himself a push and slid down the steep incline at a rapid clip. He sailed over the edge.

Leaves and branches scratched his face and hands, ripped his clothing and knocked his hat off. Then his hands closed around a thick branch. The jerk of the sudden stop felt as though it had pulled his arms out of their sockets. He hung there, swinging like a monkey on a bar. Then his dizziness left and he gradually made his way in toward the trunk.

"Come down out of there," the same voice called out and there was anger in it. "Don't make a funny play or I'll let you have it. This is the law!"

The Masked Detective groaned, and knew then why that voice had sounded both familiar and strange. It was Sergeant Gleason and the Masked Detective rarely heard him when rage got the better of his usual calm nature.

The Masked Detective slid down the trunk, landed on the ground and felt a gun jabbed into his spine.

"Turn around," Gleason's voice half snarled. Then, as the masked man obeyed, Gleason gave a glad cry. "The Masked Detective! I figured you were one of the mugs. We've got to get out of here."

But it was too late. A swarm of radio cars and fire apparatus turned into both vacant lots and their headlights illuminated everything. The Masked Detective took a long breath. "Gleason, I've got to trust you. I'm going to remove this mask because if I don't, someone else will rip it off for me."

"Hurry up, Rex, you fool," Gleason gritted. "Of course I know it's you."

Rex Parker gave a start of amazement as he tore off the mask and jammed it into his pocket.

"Then you knew I was the Masked Detective all along?" he asked.

"Ever since that note was found on Joiner's body. I compared the handwriting with yours and it checked. So I prepared another note. Wrote the damned thing myself. Even made the knife hole through it, and when I went home that night, I slaughtered one of my best hens to get the blood which made the phony note seem real. Now stop trying to talk. You came out here with me. Is that clear?"

No one seemed surprised to see Rex Parker at the scene of the fire. He walked with Gleason over to where a detective cruiser was parked, deep in one of the vacant lots.

"After you phoned me about that number, I went over to McKenna's and found our bird had flown his cage," Gleason explained. "I figured he might have prepared some kind of a death trap for you so I beat it over here. There was nothing stirring so I decided to wait. But half a second later I saw the flames and knew you must be inside. I couldn't get in. Then I saw you let a woman down and deliberately release the rope that might have saved your life—to protect her from injury. She beat it—very, very fast. Who was she? Your girl friend, Winnie Bligh?"

Parker grinned as he got into the car.

"So you don't know everything, Sarge? That woman was Mrs. Mullane. Carson took her prisoner and made Mullane give those orders about me and the Masked Detective. Doggone, I should have known I couldn't fool you. Well, what's next? A nice airy cell?"

"Airy cell, my hat," Gleason grunted. "After what you've done for me? Anything but that, Rex. You can be the Masked Detective as long as you wish, but for heaven's sake, don't let on that I know you."

"Great!" Rex Parker applauded. "We'll work together. Winnie knows about this of course. In fact she pushed me into it. You know, I'm glad things happened this way. Relieved, too—because the substitution of that note worried me. I wondered who would finally call me on it. Thanks, Sarge. I may be able to really show my appreciation soon."

"All I want is no known connection with the Masked Detective," Gleason said. "I should hob-nob with a guy who runs around socking helpless gangsters on the nose? That's against the law. Where to now?"

"Mullane's house," Parker said. "Drop me a few blocks away. Mrs. Mullane probably dusted out of the neighborhood and is on her way home by taxi."

GLEASON STOPPED the car not far from Mullane's house. Rex Parker got out and Gleason extended his hand.

"Okay, Mr. Masked Detective. I promise never to interfere in any of your plans. In fact, I don't even want to know about them, but—good luck."

Parker grinned and vanished. He reached Mullane's house, adjusted his mask and found a window wide open. He hauled himself up and into the room without disturbing the two people who had their backs turned toward him.

Mullane had always struck Parker as a hard-hearted, hard-headed man, without the least bit of sympathy in his makeup. He changed his mind about that now, as he watched Mullane and his wife.

The Masked Detective stepped forward.

"I'm afraid, Mrs. Mullane, that we were just a bit too fast for those kidnapers."

Both of them turned swiftly. Mullane's right hand darted toward his pocket, but his wife seized that hand quickly.

"Would you try to hurt the man who saved my life?" she chided.

Mullane gulped and fidgeted nervously. Then he stuck out his hand. It was trembling.

"Whatever I've said or thought about you is all changed," he announced. "I don't know how on earth you accomplished this, and I don't care. But if you ever need the help of the police—pardon me—it's the police who need your help. Anyway, call on me for anything. That goes, no matter what happens from now on."

"Thank you, Inspector," the Masked Detective said. "I came for two reasons—to assure myself that your wife was quite safe, and to learn some of the details about her kidnaping. First of all, I present you with a brief note from Attorney McKenna. When you visited him tonight, he knew your wife had been seized and even knew where she was. I—er—persuaded him to make a few notes about this knowledge. All you have to do now is find him. He slipped away from me. Now give me all the details. When was your wife taken, who contacted you—everything?"

Mullane carried a chair over and urged the man whose life he had declared forfeit only a few hours ago, to sit down. Mullane explained all he knew.

"Mrs. Mullane came to my office early this afternoon. She was going away for a few days. I phoned for a taxi to meet her in front. Apparently those crooks knew all about her plans, for when she got into the cab, someone seized her. This wouldn't have happened except that I was busy and couldn't go along to the station with her. Pritchard came, and took about half an hour of my time asking me when I'd have Trent and Neal's killers booked."

"Pritchard! the Masked Detective asked quickly. "Did he leave after your wife arrived?"

"Yes. He excused himself and left in a hurry, now that I think of it. What are you getting at, man? You don't believe that Pritchard—"

"In this case I'd believe anything," the Masked Detective said. "Now, if you want to show your appreciation for whatever help I gave your wife, don't make one move against Pritchard. Let things go on just as if nothing had happened and above all don't say I visited you. How were you notified to get rid of me?"

"By phone," Mullane groaned. "An anonymous call backed up by my wife's voice to prove she really was in the hands of the kidnapers. I didn't want to give those orders, and ever since I did, my prayers have been divided between my wife's safety and the hope that none of my men would get you. I'll rescind those orders at once."

"Good." The Masked Detective walked toward the door. "And give Rex Parker the run of the place, too. He is the only contact I have and I trust him—implicitly."

Mullane frowned. "Of course I'll do it. Parker's not exactly a man I like, but from now on I'll stand for any of his confounded kidding."

THE MASKED DETECTIVE removed his mask soon after he emerged from Mullane's home. Then he proceeded directly to the apartment house where Dr. James Trent had lived. He interviewed the superintendent, using his newspaper identification to get what he needed. When he left, there was a determined slant to his mouth.

His next stop was at Police Headquarters and he saw Inspector Mullane's car parked in front. The desk lieutenant saluted this time and told Parker the inspector wanted to see him. The *Comet* reporter was instantly admitted. Mullane looked up.

"Well, Parker," he said, "I'm glad to see you. The orders I gave some hours ago have been countermanded. I want you to understand that I did not give them willingly. Your friend, the Masked Detective, helped me out of a serious difficulty and should any occasion arise in which I can aid him, you may ask any favor he wishes."

"Thanks." Rex Parker grinned. "We'll both be grateful. You know, maybe I've been dead wrong about you. I figured any man who got your position through politics didn't deserve it, but I've changed my mind. You're a cop now—and a good one."

Sergeant Gleason was in his office, studying the confession which McKenna had written. Parker closed the door and they spoke softly. Gleason held up the confession.

"Mullane hands this to me with orders that McKenna is to be picked up and sweated until he admits that everything on the paper is the truth. That's no job for an ordinary mortal, Rex. McKenna is smart, and he knows every loophole of the law. Besides, I haven't the vaguest idea where he is hiding. Do you think this confession would hold him? I don't!"

"It will if we back it up with facts," Parker said. "Which is exactly what I hope to do. We're closing in, Sarge. Carson and McKenna are on the run. Carson's various methods of making things easy have been broken to bits, but we haven't got our real brains yet. To get him we'll have to operate much as he does—by stealth. I have an idea. It needs your cooperation, so open those ears and listen."

Parker talked for ten minutes while a slow smile crossed Gleason's face.

"It might work at that," the detective-sergeant admitted. "Won't be too easy, either your part or mine, but it's worth the risk. I'll handle it. And Rex—did you destroy that piece of blood-stained paper?"

Parker nodded. "Burned it and rubbed the ashes into the gutter. So everything is set now. By this time tomorrow we'll have our man tied up in knots, with enough evidence to burn him just as surely as I destroyed that paper."

CHAPTER XX

TROUBLE AHEAD

B Y THE time Parker returned to the newspaper offices, it was after midnight. Despite the hour, Winnie was there.

"I didn't want to leave until I knew you were safe," she said. "What's happened?"

Rex Parker told her the entire story of the kidnaping and the subsequent rescue.

"One thing I'm positive of now is that there really is a clever mind at the head of the gang. I sensed it from the beginning. Now I have the proof, but not the kind of proof that would stand up in court. Don't ask me who the man is, because I might be wrong."

"McKenna?" Winnie tried to wheedle it out of him. "He's a natural crook and a good organizer. Elijah Squires? He's one man I'd like to see stripped of that phony Blue Law attitude he shows. Or maybe some of those other men on the committee—Adams the banker, Ingerman who heads the city buildings, Pritchard the high and mighty, or even Weaver the importer? I've run through the list, darling."

"And run right over the name of the man I suspect." Parker chuckled. "Nothing doing. Until I've got the proof I need, my mouth stays shut, even to you. By the way, Gleason knows I'm the Masked Detective. He caught me red-handed tonight, but he knew even before that. Gleason substituted another blood-stained note for the one I worried about so much."

Winnie gave a long sigh of relief when she heard that.

"You don't know how much that worried me. Now I'm glad Gleason knows, because he can help you. But understand this, Rex Parker—I help too. This is as much my fight as it is yours."

Parker took both of her slender hands between his own and looked straight into her eyes.

"I'm at your service, Captain Bligh. You know that. Now I have a story to write—a most important story. If it works out right, we'll begin squeezing our clever mind until he hollers. I won't be ten minutes, so wait and I'll take you home...."

At one o'clock the next afternoon, Rex Parker was admitted to the private offices in one of the biggest museums. Pritchard was there, at the head of a conference table. Around it were gathered the other members of the committee. Leonard Adams, Elijah Squires, Ingerman and Weaver. All but Squires greeted the *Comet* reporter with enthusiasm. Squires arose to protest.

"Why should we allow this reporter to know all of our plans? Why don't we include representatives of the other newspapers? In my opinion Parker isn't worthy of getting a complete scoop."

"He won't get one," Pritchard said. "Not complete, anyway. I feel that we owe Parker something for the insult your suspicions created. Furthermore, I'm sure he can help us to go through with this new proposition. You're only one man, Squires. We've out-voted you."

"And I'll remove myself," Squires raged. "I want nothing more to do with any of you. However, I insist that I be given proper credit for my work in assembling these masterpieces. My name must appear on the plaque or I'll sue. And one more thing: This man Parker is an intimate of the Masked Detective. How do we know this masked man isn't a crook, either hoodwinking Parker or collaborating with him in some stupendous crime? What if they were to steal those masterpieces? They are irreplaceable. Don't say I didn't warn you after it happens."

SQUIRES STALKED out. Hamilton Weaver laughed derisively.

"I'm glad the old fool is gone. That stuffed shirt attitude of his gives me a pain. Now let's get on with it, Pritchard. Tell Parker why we called him in."

Pritchard held up an early edition of the *Comet* and pointed to an item, boxed in blue pencil.

"I read this story of yours with considerable interest, Parker," he said. "So Raoul LeFond is actually coming to this country. Are you sure of this?"

Parker sat down in the chair which Squires had vacated.

"Unless LeFond's press agent is a liar, I'm sure," he told the committeemen. "Also I think I know just what's up your sleeve. LeFond is one of the world's greatest connoisseurs of all kinds of art. You want him to examine and appraise the stuff you've collected. Am I right?"

"Good guessing," Weaver put in. "That's it exactly. LeFond has a worldwide reputation. If he will examine the various pieces we have assembled, then gives you a story in which he admires our choice, it will practically make us and all those who backed the deal. It's just the kind of publicity we need. Will you contact his agents and arrange things?"

"Why not?" Parker answered. "More grist for my typewriter, and I'm glad to give you gentlemen a break. All press agents are susceptible to influence from the press so I'll get in touch with LeFond's man and have everything set. He arrives on an Italian liner at five o'clock this afternoon. I'll use ship-to-shore telephone service. Rest easy, gentlemen, he'll be here."

THE MEETING adjourned. Rex Parker walked out with Hamilton Weaver, discussing the art objects which had been so painstakingly accumulated. They headed down the street toward the business section where Weaver had his offices.

"A year's work about to reach its culmination," Weaver sighed. "You don't know how hard it is to contact people these days, Parker. With the war in Europe, the trouble in the Orient—I've been at my wit's end. Then worry, worry, every second while the goods are being sent here, for fear that a torpedo might sink the ship. The only consolation lies in the fact that I purchased the goods for just about two-thirds of their value. War makes bargains in things like art."

They crossed an intersecting street while Weaver described some of the pieces.

"An earthernware punch bowl, warranted to have been used by Nero. There are two alabaster perfume jars taken from a tomb in Egypt—worth a fortune in themselves. Powder boxes, trinkets, everything to give a true picture of the life and times of the Pharaohs. Then some exquisite examples of Sung and Ming dynasty pottery from China. Painting and tapestries created during the Dark Ages. I tell you this display will be the talk of the world! Nothing like it has ever been attempted before and—"

Suddenly Parker gave a leap. His arms wrapped around Weaver and he pulled him to the sidewalk. A sedan had been following them for the last hundred yards, traveling slowly. Now it headed in toward the curb and Parker saw the gleam of a gun. Two shots roared—then four more.

Pedestrians fled and Weaver let out a moan of fear.

"Lie still—pretend he got you," Parker warned in a whisper.

Two more shots belched from the gun muzzle and then a taunting laugh made Weaver's blood run cold.

"You asked for it, Nosey Joe. So there it is!"

THE MURDER car spurted forward, took the next corner on screeching wheels and had a three-minute advantage before radio police began their pursuit.

A detective cruiser pulled up several minutes later as Weaver, shaken and numb with terror, was helped over to a stairway by Rex Parker. Both sat down.

Sergeant Gleason jumped out of the detective cruiser and rushed up.

"I got a radio broadcast about the shooting! What happened?"

Parker brushed off his clothes.

"Seems as though our friend Cal Carson almost made another of his fatal mistakes. He mistook either me or Mr. Weaver here for some mug known as Nosey Joe. At least that's the name the killer yelled."

"Nosey Joe," Gleason grunted. "I figured his number was up as soon as Carson started his murder campaign. Come to think of it he looks something like Mr. Weaver—about the same build anyway. I'd better take you men home."

Weaver found his voice. "Thanks, Parker. You saved my life that time. I didn't even notice that car pulling up. If you hadn't knocked me over, I'd have been right in the line of fire. And Sergeant Gleason, I—I think I'll accept your offer of a lift. Just in case those—those devils decide to come back and rectify their error."

Parker helped him into the car. Gleason used the siren to clear a path through the stalled traffic. Rex Parker frowned deeply.

"If those bullets had found their mark, you'd have been the third man to die because of mistaken identity, Mr. Weaver. One instance of that kind looks funny, two instances make it too damned coincidental. But three—it simply proves that Carson and his mob are not after the men whose names the killers yell out. Nothing of the kind. I'm convinced that Carson really wanted to murder Dr. Trent, Buck Neal—and you. Why? Maybe you can answer that, Weaver. You're the only man they missed."

"But I don't know," Weaver replied. "I have never seen this Carson, nor any of his men, to my best knowledge. I haven't been instrumental in having them arrested at any time. I'm sure I haven't even gone so far as to condemn them publicly. That's the truth—I'll swear to it."

Parker shook his head slowly from side to side.

"It's got beyond me, but it does seem that all this has something to do with those pieces of art work you brought into the country. Trent had a knowledge of them, so did Buck Neal, and so do you, Weaver. I wonder if Carson is foolish enough to be setting the stage for a grand robbery?"

Weaver grunted contemptuously at that and said:

"I'd like to see him try to get his filthy hands on those pieces! We maintain a twenty-four hour guard of a dozen armed men who never leave the objects out of their sight."

CHAPTER XXI

THE MAN FROM FRANCE

UNAWARE THAT this new attempt at murder was taking place, Winnie Bligh was busily engaged in following Rex Parker's instructions. She boarded a cutter to meet the Italian liner due in at five o'clock. There were a dozen and a half other ship's news reporters on the ship, kidding her unmercifully about the *Comet's* tightwad methods in sending a beauty column writer to get ship news.

When they boarded the liner, Winnie held a small black bag in one hand and she went immediately to the purser's quarters. There she displayed a letter which bore the imprint of the Metropolitan Police Department.

"I'll want a vacant cabin if there is one," she explained. "If not, wait until some passenger vacates as the ship docks. Post a steward near the gangplank and when a man named Rex Parker appears, he is to be brought to this particular cabin at once. And add to your list of passengers the name of Raoul LeFond from Paris. When the reporters want to see him, he has given instructions that there is to be no interview. Do you understand everything?"

"Quite." The purser bowed. "This is some tremendous coup, eh? Be assured that all will be taken care of."

Winnie was escorted to a vacant cabin and she sat down, anxiously awaiting Parker. She opened the black bag and took a photograph from it, studying the features carefully and from all angles. When the *Comet* crime reporter appeared, she was ready for action.

He stripped off his coat, vest and tie, sat down and Winnie first plastered his hair with a dye to make it very black. Then she combed it differently. She worked on the eyes, giving them the illusion of being much wider. She added a bit of gray coloring to the temples, fixed a heavy black beard in place and stood back to admire her job.

"Rex, you take to disguise perfectly. Look at the picture of Raoul LeFond, and then check it with your own reflection."

"Perfect!"

Even Parker was startled by the drastic change in his appearance. He stepped into the adjoining cabin of the suite, carrying the black bag with him. When he emerged, he wore gray striped trousers, a long black coat and a wide black hat. He carried a gold-topped cane. A white pocket handkerchief was prominently displayed in his breast pocket and carried the initials R. LeF.

"Maybe I take disguise perfectly, Winnie, but the credit goes to you for arranging everything and making me look like this. It's got to work. If I fail now, the whole thing will tumble, and someone is due to collect sixteen million dollars. Now you know what to do. Daytimes stay in the office, nights camp near your apartment phone. Now I think Monsieur Raoul LeFond will go ashore and brave the dangers of the New World. Wish me luck, darling—and don't worry."

The Masked Detective, in a new and unmasked rÔle walked out on deck. A cluster of reporters followed him. As Rex Parker, he knew every one of them and when he passed their inspection, he was positive his disguise couldn't be penetrated. He refused an interview by shrugging his shoulders and finally waving the reporters aside. He walked serenely down the gangplank and paused as if he expected someone, and yet was not sure just who.

Two men hurried up.

"Welcome," they chorused. "We've got a car ready for you. No mistaking you, sir. You sure look like your picture."

THE MASKED DETECTIVE nodded gravely and walked between the pair until they reached a heavy sedan. He got in and each man parked on either side of him.

"I am a very busy man," he said with a perfect accent. "But when so many of the world's treasures are gathered under one roof, I must see them. We proceed there at once—*oui?*"

"Sure, sure," one of the escorts assured him. "It's kind of a long ride and we go through the slums, but you got nothing to worry about. Just sit back and relax."

The Masked Detective sat back and did anything but relax. Those two men were phonies and as evident as the sunlight. He did not know if their orders were to murder him and dispose of his corpse, or to bring him to a certain gang headquarters, willingly or not.

As the car sped through some of the poorer sections of the city, the man who usually wore a disguising velvet mask realized that he was to be taken alive, and he felt considerably relieved. If these two men started to work on him, he would have been compelled to fight back and possibly reveal himself. Such an act would have meant an upheaval in his plans.

The car suddenly took a sharp right-hand turn and rolled through the doors of a run-down garage. The Masked Detective, acting his part, gave a startled exclamation. Instantly two guns dug into his ribs.

"Just act nice, Frenchy, and you won't get hurt. Climb out now and no tricks, understand?"

"But—but this is incredible!" the Masked Detective cried out. "I do not understand."

"Yeah," one of the thugs laughed harshly. "Incred—incred— Say, they got words for everythin', ain't they? Come along, Whiskers, or would you like a sock right on the button?"

The Masked Detective marched between them, crossed the wide length of the garage floor, and entered a small office. Carson and McKenna were there. Carson motioned to a chair.

"Okay, Frenchy," he said. "Just have a seat. We'll tie you up for a while and if you act right, you go free."

"But—but I do not understand," the masquerading Parker protested. "I was invited to come to your country in order that I might make arrangements for the purchase—"

He stopped abruptly and looked down at the floor.

"Purchase of what?" McKenna stepped forward, "What are you talking about? Out with it."

The Masked Detective shrugged. "It seems that my mission is not only secret, but also dangerous. If I do not answer you, then I am to be injured, *oui?* I can see as much in your faces. Therefore, what can I do but tell the truth? I came here at the invitation of one Hamilton Weaver to negotiate for the purchase of certain *objets d'art*. You will please explain why this has happened to me."

"We'll explain all right," Carson snarled. "But not to you, Frenchy. Come on, McKenna, we're going to pay a nice little social call."

Carson drew a gun and spun the cylinder significantly. He called for the two men who had kidnaped the man they believed to be LeFond and gave them orders to watch him.

"If Weaver says we're a couple of liars, we'll let him listen to this bozo spill the beans. Let's go!"

THE MOTOR of a car whirred and tires squealed over the concrete as Carson gave her the gun. The Masked Detective leaned back in his chair in the room in which he had been left, and looked at the two men who guarded him. Neither thought the show of a gun necessary. This foppishly dressed, middle-aged man certainly did not look like a menace. In fact he seemed so scared as to be unable to move.

The two thugs liked that. They enjoyed their power over an individual. Their prisoner watched them narrowly, checking off minutes in his mind. Finally he reached toward his vest and like a flash both men went for their guns. Then they relaxed. The Masked Detective began fingering a gold watch-chain. Casually he drew out an old-fashioned watch fob, made of gold with a stone that glistened like a diamond, imbedded in the center.

One of the crooks nudged his companion and spoke in a hoarse whisper.

"Did you see that rock? Carson won't care if we cop it. What do you say?"

The second man looked as avaricious as he felt.

"Sure, why not? It's a pip, and anyway this bozo will be bumped sooner or later."

They approached the be-whiskered Masked Detective, grinning broadly.

"How about lettin' us take a squint at the rock, Frenchy? Nice little trinket, ain't it?"

The supposed LeFond quickly pressed a hand against his vest pocket as if to protect the jeweled fob. One of the thugs leaned forward. The next instant he went hurtling across the room with a pain shooting through his abdomen like fire.

The second crook made a grab for his gun. The Masked Detective leaped from the chair, sent a hard-right fist skyrocketing upward and clipped the thug a glancing blow on the chin. It bowled him over and his attacker landed on top of him. He measured the victim for a knock-out blow and rapped it home.

"Okay, wise guy!" The first thug was on his knees, but he had managed to draw a gun. His face was creased with pain. "Stick 'em up! If Carson didn't say you was important alive, I'd let you have it right through the heart."

The Masked Detective backed away a step and raised his hands. The thug struggled to his feet and swayed, clutching at his stomach with his free hand. He advanced a few steps. "Le Fond" eyed the gun and the distance between himself and the thug. Then his right foot went up so fast that it was just a blur. The gun flew out of the thug's hand and a mighty fist crashed against his jaw.

But all this had made a terrific racket and the Masked Detective who had hoped to dispose of both men fast knew that the slightest delay would bring other members of the mob hurrying to the aid of their pals. He picked up the gun he had kicked out of one thug's hand and spun around just in time to see the door open and two men in overalls rush in.

"Reach!" he barked.

They obeyed promptly. He ordered them against the further wall, removed their guns, then forced them into a wash-room. He locked the door, darted into the garage proper and saw two more thugs maintaining a vigil at the big doors. Apparently they had heard none of the racket.

Ducking behind a car, he moved forward cautiously and gripped his borrowed revolver by the barrel. He made a leap, brought down the butt and sent one of the guards sliding to the floor. The other went for his gun, but froze into immobility. The Masked Detective flipped his weapon into the air, spun it once and caught it on the way down. He had practiced that trick many times on the police range, never realizing that it would prove useful.

"Turn around," he ordered. "Now don't move while I frisk you."

THAT DONE, he backed the thug into the middle of the garage, pulled down the hook of a small tackle and fastened it securely into the thug's pants. He hoisted the man as high as possible, waved to him and got into one of the cars. He rolled out of the garage, turned right and shot away. At the next corner he saw a patrolman. He brought the car to a stop and hailed him.

"In the garage back there,"—he pointed out the place—"kidnapers and murderers. Members of Carson's mob. If you work fast, you can nail every one. Three are unconscious, two are locked in the wash-room and another hangs high—by the seat of his pants."

Without giving the patrolman a chance to ask questions, the man the policeman could not guess was the Masked Detective sent the car moving away. In the rear view mirror he saw the patrolman blow a blast on his whistle, and then streak for the garage.

He traveled fast, paying no attention to traffic lights and possessing the luck that usually follows those who deliberately break traffic rules. Not a policeman was in sight. He dashed across town, turned into an avenue and stopped just behind the car which Carson and McKenna had used.

CHAPTER XXII

THE MASKED DETECTIVE INTERVENES

VASTLY ENRAGED, Hamilton Weaver stood in the middle of his living room with his hands raised shoulder high and a look of intense rage on his face.

"You stupid dolts!" he barked. "I don't know what you're talking about! And bringing up the subject of a double cross—what of that attempt to kill me?"

"You're nuts," Carson growled. "We didn't send anybody to gun you out, but how I wish we did. You're the rat! You sent for some French guy to come here and buy the stuff. Don't argue—we got him and he squawked all over the place. You were going to sell out, take the dough and leave us holding the bag. Only it won't work, wise guy. I'm moving in. Me and McKenna. We get the boys together, push over them guards at the museum and take the stuff for ourselves. We'll make the Frenchman buy it and pay right through the nose. As for you—how will you take it, through the chest or the belly?"

"Wait!" Weaver begged frantically. "I tell you this is all a set-up. Someone really did try to gun me out this afternoon. Damned near succeeded, too, and... I've got it! I know the answer to all of this. When I was shot at, Rex Parker was with me. He knocked me down and pretended to save my life."

"For what?" McKenna broke in. "Stop stalling, Weaver. It won't get you the slightest mercy. Go ahead, Carson."

"Let's hear what this is all about," Carson countered. "That guy Rex Parker being in this means that the Masked Detective was around. Maybe we all got the double cross."

"That's it," Weaver half screeched. "I see through his whole scheme now! He suspected I might be the real head of your gang. He and the Masked Detective planned to make me think you boys were trying to gun me out. He thought I'd get sore and give the whole thing away. That must be it. You've got to listen to reason."

McKenna's lips curled in scorn.

"Did you expect us to believe that? We heard nothing about the attempt on your life and if the Masked Detective figured you ran this outfit, he'd have cracked down on you before this. You know he doesn't fool. Sorry, Weaver. When we agreed to work for you, we were sure it was for a right guy we could trust. You're nothing but a heel, ready to make us do the dirty work and then take all the profits. Okay, Carson. No use waiting any longer."

Carson scowled and raised his gun, sighting it against Weaver's chest. A chair tipped over somewhere behind him. Carson swore and turned. He lowered the gun and all the blood drained out of his face. The Masked Detective stood behind him, gun in hand.

"Drop your weapons, gentlemen," the Masked Detective said grimly. "I'm exactly in the mood for gun play, especially with you two standing in front of me. No, Weaver—you're included for the moment. Just pretend that friend Carson is still drawing a bead on you."

Carson and McKenna let their weapons fall to the floor. The Masked Detective walked closer and kicked the guns into a corner. He moved over beside Weaver.

"What'll we do with 'em, Weaver?" he asked.

Weaver looked startled. "You mean—I get a break?"

The Masked Detective's shoulders moved.

"Why not? But I warn you, it's going to be expensive."

"Give me that gun," Weaver snarled. "Calling me a rat—I'll show those dumb clucks."

"On second thought," the Masked Detective said, "I'm a little afraid to turn over a weapon to you, Weaver. It might be possible that you'd put a bullet through me, too. Forget them for the present, and I promise you they won't walk out of this house under their, own steam. Tie them up—very firmly."

WEAVER NEEDED no second invitation. He tore down a window drape, ripped it into strips and fastened Carson and McKenna so tightly that they groaned in agony. He stepped back beside the Masked Detective.

"I always figured you weren't in this for love," he said. "What's your proposition?"

"Fifty percent," the masked man replied. "After all, I did a lot of work in running you down, my friend. You were clever. Of course, you never used those funds to purchase art from Egypt, China and Europe. You simply faked the whole process and had some duplicates made. In order to make certain they wouldn't be detected, you proceeded to murder Dr. Trent, who would have recognized the Egyptian stuff as faked. Buck Neal would have spoiled everything concerning your European paintings and tapestries and Arnold Marquod would have made a fool of you, once he laid eyes on the Chinese pottery.

"With them out of the way, the committee would be forced to take the word of men you already had planted in the museums, that the pieces were authentic. You managed to convince the members of the committee that premature publicity would lessen public interest in the new acquisitions. That was to protect yourself. Once everything was set and the last dollar turned over to you, as the agent who brought the goods over here, you could travel fast and far. The money has been turned over to you. Where is the money, Weaver?"

"In my office," Weaver replied quickly. "In my big safe. I'll gladly give you half with the consideration that we join forces. I know every angle of gang organization. I brought Carson here to act as the apparent head of the mob. But when this business turned up about the art purchasing, I horned in. My cover up was that of commission merchant dealing in art works, so it was easy. We can take that money—you and I—and travel. I'll have plastic surgery done and we'll set up a gang, the likes of which no nation has ever seen."

"Ambitious," the Masked Detective said. "I'm right with you. Weaver, but first I want to see the color of your money. Shall we go?"

Weaver motioned toward Carson and McKenna. "What about them?"

The Masked Detective let a cold smile cross his lips. He waited until Weaver donned his hat and coat. Then he took the crooked commission merchant by the arm and held him securely, forcing him out of the room. He aimed his gun and fired four quick shots, but at what targets Weaver could not see. Carson gave a yelp that sounded like a dying man's last wail.

"That," the Masked Detective said coldly, "is that. Let's get away, Weaver, before those shots are reported."

Weaver drove his car carefully and kept glancing out of the corner of his eyes at the masked man beside him. He had suspected all along that the Masked Detective was, in fact, a crook.

For the moment the masked man certainly held the upper hand, also, but Weaver was not defeated yet. Even if he could not overpower the Masked Detective he would still retain fifty percent of the loot. Which was enough. Then, also, he would have a first-class partner in crime. Weaver was trying to figure out the best angle.

"Don't stop in front of your office building," the Masked Detective warned. "Someone might see me. The mask is a dead give-away. We'll use the freight elevator. And Weaver—watch your step. I don't exactly trust you and won't until you count half the money into my hands. I killed two men just a few minutes ago and I certainly wouldn't hesitate with you."

Weaver looked properly hurt.

"But I don't want to play any tricks," he protested. "All I ask is that we operate together from now on. Well—here we are. Down the alley to the rear platform as you said."

CHAPTER XXIII

CAPTAIN BLIGH IN COMMAND

QUIETLY, WEAVER brought the car to a stop. The Masked Detective got out, held his gun ready and watched Weaver emerge. He let the crooked art dealer precede him into the building and they rode the freight elevator to the sixteenth floor where Weaver maintained his suite of offices.

Weaver removed his keys from his pocket most carefully. He remembered how cold-bloodedly the Masked Detective had shot Carson and McKenna. More and more Weaver began to realize just how big a break all this was. If the masked man had been a minute later, Carson and McKenna would have held all the cards.

Weaver turned on the lights, crossed the reception office and entered his swanky private quarters. There was a huge safe against one wall, but he did not approach it immediately, nor did the Masked Detective order him to do so.

The art dealer sat down behind his desk, placed his hands palms up on the surface and smiled.

There is just one thing I'd like to know before we culminate this deal," he said to the Masked Detective. "Where did I slip? How did you stumble onto my identity?"

The Masked Detective kept his gun trained on Weaver as he answered.

"You contacted Joiner Seddon first, gave him plenty of cash, and set him up in the same apartment building where Dr. Trent lived. You even provided Joiner with clothes identical to those Trent always wore. Both men were much alike in build.

"Then you ordered Carson to have his men get Joiner. You knew that Trent was due at a lecture, knew the exact time he would leave the house. The men who actually did the killing didn't know Joiner and naturally, provided with Trent's description which you told them was Joiner's, they mistook Trent for Joiner—and committed murder. Shortly after that I interviewed Joiner Seddon. I warned him he was in danger and while he showed fear, thinking possibly that you'd get him anyhow, he didn't seem quite frightened enough.

"I left him for a moment to arrange the getaway. While I was gone, he phoned you—directly. In those apartment houses the switchboard operators keep a record of each call. You made a serious error in letting Joiner know your identity. Of course, you planned to murder him, so you had an idea it wouldn't make much difference."

Weaver grinned.

"So that was it," he murmured. "A point I'll have to remember. Yes, Joiner phoned me and asked what he should do about you. I told him to follow your orders, and I rushed over. I trailed you to Police Headquarters, killed Joiner and took the confession off his body. That was clever, don't you think?"

"Very," the Masked Detective agreed. "But in this new partnership of ours, I'll take command. You think fast, but not thoroughly. And kidnaping will be entirely out of our line. No more snatching of police inspector's wives. Such things simply intensify the police in their hunt for crooks. Yet I will grant you it was accomplished with dispatch."

Weaver arose and started to pace up and down.

"Pritchard was coming out of Inspector Mullane's office when I met him," he explained. "He told me Mullane's wife was going away and that a taxi had been called. I had been looking for a method of tying you up in knots, of breaking off your connection with the police, so I arranged a taxi of my own. Now it all seems so funny—knowing now that you were doing the same thing I tried to do; get the confidence of the police to learn how the chase was progressing."

The art dealer stopped pacing, and moved over to the safe, stopped in front of it.

"Well, my masked friend," he said, "I'm going to open the safe. Sixteen millions of dollars—or very nearly that sum. I haven't had a chance to collect on some of the pieces, but we can't have everything."

WEAVER TURNED the dial slowly. He was still thinking hard about whether or not to dispose of the Masked Detective and take all the loot for himself, or if there was a way to dispose of this masked man. It was a difficult problem, for Weaver had plans to carry on his campaign of crime, and an assistant like the Masked Detective would be invaluable. Perhaps dangerous too. Weaver wanted to be in full command and this mysterious figure would hardly approve of that.

The safe door swung open. Inside were two suitcases, jammed with bills of high denomination. Weaver reflected how cleverly he had arranged to get all this cash. It had come from banks all over the East. He had purposely opened many branch offices so that the accumulation of all this cash would not be noticeable.

His eyes fell upon a big automatic, lying on a shelf and partly covered by a sheaf of papers. He had placed it there for just such an emergency. Now, with the Masked Detective believing he, Weaver, had fallen in with his suggestion and the masked man was certainly off guard, the art expert could grab the gun, whirl and shoot down the Masked Detective before he could pull the trigger of his own gun.

Weaver's crooked mind rejected the idea of a partnership. After all, he had enough cash to live on majestically for the remainder of his life. Why part with half of it?

He knew, however, that by stalling he might give himself away so he picked up one suitcase and thrust it between his legs. The Masked Detective's attentions would be completely centered on the loot. Weaver's fingers closed around the butt of the gun. He whirled, with a nasty grin on his face.

A gun roared. Weaver's automatic dropped from a bloody hand, smashed by a .38 slug. Weaver hardly felt the pain. For his whole system was stunned by a new shock.

The Masked Detective had completely vanished and in the middle of the office stood Sergeant Gleason and Inspector Mullane. Gleason's pistol smoked slightly.

"The next one will hurt more," Gleason snapped. "You're under arrest, Weaver, and I won't tire myself out by telling you for what crimes. Walk over to the wall and keep that good hand of yours lifted high. Frisk him, Inspector. He may travel heeled with a couple of gats."

Mullane searched Weaver, pushed him against the wall and restrained his temper with an effort.

"But this—this is all a mistake," Weaver protested shrilly. "I don't know what in the world you're talking about!"

"We do," Gleason grunted. "So the dough is in those suitcases, all nice and handy for the run-out. Maybe you can explain that, Weaver."

"Of course," Weaver cried. "The money is rightfully mine. I can prove it. You have nothing on me. This is—is all so impossible. There isn't a shred of evidence to connect me with any crime."

Mullane walked over to the door leading into the reception room. He gestured, and two patrolmen dragged in Carson and McKenna. Both of them shouted shrill accusations.

"He'd rat on himself!" Carson yelled. "Sure he's the big shot. I know this means I go to the chair, but that's okay so long as he goes, too. He built me up, gave me the dough to get my own gang and rub out the opposition. Then he heard about them art things and got set to pull a big job. Only he double-crossed us. He told the Masked Detective to rub us out, but all that masked guy did was plant a couple of bullets in the floor."

THE ART connoisseur, who looked as though he were seeing a couple of ghosts, tried to protest. Gleason snapped a handcuff around his unhurt wrist and jerked Weaver toward the door. Mullane picked up the two suitcases of money and the whole group marched into the reception room where a dozen submachine-gun-armed patrolmen were waiting.

"A trap!" Weaver moaned. "The Masked Detective led me into it. Damn him!"

Weaver's curse was vehement, but at the moment the Masked Detective would hardly have heard it if Weaver had stood two feet away and bellowed the word. The velvet mask was in Rex Parker's pocket and both his hands and both his arms were busily engaged in holding Winnie Bligh close to him.

"What a shock Weaver must have received," he murmured, after he had looked into her eyes for a long, long time, until she begged to be told all that had happened. "Gleason and Mullane had Weaver's house covered. I pretended to gun out Carson and McKenna after I let Weaver prove to them just what kind of a rat he really was. It's one way of getting what you want—by splitting the forces of gangland and making them suspicious of one another.

"First of all, I had Sergeant Gleason fire a few blank cartridges at Weaver to scare the daylights out of him and put doubt in his mind. He thought Carson and McKenna were trying to get all the money by rubbing him out. Then, as Raoul LeFond, I put a bee in the ears of Carson and McKenna to indicate that Weaver was selling them out.

"That way I located those two fugitives and sent them to Weaver. Their mutual suspicions of one another turned them from allies to deadly enemies. I let Weaver get the upper hand and he showed his true colors. Carson and McKenna started talking the moment Gleason and Mullane came in after I left with Weaver. The case is air-tight. Weaver's plans to loot charitable men by taking their money and duping them is broken up. So is Carson's mob of murder-mad thugs."

"I was so sure it would be Elijah Squires," Winnie said, shaking her head.

Rex Parker laughed. "So was I. Weaver actually seemed to be trying to help the law, while Squires yowled all over the place. That snuff box I told you about really belonged to Squires, of course. The little guy we named Dirty Neck lifted it off Squires while the old crank was administering one of his heart-to-heart talks about the futility of crime. So—it's ended. The Masked Detective crawls back in his little shell and Rex Parker writes one beautiful yarn to scoop the town."

"Rex," Winnie said softly, "are you really going to quit—forever? Is the Masked Detective really going to die with the finish of this one case? You don't believe the city is free of crime, do you? Weaver, Carson and all the others were only a fraction of the men who live by their wits and by violence."

Rex Parker looked straight ahead.

"There's a lot of satisfaction in rounding up those killers," he said, in a far-away voice. "More than I thought. The police need help—the kind of assistance we gave them. Crime has to be fought with its own ruthless methods. As the Masked Detective I was ruthless too, but do you know, I never fired a shot with the intention to kill—not even Carson and McKenna. It proves that gangland is vulnerable when the right methods are used."

"Then you will keep on, Rex?" Winnie asked.

He nodded slowly.

"When something else breaks, I'll do what I can. With you and Gleason to help me, how can I fail? I.... Say, that was smooth propaganda you pulled. You pushed me into saying I'd keep on."

Winnie nestled a little closer to him as he started the car and headed toward the newspaper offices.

"Just call me Captain Bligh," she said contentedly.

II

THE MASKED DETECTIVE'S WARNING

CHAPTER 1

PAYMENT IN BLOOD

S **TANISLAW NOWAK** wasn't smart and no one knew this any better than himself. When a man works as an unskilled laborer for twenty-two years, it is emphasized each pay-day.

Nowak drew his envelope now and slowly fingered through the thin sheaf of bills. A ten, a five, a one and some silver. Sixteen dollars a week wasn't much, but it kept starvation away from his door. And Stanislaw Nowak was a proud man. He had never known charity, and would never accept it.

Anyway, as he so often reflected, he had three healthy boys and a girl who brought home fine report cards from school. Soon they'd be grown up, working and bringing in a little money. Not that Nowak intended for them to work for him—just a little something from each, to pay for food and the rent. When that day came, he could stop worrying every time he drew his pay for fear that a pink slip might send him pacing the streets in search of another job.

Nowak thrust his lunch bucket under one arm, gravely saluted the gate tender of the big factory and walked out. Before he was a block away, two men fell into step with him.

"How goes it, Nowak?" one said grinning. "Boy, if every day was only pay-day! Let's have that usual five-spot, pal."

Nowak frowned, deep furrows in his already lined forehead.

"But this week—no," he said. "My Teddy, he needs a new suit for graduation. My girl, she cannot forever have her shoes fixed. This week—nothing. But I catch up. Eleven dollars a week until I am even again, eh?"

One of the men grabbed Nowak's arm and jerked him around.

"Listen, we said five bucks and we mean it! If you got to get yourself in debt by borrowing dough, you got to pay it back, understand? We can have you slapped in jail, but we're easy-going guys. We don't like trouble for us or for our clients. But you crash through with that five-spot or you'll wish you had."

The word "jail" used to frighten Nowak until he virtually cringed. To him it meant eternal dishonor and the blackening of his children's names. But he had changed recently. Even jail was nothing compared to this everlasting dunning by men who had been born in this great nation, educated here, and yet couldn't even speak the language except like gangsters.

NOWAK JERKED himself loose of the restraining grasp.

"Now you wait," he protested. "I am a good man. I pay my bills, and I have paid you. But I only took from you twenty-five dollars and I have paid you back five dollars each week for almost a year. You give me no receipt—nothing to show I pay. But I trust you. Last night my boy figure. He's smart—he tell me I pay too much."

"Now listen,"—one of the men thrust his face close to Nowak's—"when you needed twenty-five bucks, we didn't stall, did we? We didn't ask for any receipt, did we? No, we were soft-hearted and we handed you the dough so you could pay the doctor like you wanted to. All you been paying us is interest. You haven't even made a dent in the twenty-five you borrowed, but do we ask for that? No, we let it ride because we're good guys. But listen, dumb-ox! You pony up with that five bucks or we'll take it away from you! And if you squawk, we'll tell your boss and he'll give you the gate."

"Aw, why argue with the half-wit," the other man snarled impatiently. "We got a lot of other guys to see. Hold him while I take it."

Nowak struggled frantically, but the pay envelope was taken from his pocket, the five dollars extracted and the rest allowed to drop on the sidewalk. It flew in all directions and Nowak spent two minutes hastily picking it up. By the time he had gathered what was left, the two men had vanished.

Nowak slowly put the eleven dollars and the odd silver into his pocket. He was a patient man, but these men had gone too far now.

Nowak plodded home and merely nodded to his wife as he passed through the kitchen. He didn't stop to sniff the aroma of stew which he liked so well. Instead, he went directly to his oldest son's room and closed the door.

"Teddy," he said hesitantly, "I am in trouble. Those men who make the loan, they took five dollars today even when I said no, they could not have it. You are in high school, you are smart—sure. Last night you write down numbers. You say I pay too much. Good American schools make you smarter than your father. Now I ask one more thing, and you tell me the truth. Maybe these men are crooks. They say if I tell, they tell the boss and make me fired—but I don't care any more. I work hard and they take my money. Teddy, I go to the police, eh?"

"That's what you ought to do, Pop." Teddy was sixteen, a bright-eyed youngster with ambitions. "But I've heard about those crooks, Pop. They're bad. If you go to the police, maybe they'll hurt you—beat you up. I know you can't afford to keep on paying them, and it's not right that you should pay five dollars a week for almost a year as interest on a twenty-five dollar loan. Honest, Pop, I don't know what you ought to do."

"I go to the police," Nowak said stonily. "Always when there is trouble or something we do not understand, the police—they help. They are good men. After dinner I go, but you say nothing to Mamma. I do not want her to worry. Come—we eat."

Nowak didn't seem to relish the stew as he usually did and his wife knew that something worried him, but she asked no questions. Nowak read his evening newspaper printed in his native language, then calmly put on his hat and went out.

HE KNEW that his son Teddy had been right. These men who were hounding him did beat up some of the people who were unable to meet their payments. But Nowak, slow to anger, was now thoroughly aroused. Nothing short of death could stop him. And he could not guess that death even then, an invisible shadow, was moving along beside him.

For as Nowak left the house, the two loan sharks were watching. One nudged the other.

"I told you it was a mistake to ride that Bohunk too far. We shoulda let him skip this week like he wanted to. I'll give you three to one he's on his way to the cops right now."

"I won't take the bet," the other man snarled. "But he won't get to no police station. Let's go. Look—if you're right and he is heading for the cops, we can drive ahead of the bum and grab him before he knows what happened. Just as soon as he starts to turn the corner of the block where the precinct is, we go to work."

Nowak did not see the car drive slowly past him, nor did he glance at the driver or the man seated beside him. Nowak was too busy with a mental rehearsal of how he would explain things to the police. He should have brought Teddy along, but when his son had mentioned the trouble those loan sharks could start, Nowak had decided to risk only his own hide.

He turned the corner, saw the green lights of a precinct station just ahead of him, and picked up speed.

He passed by a car parked at the curb, but sensed no danger until a flabby hand was clapped across his mouth and a blackjack brought down against the back of his neck. Nowak was along in years and the blow took full effect. He passed out....

When Nowak opened his eyes again, he knew he was somewhere in the country. The air was sweeter and cooler, for one thing. He also was well aware of the fact that he was in serious trouble. He lay on the floor of a moving car and as he tried to straighten up, the toe of a shoe collided with his face and sent him limply back.

Finally the car turned off the main road and stopped alongside a dark, lonely lane. Nowak was hauled up and propped against the rear fender of the car.

He recognized the two men who grimly faced him, and his heart missed a few beats.

"So you were gonna pay us back for all the good we did you by going to the cops, eh?" one of the men raged. "Okay, Bohunk! We treat double-crossers like this!"

His fist smashed against Nowak's nose. Blood spurted. Nowak gave a soft cry of pain, raised his fists, and did his best to fight.

He did not even land a blow. But he took them—scores of terrific punches that landed all over his body. Once he thought his whole chest had caved in, and then he knew that his jaw was broken. And he could not see any longer because his eyes were puffed so badly, so he did not know that both these men were using brass knuckles.

The two strong-arm men seemed to be enjoying their task and did not let up until Nowak lay unconscious on the ground with blood streaming from his mouth, and a dozen or more deep lacerations on his face.

"Let him stay here." One of the thugs put away his brass knuckles. "It'll teach him a lesson and he'll pass the word on to the other suckers who may feel like renegin'. We oughta do this every time one of them saps opens his mouth. Come on—let's go back to town. We got plenty of work to do."

HOURS LATER, Nowak managed to crawl to the main highway. It was cold. His chest hurt badly. Every movement of his body brought agonizing pain from a dozen different parts of his anatomy. He hardly knew what he was doing except that he was possessed of an urge to reach the highway and stop one of those cars that roared by every few minutes.

He finally lay on the road shoulder, raising one hand in an appeal for help. But the cars were traveling too fast for anyone to see him. It was not until a dilapidated sedan rattled toward him that Nowak's prayers were answered.

The sedan stopped and a farmer climbed out. He took one look at Nowak, then stopped a faster car by waving his arms madly.

"Must have been hit by some skunk who didn't stop," the farmer said. "Got a blanket so we can keep him from spilling blood all over your car, mister?"

Then Nowak peacefully slumped into merciful unconsciousness. He did not awaken while doctors in the emergency ward tried to estimate the full extent of his injuries.

"This man wasn't hit by a car," one doctor offered. "Somebody smashed him with a lead pipe or something. His ribs are caved in—lungs punctured. X-ray immediately—and have surgery prepared. Miss Collier, please notify the police that we have an aggravated assault case here, and if they want to get this man's statement they'd better get right up here. He won't live until morning."

CHAPTER II

DUAL IDENTITY

IN A three-room apartment in the heart of Greenwich Village a rather strange scene was being enacted. A pretty girl with a supple, graceful figure stood at one end of the room with both hands poised and ready. She had raven black hair, worn short. Her eyes were clear blue and no makeup artist could have improved on her lips.

She wore a funny-looking hat which was now perched precariously on one side of her head. This was Winnie Bligh who, oddly enough, conducted the beauty column on one of New York's biggest newspapers. And in that capacity none would have imagined that her hobby was jujutsu, nor that she took every opportunity for practice of the art—as now.

She seemed to be braced for an attack and it came, with a savage rush. A man charged clear across the room with one arm stuck out its full length. The idea was for him to get that arm as close to Winnie Bligh's head as possible, and still stay on his feet.

He was tall and long-legged, so that his rush was performed with amazing speed. But Winnie Bligh's hand moved just as fast. It caught the attacker's arm, twisted it, and his feet left the floor. He flew up and over in a beautiful somersault, flopped hard enough to shake the whole building and lay there puffing.

Someone in the apartment below banged on the ceiling.

"Looks like they've had enough," Winnie murmured, and stepped before a mirror to straighten her hat. "I think you've had plenty too, Rex. I didn't break your arm, did I?"

Tall, long-legged Rex Parker got up with a wry expression on his face.

"For an undernourished dame you sure can handle your dukes, Cap'n Bligh," he murmured. "I've got to hand it to you. I didn't believe you could take me."

Winnie gave an exasperated sniff, walked over and waved one finger under Rex Parker's nose.

"I've asked you again and again to stop calling me Captain Bligh. I don't like it. I don't keep pushing you around as you indicate I do. I—I don't even care if you never do anything but be a reporter the rest of your life. It absolutely doesn't mean a thing to me."

Rex Parker leaned against the wall, stuck a cigarette between his lips and lit it.

"Not much you don't shove me around," he jeered. "If you had your way, I'd be working twenty-four hours a day. Twelve as the *Comet's* star reporter and twelve as the Masked Detective. Oh, I'm not denying we had fun with those rats we rounded up a few weeks ago when you talked me into putting on a black velvet mask and naming myself the Masked Detective. You egged me into solving a tough case.

"Sure I got a good story out of it—and also a few headaches. I can still feel a lump on my skull from one mug's gun butt. The trouble is that ever since you've been after me to wade into another case. But no soap. Why? Because I don't handle small stuff. The Masked Detective takes only big cases—where some important guy is knocked off, or a bank is robbed. The cops can take care of the small cases."

Winnie Bligh stepped back, hands on her hips.

"Of all the conceited men! Rex Parker, you enjoyed every moment working as the Masked Detective. Even when you thought the killers had the upper hand, you were in there, punching with all your strength."

REX PARKER, leaning indolently against the wall, suddenly stood erect. His right foot flashed upward, like a chorus girl's high kick, but much faster and with many more times the strength behind it. The foot flashed within half an inch of Winnie Bligh's face.

"Punching did you say?" Rex grinned. "I kicked my way through that mob. You can have your jujutsu—give me *la savate* every time. It's a dirty way of fighting, but the mugs I tossed around had dirtier ways than that. And were they surprised! Why, I never even used a gun on any of them."

"Rex," Winnie said, "if the Masked Detective doesn't take a hand in some case or other, he'll lose the prestige he built up. All the crooks in town were afraid even to mention his name. Now you stand there and tell me you won't work again as the Masked Detective until some big shot gets killed or a colossal crime is pulled off!

"Don't you realize that rackets are colossal and stupendous? A man, or band of men, robs a bank, gets a quarter of a million dollars and the newspapers—when they can find room between the war news—whoop it up as a gigantic crime. Yet nobody ever pays much attention to the mugs who walk around in two-hundred-dollar suits, drive five-thousand-dollar cars, and milk the public of millions every year.

"There's your chance to do something really big, Rex! Squash them—show them that the Masked Detective fights all kinds of crime and criminals."

Rex Parker put out his cigarette. He moved with a lazy grace, for Rex Parker was essentially a lazy man. He had a knack for getting news without too much effort and at the same time keeping up his reputation as the city's best crime reporter. Only Winnie Bligh could drive him and that was why he called her Cap'n Bligh.

She had been responsible for the creation of the Masked Detective. When police had found their hands tied by red tape, he had donned a black velvet mask and had sallied forth to beat crime with its own weapons. To his amazement he had not only been successful, but had found the work highly interesting. Winnie, because of her long affiliation with a beauty column, knew cosmetics, and the art of disguise had come to her with remarkable readiness. Rex Parker had discovered that his features took disguise easily, and with Winnie to put on the final touches, he could work without fear of detection.

But Rex Parker was also a reporter. That work was in his blood. As the Masked Detective he fought crime and criminals, and as Rex Parker he wrote amazing stories of the Masked Detective's deeds.

Rex was known to be the only contact which the mysterious masked man had with the rest of the world. Still no one suspected, in even the slightest degree, that Rex Parker in fact was the Masked Detective, or that the bizarre stories he wrote about the avenger of underworld crimes were his own adventures.

Aside from Winnie Bligh the only other person who was aware of his dual identity was detective-sergeant Dan Gleason of Homicide. Gleason, a hard-headed, hard-hitting police officer, knew the value of the Masked Detective. Some day many cases might come to the Masked Detective through Gleason, but not the one that was now fomenting in the operating room of a big hospital.

PARKER REACHED for the phone on the table beside his chair. He grinned at Winnie.

"Routine call to Headquarters. If something *has* happened, perhaps you can put those messes of grease and dyes on my face again. That's what you're aching to do—experiment with my puss and then write funny articles in your column telling women how to look like what they ain't."

"Make your call," Winnie said in a low voice, "and stop riding me or so help me I'll put a hammer lock on that silly neck of yours so you won't be able to talk for a week."

Rex Parker dialed Headquarters.

"Everything is dead, Rex," the desk lieutenant reported. "A couple of the boys just rushed up to the Goldman Hospital. Some poor guy was taken into the country and beaten up so badly he's going to die. Outside of that, no business."

Parker smiled contentedly. No business meant no work. He hung up.

"See? The town is dead. Only report is about the beating up of some sucker. Poor guy is going to kick out too, but that's hardly enough to interest the Masked Detective, eh? Wait until somebody with twenty million bucks gets his head separated from the rest of his body. That's the kind of stuff that makes news."

"Rex Parker"—Winnie jumped to her feet—"sometimes I wonder how you ever keep a straight face when you draw your week's pay. How do you know what kind of a story is behind this case? How do you know whether or not the dying man isn't a big shot, or hasn't a million dollars? Listen to me! Get that lazy shape of yours inside a coat. We're going to the Goldman Hospital."

Parker groaned, but he knew better than to disobey. Winnie had a compelling influence on him.

Her car was parked in front of his apartment house, and within three minutes she was driving toward the hospital. Both showed their press cards, walked to the surgery anteroom and sat down alongside Casey and Johnson, the two plainclothes men who had arrived from Headquarters.

"What's it all about?" Parker asked.

Casey shrugged. "Guy by the name of Stanislaw Nowak, a mill laborer, was hammered to pieces by a couple of mugs. Seems he owed 'em dough—the old stuff—loan shark racket. He didn't pay this week, so they taught him a lesson and gypped themselves out of some more gravy because dead men don't pay bills."

Parker leaned closer to Winnie and whispered:

"Big shot—millionaire! What a hunch you had!" He turned back to the detectives. "How'd you get your dope if Nowak is dead?"

"He ain't—not yet. But he will be in half an hour or so. We're sticking around in case he wakes up and can tell us the names of the mugs who busted him up. His oldest son and his wife are in the waiting room. There's a sob story in it."

WINNIE TOOK a firm grip on Rex Parker's arm and propelled him down the corridor to the waiting room. They found a woman, worn out by a life of hard work, crying softly. A boy, bright-looking and neat, was staring out of the window. He turned as Parker and Winnie entered.

"We're reporters," Parker said. "How about the details of this?"

"Details?" the boy cried. "The only details are that my father is going to die—that he was murdered because he wouldn't pay a third of his week's pay to the rottenest band of chiselers in creation! A year ago—fifty-two weeks ago—he borrowed twenty-five dollars because he wanted to pay the doctor when Mom was sick. They gave it to him and said he had to pay five dollars a week until it was cleared up. He paid it—for fifty straight weeks. Two hundred and fifty dollars for a twenty-five buck loan.

"He was going to the police to make a complaint, but they got him—like I knew they would. Pop isn't the only man who is scared of those money sharks. They wanted to kill him! They want everybody to know that if they don't get their money on time, something like this will happen."

Rex Parker was frowning angrily and deeply.

"You say he paid two hundred and fifty dollars interest on a twenty-five dollar loan? What kind of a racket is that, anyway? Do you know the men who tried to kill him, son?"

"No, but Pop does. The same two met him every pay-day, as soon as he got his envelope. He knows 'em all right, and I hope they get the electric chair. I hope they get beaten up first, like they beat up my pop!"

"Shh!" Mrs. Nowak looked up. "No speak that way, Teddy."

Suddenly Rex Parker turned on his heel and stalked out of the room. Winnie had to run to catch up with him. She clutched at his sleeve.

"Rex, what are you going to do? What's got over you?"

"Did you hear what that kid said? There are a lot of other people who will be intimidated by this Nowak's murder. That means there must be plenty who are paying something like a thousand per cent or more interest on everything they borrow from these rats. What am I going to do? First of all write a story that'll blast their ears off. And then, Winnie, old gal—the Masked Detective is going to kick in a few faces!"

PARKER SAT beside the two detectives again.

"When he wakes up—if he does—give me a chance to talk to him, boys," he asked. "I just found out what this is all about, and I know of a certain party who might be interested."

"You mean the Masked Detective, huh?" Casey asked. "So help me, Parker, I'd give my next month's pay if he'd polish off these sharks. The beating the poor saps get who don't come across gets us.... The doc said he'd be out in a minute. Stick around."

The doctor emerged, but not until thirty minutes had passed.

"You can see him now," he told the waiting detectives. "He's conscious and in a fairly good state of mind. Knows he's dying and wants to talk. He'll last only a short time."

Rex Parker went in with Casey and Johnson and sat down beside the bed. But he had to close his eyes in horror at the sight of Nowak's battered features. When he opened them, Nowak was looking at him with silent, gentle appeal.

"We'll get the men who hurt you," Parker said gently. "They'll get what's coming to them. Who were they? How did you borrow the money they were after?" He knew that he had to ask questions fast.

"Bad men," Nowak mumbled. "Turk Pasha one—Joe Dackey, other. I get money from Globe Finance Company. I go to police, but Joe— Turk—stop me.... Where is my poor boy, Teddy?"

Winnie brought the boy and also Nowak's wife. She closed the door after them softly, when the three men had filed out. Rex Parker's face was hard, his eyes brittle and cold.

"Run along home with me, Winnie," he said seriously. "I need your help."

On the way, Winnie glanced at him out of the corner of her eyes.

"But, Rex, I thought only something big would interest you. Like the murder of a millionaire?"

"Well, think again," Parker retorted. "Think I'm going to let those yeggs get away with killing that poor guy? And bleeding every sucker they can get to borrow a measly twenty-five bucks from them? I'll bust that racket wide open—and do it by morning! There won't be much of a story in it, and no glamour for the Masked Detective, but, lady, there'll be plenty of satisfaction. Can't you make this crate go any faster?"

Winnie smiled. "Rex—you're sweet."

"Sweet, my eye," Rex Parker snapped. "I'm mad!"

CHAPTER III

SHADOW IN THE DARKNESS

AT ABOUT eleven o'clock at night a fair-haired, ruddy-faced man walked into the dismal lobby of a downtown building which housed the offices of questionable attorneys, bail bondsmen, loan sharks and others of that ilk. Not even Sergeant Gleason, who could spot a phony a mile away, would have recognized this man as Rex Parker. Winnie had put plenty into that disguise.

Parker was not planning to fool anyone with the makeup, however. The Masked Detective's velvet mask lay in one pocket. The disguise was only in case that mask was torn off him by accident. Above all things he did not want his dual identity known. And he had picked this late hour so he would not be disturbed.

His hat was dilapidated, his tie loose, and on his features was a hangdog expression as he timidly rapped on the door labeled:

GLOBE FINANCE COMPANY

LOANS WITHOUT SECURITY

A harsh voice called out an order to enter. Parker opened the door and found himself in a small, cheaply furnished office. Cigarette butts were thrown carelessly on the floor. The furniture had not been dusted in weeks and the two men in that office certainly were not suave.

"I want to get some money," Parker said timorously, "I ain't got no security, but I work steady."

"Where?" one of the men demanded.

Parker recognized him as Turk Pasha. He had been dragged to Headquarters more than once, but usually had been able to get bail quickly, and to beat the rap on minor charges. The name the thug used was a phony he had picked up because he figured it made him sound tough. He was, in reality, the direct opposite of a Turk, for his face was soft and bland, his hair yellow, and his eyes a greenish blue. But he was powerfully built, and plainly vicious.

The second man, who kept his twenty-dollar shoes parked on the edge of the cheap desk, was Joe Dackey, an out-and-out gangster well known to Headquarters and to the reporters who saw such men booked. He paid a hundred and fifty dollars for his suits and they looked like bargain basement specials on him.

Rex gave them the name of a factory that employed great numbers of unskilled workers.

"I need fifty dollars," he explained. "I saw the sign on your window and I came up. I'll pay it back—honest I will. I make eighteen dollars a week." Turk slid open a big drawer that was completely filled with crumpled currency. Cash came in so fast that the crooks were unable to keep it neatly stacked.

Turk threw ten five-dollar bills across the desk.

"Okay. You give my pal your name and where you live. Also your social security number and card. You pay us back ten bucks every week, understand?"

"Sure, sure," Parker agreed quickly. He tucked the money into his pocket. "What do I sign, mister?"

"Nuthin'. We don't need signatures." Turk let his feet drop to the floor. "You're an honest-lookin' guy, so we let you have it anyhow, see? Now show that security card and scram. We're ready to close up."

REX PARKER decided this had gone far enough. He knew that neither of these two men had the remotest idea that Nowak was dead and had identified them as his murderers. Had they thought this, they would have been in mad flight by now.

"Come on," Joe Dackey half snarled. "You got your dough. What's the name and address?"

Parker sat on the edge of the desk.

"The name is Stanislaw Nowak, brother. Know how to spell it?"

Joe Dackey snorted. "Sure. We can spell them names easy. Stanislaw No—wak.... Hey, what kind of a gag is this?"

He jumped to his feet, doubled one fist and advanced menacingly. Parker grinned at both of them, stood up himself, and carefully massaged his right fist.

"I've got fifty dollars of your money, gentlemen. You have a right to know my name. It's the Masked Detective!"

Turk yanked open the top drawer of his desk and reached for a gun he kept there. But Turk heard a whizzing sound and looked up. The whizzing stopped abruptly—as a fist smashed him full in the face.

Joe Dackey had already dropped one hand into his coat pocket, but not after a gun. He figured this straw-haired sucker was just going to act nasty, and Dackey knew how to handle birds like that.

His brass knuckles around his fist, he lunged for the Masked Detective, swept a hard, swinging blow toward his jaw, and then he suddenly discovered that his feet were no longer on the ground and that there was a terrific pain in the pit of his stomach.

The Masked Detective's foot had moved so rapidly that Joe hadn't even seen it. For Rex Parker, the Masked Detective, had studied the little-known French form of fighting with the feet until he was a master of it.

The Masked Detective walked around the desk, searched Turk who was slumped in his chair, moaning in pain. Then he knelt beside Joe Dackey and took a revolver away from him. Finally the Masked Detective pulled up a chair, sat down and crossed his legs. He lit a cigarette and waited calmly until both men were on their feet again.

"You got us wrong," Turk protested shrilly. "We ain't done nothin'. We run a nice little business here and when guys need dough, they can always get it."

"Like Stanislaw Nowak got it?" the Masked Detective asked gently. "You took five dollars a week away from him for almost a year. He paid two hundred and fifty dollars interest on a twenty-five dollar loan that your generosity forced you to lend him. But—Stanislaw Nowak is dead, boys. His murderers are headed for Sing Sing, and a most uncomfortable chair they keep for visitors of your kind."

Joe Dackey sank into a chair, trembling with fear. Turk tried to speak, but only gibberish came from his palsied lips.

"I think," the Masked Detective said calmly, "that we'll take a walk to Police Headquarters. And remember, boys, I'm not a cop. There isn't a thing to restrain me from putting a slug through your rotten heads.

In fact, I'm hoping you'll give me the chance. Come on—get on your way and start moving."

Turk found his voice at last.

"No—no, listen! We'll make a deal. We know the Masked Detective don't monkey with small stuff, so you know this is a big racket. Give us two hours for a getaway and we'll talk."

THE MASKED DETECTIVE shook his head.

"I don't make deals with rats like you. However I am prepared to give you one little break. The only guns I have are your own. Watch me unload them and throw the slugs out the window. Like this. Now you have four hands against my two. We're all armed the same way—as nature meant us to be armed. If you can fight your way out of here, the door is open. If you can't, I'll smear you all over this place and dump you in the gutter for the cops—after you talk about this racket. Which is it?"

Turk walked around to the front of the desk.

"Give us a break, will yuh? We got dough. Wait—I'll show you."

He made a motion toward the desk, but not the drawer crammed full of money. He grabbed a metal date pad, and with an oath, flung it straight at the Masked Detective's head. It did not connect, because the Masked Detective had been prepared for something exactly like this. Joe Dackey jumped up and rushed forward as Turk prepared to floor his enemy by kicking him on the chin before he could arise from his chair.

Turk did kick out. He missed the Masked Detective's jaw and his ankle was seized in a painful grip. He was lifted completely off the floor and swung like a sack of flour, in a circle. His shoulders hit Joe Dackey and sent him reeling. Then the Masked Detective let go. Turk hurtled across the room, hit the wall and fell limply.

Dackey made a wild dash for the door. An arm curled around his neck, dragged him back and held him in a tight embrace. The Masked Detective's other hand connected with Joe Dackey's nose, then his eyes, and finally centered on his chin.

The thug was whining and trying to wriggle free. Those fists kept banging him on the face, not hard enough for a knockout, but each one sending stabs of pain through his body.

"That's how Nowak felt—only worse." The Masked Detective's voice was brittle. "He died. But don't worry—I wouldn't cheat the state executioner out of his fee. I want you rats to mope in jail and wait for the day they'll come for you. Nowak identified you—you haven't got a chance. This is a taste of your punishment."

When Joe Dackey went limp in the Masked Detective's embrace, Rex let him drop to the floor. Then he divested each man of his coat and vest, ripped the ten-dollar shirt off each and tore it into strips. He tied them with these firmly, and not caring whether the bonds were painfully tight.

The Masked Detective could still see Stanislaw Nowak, battered beyond recognition, dying slowly in his hospital bed. He could see the tear-stained face of the widow, and hear the righteous condemnation of her son.

Finally the Masked Detective walked around behind the desk, sat down and began straightening out some of the crumpled bills. When he had a thick sheaf of tens, approximately four thousand dollars in all, he fastened them together with an elastic.

He made a parcel out of the bills, then started searching the untidy drawers.

IN ONE he found a cheap imitation leather ledger containing the names and addresses of those who had borrowed from the firm. That was the only record in existence. The Masked Detective pulled the metal waste basket closer, ripped the book into shreds and set the pages afire.

There was a letter in the drawer also, postmarked this same day. He unfolded it and whistled softly as he read:

Pasha and Dackey:

Not entirely satisfied with your loans. Collections are okay which is to your credit, but I want to see a hundred and fifty thousand in new business before the end of the year. The money is ready any time you need it and I'll tell Manny Delisse to provide it. You know my rules. Results, or you get out, and leaving this business is accomplished in only one way—by death. So get on your toes and produce.

There was no signature and the letter was typed. The Masked Detective put it into his pocket.

"So Dackey and Turk are just running a branch agency," he muttered. "That means somebody big is furnishing the capital and taking the biggest cut. There's the man I must land."

CHAPTER IV

THE MASKED DETECTIVE— MURDERER!

THE MASKED DETECTIVE took a last look at Turk and Dackey. They were still unconscious. He made sure the fire in the metal waste basket had died out, then picked up the parcel of money, stuffed it into his pocket and called Police Headquarters, using the phone on the desk. As always, he had covered his hands with black silk gloves so there would be no prints.

"Gleason," he said, when he got the Homicide sergeant, "this is the Masked Detective. The two men who murdered Stanislaw Nowak are in their office in the Williams Building on Bidwell Street. The Globe Finance Company—on the second floor. I handled them a little roughly, but I think there is enough left to throw into a cell."

He hung up and left the offices abruptly. Gleason would give him time to get away before he sent out a radio alarm.

The Masked Detective stopped at the next corner, leaned against a wall and watched the entrance of the building until the police arrived. Only one man emerged before them—a portly man with a briefcase thrust under one arm. He looked around intently for a moment, then walked briskly north. The Masked Detective did not know him, but absorbed every detail of the man's features.

Two minutes later a radio car howled up and the Masked Detective quietly faded away. He took a taxi to Stanislaw Nowak's home. When he rang the bell, Teddy Nowak let him in. Mrs. Nowak was weeping quietly. The daughter, with eyes red-rimmed, tried to comfort her mother. Teddy's face was drawn, too.

"What do you want?" Teddy asked. "My—my father just died. That's why my mother is crying."

"Yes, I know. A friend of mine spoke to him before he died. I'm the Masked Detective, Teddy. The two men who murdered your father are under arrest now and they also had a sample of the treatment they gave your father. The real reason I came is this." He put the package of money in Teddy's hands. "Never mind where it came from. So far as you are concerned, it's honest money, do you understand? Your father paid two hundred and fifty dollars interest on a twenty-five dollar loan. I've made that interest your father parted with into another loan. The two-fifty is in this package with some more, at the same interest he was charged. It won't bring your father back, but it may help his family."

"Gee—thanks," Teddy said. "We thought the city would have to pay for the funeral and Pop would never have liked that. Thanks—a lot!"

The Masked Detective walked away from Nowak's house slowly and the warm feeling in his heart was more satisfaction than if he had just brought the murderers of a dozen multimillionaires to justice.

But the Masked Detective lacked knowledge of one significant thing. Before he was halfway down the steps of the building where the Globe Finance Company had an office, a shadowy figure came slinking along the dismal corridor, opened the Finance Company's door with a key and closed it behind him. He remained inside for about three minutes and when he emerged, one shirt cuff was bloodstained....

BACK HOME, Rex Parker removed the disguise he had assumed, changed his clothes and took a subway uptown. He walked to the offices of the *Comet,* shouted cheery greetings to the night staff and entered his own cubby-hole of an office.

He sat down before a typewriter and for forty-five minutes he pounded out a grim story. Then he slid a new sheet into the machine and wrote another. It would be plastered on the front page, ousting some war cable for once. For the Masked Detective was always big news, and this time what was written was bigger than ever. Rex Parker put his very soul into writing:

THE MASKED DETECTIVE'S WARNING

Certain elements have been conducting illegal loan businesses in this city. I know they operate many branches and that they are headed by a man with business ability. To him and to all his associates in this vicious racket, I extend a warning. Turn back all the money that has been mulcted from unfortunates. Close your offices and have the thugs who enforce payments of interest leave town. Unless this is done at once, I shall take steps to see that the entire foul business is broken to pieces and those who head it shall feel the wrath of vengeance.

"Boy, oh, boy!" someone said in Rex Parker's ear. "Is that telling 'em!" Parker looked up into Winnie's smiling face.

"You said it, beautiful. The Masked Detective contacted me a short time ago and gave me the lowdown. Say, send young Tim Cadwell in here, will you? He's a cub and needs a break. I'll have 'em put him on the story of Nowak's murder. Maybe he can ferret out some other human interest angle."

Winnie sent the cub in promptly while Parker got the managing editor's permission to use young Cadwell.

Tim Cadwell was about twenty, eager and bright-eyed. He listened to Parker's story and orders. Then he grabbed a wad of copy paper, folded it and rushed out, all excited. He would probably earn a by-line with this if he were lucky. He kept on rushing, too but Tim Cadwell had no idea that he was rushing to keep an appointment with death!

Rex Parker liked to gloat over the stories apparently provided by the Masked Detective. He enjoyed seeing the faces of his colleagues fall when they heard of another sensational newspaper beat. So he walked over to Headquarters to look some of them up, waved to the desk lieutenant, and wondered why he received only a stony stare in reply.

He kicked open the press room door and sauntered in. More than a dozen reporters were playing rummy or just sitting back and napping. All looked Parker's way when he entered. Dolan, of the *News,* had a peculiar expression on his face.

"Seen your pal, the Masked Detective, lately, Rex?" he asked.

Parker grinned. "Spend three cents in the morning and read the latest news, boys. Sorry to have another exclusive on it, but you know me."

"Yeah, we know you," Dolan countered. "Gleason is anxious to see you, too. Seems the Masked Detective called him and said there were a couple of prisoners downtown—men suspected of murdering some guy or other. When the cops got there, they didn't find any prisoners—just a couple of stiffs who had been stabbed to death and not nice either. They must have been conscious when it happened, the doc said. What got into your pal, Rex? I didn't figure him as a torture-killer."

REX PARKER'S smile died. He pivoted and walked quickly to Sergeant Gleason's office. He closed the door behind him, turned the lock and sat down opposite Gleason.

The Homicide sergeant was bulky, gruff and never minced words.

"Rex, what on earth happened? Oh, I know you didn't knife those rats, even though they deserved it. But someone did, and like a fool, I explained that the Masked Detective had phoned and told me to send for those birds. Everybody thinks he killed them. The boys in the press room have already flashed word to their papers that the Masked Detective is a killer."

"I don't care about that," Parker tensely. "But I had hoped we could make Turk and Dackey talk. That's why they were knocked off—to seal their lips. Look, Sarge, we're not fighting a small-time loan racket. It's big! Darn near as big as the legal banking business, I'll bet. There's somebody at the head of it who knows how to handle tough guys like Turk and his pal.

"They bleed the suckers who borrow, but in order to have dough to lend, you've got to be backed financially. Those mugs who run the branch offices couldn't keep twenty bucks a dozen feet away from a crap game. It's easy come and go with their likes. So we've got to find the banker! Then we'll have the killer, too, or I'm dead wrong about the whole business."

"I know," Gleason argued. "I'm glad you've made up your mind to fight that lousy racket. But it doesn't help in the present state of affairs. Even my superiors believe the Masked Detective killed those rats. The building was practically empty. The janitor was cleaning up and reached the second floor just as the door of the Globe Finance Company's office opened and a man with a black velvet mask over his eye came out.

"The janitor ducked and wasn't spotted. Before he could open the office door, after the man in the mask was gone, the radio men arrived. Can't you see how concrete such evidence is? The Masked Detective phoned me. That's admitted. The janitor saw a man with the Masked Detective's characteristic mask on his face emerge—and two minutes later, two men were found inside, dead."

Parker dropped his voice to a whisper.

"They were alive when I left them, and I wasn't wearing a mask, Sarge. I had a disguise and didn't need one. I beat them up a bit—which they deserved—but they were plenty alive when I left. Also, I wouldn't knife any man unless my life was at stake. I wouldn't even shoot one. You know that."

"Sure I do. But I'm supposed to give you the third degree, Rex—make you tell who the Masked Detective is, and where we can find him. What am I going to tell the higher-ups?"

"Stall," Parker said. "Stall with all you've got. The morning editions will carry a letter from the Masked Detective, a warning to those rats who run loan rackets. There will be no statement of the Masked detective's innocence until it can be proved by the arrest of the actual killer. I'm going to work—and I've got a clue. What do you know about a mug named Manny Delisse? There was a letter in the Finance Company's office mentioning his name."

GLEASON LEANED back, and his swivel chair squeaked protestingly.

"Delisse," he said, "is one of the rattiest vermin to walk the face of the earth. He's never been in prison, but I'll bet he's committed a thousand crimes—half of them felonies. He's clever and he's educated. He knows all the legal loopholes and he has plenty of money and nerve.

"By glory, there's the man who killed Turk and Dackey, who financed this loan racket, and who bosses the whole works! He lives in a swanky apartment hotel. The management is afraid to kick him out so you can gather just how dangerous Manny can be. They tried once and somebody heaved a bomb back of the bar one night. Manny told the management that they ought to let him stay because with him there, nothing like that would ever be pulled again."

"Maybe you're right, Sarge," Parker said. "Manny could be the backer of those loan shark businesses. We'll find out later. Right now, what's to be done about the Masked Detective?"

Gleason shrugged.

"I'll report that I demanded that you tell me the identity of the Masked Detective, and you couldn't—that you stated he merely contacts you, and doesn't reveal his identity. What else can I do, without putting you on the spot, too? I wish I didn't know you were both Rex Parker and the Masked Detective. It's going to be hard keeping a straight face when they start pumping questions at me. But run along. And for the love of Mike, nail the murderer!"

CHAPTER V

THE ANSWER

REX TOOK a subway to the station near his apartment and walked the rest of the way slowly, deep in thought. The murderer must have known he was in Turk's office, must have heard or seen the bit of action there. He had probably been afraid to tackle the Masked Detective and had waited to silence his own men and pin the blame on his enemy.

The janitor probably saw a mask all right, but it must have been a crude one hastily cut out of some material. As soon as the Masked Detective's name was mentioned, the janitor had jumped at conclusions.

Still that could not soften suspicion. And Rex Parker had an idea now that his work would be made doubly difficult by a police order to have the Masked Detective picked up.

When he reported to his office the next morning, he refused to answer any questions about the affair of the night before. Walton, the publisher, sent for him just before noon. Parker found two men in the office with Walton. He knew them both.

One was a scrawny, thin-faced man with a pair of enormous, shell-rimmed glasses—Professor Benson of a local university, where he occupied the chair of economics. Benson had fought loan companies, legal and illegal, with all the vigor his slender body could provide. Benson classed himself as a humanitarian and his life work was to eradicate all such loan businesses.

He had some rather complex theories on the solution of the whole business. For the most part he favored a plan of placing all such small loans into the hands of banks.

The other man, Adam Spencer, was powerfully built, with silvery hair, and brown eyes that usually twinkled because he enjoyed all the good things in life. He had the reputation of having a heart as big as the outdoors. Spencer owned the largest legal small loan company in the city, and ran it according to his own ideas. He made loans, on fairly sound security, and never pressed his clients for money unless they were out-and-out chiselers. There were many that said Adam Spencer was a fool, and that a banker with a heart was just no banker at all.

Spencer stepped forward and took Rex's hand in a firm grasp. "I'm shaking hands with two people at the same time," he said pleasantly. "Rex Parker, and the Masked Detective—by proxy. You, as the Masked Detective's agent and only contact, must accept part of this handshake for him. I read his warning in this morning's paper. If he can clean out those rotten loan sharks and put this business on its proper level, every working man in the nation will be grateful."

"If he put you out of business too, you mean," Professor Benson cut in, with a sour look. "You also exact too much for your loans. A man who is forced to take out a twenty or fifty dollar loan can't afford to repay with the interest rates you charge."

Spencer shrugged. "We've been over that a thousand times, Professor. We don't agree, but that doesn't make any difference. We do agree that we came here today to extend to the Masked Detective any possible help that we can offer. We must do this through Rex Parker."

"But when I agreed to that," Benson protested, "I didn't know that the Masked Detective was a murderer. Now I wash my hands of the whole thing. I don't want to contact a killer."

"Damn that suspicion of murder," Spencer shouted heatedly. "The two men who were killed deserved it, didn't they? They were murderers themselves! If the Masked Detective put an end to their miserable lives, he did the State a service."

BENSON SAID, "Bah!" and sat down. Walton motioned Rex into a chair.

"I'll be frank with you, Rex," said the publisher of the *Comet.* "Your friend, the Masked Detective, got himself in a pretty bad jam. Apparently he killed two men while they were helpless. I'm sure you know nothing about it, but you must realize that the Masked Detective being, through you, an exclusive source of news for the *Comet,* isn't doing the paper any good…. Now hold that temper of yours! I, personally, would bank on it that he did not murder those men. I think they were killed after he left, that the murders were committed to make sure the two loan sharks wouldn't talk. Therefore, I want you to contact the Masked Detective—get his side of the story. Help him prove his innocence, and believe me, we'll print it—in headlines. My idea is that you…. Excuse me—the phone."

Walton picked up the instrument, said something, then looked up at Parker.

"Receiving clerk says there's a barrel just come in for you. What's to be done with it?"

"Barrel?" Parker asked in a puzzled voice. "I don't know anything about it. I'll go down and see about it. And thanks, Mr. Walton, for having faith in me. You, too, Mr. Spencer, and you, Professor."

Winnie Bligh maintained a rather elaborate office because of the many women visitors who showed up from all over the country. Winnie's column was syndicated and widely read. As Rex Parker passed by, she called to him and he entered.

"I heard what happened, of course," she said. "You'd better tell your friend, the Masked Detective, to be more careful…. Doing anything tonight, or haven't you got the price of a good dinner?"

"Sure," Parker said. "See you at six, huh? Say, has Tim Cadwell shown up since he went out on that assignment? I thought he'd have a story in this morning's edition."

"He hasn't passed before my lovely glance," Winnie said, smiling. "Don't forget—six tonight."

"Relax," Delisse said. "All you can do is listen to me."

Rex Parker walked downstairs to the receiving room. A clerk motioned toward a barrel standing in the middle of the floor. Parker's name was printed on it in red letters, but that was all. No address, no return address.

"The oldest truck I ever saw just delivered it, Mr. Parker," the clerk said. "What's in it—fish?"

"Get a hammer and we'll find out," Parker told him. "I didn't order anything that would come in a barrel."

The clerk carefully extracted a number of nails until the head of the barrel was free. He lifted off the top, gave a screech and fell over backward. Parker looked inside, shuddered, and slowly turned his head. His eyes were blazing. His fingers clenched and unclenched.

The reason why young Timmy Cadwell, cub reporter, would never file his story was inside that barrel. It contained Tim Cadwell's corpse. He had been strangled to death with a strand of crimson-colored silk that had been rolled into a crude rope.

Then Parker saw something white pinned to Cadwell's coat. He reached down and ripped it off. It was a typed note that was terse and to the point.

TELL THE MASKED DETECTIVE
THIS IS OUR ANSWER TO HIS WARNING

REX PARKER waited impatiently until Sergeant Gleason and the medical examiner appeared. While the doctors supervised the removal of the corpse from the barrel, Parker spoke in a soft voice to Gleason.

"I can't imagine what young Cadwell found to make his death essential to those rats—or whether he found anything. They may have killed him just out of sheer defiance, but so help me, Sarge, I'll find the men responsible for this and when I do, you won't need the wagon to haul 'em in. It'll be either hearse or an ambulance. I don't care much which. Soon as your men are finished, let me have a look, will you?"

Gleason nodded somberly.

"It puts a new light on this business, Rex. If those mugs resort to wanton murder like this to protect their interests, or risk the chair just to defy the Masked Detective, you can bet their business is a lot bigger than we've estimated it to be.... Sure, do what you like with the body. After you finish, I'll set my fingerprint boys to work."

Parker got several pieces of white paper and a small penknife. He examined Cadwell's shoes and scraped tiny particles of dust and debris from the instep and from the space between the sole and the last. He carefully folded the debris in the papers, labeled them, and tucked them away.

He then went over the body inch by inch, studying the clothes, the face and the hands. He found only one thing of significance. Cadwell's right thumb was smeared with a purplish substance that looked like a peculiar shade of ink.

"Let's go over to Headquarters," Parker suggested to Gleason. "Your boys can handle the rest of the investigation. Of course, you'll have them try and check on the expressman who delivered the barrel—though I don't expect they'll find him."

Sergeant Gleason drove Rex Parker over to the police laboratories where the *Comet* reporter requested and got the use of all the equipment.

Young Cadwell had been working on the assignment several hours before his death because the medical examiner reported he had been dead not over two hours at the most. There was a possibility that he had been taken prisoner and held for some time, but Rex Parker doubted this.

If he could only find out where Cadwell had been while he snooped around! What he had uncovered, and how he had crossed tracks with the killers!

CHAPTER VI

WINNIE GETS HER WISH

EVEN BEFORE his wildest dreams could have included such a being as the Masked Detective, Rex Parker had familiarized himself with all the scientific methods of running down killers. He had spent hours in this same laboratory, watching the experts work and stowing into his keen mind all the methods they used.

"Shoes show lots of things," he told Gleason. "They pick up dust and debris with every step. I'm hoping Cadwell's will show me where he went after he was sent out on assignment."

"That's all very well," Gleason protested. "But, Rex, you've got no business monkeying with these things in here. It's against police rules."

"Cadwell's murder was against the rules too," Parker said grimly. "Try and stop me, Sarge. Now move that fat shape of yours a little while I have a look through the microscope."

He carefully spilled the contents of one paper onto a glass slide, put it under the high power of the microscope and studied the substance for color, texture and other qualities. Immediately he saw tiny strands of crimson substance resembling small bits of thread, almost invisible to the naked eye.

"That's odd," he said. "Cadwell apparently got into some place specializing in silk. He was murdered with a strand of crimson silk, and he stepped into particles of the same stuff. Look! Have the lab men compare the murder silk with the particles under the mike now. I'll bet they correspond.

"We've got to find a silk merchant who handles this particular grade of the stuff. But leave that to me, Sarge. There are other interesting particles in the sample too, but I haven't the time to study them closely. It's darn near six o'clock and I've got a date."

Gleason nodded. "I'll have 'em take care of the rest of it, Rex. You going to be around tonight?"

Rex smiled and shook his head.

"I think I'll spend a quiet evening at home, but you might stick around your office in case I get lonesome and want to talk to somebody. No telling what will happen. The murderers of young Cadwell might be placed right in your hands."

Gleason knew what Parker meant. The Masked Detective would swing into action soon.

Gleason sighed as Rex Parker walked out of the laboratory. Cadwell had been a good kid, an enterprising worker too, with an excellent chance of making a star reporter of himself. Now he was on a morgue slab. Gleason understood the rage that gripped Rex Parker.

Parker met Winnie outside the newspaper building. They walked in silence to a cafe which they often patronized, where he asked for his usual booth. He leaned over the table and picked up both of Winnie's hands in his own.

"They've taken up my challenge," he said bitterly. "I wish it had been some other way, but of course, Cadwell stumbled onto something. Just what it was, I'll do my best to find out. If I could trace his movements, I might find the same thing that caused his murder, but I'm telling you, Winnie, it won't cause mine."

"Have you any plans, Rex?" Winnie asked in a low voice.

"Only one clue—a high class mug named Manny Delisse. He's mixed up in this somehow. He may even be the big shot of the whole rotten racket. If he isn't, it's possible that I can find the real boss through him. I've got to locate that man! Now let's forget all about murder and loan sharks. It interferes with my appetite."

HE GLANCED around and held up a hand for the waiter. As he did, his eyes flashed across the long bar. There were only three men standing there. The one nearest was looking straight into the mirror, but that didn't fool Rex Parker. He knew that this man was watching him in the mirror—a man who looked like a dressed-up thug.

Rex gave their orders to the waiter and made a mental picture of the thug who was on his trail. Parker was sure he would recognize the man no matter where he saw him, for in spite of his expensive clothes the man had some outstanding features, included among which was a scar that ran from the base of his nose straight across the left cheek and ended close to the ear. Rex Parker and Winnie ate slowly, each occupied with thoughts of Cadwell and the fiendish murder. Finally Parker finished eating and leaned back.

"I'm going to look up Manny Delisse tonight, but first I'm going back to the Globe Finance Company's office. There's a little matter of squaring a double murder pinned on the esteemed name of the Masked Detective. I think Cadwell may have gone there, too, and I might stumble across his trail."

"Where do I come in?" Winnie asked. "You're not leaving me out of this, Rex. And if you think I can't handle myself, see how stiff your arm feels—the one I used as a lever to throw you yesterday."

Before he could answer, the curtains were pulled apart, a waiter appeared beside the table, and smiled at Winnie.

"Your office is calling, Miss Bligh. Number Three booth. You know where it is?"

Winnie set her lips tightly together for a second.

"All right, I'll be there…. Rex, if this is a trick of yours to get me out of the way, I'll never forgive you."

"Go on—answer the call," he said. "Remember you're a newspaper woman. Somebody may have invented a new lipstick with a nice new fancy name like Posey Rose and your millions of avid readers are curled up in excitement waiting for you to break the news. Beat it!"

Winnie leaned across the table after she had risen.

"My column is just as important as the crime news you write," she declared defensively. "I'll bet if we took a poll, more people read my stuff than read yours. But I still think this is a trick and when I come back, you'll be gone."

She went toward the hall, and Parker heard her high-heeled shoes click as she crossed the floor to the phone booths. He slowly rotated a glass of Chianti, trying to pull his thoughts away from young Cadwell, but the young reporter's swollen, livid features seemed to be reflected back at him from the surface of the deep-colored wine.

RUNNING DOWN a loan racket was, in itself, a worthy task, especially when the sharks resorted to killing one of their clients to show others they meant business. But when they murdered a green kid—a likable chap such as Cadwell had been—then the thing became personal. The fact that whoever was behind this business actually dared the Masked Detective to act was enough to make Parker over-anxious to get started.

Manny Delisse was the next logical means of running down a clue. There was someone else, too—someone Parker did not know—the man Parker had seen emerging from the building in which the Globe Finance Company had an office, just before the police arrived. There was more than an even chance that he was the killer.

Someone sat down opposite Rex Parker, but for a brief moment he did not look up. Then he heard a hard laugh. He raised his head and looked, startled. Winnie had not returned. Instead, a man of about thirty, suave, sleek and carefully tailored sat across from him.

On first glance he looked like a prosperous bond salesman. He was actually good-looking too, except for his eyes. They dominated his face. His lips wore a warm smile, but those eyes were deadly.

"Who the devil are you?" Parker demanded.

"My name is Delisse—Manny Delisse, Parker. You don't know me, even though you've written a lot of nasty stuff about me. That's your job and I don't hold it against you. Just now I've come to deliver a message."

"Go on," Parker said coldly.

"The little lady who came to dinner with you," Delisse said, and the next moment Parker saw, as he jumped out of his chair, fists clenched, the small snub-nosed revolver in the man's hand.

"Sit down and relax," Delisse ordered, smiling coldly. "There isn't a thing you can do except listen to me. The girl has been escorted away from here by a friend of mine. I'm going to keep you company until he has a chance to put a few miles between himself and you, Parker.

"Here is the set-up. You are the only man who can reach the Masked Detective. We'll concede that you have answered in the affirmative. Now, I want you to deliver a few words to your friend with the mask. Unless you do, and unless he does what I wish, the little lady may never be seen again. Alive, that is."

"You filthy scum!" Parker said tensely. "Working through a helpless girl. You know this is kidnaping! There's a law in this State that makes a capital offense of it."

"When it's proved—yes," Delisse sneered. "Now shut up and listen to my proposition. The Masked Detective is a pal of yours. He'd do anything for you. Now, you tell him to be at the corner of Blain and Moffett Streets at precisely midnight tonight. That's five hours off. If he shows, the girl will be allowed to go free. If he doesn't—you can easily guess what will happen.

"One other thing—you and the girl are on the spot from now on. Make a crack in your newspaper about this, or tell the cops, and so help me both of you will kick off faster than you ever think. That's all I've got to say, my friend. Just sit quietly for the next five minutes and then get busy and deliver that message."

"Wait a minute!" Parker brought Delisse back into his seat. "What's this all about? Why do you want the Masked Detective to meet his death on a street corner? What's he done to you?"

"What's he done?" Delisse snorted. "Don't you read the stuff you write? He killed two friends of mine—Turk Pasha and Joe Dackey. I liked those boys because once they took a rap for me. They didn't have to, but they knew I'd take care of them. The Masked Detective knifed those boys and I'm going to pay off.

"Nobody can reach the Masked Detective but you. I know what you think of that girl, too. A man has only to watch the way you look at her to tell that. And, oh yes—you might tell your pal that the girl won't be anywhere near the spot where I want him to show up. He can't rescue her by trying any tricks. I'm the only man who knows where she is— except the fellow who took her away."

Delisse backed away from the table. Parker did not move for a full two minutes. Then he dumped the rest of the Chianti down his throat, set the glass back on the table and unconsciously his fingers crushed it to pieces. Winnie was certainly having her wish not to be left out of the case.

This threw a big monkey-wrench into Rex Parker's plans. Everything else was off now—everything had to give way to the rescue of Winnie.

But he had nothing to go on. He could not simply grab Delisse, because the man was always well protected by his hoods and he was also smart enough to have made some arrangement whereby his disappearance would be Winnie's death warrant.

CHAPTER VII

THE MASKED DETECTIVE'S TRICK

WHEN REX PARKER left the cafe, in his mind was a picture of the scarred thug who had been standing at the bar. Without question he had been Winnie's kidnaper.

Parker wanted to walk slowly and reason things out, but he found himself pacing the sidewalk at a terrific rate. The pent-up anger in him was trying to escape in this manner. He knew one thing—somehow Manny Delisse must be made to contact the place where Winnie was held. In no other manner could she be saved. Except, maybe, by Rex donning a black velvet mask and strolling to the corner of Blain and Moffett Streets where he would be met by a hail of bullets.

That was a last resort—to buck almost certain death. Yet he knew that if everything else failed, he would do exactly that.

The problem seemed almost impossible of solution. Delisse had mentioned nothing about the fact that the Masked Detective threatened to wreck the whole loan racket, so it may have been true that he was only seeking revenge for the murders of his pals.

Rex Parker frowned. Those two men had been killed so they would never talk. Didn't Delisse know that the Masked Detective was not the murderer? Didn't he know the identity of the actual killer or killers? Parker determined to check on Delisse's statement of the debt he had owed those two dead men.

Still, if it were true, it did not solve his problem of saving Winnie, and that was foremost. There was not much time either, and Parker was sure that Delisse would carry out his threat no matter what the consequences.

Rex Parker went to his apartment and phoned Sergeant Gleason.

"Winnie has been picked up and held," he explained. "You can guess why. I need your help, Sarge, more than I've ever needed it."

"Anything—from plain shooting up of those mugs to putting the collar on Delisse," Gleason said. "You name it."

"Strong-arm stuff won't work, Sarge. We've got to be subtle. Listen! Delisse lives in a hotel, and unless he has a private wire his calls must go through the switchboard. You go up there and convince the necessary parties that they must keep quiet. Listen in on Delisse's calls. There'll be one sometime between ten and eleven o'clock and Delisse will sound plenty hot when he phones. Trace the number and then put the address over the air on the police wavelength. I'm going to use a car equipped with a radio. That's all you have to do."

Parker hung up and sat down in front of a triple-mirrored vanity. He kept a steel trunk in a spacious closet and when he unlocked this, he took out a number of articles needed in fashioning a disguise.

He was sure a much better job would be done if Winnie was here to apply it, for she had proved that she possessed a natural creative instinct for this work. But he had to do the best he could, even though he had only memory to go on.

Slowly and painstakingly, Rex Parker created on his own features the image of the scar-faced man who had been at the bar. He spent half an hour working at it, until he was satisfied with the results. Then he donned clothing like that worn by the crook.

He gave himself a last look in the mirror, pulled the brim of his hat down and went out to his car he had left parked outside. He drove the car to an outlying section, where he removed the marker plates and replaced them with a pair that were unregistered. This done, he proceeded to the section of the city where the family of the late Stanislaw Nowak lived.

AGAIN TEDDY came to the door in answer to the Masked Detective's knock.

"I'm the man who brought you the package of money," the Masked Detective said, "even though I don't look like him. I can tell you how much money was in the bundle, though, and what you said."

"Gosh!" Teddy was wide-eyed. "Your voice is just like his was. Say—how can you look so different?"

"A little trick of my trade, Teddy. I want you to do something for me. There are other people whom you know who were paying off on loans just as your father paid off. I want you to go and see one of these people. Find out the name of the company from whom it was borrowed. Can you do this quickly?"

Teddy was more than eager to oblige.

"Sure I can! There's a boarder living with the family upstairs. He's been paying off like Pop did and he's sore about it too. You just wait here."

Teddy came back in five minutes.

"He borrowed the money from the Loan Plan Company on River Avenue. He says somebody from that place came to see him and said if he ever needed cash to look them up. So he did. He got forty dollars and he's paid nearly two hundred on it already. Will you please come in? My mother would like to thank you for that money."

"Sorry—I haven't time," the Masked Detective said. "Now just forget all about me being here. Don't even mention it to your mother. Thank you, Teddy. I hope we'll meet again some day."

Teddy stood watching the Masked Detective disappear up the street. His mouth was firmly set. He had read about the accusation of murder against the Masked Detective, but it would take much more than newspaper items to convince Teddy his idol was a wanton killer.

The Masked Detective drove straight to the offices of the Loan Plan Company after he had checked the address in a phone book. It was located in a building of the same type that housed the Globe firm. These loan sharks did not need elaborate offices to catch their victims. Men who were willing to borrow from such places were apt to overlook anything except their financial needs.

He left the car parked nearby, walked up a flight of steps, and drew his gun. The Masked Detective usually carried a weapon, but only for demonstration. He had never fired at anyone with the intent to kill, and fervently hoped that would never become necessary.

He stepped up to the door of the lighted office and listened for a moment. He heard no voices, so reasoned there could be few people on the job. He opened the door, stepped in, and covered two men who were seated at the far end of the room. They were none too intelligent-looking thugs, apparently chosen more for their brutality than for brains.

"Hey, Al!" one of them gasped. "What's the big idea comin' here with a roscoe in your mitt?"

"The idea is that you mugs shut up and hand over the dough you collected," the Masked Detective said, his voice low and without much inflection. "Or maybe you'd rather I blew your lousy heads off, huh?"

The two thugs gulped. One of them slowly opened a desk drawer and began taking out handfuls of cash. The Masked Detective stepped close and swept this into his coat pocket until it bulged. Then he crammed the second pocket with loot.

"IF YOU guys are wise, you'll get in on this too," he said. "It's like takin' dough from a blind beggar. Think Manny will squawk to the cops? And tell them how he got the dough I'm swipin'? You guys keep your mouths shut too! You tell him I pulled this job and you'll warm a morgue slab. I'm supposed to be somewhere else, understand? I got me an alibi so Manny won't even think I pulled this job. Now, don't move, or I'll plant a thirty-eight through your dumb skulls."

The Masked Detective backed out of the door, slammed it and ran for the stairway. He raced down it, but did not emerge through the front door. Manny's two henchmen might start shooting from the windows. He knew they would notify Delisse at once, afraid of the man they thought was Al, but far more afraid of Manny Delisse.

The Masked Detective piled into his car and turned on the radio. Five minutes went by while he fumed at the delay. Every second counted. No telling what had happened to Winnie! She would not take punishment without fighting back, and Delisse's strong-armed men were not noted for their tenderness or mercy.

Then it came. The Headquarters announcer spoke just as though he were directing a car to some neighborhood squabble.

"Message—special to Sergeant Gleason's contact. Party is at Number Eleven-ninety-five Hinchley Boulevard. Eleven-ninety-five Hinchley Boulevard."

Before the announcer had finished repeating the address, the Masked Detective was turning a corner and leaning hard on the gas pedal. He had at least three miles of city traffic to negotiate and another two of suburban streets with which he was not too familiar. He had to beat Manny Delisse to that address. Unless he did, everything was lost.

The address proved to be that of a big, barnlike house without any close neighbors. The Masked Detective saw no cars pulled up in front of the place and sighed in relief. He found a good spot to hide his car, then hurried toward the front porch.

He rang the bell and banged on the door at the same time. His hat was pulled low, and unless the porch light should be switched on, he would never be recognized.

"Yeah—whaddya want?" someone asked.

"It's Manny, you fool," the Masked Detective thundered. "Open up—quick."

The door opened and if anyone had been close enough to witness that scene, two men with identical features would have been seen staring at one another.

Then the Masked Detective drove a fast fist straight to the pit of the stomach of the man whose name was really Al, and folded him up. He remedied this by hammering another to the chin, which drew Al to his full height, then toppled him over.

The Masked Detective pushed his twin into the hall, closed the door, and looked around. There was a closet at the far end. He tied and gagged Al, stuffed him inside the closet and locked the door.

He grinned as he wondered if he could surprise Winnie with his makeup. He had climbed about three steps toward the second floor when headlights of a car flashed across the front windows. He raced back downstairs parted the curtains in the little window beside the door and swore softly at his luck. He had beaten Manny Delisse, but not by enough.

The smooth-looking gang leader was piling out of his car. So were four men, all with drawn guns. They deployed, taking up stations so that every window and door was covered. Another car stopped, and five more men got out. Then Delisse, flanked by four of his gun artists, moved warily toward the front door.

THE MASKED DETECTIVE steadied himself for a moment, then flung the door wide.

"Manny!" he exclaimed, in as good an imitation of Al's voice as possible. "You didn't take long to get here."

"Is the girl all right?" Delisse asked. "Has anybody showed up?"

"Not yet," the Masked Detective grunted. "But ever since you phoned, I been thinkin' maybe there would be a try at gettin' that dame away. Say, what was the idea of askin' me on the phone if I was here, when you knew I was, like you told me to be?"

"Because the Masked Detective pulled a damn trick. He disguised himself to look like you, Al, and stuck up one of the branch offices. Let on he was you so the boys would phone me and I'd get in touch with you. I guess he hoped to trail me out here. Maybe he did, but we're going to arrange a warm welcome if he shows up. You take one of the cars and get that girl out of here. Take her to the hideout near the river. If she makes any kind of a fuss, hang one on her jaw—fast!"

CHAPTER VIII

MYSTERY SILK

BOBBING HIS head, the Masked Detective, in his identity of Al, wheeled and raced up the stairs. Delisse was giving his men orders to cover the place well and wait for his signal before they opened fire from well chosen ambush.

The Masked Detective was a little puzzled when he reached the second floor, because he had no idea in which room Winnie was held. She solved that puzzle for him by banging her feet. He opened a door and saw her lashed to a chair. He cut her loose in less than a minute, took a firm grip on her left wrist and forced her to follow him.

"Snap into it, you dope!" Manny Delisse growled as they appeared on the stairs. "The Masked Detective will be here any minute, if he's coming at all!"

Winnie heard that name and began to resist with all her might. The Masked Detective dragged her to the door, grateful that she was gagged. Then he picked her up, carried her to one of the cars, despite all the kicking she did, and deposited her in the front seat. He slid behind the wheel, started the motor and roared away.

"You and me, babe, is gonna travel to a new joint," he told her with a grin. "Aw now, ain't that too bad—you can't talk back. I'll take off the gag. I ain't such a bad guy."

He removed the gag, and Winnie's mouth opened and shut several times before she found her voice.

"You—you brute!" she sobbed. "Where are you taking me?"

"To finish the dinner our friend interrupted," the Masked Detective said in his natural voice.

Winnie, an angry retort on her lips, blinked in amazement. Then she gave a cry of joy and threw both arms around the Masked Detective's neck. The car wobbled badly from side to side.

"Hey, take it easy," the Masked Detective cautioned. "Want me to assault a tree? Now—can I make up my own face to look like somebody else's? Did you ever hear of anyone getting a girl out of a mess like I did? Not a shot fired! They even ushered me out and provided a car. Only my own bus is parked back there, so we'll turn off and wait until Manny hightails it back to town."

Forty minutes later they saw Manny Delisse's car flash by. It was packed with his men and three were hanging onto the running boards. The Masked Detective grinned.

"I hope he hits a bump and they bust their necks. I guess maybe Manny found Al and knew we'd tricked him. Now I have something to say to you, Cap'n Bligh. How come you let that hood snatch you? I thought you could handle one of those red-hots by just batting your eye at him."

Winnie was clinging to the Masked Detective's arm with both hands.

"Go ahead—keep right on kidding me," she defied. "I deserve it. But that Al you mentioned was no gentleman. He was waiting near the phone booths and stuck a young cannon right under my nose. I thought it best if I followed my impulse to obey him. But, Rex, I was never so frightened. He told me I was being used as a plant to lure the Masked Detective into a death-trap. I—I think I've lost ten pounds since I left you in the cafe."

The Masked Detective headed back toward the house they had recently left, stopped near where he had parked his car and changed to it. They drove back to town and he dropped Winnie off at her apartment.

"We were lucky this time," he cautioned her. "But watch yourself. Delisse won't be floored by one failure."

He waited until she gently opened a window in her apartment seven stories up and waved to indicate everything was all right. Then the Masked Detective headed toward Greenwich Village. Parking in a deserted street, he removed as much of the makeup as possible and put back the registered marker plates. Then he drove the car to the garage where he kept it, and sauntered to his apartment.

Delisse might be waiting and Rex Parker was ready for that. But nothing happened and he hastily removed all traces of his disguise, changed clothes and made sure his mask was in his pocket. Then he taxied to the building where the Globe Finance Company's office was located.

He worked openly now. As Rex Parker, he had a logical reason to check up on the murder of Tim Cadwell.

It was after midnight and the building was in darkness, but he found a rear door open and walked in. He heard the night watchman coming his way, and stepped out of sight until the man went by.

In the lobby, he studied the listed names of occupants and found one name that interested him immensely. The tenant was Frank Griffin, dealer in imported silks. His office was directly above that occupied by the Globe Finance Company.

Parker climbed the stairs to the third floor, approached the silk exporter's door cautiously and listened, even though no lights shone through the glass upper half of the door. He tried the knob, but the door was locked. Parker was no expert at picking locks, but this building was old, as was its hardware.

He got out his penknife and wiggled the big blade into the framework of the door. He reached the latch, forced it back and had the door open in less than five minutes. He closed it again, lit a match and held the tiny torch high until he spotted a small desk lamp.

Turning this on, he inspected the place. Bolts of expensive silk were neatly arranged on shelves. Some of it was bright red—exactly the color of the strip that had been used to kill Cadwell. There were pieces of it on the floor, too, and only the red silk at that. Apparently a great deal of work had been done with that particular shade and the remnants and threads not swept up.

Rex Parker realized one thing—Cadwell had met his death in this office or close by. The silk used to throttle him had come from this room.

He examined the old-fashioned roll-top desk, but found nothing of interest. Appropriating a piece of white paper, he swept up some of the dust and threads from the floor and tucked this into his pocket.

Seated in the old reed chair behind the desk, he shut off the light and tried to figure out just what Cadwell could have found to make his murder so necessary. Parker could not give credence to the idea that Cadwell had been killed merely to have his corpse serve as an answer to the Masked Detective's warning. The true facts must be that Cadwell, intent on getting all the facts for his article, had come to this building to begin the work. He had found something, too—something so important that his life had been taken to prevent him from revealing that secret.

Parker gave up trying to solve the puzzle, arose and headed toward a small stockroom off the main office. He was fumbling around in his pockets for a match when he heard a clicking sound at the door. Quickly flattening himself against the wall, he was glad that he had turned out the desk light.

THE DOOR opened and a man came in, replacing a key in his pocket. And when he snapped on the desk lamp, Rex Parker saw Manny Delisse!

Delisse walked directly to one of the shelves, moved several bolts of silk and took down the bottom one. It was a pale blue in color. He tucked this under one arm, gave the office a last cursory glance, and put out the light. Then he left the office, closing the door carefully after him.

Parker came out of his hiding place, ran softly across the floor of the dark office and opened the door. He could hear Delisse's footsteps descending the staircase. Parker was after him quickly. Why had Manny Delisse had a key to that silk importer's office, and why had he taken away that one certain bolt of silk?

The reporter reached the main entrance of the building, turned the spring lock that closed the door from inside and stepped out onto the sidewalk. He had taken about two paces forward when a gun was jabbed into his back.

"So the famous Rex Parker, crime reporter, is doing a little detective work on his own, eh?" Manny's smooth voice was sleeker than the bolt of silk he had taken. "You're not so clever at this sort of thing, Parker. I didn't see you in that office, but I knew someone was either hiding there or had just left because when I switched on the desk lamp it was still hot, and old man Griffin never comes to the office at night. So I parked here to wait and see if anybody would come out instead of giving you the advantage up there. Suppose you and I take a little ride, eh?"

Parker shrugged. "Why not? I'm in no hurry to get any place." He glanced sideward at Delisse. "I understand the Masked Detective didn't keep a rendezvous with you. Look, Manny—you can't fool that guy. Sometimes he even knows what I'm thinking about before I open my mouth. Where are we going?"

"Just to some nice, quiet place where we can chin a little." Manny Delisse chuckled. "It's too public here. People might object if I put a slug through your back. The noise would wake them up. I'm all alone, so if you don't mind, I'll let you drive my car. Remember, this gun is loaded and your skin isn't armor plated."

Rex Parker got behind the wheel, started the motor and, following Delisse's orders, drove out of the city until they reached an isolated section. Under the crook's directions, he pulled over to the side of the road, stopped and shut off the headlights.

"It would be healthier if you kept your hands right on the wheel where I can see them," Delisse said. "Now—what were you doing in that office?"

"Looking around," Rex Parker answered quietly. "A friend of mine was murdered this morning, by a piece of silk twisted around his throat. I remembered that there was a small silk business in the building where those two friends of yours were murdered. Naturally, I associated the ideas and had a look for myself. Seems I wasn't the only one interested."

Manny Delisse was gazing at him thoughtfully.

"The Masked Detective put a fast one over on me tonight," he said, "but I haven't played all nine innings yet. If I hadn't had you checked and double-checked, Parker, sometimes I'd think you might be the Masked Detective. But you haven't enough brains to pull a job like the one the Masked Detective pulled tonight—and you're too lazy to do any of his stunts. But you got in my way tonight and I can't permit you to print a story about me being in Griffin's office. There is only one way to…. Quiet now! There's a car coming this way."

PARKER SAT rigid, every muscle and nerve tensed to take action the moment he found the slightest opportunity that would not be deliberate suicide.

"May be police," he said calmly. "Looking for you, too. As soon as Winnie Bligh was released by the Masked Detective, I called Head-quarters and filed a formal kidnaping charge against you. They put out a dragnet for you at once."

"Thanks for the information," Delisse growled. "But your luck's run out, brother. That wasn't a police car, and beside, we look like a couple of neckers and nobody would bother us." Another car was heading down the road. Delisse jabbed the gun against Parker's ribs to insure his silence. He muttered a curse when the car slowed. It was painted pure white with "POLICE" printed on it. Manny Delisse held his breath for a moment, then the white car picked up speed again.

"I wouldn't want to be cheated out of the pleasure of killing you, Parker," the crook said coolly. "But I'm very careful and after you're finished, there won't be a clue. I'll have an alibi arranged and if the cops pick me up, they'll get nowhere. I never flirt with the chair, you see…. Well, I can't kill time here, so get ready. Even if you hadn't spotted me in that silk dealer's office, I'd still be gunning for you, because you are the Masked Detective's contact. He'll have a hard time developing another."

"Before you pull the trigger," Rex drawled calmly, "suppose you have a look in the rear view mirror. That police car did stop. It's backing up. If you plugged me now, you wouldn't have an alibi, Manny."

CHAPTER IX

BACKGROUND FOR MURDER

PUSHING HIS gun hard against Rex Parker's side, the crook turned, and swore. The police car was backing up.

Manny Delisse hesitated. He could kill this nosey reporter and take a chance on running for it. But those radio cars were equipped with spotlights. They might identify him, even if he escaped their guns. Then, too, this was his car. It would tie him solidly to the crime of murder.

Manny Delisse was no fool. And he'd had nightmares about the electric chair too often to stick his neck out. Suddenly he raised the gun and raked it across Parker's skull.

The reporter slumped sideward. Delisse fumbled on the floor for the bolt of silk he had thrown there. He found it, but it had become unwound somehow. With a savage wrench he tore the loose end free of the bolt, jumped out of the car and sprinted toward the heavy forest growth beside the road. Someone called out for him to stop, but he had already vanished into the darkness.

Rex Parker raised his head and groaned. A flashlight centered on his face. Behind it was a state trooper.

"What's this all about?" the trooper queried. "And keep your hands up! I've got an idea you and your pal are silk thieves."

"I'm Rex Parker, reporter on the *Comet*," Parker mumbled. "The man who ran away was Manny Delisse—wanted for kidnaping. He brought me out here to kill me."

A second trooper shoved his head into the car.

"He's Parker all right."

"What's the idea of about fifty yards of silk hanging from the car and trailing way out across the highway?" the first trooper demanded.

Parker managed to grin despite the pain that ran like a flame across his skull. He knew well enough why these troopers had believed silk thieves were in the car.

"Manny swiped that silk," he told them. "He threw it on the floor of the car after I got in. It landed on my feet. When I knew he was set to take me to a quiet spot and gun me out, I opened the door on my side of the car, unrolled the silk and let the loose end fall out. It didn't start to unroll, though, until we were close to this spot. I'd hoped enough of it would have been flying out when we passed through the city to attract attention…. Look on the floor, will you? I want the rest of that bolt."

The trooper played his flash on the floor.

"The bolt is gone. Looks like Manny saw what had happened, ripped the loose end off, and probably has the whole business by now."

Rex Parker groaned. "There goes my first and only clue to the murder of Tim Cadwell that was worth its salt. If you don't mind, I'll drive Manny's car to Headquarters in town. I'll file a report of this too…."

Parker awoke the next morning to the insistent jangling of the telephone. It racked his still outraged head. Sergeant Gleason was on the wire.

"If you hadn't answered in another second, I'd have sent radio cars over," Gleason barked. "Thought maybe Manny Delisse had paid you a visit to finish the job he started last night. The alarm for him hasn't produced him, but I have Frank Griffin, the silk merchant, here in my office. You'd better get down here fast, because Griffin doesn't like police stations and he's already called a lawyer to rescue him."

"Be right down," Parker said.

He jumped out of bed, reeled a few steps, and sat down weakly. That bang on the skull had been more serious than he thought. There was a good-sized lump on his head.

HE REMEMBERED driving Manny Delisse's car to Headquarters and getting Gleason out of bed to tell what had happened. So now Gleason had the ball rolling. Maybe Griffin could give some reasons why Delisse had slipped into his office after midnight and stolen a bolt of blue silk.

Before he got dressed, Parker phoned Winnie at the *Comet* office.

"Of course I'm all right," she answered his query. "I thought you might have called me last night—or this morning before I left for work."

"I went on a binge," Parker groaned. "I inhaled one sweet cocktail, the most potent ingredient of which was a revolver butt. My head is still ringing. Tell you all about it later. Manny is on the loose, beautiful. I gather that he doesn't like you or me very much. Better send out for lunch."

He felt a little better after he had showered, dressed and bolted a quick breakfast. When he reached Headquarters, Gleason was in his office trying to pacify two men. Parker drew a sharp breath. He didn't know which was Griffin, but one of them, he was positive, was the man who had emerged from the building he had been watching just before radio cars arrived, and Turk Pasha and Joe Dackey had been found murdered.

"Meet Mr. Griffin," Gleason said, and indicated an elderly, highly agitated man. "His friend is also his attorney—Mr. Jacklin. Griffin has this thing all wrong. He thinks he's arrested."

Parker eyed Jacklin narrowly—a middle-aged man, portly of build and with a double chin and thick lips. Jacklin's eyes were small and piggish. He reeked shyster. This was the man of mystery, the man who had walked out of the building just after Turk Pasha and Joe Dackey were murdered. "I am Griffin's attorney," Jacklin announced importantly. "Unless there is a charge against him, he can go free whenever he chooses."

"Of course he can," Parker said. "We're interested only in finding out from him certain facts about a burglary performed in his office last night. A bolt of silk was stolen."

Griffin looked amazed.

"But I have missed no silk!" he said excitedly. "One look, and I would know if any was gone. There is a mistake."

Rex Parker pulled a thick wad of silk from his pocket, part of the streamer he had allowed to streak out from Delisse's car.

"This is part of it," he said. "Are you sure it's not your property?"

Griffin felt of the silk, held it to the light, and then hunched his shoulders.

"Silk of this kind I have never had in my office," he declared. "It is cheap—poorly dyed. I would have nothing to do with stuff like this. I deal only in the best. Now, if this nonsense is finished with, I can go, eh?"

"You can go," Gleason agreed. "If we want you again, we'll call your lawyer up first and save you a lot of trouble."

Jacklin wrinkled his nose in derision, took Griffin's arm and towed him out of the office. Rex Parker sat down heavily, threw the piece of silk on Gleason's desk, and swore.

"**DAMN IT,** Sarge, I could have sworn we'd get a lead through Griffin. I don't think the old duffer is lying, either. Know anything about Jacklin? He must have changed his name from Jackal. He certainly looks like he's related to a wolf."

"He's an honest man." Gleason grinned. "You can take his word, just as surely as you can those of a dictator. Jacklin wouldn't lie—unless there was a plugged nickel in it for him. He's been around for a long time. His clients are dope peddlers, petty crooks and the like.... Oh yes, Rex! Adam Spencer phoned and wanted to know if you'd like an interview. He's a little hot about your starting some series of articles concerning small loan companies. He called the office first, and then your apartment, but you'd left to come down here."

"I'll see him after I visit your laboratory again," Parker said. "Got some more dust to check."

He spent half an hour bent over a microscope, comparing the samples of dirt he had taken from Cadwell's shoes with the sample he had swept up from Griffin's office. The same minute strands of red silk were evident. Parker was more positive that Cadwell had gone to Griffin's office for some purpose.

But there were other almost infinitesimal particles in the sample from Cadwell's shoes. These were not present in the dust from Griffin's floor. Those particles shone dully, like faintly colored glass, but there wasn't enough for an analysis.

Rex Parker was still a reporter who had to work for his week's pay. Adam Spencer offered possibilities of an interesting series to bring to light all the shyster policies of unlicensed loan sharks. Spencer was one himself, in a way, for he made small loans and charged high interest. The *Comet* man wanted to get a good slant on this apparently highly lucrative business.

When he arrived at the building housing Spencer's business, he was instantly admitted to Spencer's private office which he found to be luxuriously outfitted, even to a Stradivarius in a glass case. This was flanked with portraits of great artistes. Spencer was evidently musically inclined. Even his desk lighter represented a harp, reproduced in miniature so perfectly as to be almost amazing.

Spencer pushed a comfortable chair close to his desk and Rex Parker sat down. The loan broker proffered a fat cigar, but the reporter settled for a cigarette. Spencer blew a column of smoke toward the ceiling, then looked at Parker intently.

"I think you and I can help one another," he said frankly. "I've made a lot of money in this small loan business. I have branch offices all over the East. But mark you—every office is operated under state license and my interest rates are below those prescribed by law. There are people who have firmly convinced themselves that our rates are excessive, but before I'm through, I can show you that our margin of profit isn't large on individual loans.

"We make a thorough investigation of each applicant. If he sizes up to our specifications, he gets his money. If he becomes ill or loses his job, payments are suspended and the interest is no longer charged. We try to be fair.

"But lately these unlicensed loan sharks have been eating into our business. Naturally they get a certain percentage of the people we reject, but recently they've been getting some of our best clients. They get stronger and stronger every day, while the reputation of this business is undermined by their methods."

PARKER CONSIDERED thoughtfully.

"How much would you figure the unlicensed loan sharks profit annually?" he asked.

"In this city, I'm not sure. However, we're many times bigger than the city of Dallas, for instance. Figures released in Dallas show that an estimated one million, two hundred and sixty-two thousand, four hundred and twenty dollars is paid in illegal interest annually. Loan shark interest rates in that city average—just average, mind you—two hundred and seventy-one percent. The highest they found was one thousand, one hundred and thirty-one percent.

"That's just one example, Parker. It shows you a background for murder. We've got to kill that rotten traffic—drive out the rodents who manipulate it! I'm willing to help, with everything at my control. I've had a detailed statement made. My secretary is typing it now. She'll give you a copy on your way out. If you will print it, play up the methods of those sharks to the fullest extent, I shall be indebted to you for life."

"Thanks," Parker said. "I'll play it up, all right. This thing has become personal so far as I'm concerned. One of those loan sharks took me for a ride last night. He meant to murder me, and only the luckiest break saved my life.... By the way, do you think Professor Benson might give me some interesting dope about all this?"

Spencer spread his hands in a hopeless gesture.

"See him, by all means, but I warn you, he'll be just as hard on me as he is on the real loan sharks. He's obsessed with the idea that all small loan companies should be driven out of business. I hope you won't play up that idea."

Parker grinned as he got up and casually put his hands in his pockets. He shook his head slowly, thoughtfully.

"I won't. Everybody knows how fairly you run things, Mr. Spencer. But I'm puzzled. Suppose Professor Benson gets the proper backing in the legislature and puts through his idea of a bill controlling your interest rates. If that happens, he'll drive you out of business and drive the loan sharks with their excessive interest rates right in. He's really working for the loan sharks in trying to beat you, isn't he?"

Spencer nodded somberly.

"Exactly, but you can't reason with the man. He deals in figures, not human nature. He thinks that if he drives us out, the banks will have to take over. Did you ever try to borrow fifty dollars from a bank—without collateral?"

"Heaven forbid that I ever have to try," Parker said, and laughed. "I know just what would happen and it's bad for the reputation to be kicked out of a bank. No, I'm convinced such loan companies as yours not only have the right to exist, but are a definite advantage to the public in keeping out the chiselers. I'll pick up your statement on the way out, Mr. Spencer, and thanks for the help."

"Don't mention it." Spencer shook hands with the reporter. "I do all I can for the common good. I spend a good part of my income in music schools for the underprivileged who show any talent. Music is my hobby—although I hardly have to tell you that."

He waved his hand at the portraits and the glass-enclosed violin.

CHAPTER X

THUNDER AT HIS HEELS

ON HIS way out, Parker picked up the statement, and studied it as he rode the subway to his newspaper office. Spencer was certainly on the right track. He had concrete evidence which showed exactly how the loan sharks work. It was an amazing revelation.

It did not solve the murder of Tim Cadwell, however, nor remove the suspicion of homicide against the Masked Detective.

Parker determined to write his story and then concentrate on finding Manny Delisse. That crook was still the only real clue Parker had, although Professor Benson required some study as to why his efforts were devoted in the loan shark's favor. Griffin, the silk dealer, was not in the clear, either, and most certainly his attorney, Jacklin, had things to explain. If he had been in his office the night Turk Pasha and Joe Dackey were killed, he must have caught a glimpse of the killer as he fled.

Parker also wondered why the janitor, who had hidden himself in the gloom of the corridor, had not admitted having seen Jacklin come down the steps. There was no elevator in the old building and Jacklin could not have escaped his eyes.

Rex Parker also was aware that every minute he wasted meant scores of new clients who borrowed a paltry sum in an emergency and then slaved for years to pay the interest—or be cruelly beaten up. Parker had not forgotten Stanislaw Nowak. His death had been avenged to a certain extent, but the man responsible for the methods of Turk and Dackey was the real culprit.

Neck-high in a welter of suspicions, Parker needed facts—evidence to convict, to show why young Cadwell had been strangled to death, why Manny Delisse had appropriated a bolt of blue cheap silk, why Griffin's silk shop had been picked on, and what Jacklin was doing in the building so late the night of the double murder.

The Masked Detective would be on the prowl soon. Rex Parker needed no pushing around by Winnie to sail into this case.

When he arrived at the *Comet* office, he found a visitor waiting, a well dressed young man of twenty-seven or eight. He arose when Rex Parker entered, and extended his hand.

"My name is Bart Abel—Bartholomew if you want the business in full. I'm one of the so-called idle rich, but I got sick of being idle so I started a little business which has been my life-long ambition. I operate the Apex Detective Agency."

Parker shook hands with him, motioned to a chair, and sat down behind his desk.

"I've heard of you. Exceptions to the rule always stand out and when a man with enough money to insure himself against ever having to work deliberately goes out to create a job for himself, I remember things like that. What can I do for you?"

ABEL WALKED over and closed the door. Then he faced Parker with a serious expression on his face.

"I suppose all kinds of people come to see you, as the Masked Detective's contact. They probably want all manner of things. That's me, too. Ever since I read the Masked Detective's warning about those loan sharks, I've been wanting to reach him.

"You see, in my business I have to hire various types of individuals. Among them are a couple of men who are indebted to these wolves—paying off at several hundred per cent interest. That didn't bother me until I was directly approached and told that a lien would be slapped on their wages unless they speeded up in payments. I decided to make an investigation of the racket, and I found enough to make me pretty hot under the collar."

Parker grinned. "You're not the only one. What, exactly, do you want with the Masked Detective?"

"Let me finish," Abel begged. "I discovered that these loan sharks are in the habit of phoning neighbors of the people who owe them money. They ask to have the debtor come to the phone and actually divulge to these neighbors the fact that the man is in debt. Sometimes they call offices where the unfortunate borrowers work and threaten them for ten minutes at a time, making them almost go mad for fear their friends will find out about it.

"They have another neat little trick, too. They often phone their so-called clients in the middle of the night and warn them what will happen if they don't pay up. It drives some of these people into a frenzy. I feel as though I ought to do what I can to help them—so I want to join forces with the Masked Detective."

"I don't blame you for wanting to fight those rats," Parker said. "Just what have you to offer the Masked Detective if he does decide to see you?"

"A list of more than fifteen holes-in-the-wall where the loans are made and where clients are forced to go and make payments. They operate under all kinds of fantastic names—like the Business Men's Fund, Incorporated; the Finance Advisory Committee; things like that. I've spent time and money getting this dope. It should be useful to the Masked Detective. I cannot fight these men alone. I have to obey legal red tape to the letter, while the Masked Detective—well, he rather makes his own laws as he goes along. Do you think he might be interested?"

Rex Parker raised his eyebrows in an unspoken doubt.

"I'll tell him. That's all I can do. Suppose you stay in your office tonight—around nine o'clock, let's say. If he wants to meet you, I'll tell him you are available at that hour. And thanks for the interest you've shown. We need all the help possible to beat those vultures."

Abel left and the reporter rubbed his chin thoughtfully. Coming out of a clear sky like this, an offer was decidedly suspicious, no matter who made it. Abel was wealthy, but no man dislikes getting more money. He possessed business acumen above the average.

Why, then, shouldn't he also be a suspect? If the boss of the money ring wanted to trap the Masked Detective, Abel's method was clever—to bring the Masked Detective to a certain place at a specified hour.

Parker walked in on Winnie, who was at work pounding out the last paragraphs of her column.

"Umm," he said, looking over her shoulder. "Who would have thought that you can buy false eyelashes almost three quarters of an inch long! I often wonder why they print crime and war news on the front page, when they can get hot stuff like that."

"Park," Winnie snapped, "while I finish this, and I'll give you a piece of my mind."

SHE BANGED the last period, swung around in her swivel chair and glared at him.

"You want something, and I ought to refuse, point-blank, to have anything to do with it. I'm surprised at you, Rex. Days have gone by and you've got nowhere in your work against the loan shark racket. They've had the upper hand from the start, and you hang around the office kidding me and my column. Why don't you go out and do something? Break up their offices! Get stories from the victims and blow the racket wide open! If you don't start pretty soon—"

"I've already begun, Cap'n Bligh," Parker said, and chuckled. "I've been wondering when you'd start to ride me again. But, joking aside, I want you to locate as many of those loan offices as possible. Not licensed ones, but those dumps where they take in thousands of dollars a week illegally. You and I think alike, my sweet. For a beginning, as soon as you get me the dope I need, those joints will be torn apart from stem to stern. I'll put those rats on the defensive, make them come out into the open and fight. Once they show themselves, half the battle is won."

"I can check with the Better Business Bureau," Winnie said eagerly. "They'll give me a list of all loan agencies and I'll take a look at them. When do you need the first batch?"

"By morning. I'm sorry I must break our usual dinner date tonight, but there is work to be done and it's late now. That's why I want you to do that checking for me. And suppose you slip into my apartment in half an hour or so. There's a swell chance for you to experiment with those rouge pots and fake whiskers. Okay?"

"Okay." Winnie smiled. "I'm glad to see you're anxious to get started."

Forty-five minutes later, Rex sat before the triple-mirrored vanity with a towel tucked under his collar while Winnie applied a skin-coloring.

"Had a visitor today—nice-looking guy, so keep away from him," he told her. "A private detective named Abel. Says he wants to work with the Masked Detective in killing off the loan shark racket. His offer sounds interesting, too. He's dug up the location of several joints such as those I asked you to check on. He openly suggests they be ripped apart, but admits he can't do it and stay out of jail, the way he wants to go after them."

Winnie affixed two small pieces of a special wax which made Parker's nose look broader at the base.

"But, Rex, are you sure of him? What if he's setting a trap? Ever since one of Manny Delisse's men snatched me, I've been afraid. A gangster like that won't give up easily."

"I've thought of all that. When I go into Abel's parlor, it won't be as an unsuspecting fly, my dear." Parker looked in the mirror and sat erect. "Hey, what are you trying to make out of my face? I look as if I'd just landed off an immigrant ship."

"Exactly how I want you to look," Winnie retorted. "Now, a little dye for the hair. It will wash out easily— I hope."

When he got up from his chair, he looked down into her eyes, and marveled at their clearness.

Winnie was safe!

"Winnie, I owe you a lot—and I won't forget it. You created the Masked Detective and you risk your pretty little neck to help him. You've taught me many of the important tricks that go with this business too. The only thing I regret is that it keeps me from seeing you often enough."

"Stop being so serious," Winnie chided. "If you want to pay me back for anything I've done, go and beard the lion in his den."

Parker opened the door.

"If I only knew who the lion was.... Good night, Cap'n Bligh. I'll see you in the morning."

"That's, more like it," Winnie laughed. "For a minute you sounded like the long, last farewell."

CHAPTER XI

LIGHTNING STRIKES

LEAVING WINNIE, Rex Parker headed for Bart Abel's private detective agency office. Somehow he felt as if he were walking into danger, that there was thunder at his heels, with a bolt of lightning hidden behind some dark cloud ready to lash out at him in fury.

One thing he knew. His closest friend would not recognize Rex Parker in the disguise Winnie had evolved. His face was broader, heavier, and the complexion lighter. His hair was a light brown and even his lips seemed thicker.

He took an elevator to Abel's floor, looked around to see if a lookout was hiding somewhere, then walked into the reception room. It was empty. He dropped one hand to the butt of his holstered gun and half drew it. Suddenly the inter-office door opened. Abel stood there, looking at him with a frown on his face.

"Sorry," he said. "We're closed for the night. Can't you return tomorrow?"

Parker was looking over Abel's shoulder into the private office. A big mirror behind Abel's desk gave him a good view of the entire room, so he could see that no one was there.

"I could"—Parker smiled—"but the Masked Detective likes working at night much better, thanks."

Abel's jaw dropped. "You? The Masked Detective? Why, I—I.... Come in. Say, for a little while I was afraid you weren't going to accept my invitation."

Parker sat down in a comfortable leather chair and accepted a cigarette.

Abel walked around behind his desk.

"I know you don't want me to waste time," he said. "Because you have consented to visit my office, I know that Rex Parker told you about the circumstances which impelled me to ask for your aid. I have the addresses of several loan shark offices. You can do what you like with them, and I hope that will do what's buzzing around in my head to do."

"Smash them?" Parker nodded. "That's what I plan to do. The more of those places we can ruin, the less they'll get their claws into more victims. But you are a bit impetuous, Mr. Abel. I could be a loan shark posing as the Masked Detective. If I were, you'd be in rather a bad spot. You accept things too easily."

"Are you the Masked Detective?" Abel asked quietly.

His right hand rested on top of a folded newspaper.

"I am," Parker said. "I can tell you exactly what you told Rex Parker, which should be proof enough. I only wanted to emphasize the seriousness of this business."

Abel flipped over a section of the folded newspaper and revealed a cocked revolver pointed straight at the Masked Detective's chest.

"I was ready to ask certain questions," he said, and smiled thinly. "If you couldn't answer them, the chair you occupy is placed in such a position that I couldn't miss with this gun. What else did I say to Parker?"

The Masked Detective threw back his head and laughed.

"I made a mistake, I see. You told him you went into this business because it was your ambition to be an investigator, that certain of your men had become involved with the loan sharks, that—"

"Enough," Abel slowly released the hammer of the pistol. "I'm satisfied. Will you help me—or rather let me help you?"

"Let me see your list," the Masked Detective suggested.

Abel handed him a neatly typed card. He studied it, then looked up at Abel.

"Very good. Suppose you tag along and see just how this is done. You don't have to involve yourself—just hang around as a lookout. We'll tackle these joints in the order you've listed them. They stay open half the night. Remember—you can refuse. You'll be breaking the law by traveling my road because I mean to loot those places. I'll let you seal envelopes full of cash which I take from them and address them to the Red Cross, shall we say? They need it more than the loan sharks do."

Abel whacked the desk with the flat of his hand and laughed.

"It will be a pleasure. Let's go!"

CONTINENTAL SECURITIES, INCORPORATED had a fancy name, but not a fancy office. The Masked Detective and Abel made the wooden floors of the old building creak as they climbed to the third floor.

"Here is where you park," the Masked Detective said. "Your job is to see that my retreat isn't blocked."

Abel wrinkled his nose. "I'd rather go along and see the fireworks, but I know that's impossible."

The Masked Detective put on the black velvet mask.

"Whistle if there's any sign of interference."

Ten minutes later the Masked Detective sauntered out of the office. He held the door open for a moment and Abel grinned when he saw one man lying across the desk and another squatted in the corner with a waste basket over his head. The Masked Detective was carefully thrusting a thick wad of bills into an envelope. He gravely presented this to Abel.

"The fruits of our first raid. Now we'll have to step on it. These babies I tossed around will probably notify the other branch offices and they might be ready for us. Where's the next victim?"

Abel consulted the card. They taxied to the next place and once more the Masked Detective adjusted the strip of black velvet to cover his eyes. The office he sought was located on the third floor of one of the oldest, most dilapidated buildings the Masked Detective had ever seen. Apparently all the other offices were vacant, for lights gleamed only in the windows of the one marked with another fancy title.

He left Abel on the second floor landing and climbed the protesting steps of the old fire-trap as lightly as possible. The Masked Detective enjoyed giving these thugs a taste of their own bitter brand of medicine. They lived by brute force and intimidation and fear. They cowed their victims in much the same manner that whole nations have been cowed in recent world history.

Then the Masked Detective paused. That same feeling which he had shrugged off just after he left Winnie came back stronger than ever. He forced it away, and walked up to the door. No sound came from behind the panels. He turned the knob slowly, threw the door wide and got set for trouble.

A cigarette was still burning on an ash tray, papers were strewn around on top of the old desk. But the office was empty! To all appearances the thug in charge of this office had merely stepped out for a moment. Certainly no danger seemed to beckon from an empty office. The Masked Detective stepped into the room, walked over to the desk, and picked up several of the papers. They related to the day's collections, listing names and addresses.

SOMETHING MOVED behind him and he turned quickly. The door, which he had left open, was closing of its own accord. The locking mechanism clicked. A scraping sound brought the Masked Detective's attention to the one window in the office.

A sheet of steel was sliding down to cover it. He leaped for the door and struck it a terrific blow with his shoulder. He was thrown back and a stab of pain ran down his side.

He drew his gun and tapped the door with the butt. It was made of steel, cleverly disguised to look like weather-beaten wood. Nothing short of an oxyacetylene torch would go through it. The Masked Detective was certain that it had been locked electrically, too.

He rushed over to the window, prying at the steel curtain that had dropped into place. If he had a crowbar, he might have attacked it successfully, but crowbars were not among business office fittings.

The Masked Detective broke out in a cold sweat. He was trapped! More securely than he had ever been before!

He walked around the desk and his eyes fell upon a piece of paper on which something had been printed in big block letters. He read the grim message, and his lips tightened.

FIVE MINUTES AFTER THE DOOR CLOSES, THIS PLACE WILL BE BLOWN TO BITS. WE HOPE YOU DIE HARD— MASKED DETECTIVE!

Then they had known he was coming here! That meant that Bart Abel must be involved. Had he cleverly managed this whole plot, sent the Masked Detective into a trap from which escape was impossible? Who else had known of that list of Abel's?

The Masked Detective seized a chair, ran over to the door and smashed at it. All he accomplished was to prove what he already knew, when some of the paint cracked off and revealed the silvery surface beneath. There were only two exits and both of them were sealed. He had about two more minutes before whatever kind of infernal apparatus was planted here let go with its death blast. The Masked Detective began searching the place frantically, looking for the death machine. He yanked open drawers, ripped up the worn rug, tore down two old-fashioned pictures and raided the contents of a small supply closet. He found nothing!

His heart was pounding in unison with the ticking of his wrist watch. Each tick meant that he was just that much closer to death. He had no idea from what direction the blast would come, but it probably would tear the whole room to pieces.

All he could do now was shield himself as much as possible. He dragged the desk into one corner, praying that he wasn't selecting the spot beneath or above which the bomb had been placed. He tore up the rug, threw it over the desk. Ripping the supply closet door from its hinges, he fashioned a crude, but highly vulnerable roof. Then he crawled under this, pulled the rug around him and held his breath.

The next twenty seconds seemed an eternity. The Masked Detective was no coward, but death like this, without a chance to fight back, sent waves of horror through his brain. The agony could not last much longer.

THEN IT came. A terrific explosion rocked the whole building. The floor beneath him sagged dangerously. Chunks of plaster from the ceiling banged down on the rug over his head. Large pieces of wood smashed through the flimsy door he had made his roof, but the old rug gave under their impact, and they didn't break through.

The roar of the explosion all but knocked the Masked Detective out, for the concussion was terrific. The old desk gave a lurch as the floor caved in beneath it. Then, with a grinding protest, it slipped through the hole torn in the floor.

The Masked Detective struggled up carefully. This building must have been deliberately selected for the trap, because its time-worn supports must have been almost ready to cave in of their own weight.

Then the Masked Detective heard a sinister crackling and acrid fumes reached his nostrils. He threw off the rug, pushed the splinters of the old door away and set his back against the wall.

He saw the results of the explosion then. Apparently several bombs had gone off simultaneously, for not only was the floor blasted to pieces, but the ceiling had been blown out too. The Masked Detective could look straight up to the top floor.

CHAPTER XII

TRIAL BY FIRE

SMOKE BROUGHT the Masked Detective back to the reality of his predicament. The whole place was on fire. Some of the bombs must have been incendiary, for the fire was blazing in a dozen different places. Blasting the ceilings through had made a draft for the fire.

The Masked Detective edged his way carefully toward the center of the wall. He couldn't cross the floor because there wasn't any, just a jagged hole through which flames shot higher and higher. The walls had not been blasted out so there lay no hope of escape there. If he took a chance and jumped through the flames to land on the second floor, he would most certainly be worse off than he was here—if such a thing were possible.

The Masked Detective looked upward. The ceiling was much too high to reach by leaping for it from a standing position. Besides he had no more than three feet of floor left between him and the blasted-out portion.

Then he realized that he could look clear up into the hallway of the top floor. The smoke was not so thick that it prevented him from making out objects there and the blaze furnished light. He saw a fire hose, neatly folded and held in place against the wall by a strip of leather which was fastened to a big hook. One end of that hose was securely screwed to its water connection.

The Masked Detective drew his gun. There was no time to waste. Within the next five minutes the whole building would be an inferno which could defy even the efforts of the entire fire department.

He steadied the gun in the crook of his left arm, sighted the big hook and sent a .38 steel-jacketed bullet on an errand of aid. The hook holding the hose was bent by the impact, but that was all.

Grimly the Masked Detective aimed again. This time he missed, for the flickering flames made the hook a tantalizing target. The third bullet smashed against the hook again, but the hose stayed in place.

He used up three more shots, and realized that there were only three more bullets in the magazine of his automatic. Three bullets between life and death!

He fired again and groaned, for it was a complete miss. The flames were growing, and revealed the target better. He snapped his next to the last slug. It struck the hook squarely and the already battered piece of metal was blown in half. The hose came down, just missing the edge of the ceiling. It dangled four feet from where the Masked Detective stood.

The only way to reach it was by a jump straight across the pit of fire. If he missed his hold, death was sure. He replaced the gun and took a long breath of the smoke-tainted air. Then his supple, trained leg muscles sent him flying out in a perfect leap. Strong hands seized the hose while he prayed it was not as old as the building, and would support him.

It did, but fire licked at his ankles. He reached up with one hand and pulled himself out of range of the flames. Slowly, for fear that his precarious life-saving apparatus would break, he climbed the hose until he finally stood on the more or less questionable security of the top floor.

He pulled the hose up before the flames consumed it, then started to inspect his new position. The stairway was burning fast. There seemed to be no opening to the roof. The Masked Detective raced down the corridor. In the gloom of smoke and darkness, he stumbled over something and fell heavily.

HE GOT up, and reached for his gun. But when he lit a match and examined the object which had tripped him, he realized that no weapon was necessary. It was a man—with half his shoulder blown off. He had died instantly.

The Masked Detective looked down at the pallid face and recognition dawned. This was one of the loan racket thugs. Apparently he had been assigned to operate whatever devilish mechanism controlled the closing of the steel door and the lowering of the steel window shutter. He had been trapped in a net of his own making.

The Masked Detective ascertained that the man was quite dead, and beyond any reason for being removed from the fire. Then he heard sirens screeching and it seemed to him that the fire department had taken hours to reach the scene. But subconsciously he knew that not more than three or four minutes had passed since the explosion.

He found an office door and smashed it with two husky assaults. A window offered some hope, and he raised it. He looked out into a rear courtyard. Racing back to where the hose lay, he dragged it behind him. He lowered it as far as it would reach, slipped through the window and went down it, hand over hand. When he let go, he landed lightly, and was up in a flash, racing into the darkness.

He vaulted a fence, stopped to get his breath, and hastily peeled off the disguise Winnie had put on his face. His hair was still dyed, but that would hardly be noticed when he pulled his hat down as far as possible. The coloring matter which changed his complexion was still on too, but he found an outside faucet on a nearby house and squatted there, laving his face and wiping it dry with a handkerchief.

He was once more Rex Parker.

One minute later he was on the street, brushing the white dust of plaster from his clothes. A fire truck came screeching down the street. The firemen were clustered around the front of it, and no one noticed when Parker leaped aboard the tail and clung to one of the brass supports.

When the fire truck went through police lines, Parker jumped off as the truck stopped and rushed up to a group of fire officials. But they

did not notice his involuntary shudder, which was for what he had escaped as he saw the building blazing furiously, and from so many places that it was almost lost from view in the red and yellow tongues of flame.

"Looks incendiary to me," Parker commented.

A fire marshal nodded as he recognized Rex Parker.

"What's worse," he said, "there's somebody inside. Just before an explosion set off this fire, two people saw a girl enter the place—a tall, slender, blond girl."

Rex Parker's heart stopped beating. That description fitted Winnie Bligh! Had she been lured into this same trap?

Rex Parker hurled
the bottle at his
nearest adversary.

WHEN WINNIE had watched the Masked Detective disappear down the street, she had smiled happily, for at last he had all but admitted that his feeling for her had changed from friendship to love. That was the way she wanted things. It might serve to make him more cautious and then, some day—Well, her dream might come true. She and Rex....

With her thoughts in the skies Winnie had left Rex Parker's apartment and walked resolutely to the subway station a block away. She would do as Rex Parker had requested, and not become involved in the case at this moment. There was nothing she could do anyway except go back to her office in case he called for help. She did stop at the offices of the Better Business Bureau and secure a list of all loan companies.

Winnie frequently worked nights, so that she aroused no curiosity from the night staff as she entered her office. An hour passed while she studied the list, checked addresses, and listened for the telephone.

Someone tapped on her door. One of the copy boys stuck his head in.

"Seen anything of Rex Parker, Miss Bligh? There's a party wants to see him—says it's awful important. But if you should ask me, he looks like a bum looking for a handout."

"Bring him in here," Winnie ordered.

The copy boy motioned a hesitant, hand-rubbing man into the office. He was poorly dressed and seemed highly agitated.

"Mr. Parker isn't here at the moment," Winnie exclaimed. "Perhaps I can help you."

The man shook his head stubbornly.

"No, I see Mr. Parker. He come pretty soon, yes? He is the man who write all the time about these loan sharks? I want help."

"What kind of help?" Winnie tried to draw him out. "I work with Mr. Parker and I know all about those rackets. Have some of those men threatened you?"

The man bobbed his head in assent.

"Yes, yes. They say I no pay, they kill me. I have no money. I can't pay. I am afraid. Here"—he dropped a soiled piece of paper on Winnie's desk—"that is place where I supposed to pay. You tell Mr. Parker and he do something, yes?"

"Yes, indeed." Winnie brightened. This added to her steadily growing list of questionable loan offices. "Here is what you do. Go to the police— at once. Tell them you have been threatened and they'll take care of you. Come back tomorrow, after work."

Winnie got up and put on her hat. There was something to do after all. This newly found address might be just what Rex Parker needed. If she could have a look at the place, see who came out, she might supply some vital information.

Winnie took a cab to the place. It was not a particularly inviting building, but Winnie had plenty of courage. The lobby door was open and she walked into an ancient hallway. She noticed that the floor directory contained no names at all and, as she now recalled, not a light had shone in any of the windows. Still, this was the address which that worried laborer had provided.

Winnie started to climb the steps.

Suddenly the whole world seemed to come to an end. There was a gigantic roar and a livid sheet of flame stretched from the lower hallway, clear up to the third floor.

The force of the explosion swept Winnie off her feet. The concussion made her senses reel. She left herself falling, and with a frantic gesture seized the bannister and clung to it. Her knees buckled, and she slowly sank into a heap on the stairs.

Some miracle prevented her from falling off, but every second the flames advanced closer and closer!

CHAPTER XIII

"THE MASKED DETECTIVE IS DEAD!"

GAINING THE outside of the burning building, Rex Parker elbowed fire officials aside and streaked across the cleared space in front of the building. Voices screamed at him, shouting for him to come back, but he kept on going. Luckily he remembered just where the doorway was, for it was no longer visible in the columns of smoke that billowed in all directions.

His brain was reeling under the impact of the horrible knowledge that Winnie was somewhere in this inferno. He did not realize his own danger. Nothing mattered except to find her. He could not even feel twinges of hate for the men who had planned and sprung this fiendish death trap.

As he barged through the open door, a wall of fire blocked the way to the staircase, but his eyes penetrated it and he saw the crumpled figure huddled halfway up the stairs. Part of the steps had already burned away and the flames were licking at Winnie's feet.

Parker went through the fire, felt his hair and eyebrows singe, felt the scorching heat against his flesh before he reached her. Eagerly he lifted her in his arms, gave a leap and shot through the fire to land just inside the exit.

Another second and he was through. Winnie was safe!

Behind him there was a crashing roar as floors and wall gave way. He staggered toward the firemen who were running to help him. They took Winnie and placed her on a stretcher. Parker knelt, patting her hand, and nothing else mattered but for her to open her eyes and smile at him.

As if she had unconsciously heard his prayers, her eyelids flickered. They opened, and she gave a short, happy cry before she passed out again. Rex Parker heaved a great sigh, wiped soot from his face, and walked slowly back to the fire lines as the stretcher bearers carried her to a waiting ambulance. She would be safe now, but his place was here. There was work to do.

His eyes flickered strangely and he moved over beside a thin, spectacled man who was watching the blaze with the gaping interest of a pyromaniac. It was Professor Benson.

"Hello, Professor," Parker said quietly. "What brings you into this neighborhood?"

"Don't bother me!" Benson did not even look at the reporter. "The roof is going to cave in any minute! Why, this is one of the best fires I've ever seen!"

Rex moved away, but there was a growing suspicion in his mind. If Benson was the shy, retiring scholar he professed to be, he would not be prowling around a section like this in the middle of the night. Had he purposely come to enjoy a spectacle, believing that a man—the Masked Detective—was being roasted alive in those flames?

Parker picked up speed as he spotted the ambulance into which Winnie had been placed, and saw that it had not left. Winnie was inside it, sitting up, and trying to convince an intern that she was all right. Parker climbed into the vehicle and grinned at her.

"Playing with matches again?" he asked. "I thought I told you to stay away from fires."

She rolled off the stretcher, paying no attention to the doctor's protests. She held tightly to Parker's arm after they were out of the ambulance.

"Oh, Rex, it was horrible! I don't even know what happened. There was an explosion, and then everything turned black. They told me how you waded into the building after me. I—don't know how to thank you."

"Forget it," he scoffed. "If I didn't have you around to nag me, I'd grow cobwebs. Anyway I'm the big hero. My picture will be in all the papers tomorrow."

HE LED Winnie toward a cab.

"That fire nearly got me too," he told her. "It was set for the sole purpose of making a nicely browned hamburger out of the Masked Detective. Now—just how come you were in it, too?"

"A man—somebody the loan sharks had been threatening to beat up—came to see you. I got him to talk. He mentioned this place, said it was where he had come for his loan. I came down to have a look at it."

Parker's face grew hard and his eyes glittered.

"They decided to use the same means of wiping you out," he said flatly. "That means Manny Delisse had a finger in the pie. He knows that your testimony can send him away on a kidnaping charge. Therefore he was trying to clean his own slate by getting you out of the way. A dead witness is no good in a court. He knew what you would do when he had that man plant that story. He must have known, too, that when I wasn't in the office, an insistent visitor would be turned over to you. When I get my hands on that mug, I'll tear him apart and see what kind of granite his heart is made of."

He helped her into the taxi, gave the driver orders to take them to her apartment, and settled back beside Winnie.

"Did you know that the Masked Detective is dead?" he asked her quietly.

Winnie stared at him. "You mean—you're through?"

"I'm just beginning. One of the rats who closed a trap around me is still in that building. He was blown up by the explosion he set off. There must have been a time element on the bomb, or at least that dead man thought so. It's possible that Manny had the remarkably clever idea of killing off his bomb maker too. Anyway that man is very, very dead. I shoved my mask into his pocket. If it doesn't burn, they'll think he is me—which is not good English, but it serves.

"I want those crooks to think the Masked Detective is dead. They'll really go to town then. Haven't you noticed that since I began kicking them around, there have been no more intimidations of debtors? I scared them, but that's nothing compared to what I'll do when the right time comes."

"Where are we going now?" Winnie asked.

"You're going home and you're going to lock every door. If Manny's chumps were watching that fire, they know you're alive, and they may try again…. Remember I told you about Bart Abel? He was with me when I entered that building. I left him guarding the stairs, but you can bet your life Abel isn't in there now. I want to know what happened to him."

The taxi pulled up in front of Winnie's apartment.

"But how will you find out?" she asked him.

"By requesting Mr. Abel to inform me what the devil he did with my pal, the Masked Detective. They'll have found the body of that crook by now, the way those firemen were going after that blaze, and word will be flashed to Headquarters that the Masked Detective is no more. Then Rex Parker can demand that Abel talk, because I know the Masked Detective saw him tonight."

PARKER WAS right. When he reached Headquarters, the desk lieutenant blurted out the news.

"They just found his body," he added. "The mask was in his pocket, burned, but recognizable. They got the fire out before the floor he was on burned through. But his face was burned to a crisp, and his hands—can't even be fingerprinted."

Parker allowed a serious expression to cross his face.

"He was bound to get it sooner or later, the way he waded into those crooks. Maybe you don't believe this, Lieutenant, but I don't know who he was. He just worked through me, that's all."

"Say," the lieutenant said, "all the other boys went back to their offices in nothing flat when they heard the news. Looks like they've beat you, and if anybody was entitled to this yarn, it was you."

"Let 'em," Parker said stonily. "I hate obituaries."

He went to the wash-room assigned to the reporters. Making sure it was empty, he pulled off his hat, rinsed the dye out of his hair, combed it, and surveyed what was left of his eyebrows. There wasn't much.

Then he ambled out of Headquarters, checked Bart Abel's office phone and called. There was no answer. He got Abel's home address and went there by cab. Lights indicated that someone was awake. He punched the bell.

Abel himself answered, and stared at Parker with a harrowed expression on his face.

"Oh—it's you. Come in, Parker."

Abel escorted him to a richly furnished study. They sat down and for the first time Parker noticed that Abel's head was bandaged.

"I suppose you heard the news," Abel said bitterly. "And you wonder what happened. I'll tell you—and fantastic as it sounds, this is the Gospel truth. The Masked Detective and I were raiding those loan shark offices. That is, he did the raiding, while I watched. A fine lookout I turned out to be! We went into that building which burned down. The Masked

Detective left me in the lobby. One minute later somebody stepped out of a nook and slugged me on the head.

"When I woke up, I was lying in the grass in Fairlawn Park—exactly seven miles from where I had been attacked. I don't know who slugged me. I didn't know what happened to the Masked Detective until I heard a news flash a few minutes ago. I—feel responsible for his death. If only there was something I could do." He looked at Parker's set face. "You believe me, don't you?"

"Why shouldn't I?" the reporter countered. "There is a bump on your head. I don't think you knocked yourself silly."

"I could have, you know," Abel said. "It's been done."

Rex Parker arose wearily.

"Not by your type, Abel. What happened tonight couldn't have been your fault, but it certainly has jammed the gears on our plans for busting up that racket. It will flourish now, more than it ever has. There is no Masked Detective to step in and show those rats up."

Abel arose also and his face was dark with passionate hatred.

"It will not stop!" he promised grimly. "If it takes my last cent—even my life—I'll run those devils to earth! Not the thugs who beat up those poor fools who borrow money, but the bigger men behind them. The real brains—those who actually reap the profits. That, Parker, is a promise!"

CHAPTER XIV

THE MONEY LENDERS

JUST AS soon as he returned to his office, Rex Parker called Winnie. Assured that she was safe, he sat down to write a story of the Masked Detective's death. He put his heart into it, but that required little effort, for Parker had been so close to death he could almost believe the mythical figure of the Masked Detective had really departed from the earth.

He exhorted victims of the loan shark ring to rebel, to refuse to pay up, and to report any threats made against them to the nearest policeman. Then he finished it off with a blast against Manny Delisse and his kind.

He was so exhausted when he finally went home and crawled into bed, that he fell asleep in nothing flat. The next morning, however, he rose fresh and ready to work.

A vague plan was in his mind that took firmer shape while he forgot to turn the toast. The acrid fumes, reminding him of the fire and his close call with death, brought the plan to solidity.

If the loan sharks believed the Masked Detective dead, they were bound to burst forth afresh. They were ready to defy the police because they knew very well that the hands of the authorities were tied by red tape. Racket victims who had gained enough courage to refuse to pay up would suffer now.

Parker could not afford to lose any time. He must put his idea into motion at once. He needed Winnie, but he did not have to call her. She arrived three minutes after he had formulated his plan.

Over coffee he told her about it.

"The way you fixed me up last night to look so much like a stolid, ignorant laborer gave me an idea. I want you to disguise me like another man of the same type—more simple-minded than I am naturally, if that's possible. I'm going to establish a private fifth column of my own and bore at those money lenders from within. I'm going to get a job as a manual laborer, darling. Then I'm going to borrow some money and try a little scheme I have in mind. It will take a couple of days to put it through—but then I'll have the brains of this rotten outfit right in the palm of my hand. Like this!"

He extended one hand, palm upward, and slowly closed it into a tight fist.

"He won't be able to wriggle out, no matter how many lawyers he retains. First of all—run down to the bank and get me four hundred dollars in fives. Not new bills but fresh ones, not too badly wrinkled."

"Have you got four hundred dollars in the bank?" Winnie gaped.

"Me? Of course not. Don't bother me with petty details. You have. You boasted about it a couple of weeks ago. Bring the money back here, put that disguise on my face and then check me out at the *Comet* for a couple of days. Winnie, this is a swell idea—if it works." His face grew sober. "It's got to work. There's no other way to reach the head man of that outfit."

"Don't you suspect anyone yet?" Winnie asked.

"Sure—everybody. Did I tell you that the estimable Professor Benson was at the scene of the fire and extremely happy to watch the flames? Looks funny, doesn't it? Then we have Adam Spencer and Frank Griffin, the silk merchant, and Attorney Jacklin. I almost wish he was the man

I'm after. There is also our good and almost too devoted friend Bart Abel. He seemed to tell a straight story last night, but in this business—don't believe anybody. Now will you get that money, or do I have to marry you to lay my hands on it?"

Winnie laughed softly. "Maybe I could blackmail you that way, but I know you're too busy right now to get married. But listen—I want it back, understand?"

"Easy enough," said Parker. "If there's no reward goes with success on this case, you've got a lien on my salary right now. Man—you don't want to make *your* sacrifice for humanity, do you!"

WINNIE MERELY sniffed at him, and when she was gone, Parker continued to plot his scheme. Then someone rang the buzzer. It was Sergeant Gleason, and Parker asked him to come up.

Gleason came in, sat down, and grinned.

"I came to get all the dope on the murder of the Masked Detective," he said. "It gave me quite a start when I heard the news. Then I learned that Rex Parker was still around, so I knew everything was under control. Exactly who was that scarred corpse taken out of the burned ruins?"

"Some mug," Parker explained. "He practically killed himself. I'm allowing the Masked Detective to stay dead temporarily, so the loan sharks will bloom again and give me something to work on. They've crawled into their holes lately. Sarge, I'm glad you came. Manny Delisse told me that Turk Pasha and Joe Dackey were his pals—that he was after the Masked Detective because he killed them. So of course Delisse claims that he knows nothing about that double murder. What about it?"

"I know what you're driving at," Gleason said. "If Manny didn't kill those mugs, the man higher up in the racket did and doesn't want Manny to know about it. I guess Manny was telling the truth about Joe and Turk. About seven years ago in a big stick-up Turk and Joe Dackey shot it out with the cops to cover a third man who escaped. They refused to tell who he was and took a fairly stiff rap on that account. Manny spent thousands getting those boys out of prison. We always suspected the third man was Manny Delisse, but couldn't prove it. He did owe those two rats something."

"Now I have something to go on," Parker said hopefully. "There is one more thing you can do for me. I'm looking for a job—a laborer's job in some big plant. You've got lots of friends. See what you can do. I'll apply under the name of William Ramsey and say that I'm a corn-fed farmer's boy from the Middle West. I'm depending on you, Sarge."

Gleason had been gone a long time when, almost two hours later, Winnie finished putting on Rex Parker's new disguise. When he had his first look at his own reflection, he could almost smell the new mown hay.

Then he sent Winnie back to her work on the *Comet*. Gleason phoned shortly after and gave him the name of a factory and a foreman who would hire him. Parker spent another two hours in some slow, exacting work which concerned the five-dollar bills that Winnie had provided.

Immediately after lunch he contacted the foreman and got a job wheeling stock around a shipping room. By quitting time he knew most of his fellow workers and was on friendly terms with them. He led one man aside.

"I'm in a little trouble, financially," he explained. "In a few days I'll get four hundred dollars from my uncle's estate, but until then I haven't got enough to get a room and feed myself. I was wondering—maybe you or some of the fellows know of some place that lends money. You know—a small loan company."

"Stay away from them," Parker's new friend warned. "You're new in town and you haven't been reading the newspapers—especially the *Comet*. Guy named Rex Parker on that sheet has been taking those loan sharks over the coals. Take my advice and don't let them get their hooks into you. Anyway I don't know any places."

BUT PARKER had accomplished what he wished. Several other workers had overheard the conversation. When he punched the time-clock at the end of the working day and was walking slowly toward the factory gates an undersized, dirty-looking man fell into step with him. Parker remembered seeing this man in the same room where he worked.

"I heard you talking to Ed Thornley," the man said in a hoarse whisper. "If you need dough bad, I know a place. They treat you okay too. Want me to introduce you?"

"Sure." Parker looked properly grateful. "I need money and I'm willing to pay plenty for the use of a hundred bucks for a few days."

His new friend escorted him to one of the usual loan shark offices. Two men there listened to his story.

"A hundred bucks is a lot of dough, buddy, but I guess maybe you're okay. Tried any of the regular small loan companies yet?"

Parker nodded. "They all turned me down—said I didn't even have furniture they could take if I didn't pay."

The man behind the desk opened a drawer, grabbed a handful of bills and counted out an even hundred. He passed this into Parker's eager hands.

"You pay us back every week, understand? We'll tell you how much when you come in later. I haven't got time to figure it out now."

The self-styled friend who had brought Parker to the office, meekly accepted a one-dollar bill as his fee for furnishing a new client.

Parker was amazed at the open manner in which these men worked. And why hadn't he been asked to sign anything? How in the world could they trust new clients without making some kind of an investigation of their ability to repay the loan? These men had merely taken the word of a cheap chiseler who brought a prospective borrower to their office.

"Thanks—thanks." Parker tucked the money into a vest pocket. "I'll pay it back in a couple of days—I hope. I got four hundred dollars coming from an estate and it'll be here pretty soon."

But the lender didn't even seem to hear what Parker said. He was busy studying a racing form and making red penciled notations about horses he picked to win. Parker felt a tug at his arm. He nodded to his fellow worker and followed him out.

"They ain't so tough when you pony up the dough every week," the little chiseler told him. "Did you see him hand me a buck? I get one every time I bring a client in."

Parker didn't show what he thought of this man. He was wondering if the man might not serve him further. However, he did nothing about that except lay the groundwork.

"I'm grateful to you for showing me that office," he said. "If you get into a jam, just let me know. I'll have plenty of dough pretty soon."

Leaving the man, Parker made his way to his apartment by a devious route. There he removed the disguise, then taxied to the *Comet* offices. There was an air of general confusion about the place and Parker got all the details when he found Winnie.

"IT'S MANNY DELISSE and his mugs," she said bitterly. "They threw an incendiary bomb into the back of one of our delivery trucks—or at least everybody thinks it was the Delisse mob. The driver is in the hospital, badly burned. Manny—they're sure the anonymous threatener is Manny—sent word that unless we lay off the loan shark racket, we'll get more of the same thing. Rex, I'm deathly afraid of that man! I feel as though he's just laying back and waiting for a chance to dispose of you and me so there will no longer be a kidnaping charge against him."

Rex nodded. "I'm afraid you're right, but Manny is pretty well holed up somewhere now. Doesn't dare show, with the police after him. If I could draw him out into the open, or discover where he is hidden, we'd make short work of that heel. What did the long suffering boss think of those threats?"

"Just what you might expect. He wrote a front page blurb himself, condemning the racket, and he didn't mince any words. When Manny reads that, he'll burn up and pull some other cowardly trick. He'll be bolder, too, now that he thinks the Masked Detective is dead."

For a moment Parker wondered if he'd made a mistake in killing off the Masked Detective, even for a time. It would bring the crooks into more open activity, but he had not counted on their creating a fully grown crime wave.

On his desk was a notation that Adam Spencer wanted him to phone. He dialed the loan broker's home and Spencer answered immediately.

"Something rather odd has happened," Spencer explained. "I think you ought to know about it. Professor Benson has really sunk his teeth into the loan business. He's hired an attorney to lobby against licensed loan companies at the next legislature. He's intent on driving us out, Parker—so that racketeers can move in and control every small loan made in this state!"

"He's certainly working hard for those crooks," Parker agreed. "What attorney did he hire?"

"Some shyster named Jacklin. No respectable lawyer would take an assignment of that nature."

CHAPTER XV

CRIME WAVE

HANGING UP slowly, Parker was thoughtful. So Jacklin was in the game again. With both feet this time. Just whom did he represent? Benson—the professor with a complex for kicking all small loan companies out of business? Or himself?

Jacklin was a natural for the head of a loan shark racket ring. It required a man with an avaricious nature and a great deal of cupidity to order gangsters around and keep them in line.

Parker firmly put all these thoughts out of his mind. They only served to confuse him. He had too many suspicions and too few facts. For the moment, Manny Delisse was the biggest hurdle to get over. He had tried to get Winnie and he wouldn't let one failure prevent him from trying again. Rex Parker could not afford to give him another chance.

He went down to the shipping rooms and learned that trucks loaded with the third editions were ready to roll. He discovered that one of these trucks was headed for the congested downtown area, covering practically the same route as the one which had been bombed.

Winnie's car was in the parking station at the rear of the building and Parker commandeered it. When the truck rolled out, he followed. It was more or less a long shot, but if Delisse's hoods attempted to bomb this truck Rex Parker wanted to be nearby. It was only through Delisse's own men that Parker could find him.

The truck made several deliveries to newsstands, then turned down a narrow street toward the waterfront, with Parker close behind it. The driver had been warned to prepare for trouble, and to leap from the truck at the first signs of an attack.

Parker spotted three men, standing in the street beside a black sedan, with the motor running. Parker eased up on the gas.

Suddenly two of the men sprinted after the truck. One hurled something into the back of it, then both raced to their car. It shot away, passing the delivery truck fast. Rex Parker passed it too, but called a warning to the driver. In the rear view mirror, Parker saw the news truck stop abruptly and the driver jumped not two seconds before the roof of the truck was blown off and a bursting sheet of flame enveloped it.

The bombers' car was traveling fast, but Parker kept it in sight every second, turned when they did and followed on the straight highway that led out of the city. Suddenly the car he was trailing veered sharply, passed under a crimson neon sign and stopped in the parking space beside a roadhouse. The sign indicated that the Century Club sold the best of wines and liquors, the best food, and maintained an orchestra for dancing nightly.

"A good place for Manny to hole up," Parker thought. "And a tough place to study without being spotted. It's a job for the Masked Detective, but as he is supposed to be dead, I guess Rex Parker gets the assignment."

Parker parked his car alongside the waiting cars of patrons of the place. Entering, he checked his hat and ambled along the sides of the dance floor, avoiding couples who were swaying to the music of an eight-piece orchestra. A headwaiter took him in tow and deposited him at a small table not far from the miniature stage. Parker ordered a drink and sat back to observe the place and everyone in it.

APPARENTLY THE inn was run properly and its patrons were young people of good type. But if Manny Delisse was hidden here, the roadhouse was also used to hide wanted men. Such a place as this would just suit Manny, too—he could listen to music, hang out in the bar and, when he thought it safe, mingle with the guests.

Before his drink arrived, Rex Parker got up and headed toward the phone booths. He stepped into one, deposited a nickel and got Police Headquarters. Gleason's gruff voice was a satisfactory sound to Rex Parker's ears.

"I'm at the Century Club on Route Eleven," the reporter said quickly. "Trailed Manny's boys here and I think he's holed up here. Send a raiding party and come along yourself. We may have him in the bag. How soon can you make it?"

"Five minutes to line up a squad and fifteen or twenty minutes to roll out there," Gleason said. "Don't stick your neck out, Rex. Manny plays rough. And watch to see that he doesn't take it on the lam."

Parker hung up, emerged from the phone booth and glanced quickly at the two booths on either side of it. They were unoccupied, as they had been when he had entered the center booth. There was a chance that someone in the room behind those booths might have overheard him, but Parker doubted this. He returned to his table and sipped the drink he had ordered. Then a ruddy-faced man in a tuxedo stopped before Parker's table and bowed.

"You are Rex Parker of the *Comet*, are you not?" he asked suavely. "I am Harlan Wright, owner of this club. I'm very happy to have a representative of the press among my guests. For tonight, Mr. Parker, the house is yours. There will be no check. Of course, if you mention my little place, I shall be most grateful."

"Nice place," Parker said, wondering what this sleek, fawning man was up to. "Nice crowd too. And thanks for the offer, but no go—I pay my way. I'll be glad to mention the place, however."

He chuckled to himself. If things went as he hoped, he would mention the Century Club all right. But it was doubtful if Harlan Wright would like what he wrote.

Wright bowed again and moved away. Parker looked at his watch. In about twenty minutes Gleason and his men should arrive. Yet many things could happen in that time and somehow Rex Parker had a hunch they would happen.

Not four minutes later a group of scowling men entered the big room. They split up in pairs, and moved to different sections of the place. Then, on some hidden signal, all of them whipped out guns.

"Just sit tight!" one snapped. "This is a stick-up. Nobody will get hurt if you stay wise. Gents line up against the wall and shell out. The ladies won't be bothered. Come on—snap into it."

Parker arose warily. Two of the hold-up men seemed to be paying him some very particular attention. If his phone call had been overheard and he was murdered in the course of a hold-up, who could blame Harlan Wright or the men who worked in his club? To Rex Parker, this had all the earmarks of a hastily arranged trap for his benefit alone.

He started to move toward the wall along which the other men were slowly lining up. One of the thugs stepped close and struck him across the back of the neck.

"Pick up them dogs faster or I'll smear you," he growled.

PARKER HELD his temper. He was more sure of this thing now. That man was trying to get a rise out of him—anything which might serve as an excuse to shoot. Rex Parker meant to give no such cause, but was determined to make a getaway at the first opportunity. If he could stall long enough, Gleason would be here, but if this hold-up was being staged with the sole idea of murdering him, they wouldn't wait for Gleason.

He was given a hard shove forward. It sent him careening against a table and he knocked it over, spilling food and drinks. He was struck again, a slashing slap across the face. His lower lip bled, and his eyes blazed in anger.

He doubted now that he would gain anything by stalling. He passed close to another table, upon which was a bottle half filled with wine. He stumbled, lurched against the table and suddenly his right hand shot out, grasped the wine bottle by the neck and with almost the same motion he crashed it against the head of the nearest gunman.

The blow floored the man, but Parker did not wait for him to fall. He hurled the bottle straight at the second gunman who was bringing up his weapon for some close and quick shooting. The gun exploded, but the bullet plowed into the floor at Rex Parker's feet. The thug took the bottle full across the face and was blinded by the wine and stunned by the impact.

Parker tipped over another table, skirted still another, and vaulted over a fallen chair. He was heading toward the bandstand upon a dais about three feet high. It offered some protection. The orchestra had filed off to line up against the wall.

Bullets whizzed by Parker's head, but he kept low and ran zigzag to make a more difficult target of himself. He went into a dive across the floor as he neared the dais and managed to wriggle behind it. He was unarmed and the thugs were advancing toward him. Only two men were left to guard the patrons of the roadhouse, and even they seemed to concentrate almost all their attentions on Rex.

It would not be long now. Once those killers got the range, they would blast him out.

Again Parker glanced hastily at his watch. With good luck, Gleason shouldn't be much more than a mile or two away and probably coming like the wind. If these thugs could only be held off! But with what? Fists are not much use against bullets. And quick thinking cannot help a man with his back against the wall, facing five armed and desperate men determined on his death.

A bullet tore a chunk of wood from the edge of the platform. Parker gauged the distance to a rear exit. To reach it he would have to rush across fifteen feet of cleared space. That would be suicide, but there seemed nothing else to do.

Sweat rolled down his face. His lip was swelling and beginning to ache, but he was only aware of these things in a subconscious way. All his attention was for the grim menace that slowly, inexorably closed in around him.

Everyone in the club had frozen into an almost terrifying silence. Suddenly this was cut by the jangle of a phone bell. Parker jumped in alarm. Guns blazed again and he dropped to the floor. Then he became aware of the fact that his would-be killers were hastily retreating. Firing a few more shots in his direction, they rushed through the door and piled out of the place.

Rex Parker arose warily, wondering if this were just another lure to make him expose himself. But nothing happened, and then he realized just why they had departed in such a rush. In the distance he could hear a siren's wail die. Now he *knew* the hold-up had been a plant to murder him. They knew he had called Gleason, and a lookout had been posted up the road to phone in an alarm so that the fake hold-up men could get clear before Gleason arrived.

THE COMET reporter was tottery as he walked across the floor to his table. He sat down, picked up his drink with a shaking hand and downed it. He had been mighty close to death. Rex Parker could not use the tactics employed by the Masked Detective, so at that moment Parker decided that any further investigations would be made by the Masked Detective.

Gleason came thundering into the place leading ten armed men. Others had been thrown around the building to prevent anyone from leaving. Gleason stalked up to Parker.

"I pulled a boner," the reporter groaned. "They must have heard me call you. They staged a murder party, but you came too soon for them to go into their last act. Sarge, nothing ever looked so good to me as your ugly mug does right now. The boys can search the place, but I'm afraid Manny has flown the coop. During the excitement of that stick-up he had plenty of chance to get clear."

Wright, the owner of the club, looked a bit sick as the *Comet* man strode up to him.

"There are rooms upstairs," Parker said in a brittle voice. "Manny Delisse occupies one of them—or did. If he's gone, you'd better think up an explanation fast."

He signaled two patrolmen and they stood guard over Wright. He went upstairs and found Gleason in a well furnished room where someone had been playing solitaire. The cards, still on the table, and a highball glass half filled with Scotch and soda, with ice cubes still not nearly dissolved, indicated that whoever had been here had made a quick getaway.

Parker walked over to a door, opened it, and looked into a clothes closet. Five expensively tailored suits were neatly hung on hooks. Shoes were placed in a row on the floor. Two hats occupied a shelf.

"Manny," Parker said grimly. "These are his clothes, but we won't let on that we know this. I want Wright taken to Headquarters and held without the privilege of seeing anyone or using a phone. You have the right to hold a man suspected of harboring a fugitive from justice."

Rex Parker went downstairs, glared at Wright, and then examined the phone booths. He frowned for it was impossible to overhear anything said in them. Gleason saw him prowling around and came over.

"I think I know how those bozos were tipped off, Rex," he said in a low voice. "When your call came that private detective, Bart Abel, was in my office trying to find out if we'd arrested the murderers of the Masked Detective. Naturally he heard me giving orders for the raid. He left, before I got started."

Parker whistled softly. "The tip-off could have come from no one but Abel. We'll look into that later…. Sarge, leave four men to guard this dump. Have it cleared out and make sure nobody gets in until I give the word that your guard is to be withdrawn. I've got to get back to town for some rest. A working man like me needs plenty of sleep."

CHAPTER XVI

DELISSE HAS
A VISITOR

DURING ALL the following day Rex worked hard, wondering what Winnie would think if she could see him wrestling barrels and heavy crates while sweat soaked his shirt and ran down his face and neck.

Rex Parker was putting everything he had into this game of life and death. If he failed, months or years might go by before someone else took up the crusade against the rotten business of loan racketeering. Meanwhile men and families would suffer, reports of assaults would fill police blotters and hospital wards. The more power the racketeers gained, the bolder and tougher they would act.

And all the time soft-headed fools like Professor Benson would go on campaigning against the only method in existence for removing the bane of the money lenders. No amount of legislation could abolish them, because they reveled in breaking the law, while that same set of laws would drive licensed loan companies out of business.

At noon Parker's friend, who had escorted him to the loan office, approached hesitantly and the reporter knew by looking at him what he would ask.

"Say, you said yesterday if I got into a jam, you'd help me out. Did you get that dough yet? The inheritance, I mean."

"Yeah, I got it this afternoon. Why?"

"I'm a little short—can't make my payment to those guys today. If I don't, they'll maybe bust me on the jaw or somethin'. Would you lend me eleven bucks?"

"Sure," Parker said promptly. "I'd be glad to. After all, you did me a favor. Tell you what—at six o'clock meet me in front of the loan office. I'm going to square up with them, every nickel. I bet they'll be surprised to get their money back so quick."

"Yeah, yeah—I guess they will," the other man said weakly. "I—I'll see you at six then."

He was there twenty minutes early, but Rex Parker did not appear until promptly on the hour. They entered the loan office and Parker handed his friend the necessary money which was promptly paid over. Then the *Comet* man was alone with the two men who ran the office.

"Like I said yesterday," he announced to them, "I had money coming. It arrived a couple of days early, so I can pay you back now. It's a hundred plus the interest. How much all together, boys?"

"It's ten bucks now." One of the men looked at Rex with narrowed eyes. "We don't make no short term loans. You don't have to pay us back for a year, but every week you pony up with ten bucks, understand?"

"No," Parker said firmly. "I'm willing to pay it all back now. I'll give you ten bucks for the use of that hundred for twenty-four hours. It's stiff interest, but I needed the dough at the time."

One of the thugs walked up to Parker and suddenly grabbed his vest in a tight grip.

"You heard us," he growled. "We ain't in this racket because we're good guys and soft, see? You still got six days to pay over the first interest, so beat it now. We're gonna be busy."

Parker wrenched himself free of that grasp and took a couple of steps forward. Instantly the thug moved in and clipped him a hard right on the jaw. The reporter fell into a chair, shook his head as if he were dizzy, then he bounced up again, fist doubled. The office door opened and a beefy, heavily jowled man strode in. He saw Parker ready to start something and quickly whipped out a gun.

"What's going on in here?" he demanded authoritatively. As he spoke, he pulled aside his coat slightly and revealed a badge pinned to his vest.

PARKER RUSHED up to him, heedless of the gun.

"Officer—I'm glad you came! These two men loaned me a hundred dollars yesterday, and they won't take it back. They say I have to pay ten dollars a week for a year before they let me pay off the hundred I borrowed. That's crooked, isn't it?"

The "officer" shoved him back.

"Now listen to me," he said scowling. "You're from the country. Don't ask me how I know, because it sticks out all over you. You don't know the rules in this city. I'll put you wise, see? If you borrowed money, you gotta pay it back—just as these gents say. It don't matter how much interest they charge. It's legal, y'understand? Now if you want me to haul the whole bunch of you to Headquarters, okay, I'll call the wagon. But I'm tellin' you—if these gents make a complaint, you're liable to be held on charges of tryin' to cheat them."

Parker shook his head slowly and allowed his shoulders to droop. He moved forward a few steps and brushed against the man with the badge.

He wanted a look at that nickel plated ornament. He managed to open the man's coat a bit and he did have a good look—all that was necessary. This was one of Bart Abel's private detectives. Parker spread his hands in a gesture of despair.

"All right—I know when I'm licked. But can't I pay a couple of weeks' interest now and then I don't have to come in?"

"Sure, hand it over." The thug behind the desk grinned. "We don't like to toss you chumps around, but it's the only way to make you see our side of it. Twenty bucks, pal, and we won't bother you for two weeks."

Rex Parker drew out a roll and slowly peeled off four five-dollar bills. These were brushed across the desk and into the big middle drawer, already half-full of currency. That transaction completed, neither thug seemed interested any more. The detective was looking out of the window.

Parker turned away slowly and went out. There was a peculiar smile on his face as he descended the steps.

Maintaining the same disguise, he phoned Sergeant Gleason and arranged for the release of the roadhouse owner and the withdrawal of the guard around the place. Wright, an angry expression on his face and his clothes wrinkled from a night in a cell, walked into his roadhouse an hour later. He banged the door behind him and Parker, waiting in the darkness outside, heard the lock turn. He climbed into his car, drove to an intersection and entered a gas station. He bought a pack of cigarettes and then used the telephone, calling the Century Club.

Rex Parker was no past master at the art of disguising his voice, but he knew that Wright would be upset and not apt to notice any small variation.

"This is Manny," he told Wright, when the nightclub owner answered. "Bring my clothes over and make it snappy. Where you been all day? I called half a dozen times and nobody answered."

"I been in hock," Wright replied angrily. "That big heel, Gleason, threw me in the can. I'll bring the clothes right over. I don't think they even noticed them and anyway they'd think they were mine. Only stay away from here for a while. I'm in bad enough right now. You at the usual place, Manny?"

Parker grunted an affirmative answer, hung up and hurried back to his car. He was parked at a crossroad when Wright's roadster shot by, and instantly took up the chase. It led, to his amazement, deep into the heart of the city. Then Wright turned toward the more squalid sections of the East Side.

FINALLY HE pulled up in front of a heavy steel gate and tapped his horn in a peculiar signal. A man ran from the brick building which seemed to be a small factory of some kind, and quickly opened the gates. They were closed as soon as Wright drove through. As the headlights of his car swept along the short driveway, they illuminated a small arched sign. It indicated that this was the Continental Silk Dye Works.

"So this is where some of that silk came from," Parker muttered. "I'd better get inside fast—before Manny figures out something must have been phony with the call Wright got."

He did not approach the gate. Instead he found a dark spot, first tested the fence to be certain it was not charged, then swarmed over it. He dropped safely on the other side, drew out the Masked Detective's velvet mask and donned it. Now he no longer cared whether or not these crooks figured that the Masked Detective was dead. He had brought them into the open far enough to get the lead he required. Through Manny Delisse he might even clean up the whole sordid affair.

The Masked Detective moved like a shadow toward the front door of the plant. If all of Manny's hoods had fled to this hideout, that meant that more than a dozen would be in the fight against him. The Masked Detective knew better than to battle such odds. He drew back into the darkness and waited a few moments.

Wright came out first, rushing like a madman, and followed by raucous curses from Manny Delisse. The Masked Detective's lips went grim and hard. He had waited a long time for a crack at this suave mobster who had threatened Winnie with death.

Two or three minutes passed and then three men emerged, ran around the side of the building, and three cars rolled out of a garage. They stopped beside the entrance to the place. Manny came out, darted toward one of the cars and climbed behind the wheel. Two men joined him and others headed for the remaining two cars.

The Masked Detective slipped back, following the side of the building until he reached a window. He smashed this by first wrapping his fist in his soft hat and exerting enough pressure to break the glass. He drew a gun from his pocket, thrust it through the aperture in the glass and fired two quick shots. His arm, deep within the building, made the shots seem to come from well inside. This done, he ran to the front of the place again, in time to see the men in the two cars behind Manny's pile out and rush back to find out who had fired those shots.

The Masked Detective waited only long enough for the last man to disappear through the doors. Then he ran lightly to the rear of Manny's car, took a quick look through the window and saw that Manny and two bodyguards were still there. He grasped the handle of the door, pulled it open suddenly and his gun menaced all three men.

"One sound and I'll let you have it!" he warned. "And don't gape. I'm the Masked Detective. I didn't die quite as easily as you'd hoped. You two in the back seat—get out and keep your arms high."

THEY OBEYED meekly, for the sight of that masked figure had given them the jitters. A man they believed roasted alive had suddenly appeared from the dead—with a gun in his fist. The Masked Detective ordered them to turn around and reach as high as possible. Then he slipped up to where Manny sat. The dapper crook hadn't been idle. A gun, half drawn from a shoulder holster, was almost ready to be turned on the Masked Detective. A gun butt flashed. Manny took it full on the skull and folded up with a moan.

The sound of the collision between metal and bone brought the two killers around. Together they charged forward, hoping the masked man would be too busy to meet their charge. He was not. One of them had a gun in his hand and was drawing down for a quick shot.

The Masked Detective, instead of opening fire himself and retreating as any sane man should have done, rushed forward instead. His right foot kicked upward and the gun in the killer's hand flew ten feet into the air. That same foot came up again and caught the gunman directly under the chin. He hurtled backward and landed with a crash.

CHAPTER XVII

THE MASKED DETECTIVE BAGS A CATCH

NOW THERE was no time to lose. The sound of this scuffle was bound to attract the others who had entered the factory on a ruse. The second gunman lowered his head and charged. The Masked Detective was unable to move fast enough and took the assault squarely. It sent him reeling back. The thug gave a cry of elation, tugged at his hip pocket, and kept on coming.

This time he met a completely different defense. The Masked Detective's foot rose, knee high, and shot out to collide with the pit of the thug's stomach. It elicited a yelp of pain and the crook forgot all about drawing his gun. He needed both hands to clutch his middle.

The Masked Detective moved closer, lifted the thug off his feet with a haymaker. Before he hit the ground, the masked man was racing back to the car where Manny Delisse lay draped over the wheel.

He shoved the unconscious crook to one side, slid behind the wheel himself and headed for the gate. Several small shacks had masked the scene of the fight and the gateman on duty merely thought that Manny was leaving in a hurry. He opened the gates and the Masked Detective sent the car scooting through them.

He headed north until he reached a small, dark public park. He drove into the middle of it, stopped and shut off the motor. Then he hoisted Manny Delisse into a sitting position and waited until he opened his eyes.

Delisse's stunned brain sent warnings of danger to his muscles and the gang leader made a grab for a gun that was not in its holster. Instead he found that it was leveled at a spot directly between his eyes, and that the man who held it wore a black velvet mask.

Manny Delisse shivered. "Okay—you got me, so what? You're not the Masked Detective, because I know he's dead. You're some phony chiseling in on his racket. Name your price. But remember—I'm not through with you after the pay-off."

"I have no price," the Masked Detective said, "and if you believe I am a fake, that's quite all right because it makes no difference. I'm going to ask you a question. If you refuse to answer—or reply falsely—this gun is going to go off and the muzzle will be pointed exactly as it is now. Who is the man responsible for the organization and the financing of the loan shark racket?"

"I don't know what you're talking about," Delisse sneered. "Go ahead and shoot! You haven't got the nerve and—"

The gun blasted. Delisse felt the slug whip through his hair and plow into the cushion behind him. The look of defiance he wore changed to a pallid, terrorized squint.

"D-don't do that again," he half whined. "You—you creased my skull."

"I'll try it half an inch lower next time," the Masked Detective said calmly. "And don't hope the shot will attract any attention, because this park isn't patrolled and the windows of the car are up to muffle it anyway. Who is the man you work for, Manny?"

The crook, who had been so sleek and suave, changed into a man afflicted with palsied terror. Somehow he knew this man really was the Masked Detective and that something had gone wrong with the plant in the old building. Delisse's protruding eyes could see the trigger of that gun being slowly depressed. He shivered again and held up one hand in an appeal for mercy.

"I'll talk—I'll tell you everything I know! Only it's not much. I swear it. Yes, I run the loan racket. I started it, but this guy muscled in because I needed cash. He gave me enough to set up a big business, but I never even saw the guy. He just phoned me—said he knew all about it, and if I didn't play ball, he'd have me gunned out. I laughed at him and then—then somebody took a pot-shot at me. Winged me, too. I got another call, and I listened this time because I knew the guy meant business."

"And what happened after that?" the Masked Detective demanded.

"He—he sent me a lot of cash. Big dough it was, too. After that everything was handled by mail. I can't tell you who the guy is because I don't know—honest."

THE MASKED DETECTIVE knew that Manny Delisse was terrorized to a point where he'd have spoken the truth if he had known it. Perhaps he was not revealing certain minor secrets, but the Masked Detective was satisfied that Delisse did not know the identity of the man for whom he operated the loan shark offices. That individual was crafty enough to trust no one—not even his right-hand man.

Suddenly headlights of a car appeared in the rear view mirror. They winked off once and then came on again. The Masked Detective opened the door beside him and got out. Delisse started to follow.

"Good night, Manny," the Masked Detective said, "and this is a nightcap from a friend of mine."

He rocked Delisse with a short jab to the jaw and the crook fell sideward onto the seat. The Masked Detective stopped behind a thick bush and waited while the mystery car pulled up. Detective Sergeant Gleason emerged. He was alone.

"I've got him." The Masked Detective stepped into sight so softly that Gleason reached for his gun automatically. "He's sleeping just now, and I've learned all I could for the time being. Lock him up in the quietest precinct you can find. Put him in solitary and book him under an assumed name. We'll need Manny again before this case is finished."

"But if he isn't the ring leader, what's the sense of grabbing him except on that kidnaping charge he's wanted for?" demanded Gleason.

"Because if Manny isn't around, the ring leader will have to come out of his little nest and do Manny's work. If he doesn't know where Manny is or what happened to him, so much the better. You can always prey on the nerves of a worried man much faster than on one too sure of himself. From here you take over, Sarge. I've got another bit of business to handle."

After Manny Delisse had been transferred to Gleason's car, the Masked Detective left the crook's sedan in the park. As he hurried away on foot, he removed his mask and now he bore no resemblance either to Rex Parker or the masked crime crusader engaged in striking a blow at the underworld.

A taxi whisked him downtown and he paid off the driver not far from the loan office where he had borrowed the hundred dollars. He slipped into the building and made sure the office was locked up for the night. It required three minutes work to get the door open and he drew a small flashlight from his pocket. The lens was especially treated so that it gave off only a dull light which would not be noticed from the street nor by anyone not in the same room.

He opened the desk drawers first and noted, with satisfaction, that they had been cleaned out. All the proceeds of the day's work had been taken safely away. Another drawer was locked and the Masked Detective forced it open. Inside was a filing system, alphabetically arranged.

Here were the names of the victims—those who had borrowed a few dollars and paid through the nose until interest rates soared to stupendous heights. The Masked Detective found a pad and quickly copied a score of the names. He did not destroy the filing system, and even worked on the drawer to eliminate signs of its having been forced.

He needed these names for a purpose that had already taken shape in his mind.

Then he tiptoed toward the door. As he reached for the knob, he froze into rigid silence. Someone was coming up the stairs. A heavy man, if the creaks meant anything.

UNTIL HE heard the footsteps pass in front of the door, the Masked Detective held his breath, then they continued on to the next flight. He waited until they died away entirely and then slipped out, supported himself on the bannister to lighten his weight against the noisy stairs, and reached the lobby. A small office directory was nailed to the wall. He turned the ray of his flash on it and frowned. A silk merchant was listed as having an office directly above the loan shark's place of business. Had those mysterious footsteps continued to that office?

The Masked Detective turned and started back up the steps. Despite all the precautions he took, they still squeaked. He reached the third floor, crouched and listened.

Not a sound reached his ears, but he knew someone was in one of the half dozen offices.

He crept forward until he located the one marked with the silk dealer's name. It was ajar about an inch. He drew his gun, pushed the door open far enough so that he could slip through, and slowly advanced toward the center of the darkened room. His flash played on the shelves laden with silk. This office was practically a replica of the one run by Frank Griffin in the building where Turk Pasha and Joe Dackey had been murdered.

There was even that same bolt of cheap blue silk thrust beneath the other stock.

The Masked Detective moved toward it. He had an idea that these mysterious windings of silk might spell the answer to his whole problem. Intent on getting to this piece of evidence, he forgot that no one had left the building, and the man who had made the stairs squeak must be lurking somewhere in the gloom.

The Masked Detective felt, rather than heard, the presence of approaching disaster. He whirled around, saw a confused blur of arms and the bulk of a big man's body. Then something crashed down on his head. The Masked Detective dropped to his knees, flung himself to one side as another and more vicious blow started a fast journey toward his skull again, and suddenly let his body fall forward while his arms shot out and enveloped the legs of his attacker.

He brought the man down with a resounding crash, but whoever this attacker was, he knew how to fight. He drew back one foot, forcing it out of the Masked Detective's embrace. It came back, crashed against the Masked Detective's neck and paralyzed his throat for a moment.

Before the masked man could regain his wits, the attacker scrambled to his feet, lurched to the door, and then turned. His gun centered and a single shot was fired. It struck the floor so close to the Masked Detective's head that splinters of wood were driven into his cheeks. The door slammed, heavy feet raced down the steps, and then a dismal silence hung over everything.

The Masked Detective got up slowly, massaging his throat and groaning softly in pain.

He moved over to the shelves and the groaning grew louder. The blue bolt of silk was gone!

He knew just how all this had happened. The mystery man had heard him coming up the stairs, had left the office door open as a lure, and then concealed himself somewhere in a spot from which a swift attack could be launched. The Masked Detective wheeled suddenly and darted for the door.

He raced down the steps, sought the rear exit of the building and emerged into an alley. Removing the mask, he eased his way to the sidewalk, tensed for an attack. He hailed a taxi, piled in, and was driven promptly to Bart Abel's home.

HERE WAS a good chance to learn whether or not Abel was the attacker—and the brains and bank behind the money ring! If Private Detective Abel was not at home, and could not furnish a good alibi, he would then definitely rise to the top of the Masked Detective's list of suspects.

There were plenty of lights in the big house and the Masked Detective made his stealthy way toward the illuminated windows. He rose slowly and looked into an empty living room. Two windows farther toward the rear, he glanced into a study and saw Abel seated in an easy chair, legs crossed, pipe clamped between his teeth and calmly reading a book.

A highball at his elbow contained unmelted ice.

If Abel had been the attacker, he must have acted extremely fast to set this stage. The Masked Detective returned to the street almost convinced that despite all the evidence against him, Abel seemed to be wholly innocent.

CHAPTER XVIII

MENACE IN THE DARKNESS

C **OMFORTABLE AND** at ease, Rex Parker sat in Winnie's apartment half an hour later and told her what had happened.

"So since Abel could not be in two places at the same time, therefore he is not the man behind Manny Delisse's throne. We still have Professor Benson, though, and he's just started active lobbying in the legislature to have all loan companies put out of business."

Winnie nodded thoughtfully. "Which means he opens the way for crooked loan sharks to take over the entire small loan business in the whole state. Rex, do you really think that pip-squeak of a professor is getting a cut for his work? Or is he just blinded by his own conclusions and theories?"

Parker shrugged. "He's so open about it all that it's hard to suspect him. However, even professors like to live affluently, I suppose. Benson is a smart man—in his own peculiar way. He has the necessary brains to head such an organization as we're fighting. But Benson hired Attorney Jacklin to handle the lobbying. Jacklin is the man I saw emerge from the Williams Building the night that Turk and Dackey were knifed. He would have had time enough to murder them.

"And Jacklin is a friend of old Frank Griffin, the silk dealer. I'm beginning to wonder if there is a silk dealer's office in each building where the loan shark ring also maintains an office. Because most of their business comes from the poorer sections, the loan offices are distributed largely through a section where small dealers like Griffin operate."

"I wish I could help more than I have been doing," Winnie said ruefully.

Rex Parker reached into his pocket and took out a wad of five dollar bills, of Winnie's own money, though neither of them bothered about that. Winnie knew she would get it all back when Rex Parker had completed his case, and this was one way she could help.

"You can help," he told her. "Take this money. I made a list of suckers that report to one of the loan offices. Here it is. Visit each one of those people, explain that you're a reporter and want to break up this racket, and that if they'll talk, you will provide money enough to pay the next installment on their loans. Hand them money from this roll and impress on them that they must use it to pay off the interest. When you cover a few of the names, come back to your office and wait there. I've got ideas and I may need some fast help."

Winnie took the cash, asked no questions and stowed it in her purse. She left two minutes after Parker departed.

He returned to his own apartment, whistling softly as he turned into the lobby. His mind dwelt almost entirely on the murder of young Tim Cadwell now. That purple stain on Cadwell's fingertips, the strange glasslike dust taken from his shoes, the red silk threads. All of these were clues, but what did they point to?

The reason for the red silk was plain enough. It meant that Cadwell had been inside Griffin's silk shop. But the other two things were still complete mysteries.

Parker was grateful for one thing though. Manny Delisse was now beyond any hope of wreaking his revenge on Winnie. That was a great load off the *Comet* reporter's mind.

He shoved his key into the door, reached for the light switch, and snapped it on. Still whistling, he moved into the apartment. Then he stopped. So did the whistle on his lips. A gun was pressed against the small of his back.

REX PARKER elevated his hands shoulder-high, walked forward a couple of paces, then slowly turned around. His first impulse was to gasp in amazement, but some quick thinking prevented that, and he kept a bland expression on his face.

The man behind the gun was Manny Delisse, whom the Masked Detective had left in Sergeant Gleason's custody.

"You're a smart guy," Delisse growled. "For two cents I'd have sent a slug through your back. I should have done just that when I had you in my car the other day, but I let you talk me into stalling. It won't work this time, Parker, but don't worry, you can keep on living if you do exactly as I say. First of all, who is the Masked Detective?"

Parker's mind was turning over fast. Somehow, Gleason must have been attacked and either killed or taken prisoner. Parker's first thought was for Gleason's safety, and he was willing to risk anything to reach him. There was one way—a dangerous path to travel both for himself and Gleason. It might mean the end of the Masked Detective's career, but even that seemed inconsequential compared to Gleason's health.

"I told you I didn't know," Parker insisted. "He contacts me by phone. I've never seen his face."

Delisse's lips parted in a nasty smile.

"No? Well, I have. In fact that poor sap is tied up at a certain place and ready to get the business, if you know what I mean. I just wanted to make sure he really is the Masked Detective, and you're the man to confirm his identity. Stop stalling, Parker. The Masked Detective is known to you, otherwise how could you call him in? You have one minute to talk—tell his name. If you don't, I'll leave here, but you'll stay, planted to the floor by a couple of slugs."

Manny Delisse meant this. Parker could tell that by the look in the gangster chief's eyes. Parker had to take a chance, otherwise everything would be lost. He sat down weakly, took a cigarette from a package on a table and lit it with a hand that shook very badly.

"What's there in it for me if I do tell?" he asked. "I'm not going to sell out and be rewarded with a bullet through my head. Yes, I do know who the Masked Detective is, although he'll deny it until he's blue in the face."

Delisse straddled a straight-backed chair and kept his gun trained on Rex Parker.

"My proposition is short and sweet. You and that dame of yours can send me to the pen for a stiff rap. The safest thing for me to do is bump off both of you, but I'll trade your life and hers if you face this guy we captured and accuse him of being the Masked Detective. I'll arrange it so both of you are put on a freighter that won't stop until it reaches Chile. By the time you notify the cops, I'll have cleaned up enough to retire on. Take it or leave it, Parker."

The *Comet* reporter looked up with a harrowed expression on his face.

"I've got to talk—for Winnie Bligh's sake, if not for my own safety. You'll know I'm not lying when I give you the name of the Masked Detective. He is—Sergeant Dan Gleason of the Homicide Squad."

Manny Delisse gave a grunt of elation.

"I knew I couldn't be wrong! Okay, Parker, we're going places. Gleason denies he is the Masked Detective, and before he croaks, I want you to accuse him. It'll make his death all the tougher. There's a car just around the corner and don't make a mistake by trying to pull a getaway because, so help me, I'll cut you down in half a second."

PARKER NODDED somberly, preceded Delisse out of the apartment and walked beside him to the sedan which was waiting. The driver already had his orders and he headed the car due east. Parker, looking straight ahead, seemed frightened and thoroughly cowed, but that was only an act. There was some fear in his heart. It was mostly for Gleason and Winnie. What made matters so utterly hopeless was the fact that the Masked Detective could not operate, and every loophole of escape seemed closed.

The car kept going east until it reached the river front, but far uptown and away from the congested docks. It stopped in a dark spot about a hundred yards from the river. Parker got out and was escorted to a spacious, but run-down building which had once been used as a yacht club. A faded sign even portrayed that fact.

As they neared the door, it opened and Parker went in, feeling about as low as a murderer who walks through the entrance to the death chamber. He noticed six hard-faced men watching him. Delisse kept his gun drilling into Rex Parker's ribs.

"We're going into the cellar, chump," he announced. "I'll show you how we handle the Masked Detective."

Parker descended narrow stairs into a damp, dreary basement. There seemed to be a wine cellar made of cement and containing a stout door. He was forced to approach this. Delisse unlocked that heavy door and Parker's heart sank, even though he knew what he would find there. Sergeant Gleason, firmly tied to a heavy chair, looked at the reporter, and the tiny ray of hope he had kept his courage based on faded rapidly.

"Okay," Manny Delisse ordered harshly, "do your stuff, Parker. Tell this wise guy who he is."

"You—you're the—the Masked Detective," Parker said in a strained voice.

Gleason gaped at him, and then sheer contempt crossed his features. He moved his shoulders in a resigned way and turned his head. Delisse snapped orders. Another chair was brought into the wine cellar and Parker was forced into it. He was skillfully and painfully strapped to it. Delisse grinned at him.

"We'll let you two gents talk things over for a while. And stop shivering, Parker. Gleason is tied up and won't be able to push your face in, even though you did queer his little game. Imagine—a regular cop being the Masked Detective! You fooled me, Gleason, but not for long. I had an idea you were the Masked Detective all along."

The door slammed shut, but a weak electric light bulb overhead illuminated the cramped quarters. Parker glanced at Gleason and the Homicide detective grinned.

"I'm sorry I had to do that," Parker apologized in a whisper, "but it was the only way I could find out where they had you. What happened in the park?"

Gleason wrinkled his nose.

"Was I a sap! You left me with Manny in my car, remember? I put the cuffs on him in case he woke up. Then I started to drive to the street. I turned a sharp bend, going slow along the park drive. Someone jumped on the running board and pushed a young cannon under my nose. I stopped, of course, and made a play for my gun, thinking the mug wouldn't open fire because of the noise his gun would make. But Manny woke up just then and draped his cuffed arms around me. I took a slug on the head and passed out. I woke up here."

REX PARKER was testing the ropes that held him to the chair while he talked.

"That man must have been the leader of the mob," he said. "What did he look like, Sarge?"

Gleason sighed. "At least I solved one angle to this case. He wore a mask, Rex. Something like the Masked Detective's, only a bit larger, to cover all of his face except the chin. It explains why that janitor thought he saw the Masked Detective coming out of that loan office where Turk and Dackey were murdered. Not that this is going to do us much good. Why in hell did you let them take you."

Parker's fingers were bleeding slightly from torn nails, but the ropes resisted every effort he could make.

"Never mind that," he said curtly. "I understand just what happened now. Manny knew, when the roadhouse owner came with his clothes, that he'd been tricked somehow and he called the big shot for advice. Whoever the real boss may be, he must have followed me to the park, lost me for a while and when he found Manny again, you were the only person on the scene. So both he and Manny figured you for the Masked Detective. All of which does nothing to get us out of here. See if you can twist your chair around so I can reach the knots."

"There's no use," Gleason groaned. "I can reach the knots myself, but they're like braided steel. We're licked, Rex, and Manny isn't going to be gentle about our finish either. I had hopes— Someone's coming!"

CHAPTER XIX

VENGEANCE

MANNY DELISSE swaggered in as a peg was removed from the latch on the outer side of the door and it opened. He planted his feet far apart, folded his arms and grinned at Rex Parker.

"I suppose you two boys have patched up your differences by now. So we'll get down to business. Parker, you've got to bring that girl of yours here. She's just as dangerous to me as you were."

Parker shook his head. "No dice, Manny. You can do what you like to me, but the girl isn't going to be caught—not with my help."

Gleason nodded grimly.

Delisse raised his eyebrows in mock surprise. Then he took a clasp knife from his pocket, pressed a spring and a fat, short blade snapped out. He stepped close to Gleason and gently drew the edge of the blade across Gleason's throat. Blood spurted to form a fine line.

"Gleason is still your pal, eh, Parker?" the crook drawled. "You can talk any time you like, but while you're making up your mind, I'll have a little fun. Of course, if you delay too long, Gleason here might turn into a bunch of red ribbons."

He let that sharp-edged blade sink into Gleason's cheek. The detective gave a cry of pain. Then, through set teeth, he said:

"Don't do it, Rex. He'll kill Winnie, too."

Manny Delisse attacked the other cheek.

"Parker knows better than that. I promised him something if he identified you as the Masked Detective, Sarge, and I keep my bargains.

Nothing he nor anyone else can do will save your life, because I'm keeping another bargain in killing you slowly. Turk and Dackey would have liked it that way. You didn't show them much mercy."

"Wait!" Rex Parker cried. "I'll do as you say. I'll get the girl here. I'll take a chance that you're not lying, Manny."

The crook smiled.

"Now you're using sense. After I ship you and the dame away, I'll knock off Gleason—fast. You saved him a lot of agony by agreeing, Parker. I'm going to cut you loose now, but no tricks. We'll go upstairs and you can phone the girl. I don't care how you get her so long as you don't tip her off."

He slit the ropes and Parker got up, massaging his wrists. He looked at Gleason and shuddered. The Homicide detective's head was drooping and blood flowed from the cuts, to stain his shirt front.

Parker preceded Delisse up the narrow stairs, sat down at a small table and picked up the phone. The suave gangster and his half dozen assorted thugs gathered in a half circle to listen.

Parker dialed the newspaper office, asked for Winnie and she answered immediately.

"I'm on a big case," he said. "So big that I can't leave it to write the story. We've got to make the Five Star Final and beat the other sheets, so you get in a cab and come down to the end of Pier One Hundred and Sixty-five. There's a rickety yacht club there. I'll be waiting inside. And don't tell a soul where you're going. If opposition reporters ask you any questions, disguise the facts. Under no circumstances say I called. This must be kept quiet until we get to the bottom of the affair."

"I'll come—at once," Winnie replied.

Winnie hung up slowly and sat back. Why should Parker be working on some big case when his heart and soul were fixed on breaking up the loan shark racket? Why had he said the story must reach the Five Star Final? It was almost midnight. The morning editions would be out in a few hours while the Five Star Final wouldn't close until almost six o'clock the next afternoon.

THAT HAD been a tip-off. Rex Parker was in trouble of some kind and asking Winnie for help. He had just perceptibly stressed the word disguise. Possibly he meant that he needed a disguise kit. The word "bottom" had also been slightly emphasized. Winnie could not figure that out.

She typed a full explanation of where she was going and why. She sealed it in an envelope, addressed it to Sergeant Gleason at Police Headquarters, then hurried to the street.

She went to her apartment first and there assembled small quantities of disguise material. It made only an insignificant package which she stowed into her handbag. Then, on a hunch, she took a snub-nosed automatic out of a dresser drawer and dropped that in beside the makeup kit.

She used her own car to reach the river front and parked it a block away from the yacht club. She ran down a pier close by the clubhouse, dropped off the edge, and landed in two feet of slime. When she tried to take a step, her shoes were removed by the suction. She fumbled in the mud, extracted them, and winced at their appearance. Tucking them under one arm, she made her way cautiously to the yacht club.

She studied the place from a distance. There was some kind of cellar and it contained only one window which was of solid wood instead of glass. Suddenly it came to her that Parker, by stressing the word "bottom" might have meant that he was in the cellar. She carefully approached that window, finding the ground drier and harder as she progressed. In a moment she was kneeling beside the window and wondering just what she should do next.

Then her heart stopped beating for a few seconds. A low, familiar whistle came from the other side of the window. It was Parker—no question about it. Winnie didn't wait any longer. She examined the window and found that two of the boards had become warped and pulled away from one another, making a narrow slit near the bottom. She reasoned that the window was held in place by some kind of a hook.

Fumbling in her purse, she found a long fingernail file and slipped it through the crevice. It struck the metal of a hook and hope surged high within her.

She managed to work the file under the hook, then pried gently to dislodge it, making as little noise as possible, for there might be armed guards in the room with Rex Parker. Then she almost lost her precarious grip on the nail file, for someone was coming around the other side of the building.

Winnie hastily withdrew the file, dropped her shoes, and scooted toward a small boat house, not more than three feet above the ground. It had fallen to ruins and a two-by-four piece of wood lay beside it. She picked this up, got a grip on some of the holes in the side of the shack, and forgetting her silk stockings and her dress, she climbed onto the roof. It was still secure enough to support her weight.

She looked over the edge and saw a burly man, with a submachine-gun cradled in his arms, slowly patrolling the building. He would walk close by the shack. Winnie waited until he was just below her. Then she raised the heavy club and brought it down with all the strength she could muster.

"You—big—palooka!" Winnie said hoarsely as the club made contact with the man's skull.

He half turned, made a weak effort to raise his gun, then dropped flat on his face. Winnie jumped down beside him, picked up the machine-gun and wondered just how one of these weapons was used. Parker would know, and it might prove a valuable asset to his escape.

SHE HEARD the guard stir and groan softly. Winnie found the club again and whacked him once more. The groan died away, and so did the convulsive movements. She hurried back to the window, used the nail file for a few moments, then felt the hook forced free. She pushed the window open half an inch and looked down at Rex Parker who was nearly breaking his neck by turning his head around in her direction.

She did not say a word, although when she saw Gleason there too, a little cry of fear came to her lips. She wriggled through the window, dropped lightly to the floor and began filing at the ropes. The file was long and sharp. It cut through the ropes slowly, but surely. When they fell away, Parker arose, put both arms around her and for a brief instant both of them forgot their peril.

Then he motioned for continued silence and went to work on Gleason's ropes. He mopped some of the half dried blood off the detective's face, but Gleason was grinning like a hyena and paying no attention to the twinges of pain that coursed through his system.

Their heads close together, Parker talked to the girl in a whisper.

"I knew you'd do it, Winnie! Now I've got to wipe out this idea that Gleason is the Masked Detective somehow—and at the same time insure the fact that I won't be suspected as him either. I'd hoped to nail one of the mugs, disguise him to look like me and sail into the gang as the Masked Detective.... They'd see you here, Gleason, and a man they'd think was Rex Parker too."

"I can provide a man who'll be agreeable," Winnie broke in. "I slugged him and he's pushed his face into the ground just outside."

Parker gave a soft cheer, went over to the window and found the machine-gun. He turned this over to Gleason, wriggled through the window and found Winnie's victim. He dragged him to the window, Gleason helped to ease him through, and Winnie went to work promptly.

She required no more than five minutes to make the thug's face resemble Rex Parker's sufficiently to get by in the weak light. Parker then located his black velvet mask, concealed in an especially created slit in his coat. He donned it, and waited until Gleason had strapped the unconscious thug into Parker's chair. Then Gleason sat down and Parker draped the ropes around him so that they looked secure, but Gleason could jump free of them instantly.

The reporter boosted Winnie through the cellar window, climbed out himself, and stood beside her for a moment.

"You're absolute tops, Winnie," he whispered, "and you have done wonders, but now beat it back to your apartment. There's liable to be some fancy shooting and I don't want you around."

"I'll wait in my car," Winnie countered. "It's just around the corner. And, Rex—don't forget to punch Manny Delisse's face for me. Oh, if he'd only been that tough mug I slugged!"

Parker waited until she had vanished in the night. Then he smiled grimly, made sure his mask was adjusted and started toward the entrance of the yacht club. He reached the wall, put his back against it and sidestepped toward the door. They would be on guard within the place, because they expected Winnie to appear at any moment.

The Masked Detective's finger tightened on the trigger of the machine-gun. These weapons were fairly familiar to him. But no matter how great his hatred for these men, he hoped fervently that he would kill none of them. If killing was to be done, the state had the legal right and no one else.

He was beside the door now, out of sight from any observing eyes within.

Bending down, he easily picked up a fairly large rock. He hurled this straight into the night and it hit the wooden surface of the pier with a resounding clatter.

Instantly the door opened and two men stepped out. They stepped back inside again—quickly—with the Masked Detective's gun covering them. The others, waiting in the reception room, were caught before they could act. Two, including Manny Delisse, made grabs for their guns, but the Masked Detective sent a hail of leaden death just above their heads. Hands promptly shot toward the ceiling.

Delisse's face was a picture of glowering rage.

"You're not the real Masked Detective!" he accused. "If you're smart, you'll bargain."

"All of you"—the Masked Detective paid no attention to Delisse's offer—"line up, facing the wall. Put the palms of your hands flat against the wall, too, and keep them there. Manny, you'll search your men and carefully remove their fangs. Handle the guns by the barrels only and make a neat pile on that table. Snap it up!"

CHAPTER XX

THE SECRET OF THE SILK

KNOWING CONSIDERABLE about the Masked Detective, Manny Delisse was eying the masked figure, and the look of doubt was fading from his eyes. The way this masked man worked, the firmness of his voice, all indicated that he was the genuine Masked Detective.

Delisse gave an audible gasp. Gleason must have escaped from the wine cellar somehow! That was the only answer. He obeyed the orders perfectly, for that automatic gun could mow him and his men down in a single blast. When he was finished, the Masked Detective spoke again.

"You have a couple of men held prisoners. Where are they?"

"As if you didn't know," Delisse snarled.

"I don't know, but I'll soon find out," the Masked Detective retorted. "Stay where you are, Manny. The rest of your mugs will file into that closet over on the east side of the room."

"But we can't all fit in there," one of the thugs protested shrilly.

"We'll see," the Masked Detective said. "Get moving."

They obeyed, and while Delisse stood beside the door with his hands raised high, the men entered the closet. Four of them did not seem to be able to fit, but under the influence of that machine-gun they forced their way in. The Masked Detective slammed the door, crushing them together so tightly that none could move a muscle. The door itself was sturdy enough to withstand the pressure and certainly the prisoners within could not surge against it to crash it down. They were much too tightly packed.

The Masked Detective prodded Delisse with the gun.

"Take me to Sergeant Gleason and Rex Parker. Hurry! If those men of yours happen to break out, you'll be the first one to die."

Manny Delisse gulped and sped to the cellar. He recovered some of his poise as he stepped in front of the wine cellar door.

"You're not fooling me, Gleason. You got away somehow, but I'll tell the world who the Masked Detective is. I'll break your little racket wide open!"

"The door," the Masked Detective said. "Hurry!"

Delisse lifted the peg out of the latch and flung the door wide. His jaw dropped a notch. He stared at Gleason and at the second figure tied to the other chair. There was no question in his mind but that this was Rex Parker.

His eyes bulged as he turned them from Gleason back to the masked man who stood at his side. His face drained of blood, his knees shook. Suddenly terror got the better of his judgment. With a wild shriek he broke from the Masked Detective's side and made a line for the stairway.

The long-legged Masked Detective sprinted in pursuit. The submachine-gun rose and fell. So did Manny Delisse—and he didn't move after he hit the cement floor.

Gleason was up instantly. The Masked Detective turned the rifle over to him.

"We still have to work fast," the Masked Detective said hurriedly. "Manny's boys will break out of the closet upstairs any minute. Take the gun—keep them covered. I'll send help."

"And Manny?" Gleason indicated the unconscious gangster.

"I'll take care of him," the Masked Detective said. "One more thing. I'll climb out the window. You hand up that mug Winnie knocked stiff. I'll put him back where I found him. When he wakes up, he won't know what happened, and most certainly he'll never think he doubled for Rex Parker. You can get him later on before he escapes."

GLEASON PUT down the rifle, loosened the thug's bonds while Parker erased all signs of the disguise. He passed the man through the narrow window and Rex Parker hastily put him on the ground beside the dilapidated boat house. Then, at the Masked Detective's request, Gleason shoved Manny Delisse through the window.

"I just socked him again to make sure he'll stay quiet," Gleason said, and grinned. "The mug you just stowed away awoke a couple of minutes ago and I plastered one on his chin, too. Boy—I'm having fun."

It was early morning and around this section of the waterfront there were few patrolmen and no pedestrians. The Masked Detective slung Delisse over one shoulder and made his way to where Winnie was waiting in her car. He threw the crook into the back seat, sat down beside Winnie and heaved a great sigh.

"We're almost finished, beautiful. A couple of more details and I'll write the grandest story of my career—about the liberation of a lot of poor saps who borrowed money from the loan sharks."

"Then you know who the big shot is?" Winnie asked in surprise.

"I think I do. Before morning I'll be certain. Drive to my apartment first."

"What about the load of chilled beef in the back seat?" Winnie jerked her head in Manny Delisse's direction.

"We'll unload him pretty soon. Don't waste time—and when you see a cop, slow up."

The Masked Detective removed the black velvet mask and became Rex Parker again. Winnie tooted her horn at the sight of a patrolman just getting ready to turn in a duty call at a police box. Parker leaned out of the window.

"Sergeant Gleason is at the old yacht club at the end of the pier," he called out. "He's rounded up a mob and needs help. Send for the wagon and some men and then beat it down there."

"Right you are, Mr. Parker." The patrolman saw the reporter's face plainly.

SOMEWHERE A clock struck three and like a shadowy, avenging ghost, the Masked Detective came around the corner of a squalid block and looked up at a run-down office building. The second floor windows bore the title of another loan shark office and just above it, another sign labeled that office as being the silk business of one Thaddeus Warlick.

The lobby door was locked, but the Masked Detective made short work of that barrier and was soon climbing the stairs. He passed the loan office, continued to the third floor, and forced the door of the silk business office. He stepped inside, and that flashlight which threw only a dull glow swept over the shelves of stock. He picked out a bolt of cheap blue silk, almost buried under the rest of the stock. He pulled this out, laid it down on the long cutting table and unrolled it.

The silk was carefully rolled around a thick base of cardboard. As this was revealed, a sheet of white paper fell away from it. The Masked Detective picked it up, turned the ray of his flash on it, and gave a grunt of satisfaction. It contained a long list of names and addresses.

Working furiously, he copied these, rolled the silk back as well as he could, and replaced it on the shelves. When it was called for, no one could tell that it had been examined.

He removed his mask as he reached the lobby, left the building, and ran around a corner to where his car was parked. Next he drove into the heart of the city and this time he had a more difficult problem to solve. He entered a lavish office building—utterly unlike those used by the loan sharks.

ON ONE of the lower floors, he worked on a modern lock with a bunch of pass keys he had picked up during the course of his work around Police Headquarters. They had permitted crooks to make easy entrances to places like this and they served the Masked Detective just as well. He spent about twenty minutes inside the offices and when he emerged, there was a contented grin on his face.

He made one more nocturnal visit.

But it was turning light when Rex Parker put his car away and returned to his apartment for some much needed sleep.

Shortly after noon the next day, Rex Parker met Adam Spencer, who operated the licensed loan companies and fought the loan shark racket with all he had. The meeting was by appointment and at Spencer's home. It was a lavishly furnished place, and Spencer came to the door with a violin tucked under one arm and the bow in his hand.

"Come in, Parker. I'm glad to see you. Just brushing up on my music. I'm composing a violin concerto. I'd like to have you hear it."

He led Parker through the drawing room and into a smaller room fitted with all manner of musical instruments and devices. There was a tilt-top desk in one corner and on it were pages of blank music which Spencer used to record his melodies. He had stamped in—with small rubber stamps that formed printed notes—whole bars of music.

Spencer motioned Parker into a chair, and while the reporter talked, Spencer idly rubbed rosin over his bow.

"First of all, I came to have you approve articles I've written, blasting away at the loan shark racket," Parker explained. "I'm not completely familiar with all the phases of banking and lending, so I thought you'd better give my story a once over. I'll leave it and call tonight. Is that satisfactory?"

"Very," Spencer said. "I'm more than happy to help. Have you—or your friend the Masked Detective—any more information on the ring?"

Parker smiled. "I think I've run down our man. Now don't start asking questions. It will all come out later, when I'm positive of my grounds. Sufficient to say now that every clue points to him. You've helped me there considerably, Mr. Spencer."

"Benson!" Spencer ejaculated. "You've told me enough so that I know who you must mean. That's why he's instigated this lobbying. He has built up his smelly business until he can take over the whole loan racket and run it just as he wishes. The bill he hopes to pass cuts our interest rates down to ten per cent. We can't possibly operate on such a margin. We can't split even on it. Get him, Parker, before that bill goes through. Get him and you can have anything in my power to give you."

Parker laid a sheaf of papers on the table.

"There are the articles. I'm not looking for a reward, Mr. Spencer. If I can free those poor people from the invisible chains those bandits have put around them, that will be payment enough. As soon as I know where I stand—you can be in on the kill, but mind you I'm not saying it's Benson. There are other people under suspicion."

THEY SHOOK hands and Spencer escorted him to the door. He clapped Parker's shoulder in a friendly manner.

"I'm appreciative for all this, make no mistake about that. Tonight then—after I've had a chance to read your articles."

"Good," Parker said. Then he hesitated. "Say, you don't need one page of those papers. They're just notes to be used in another story."

He hurried back to the music room and picked up the sheaf of papers. Spencer looked over Parker's shoulder and as Parker started to turn, he bumped into the man. The papers fell from his hands. He grinned sheepishly and with Spencer's help, picked them up again. He folded one and put it into his pocket.

"The excitement of this case is getting on my nerves, I guess," he apologized. "Thanks again and this time I'm really going."

CHAPTER XXI

THE CLOSING NET

QUIETLY TRYING to concentrate on her column and having no success whatsoever, Winnie was in her office when Rex Parker came in and sat down on the edge of her desk.

"I didn't have time to tell you last night," she said, "but I visited some of those poor people you had on your list. I gave them money, too, and they went to the loan offices without waiting another minute. Those places stay open late enough, don't they?"

"So they'll never miss a sucker," Parker said, chuckling. "We'll close them up shortly though. What about the Continental Silk Dye Works?"

"I checked it this morning. Rex, it's owned by Professor Benson. The corporation papers show him—Ronald Benson—as president and treasurer. The vice-president and secretary sound like phonies to me. At least I couldn't locate either of them. Another thing—I ruined a pair of shoes, a pair of stockings, and a dress last night. You also owe me four hundred nice, green dollars. Don't forget that."

Rex pulled a roll of bills from his pocket and placed it on Winnie's desk.

"I borrowed that hundred dollars from a loan shark. They were responsible for ruining your clothes, but I think you can buy new ones out of that and have enough left to blow me to a supper tonight. About eleven or midnight, let's say. As for the four hundred dollars I promise you this—either I pay it back or I'll have to marry you. I'm certainly cornered, I guess."

Winnie's hand rested on his wrist.

"Some day," she warned, "I swear I'll take you up on that. My head is getting soft with advancing age. Now get out of here and let me finish my column."

He headed for the door.

"Which reminds me—if I hope to make the morning editions with the greatest story the Masked Detective ever turned over, I've got to write it. Quickly."

In the late afternoon, Rex Parker and Sergeant Gleason were in the police laboratories. Parker got out the debris he had peeled off of Tim Cadwell's shoes and also produced another carefully folded paper containing more dust. He compared these two tiny heaps of dust under the high power of the microscope again and now both of them contained the same fine particles of that glasslike substance. Rex Parker had studied chemistry and physics in college, had majored in them before he decided to turn reporter. He had spent hours in the police labs, watching experts go about the business of solving crime by exacting analysis. Now he put all his experience to work.

He weighed out identical portions of the dust taken from each sample and used a microbalance so sensitive that it was air conditioned against air currents and temperature changes. When he was satisfied that he had assembled the dust in exact quantities, he placed two graphite sticks in a board which contained holes to fit these sticks and keep them in a vertical position.

The graphite sticks had hollowed-out ends, and in each of these he placed tiny portions of his weighed samples. Some of the dust was too fine to be picked up with forceps, so he rubbed a celluloid stick with a piece of silk until the tube was giving off static electricity. This caused the particles of dust to adhere easily and he deposited them in the hollowed-out ends of the graphite.

"THAT'S AN awful lot of careful work," Gleason broke the silence. "What's it going to get you, Rex?"

"One murderer—impaled to the wall and ripe for the electric chair," Parker said quickly. "I'm putting my samples through spectroscopic analysis for purposes of comparison. If they compare, we've got our man without the slightest loophole for escape. He can hire the most expensive lawyers in the world, and when this work I'm doing is demonstrated before a jury, the case will be in the bag—for the district attorney."

He transferred the graphite sticks to an electrode holder, hooked up the apparatus, and turned on two hundred and twenty volts of current. The almost infinitesimal particles on the ends of the graphite sticks burned. Prisms, correctly placed in the machine, broke up the light of these minute flames into wave lengths. Parker manipulated a camera with a highly sensitive film and the light from the particles, coming through the prism, were recorded on the film.

Moments later he projected these light lines through an especially created glass box. The lines seemed to leap out, casting off significant colored lines. These were spectrum lines through which the finest analysis in the world was possible. Both samples of dust had given off their individual bands of light and Rex compared these. The bands matched as to color.

"One more test," he told Gleason. "I'm satisfied now, but we might as well be positive about it."

"Well," Gleason grunted, "I thought I knew something about tracing down clues, but this stuff—it's way over my head."

"Then I'll explain. Each of these samples was taken from different sources, but they contained what seemed to be identical substances. I burned the samples with electricity and they threw off certain color and light waves which I photographed. If each sample shows the same color bands on the spectrum scale, we're sure the samples are identical. The substance I'm checking may be wood, for instance, but if the color bands showed the same, that wood came from the same block, not the same board or the same tree, but the identical block. I'm not studying wood, however."

He worked at another apparatus, a densitometer, which changed the light beams registered on the film into electric impulses. These were shot out to hit a mirror. With a piece of platinum wire, no wider than a hair, Rex traced the mirror-reflected spectrum lines. They were identical.

He leaned back in a chair, lit a cigarette and grinned at Gleason.

"I'm satisfied. There can be no question but that both samples came from the same spot. The net is closed, Sarge."

Gleason frowned.

"What I'd like to know is what did you do with Manny Delisse? Don't forget, I've got a warrant out for that bird. Those mugs I brought to Headquarters last night are just plain dumb heels. They think they were working for Manny and they're yelling like blazes to make a deal. I could plaster Manny into the chair with the stuff they've told me."

Rex Parker got up and put on his coat.

"What's the use of convicting a little guy like Manny when the big shot will only bide his time and start the racket all over again? Come on, Sarge. We've got things to do."

WINNIE WAS waiting outside Police Headquarters in her car.

"I'm not going to be left out of this," she said insistently, as Parker got in. "When are you going to expose your man, Rex?"

"Soon. You can drive me to Adam Spencer's house first. I've got a series of articles which he's been checking over. I need them for the morning editions."

"But I thought you'd print the whole story?" Winnie protested. "Listen to me, Rex Parker, if you think I'm going to be disposed of while you finish the case, you're wrong. I'm not leaving you—not for one minute. I—I—"

Parker smiled and patted her cheek.

"Right you are, Captain Bligh. I guess you are entitled to see the finish. Now will you drive me to Spencer's place?"

She parked in front of the big house a short time later, and shut off the motor.

"You can go and get your articles," she said firmly, "but I'm not leaving the car. And I can see the back of the house from here, too."

When Parker rang the bell, Spencer let him in immediately.

"I've read your stuff and it's right to the point, Parker," he said at once. "If people will absorb the information, you've struck a body blow at the loan sharks. I'm as grateful as their victims will be."

Rex threw his hat on a chair, carefully folded the papers which Spencer handed back to him, and put them into his pocket.

"Thanks for looking them over. They'll serve a certain purpose, I think, but the loan racket is ready to be blown high, wide and handsome. Read the morning papers."

Parker shook hands with Spencer and departed. Spencer watched him climb into the car and be driven off. Spencer seemed considerably relieved. He went back to his music room, picked up his violin and played over the bars he had written. Perhaps three minutes passed by and he kept applying himself to the music. Then, suddenly, Spencer gasped, as a voice came from the other room.

"A little stilted, Mr. Spencer. I don't think your mind has been on your music lately."

Spencer walked into the next room, prepared to meet almost anything. He stopped dead and gaped. The Masked Detective sat in a chair before Spencer's big desk. His feet were planked on the edge of it.

"Sit down, Spencer," the Masked Detective invited. "You and I have things to discuss."

Spencer obeyed, slowly and with a frightened expression on his face. He laid the violin on a corner of the desk and mopped his forehead with a silk handkerchief. He even managed a weak smile.

"Of course—of course. I—I'm glad you've come. I thought you might come to see me after what your friend Rex Parker told me. How can I help you?"

"It's not hard," the Masked Detective replied. "In fact, if you'll just write me a confession, it will be all over. My end of it. You've got to face the music, Spencer!"

CHAPTER XXII

PAY-OFF IN DEATH

FACE BEET-RED, then white, Spencer jumped up. His hands shook and when he spoke, his voice was venom-filled.

"What do you mean? Are you accusing me of being behind that vicious racket?"

"No, I'm not accusing. I'm telling you. Listen—and sit down. You make me nervous. Here is why I'm so sure. Tim Cadwell, a very nice lad, went out to get a story on the loan shark racket. He entered the

Williams Building, where you had just previously murdered two men. You were still there, busy at your work of placing a bolt of silk for Manny Delisse or one of his men to get. You didn't want to meet those who worked for you, and that is why you chose this method of indirect contact.

"In each bolt of silk you placed a list of names. Significant names, too. When applicants for loans at your very much licensed offices were investigated and rejected, you turned these over to the loan sharks. They then approached these people, made the loans, and intimidated the poor saps from that moment on."

"Silk? List of names?" Spencer derided. "Of all the silly things I've ever heard—"

"Shut up and listen," the Masked Detective said. "Tim Cadwell heard you upstairs in Frank Griffin's silk store. He probably went up there to see if he could get a story. He found you there, wearing a mask.

"Cadwell was just a boy. Easy meat for you. You struck him. Then you tied his hands with a piece of red silk. You smuggled him out of the building somehow, took him to your home and asked him plenty of questions. Now Cadwell was young, but he was no fool. He knew he would never get away alive so he proceeded to leave a clue and, unconsciously, take another with him. You strangled him with that red silk, packed him into a barrel and shipped him to the newspaper office as a challenge to me."

Spencer's lips curled in a sneer.

"Show me those clues. You're bluffing."

"In your music room"—the Masked Detective's voice was like the rumble of approaching doom—"is a tilt-top table on which you write your scores. You hit upon a new wrinkle there—instead of inking or penciling the notes in, you use a rubber stamp. Cadwell saw the ink pad. He pressed his fingers against it, and left his prints on the underside of that table. They are there now.

"I paid you a visit last night—one you didn't know about. The same ink that was on Cadwell's fingers is on your table with his prints. That's one clue, Spencer. The other was developed in a laboratory. Some of the debris taken from Cadwell's shoes proved he was in Griffin's silk shop. But there was something else—not enough to analyze, but it gave me an idea.

"Today I sent my friend Rex Parker to see you. Remember how he dropped papers on the floor of your music room? One of those was covered with a substance that picked up dust from your floor. It contained the identical substance that was taken from Cadwell's shoes. It was rosin. You use it on your violin bow."

SPENCER SHOULD have showed signs of fear, but the Masked Detective saw none. The first shock had passed. Spencer seemed almost too sure of himself.

"Go on with your fairy tale," he said.

"You tried to hang Benson for your crimes. You actually wanted him to put through a law which would have forced your licensed offices out of business. Then you could squawk to high heaven, but run the illicit loan rackets to your heart's content. Benson did act suspiciously too. The night your men tried to roast me alive, he was at the scene of the fire, but I've learned since that he thought himself something of a detective and used to watch the various loan shark offices, trying to get evidence against them. There's an odd streak in his make-up—it compelled him to remain and watch the blaze.

"You set up silk merchants in the building where your loan offices were located. You bought the Continental Silk Dye Works and used Professor Benson's name to do it. If that business of using silk to hide your list of victims was uncovered and the silk traced, it would lead right to Benson.

"Your guilt is known all over the city by now. Your mugs turned in their cash daily and you banked it. But today, among those bills you received were some that had been planted in those offices. They were marked with an ink that became visible before you banked them. The words stated that the passer of the bills was a loan shark. Your bank spotted them and relayed word to the police. That alone will convict you."

Spencer forced a leering smile.

"You're a clever man—stupid only at rare intervals. This happens to be one of them. Immediately behind you is my butler who happens to be in my confidence. I never allowed him to answer the door, but simply to wait and if anything like this should happen I'd still have the upper hand. That's a gun touching the back of your neck, Mr. Masked Detective. Do I still see a smile on your face?"

"You do. The game isn't lost until the final inning, Spencer. That hasn't come yet. Tell your man to come around in front. What's he afraid of—with a gun in his hand?"

Spencer rasped an oath, motioned his man to approach, and took the gun from his hand. He leveled it at the Masked Detective's chest.

"Very well, then I'll finish it—now."

"Why hurry?" the Masked Detective said languidly, but while his pose suggested the idea that he knew he was securely trapped, every nerve, every muscle was tensed and ready.

"Why not tell me all about the way you murdered Turk Pasha and Joe Dackey? You did that, didn't you?"

"Yes, I killed them. They weren't producing enough anyway. I couldn't let them fall into the hands of the police, any more than I could permit you to leave here—alive."

Suddenly a curtain at the end of the room was thrust aside and Manny Delisse came rushing out. Murder was written on his face. His voice reached a scream.

"You killed them! You killed my pals! You told me the Masked Detective did it. Damn you, I'll—"

Spencer whirled around. His gun blasted twice. Delisse stopped short, stood as quietly as a statue for a few seconds, then slumped sideward.

Spencer started to turn the gun in the direction of the Masked Detective. A foot flashed before his eyes and the gun flew out of his hand. The same foot came up a second time and hit Spencer across the chest. It sent him staggering backward.

HIS BUTLER gave a vicious snarl and lunged for the alert Masked Detective.

There was another shot. The butler screeched, clapped one hand to his shoulder, and Sergeant Gleason came from behind the curtains, smoking gun in his fist.

"Nice work," the Masked Detective said. "Now turn your back, Sergeant, because I'm going to violate the law."

Gleason snapped handcuffs on the wrists of the pain-contorted butler. While he was busy, the Masked Detective forced Spencer back against the wall and methodically rammed home a dozen hard blows until Spencer howled for mercy, screaming a full confession of his guilt and trying to cover his face from those slashing punches. Finally he sat down, most abruptly, with his back against the wall.

Gleason turned around then. Only Spencer was there. The Masked Detective had vanished. Gleason looked at Spencer's battered face.

"My, my, you must have had an accident." He cocked his head to one side and squinted. "A mighty fine accident, too. Get up, you heel. The wagon is on the way."

Outside the house, half a block from the doorway, Winnie sat behind the wheel of her car, clenching and unclenching her small fists. She saw a shadowy figure flit from a hedge, cross the sidewalk and pile in beside her.

"So you tricked me," she said. "You made me wait out here while you went in and grabbed Spencer. Rex, I'll never forgive you!"

HE WIPED sweat from his face.

"If you'd been there, I'd never have forgiven myself. It was a close shave for a moment. Spencer had a thug in the house, and believe me, the gun he had looked just as big as the one Manny's half-wit stuck under your nose. It was decidedly not a place for you, my dear."

"Did you get him?" Winnie asked.

"He's got. Gleason had Manny Delisse hidden in the house. They got in when I kept Spencer busy at the front door. Manny heard Spencer confess to killing Turk and Dackey. He certainly must have liked those boys because he pulled away from Gleason and charged right into the face of Spencer's gun. Manny is dead! Now let's go back to the office while I put on a few finishing touches to my story. A little postscript for the benefit of my avid readers."

"Never mind that now. Rex, I thought it was Benson or that shyster lawyer, or even Abel, the private detective."

"So did I." Parker grinned. "It seems that Jacklin, the lawyer, kept a small office in the same building where he used to meet some of the clients he didn't dare allow to enter his regular office. Jacklin neither saw nor heard a thing. He must have gone down the stairs just before Spencer murdered those two men.

"Benson was framed to a certain extent. He's just a man with a mission too big for his brain. Abel actually wanted to help. Some of the men he hired were planted in his organization after he started to investigate the loan sharks. These men had big ears and Abel trusted them a bit too much. He evidently heard Gleason get my call from the roadhouse and mentioned the impending raid to one of his detectives. That spy contacted Manny."

"And what's the postscript to your story?" Winnie asked.

"For the benefit of those who need money badly. It's another warning. If they must borrow, licensed loan companies are the best for their needs, and under no circumstances should anyone sign papers for loan sharks. Nor should they put their signatures on blank papers without the figures filled in, nor do business with men who demand repayment within a week or two. They'll just make the loan all over again and charge a new interest rate.

"Not to deal with men who, for a fee, will arrange a loan, nor men who seem to have no office. Nor those who require the borrower to sign a blank check even though the borrower has no bank account. That's a crime in itself. Borrowers should demand to see the state license and refuse to deal with anyone who can't display it.

"There are plenty of angles to this rotten business and the loan sharks know all of them. Their victims, unfortunately, don't. Now will you drive me to the office, if I say please?"

"Why not?" Winnie smiled and stepped on the starter. "I hope you heed your own advice, Rex Parker. Because if you haven't four hundred dollars, you'll have to go out and borrow it. That's what you owe me."

"Or else marry you, huh?" Rex Parker grinned. "Give me time. I'll think it over."

III

THE MASKED DETECTIVE'S MANHUNT

CHAPTER I

TWO THOUSAND DOLLARS—AND DEATH

PHIL VOGAN was about fifty, rich through his own enterprises, and a shrewd, calculating man. Careful, too—otherwise his butler might have noticed the suspicious gleam in Vogan's eyes as he gave his servant final instructions before leaving the house.

"I'm attending a meeting—about a new polo club," Vogan told his butler. "Probably won't be home for hours. You will stay on duty, but all the other servants have a night off as usual."

Austen, the butler, flecked an imaginary bit of dust from the lapels of his master's topcoat, stepped back a pace and bowed slightly.

"Very well, sir," he murmured. "Everything will be quite all right."

Vogan walked through the door, deferentially held open by the butler, and headed toward his car parked at the curb. He glanced over his shoulder and saw that the door of his home had been closed behind him. Vogan darted over beside the five-foot-high hedge that shielded his estate from the street and, keeping well in the shadows it offered, he made his way to the back door.

This was unlocked, but that did not surprise Vogan because he had personally attended to that while the butler had been busy on an errand up stairs. Vogan's face was stern. Above all else, he refused to tolerate dishonesty among those who worked for him.

Above stairs, Austen, the butler, was wholly oblivious of his master's suspicions. He waited five full minutes after Vogan had left, and then rubbed his hands briskly. He no longer looked like a servant, nor acted like one. In his room his bags were packed, and in the living room was a wall safe. Vogan, the fool, believed it was cleverly hidden, but Austen had seen it more than once. He had even arranged matters so that on one occasion when Vogan had opened the safe, he had been able to watch the movement of the dial and register the combination in his crafty brain.

Austen hurriedly pulled down the curtains in the living room, stepped to the fireplace and reached up into the chimney. No wonder Vogan never permitted a fire to be laid here. Austen's inquisitive fingers located a small lever which he pulled slowly. Above the fireplace one of the oak panels slowly slid away to reveal the shining surface of the safe.

AUSTEN MOVED toward it eagerly, swiftly drawing on a pair of gloves. Calmly he proceeded to spin the combination until the safe door swung back. He reached inside, pulled out a flat steel box and raised the lid. His face fell slightly for he had expected there would be a thick sheaf of bills there. He found only a thin stack of them.

He riffled these through his fingers and cursed Vogan. Two thousand dollars—pin money, yet it was cash. Enough at least, for a couple of good splurges at the race track. He might double or treble it there. All Austen wanted was a stake, he told himself.

Suddenly there was a brilliant flash of light. Austen gave a yelp of alarm, swung around on his heel, and gasped. His employer stood just inside the door and there was a camera with a synchronized flash bulb in his hand.

"You may put the money back now, Austen," Vogan said curtly. "Then get out of that livery. Put on your own clothes and wait for the police. I think I have some rather good evidence on this film. You might also tell me what pawnshop I must visit to redeem my diamond studs which I missed two weeks ago—and a set of cuff links, also."

Austen was pale, and his hands shook as he replaced the money in the steel box, and then shoved this back into the safe. He walked slowly toward Vogan.

"I—I'm sorry, sir," he mumbled, his voice whining. "I couldn't help myself. I'm weak. A butler doesn't make much, sir, and he's in constant contact with wealth and all the good things there are, sir. You can't blame a man for wanting to better himself. I was going to use the money for an—an investment, and then return what I had taken after I'd made my profit, sir. Please—not the police! I—I'll go away."

"And half of what's in this house will go with you," Vogan grunted. "You'll get yourself another job with forged credentials like those you put over on me. Then someone else will lose his possessions. Oh, no, Austen, this is a matter for the police. Look here—you can't get away with things like this. I've suspected you for days. That's why I came back tonight. I saw you watching me put money in the safe. Make a clean breast of it, Austen, and things will go better for you. Now—get into your own clothes. Pack your bag and wait. I'm calling the police now.

You won't run out. Your kind never does, and anyway how far would you get? Be sensible. Take your medicine."

Austen knew there was no use to protest further. Shoulders drooping, he marched up the stairs to the third floor where his small room was located. He went in, snapped on the lights and took half a dozen steps toward the closet. Then a gentle, cultured voice spoke from behind him.

"How now, my clumsy fingered friend? Why were you so stupid as to be caught in the act!"

Austen was a plump, red-faced little man with perfect manners, but they could not approach the suaveness and aplomb of this person who was smiling at him. Austen saw a well proportioned man of medium height, with pale, almost livid flesh, and deep eyes with arched brows to frame them. The man's face was long and slender. He looked much like an undertaker in his bowler hat and his black coat.

Austen sat down on the edge of his bed and scowled.

"You got me into this, damn you, Diggs," he accused. "You told me Vogan would be bringing home a lot of cash. You told me how to get it, too—because you wanted a cut. Do you also accept a cut on the prison sentence I'm going to serve?"

THE SUAVE visitor removed his derby and calmly dusted it along his left forearm. He did not look at Austen as he spoke.

"My dear Austen," he murmured, "people in your profession and mine always make mistakes. Yours was in being too sure of yourself. You stumbled, you've fallen, and there is normally a price to pay. However, you joined my little organization and I must protect you."

"Joined it!" Austen scoffed. "You hunted me up, came to me—said if I didn't obey you, I'd be dragged in for stealing Mrs. Wentworth Michael's jewelry. You'd found that out somehow. I had no choice. Now I've got to face that rap, and also the one Vogan will hang on me. Oh, yes—you'll help me all right. I'll see to that, because if you don't, by heavens, I'll talk—loud and plenty! The cops would be interested to hear about your little club and about you. How you have servants planted all over the country—men and women you have something on so they are forced to obey you. I'll wager the district attorney would let me go free if I told everything. So you'll help, and I'd like to know what steps you'll take."

The suave visitor allowed a slow smile to cross his face.

"You liked my organization, Austen," he reminded coolly. "You liked the profits which you shared on the strength of jobs pulled by other members. It was your turn to provide this time. You didn't. Of course you should never have stolen Mr. Vogan's studs and links—at least not without telling me about it. However, you are entitled to the protection

I offer. It's a bit startling, my dear fellow—what I mean to do for you—but perfect. Utterly perfect. I shall give you a few drops of a certain drug which I keep for such purposes. By taking it you will immediately become a victim of amnesia. You will forget all that has happened, forget your identity and even the fact that the police are coming for you.

"The effects of the drug will last for approximately two months. Doctors can examine you in any way they choose and find nothing, except that you apparently possess a blank mind. You will not be tempted to talk about me or my friends. You will be practically pardoned because, as a victim of amnesia, you will hardly have been responsible for what you did."

As he spoke, the visitor removed a small bottle from his pocket, walked into the adjoining bathroom and emerged with a drinking glass held between the folds of a hand towel. Carefully he placed the glass on the table. It was half full of water.

The small bottle in his other hand had a medicine dropper in its screw top. He allowed a few drops of the colorless fluid to fall into the glass.

"Now"—he looked at Austen and stepped back—"drink it, my good fellow. You will hardly taste the stuff—and it will not harm you."

Austen looked into those deep-set, bleak eyes that were boring into him, and shivered. Then he muttered an imprecation.

"No—I won't do it!" he refused flatly. "The stuff is probably poison. Oh, you'll fix it so I won't talk all right—so I'll never talk again. I'll take jail first." His voice rose on an hysterical note. "No! I won't take it."

The visitor's hand dipped into the outer pocket of his coat and came away holding a neat .25 caliber pistol. He spoke, his voice low, purring.

"My dear Austen, what I'm doing is for your own good. There is no time to argue, and while I hate to threaten, you will either drink the potion—or I shall send a bullet through your stupid head. Take a good look at this gun. Probably you recognize it. It belongs to Vogan. I shall arrange things to make it seem as though you committed suicide. Now—which shall it be? The drug which will prove to be harmless in the long run? Or a bullet which will kill immediately?"

AUSTEN'S LIPS were dry, his eyes crammed with the agony that tore at his soul. He knew this man in black meant exactly what he said, knew him only too well. And he was making a desperate choice swiftly. With the drug there was a chance that he would not die, but the gun meant a swift end to everything.

Austen slowly reached out. His fingers slid beneath the towel which was still around the glass on the little table in front of him. Then, with a quick gesture, he grasped the towel-wrapped glass, lifted it, and drained the contents.

Thirty seconds later Austen was stone dead!

His suave visitor hastily wiped the gun with his handkerchief and threw the weapon on the bed. Then he paused. Somehow he had a feeling that Austen had tricked him, and was trying to think how.

Then a stern, gruff voice came from the regions lower in the house. The police had arrived without delay. Austen's visitor knew that it was no longer safe to delay. He darted out of the room, moved with the stealth of a cat toward the stairway and then ducked into a small room.

He saw Vogan and a detective pass him by and enter Austen's room. Instantly the visitor who had been called Diggs emerged from the small room, darted down the steps, moving fast. Almost before the two men in Austen's room knew the man there at whom they were looking was dead, Diggs slipped out the back door and vanished in the darkness.

Sergeant Blane, who had answered Vogan's call, shook his head sadly. He bent down and sniffed of the glass on the table in front of Austen. The dead man was on the edge of the bed. His legs were beneath the bed and somehow they supported him and kept him in a rigid position.

"Looks like he took the easiest way out," Blane said. "Do me a favor, will you, Mr. Vogan? Get on the phone and have Headquarters send over the medical examiner and a couple of Homicide men. Not that we need 'em, because this is a clear-cut case all right.... Imagine a guy who'd rather knock himself off than take maybe a one-year stretch in the pen!"

Vogan nodded and mopped his forehead.

"I'm sorry, now, that I went at this the way I did," he muttered. "I should have simply fired him when I suspected he was taking things. Now he's dead—and somehow I feel responsible."

CHAPTER II

THE MASKED DETECTIVE MOVES IN

I N THE press room at Police Headquarters, three different games were going on. Four men argued over the cards dealt in bridge, two were pegging their scores at cribbage, and six were hovering around a table upon which a game of stud poker was in progress. Others crowded around, kibitzing. Good-natured arguments were cropping up every couple of minutes. All of which meant that this was a slow night so far as crime news went.

One man present did not take part in the games. He sat on a straight-backed chair which was tipped against the wall, and his feet were planked on a table two inches away from the cribbage board. The players paid no attention to this. In fact they were so used to Rex Parker, ace crime reporter for the *Comet* that he might as well not have been there.

Parker's hat was pulled down over his face and, to all appearances, he was blissfully unaware of worldly things. Everyone knew Rex Parker. He was a genial, lazy cuss until something broke. Then he became a human bloodhound. His stories, always by-lined, were considered the apex of reporting. Then, too, his frequent column about the escapades of the Masked Detective drew as many, if not more readers than the current war news.

Rex Parker was believed to be the one and the only confidant of this mysterious crusader against crime, and that was a distinction worthy of note. For a man who worked independently of all law enforcement agencies and slashed red tape to ribbons if that suited his purpose, was a dread figure in the underworld. His identity was his own secret, and even Rex Parker denied all knowledge of it. To all others he was known merely as a mysterious avenger who wore a black velvet mask. And no man had ever seen the features beneath that mask.

Unknown to the rest of the world, however, two other people besides the *Comet's* crime reporter were in the confidence of the Masked Detective and were fully aware of his identity. One was Winnie Bligh, who gathered and wrote the advice-to-the-lovelorn column on Rex Parker's paper, and Homicide Sergeant Dan Gleason, attached to Headquarters. And they knew that Rex Parker, posing as the Masked Detective's contact, was really the Masked Detective himself, and that those columns of thrilling exploits were his own experiences.

Parker had become the Masked Detective by an ordinary chain of events that had nothing of the spectacular in them. As a crime reporter he had recognized the fact that regular police were greatly handicapped in fighting crime. For though aware of loopholes through which wily criminals could slip, they were often powerless, because of legal complications, to do anything about them.

To solve an important case once—at Winnie Bligh's insistence—Parker had donned a velvet mask so that his paper wouldn't be involved in case of a slip-up. But there had been none. He had been phenomenally successful. And from then on, the Masked Detective, who apparently had risen from nowhere, had taken an active part in the solving of all major crimes.

REX PARKER wasn't sound asleep now, as he appeared to be. Dozing perhaps, but that brain of his worked overtime. Several events of recent occurrence had set him thinking. Some concerned Ralph DeLeon, Peter Lawrence, Oliver Costello—all prominent people. They made news. Yet, although each of them had been robbed by trusted servants, nothing had appeared in the newspapers about the crimes. The only reports which the police had received had come as routine from insurance companies which had paid claims for these losses.

Such robberies were not out of the ordinary, but these had been handled deftly and in each case the servants had not been apprehended. The losses had not been high—taking into consideration the financial status of the victims—and insurance companies had paid off promptly. The largest claim had been for only three thousand dollars.

But what made Parker wonder, and had set him to thinking, was the fact that in each case the references of the treacherous servants had been forged. It looked to him as though there might be a guiding genius behind the crimes—a man who directed every move. If an organization of this kind should be spread all over the country, even if the individual robberies were small, it could collect loot that might add up to surprising figures.

Each robbery had been handled in the same manner—carefully planned and executed. Parker had studied the characteristics of the thieves as finally reported to the police after each disappearance, and he had decided that they hardly possessed brains enough to pull off smooth jobs like these had been. He wondered how many other robberies had taken place and no report at all had been made. The victims were all people of wealth and influence, the kind who went out of their way to avoid publicity, and others like them may not even have put in insurance claims for the same reasons.

The door of the press room opened and a man whom Parker at once recognized as Philip Vogan, wealthy philanthropist, entered. Vogan hesitated slightly because of his unfamiliarity with things of this nature. The reporters gave him a quick glance, and then turned back to their cards, but Rex Parker's eyes slitted. He knew Phil Vogan fairly well through his contacts with the man on newspaper stories.

Parker slowly dragged his feet off the table, rocked his chair back to its normal position, and shoved his hat to the back of his head.

"Hello, Mr. Vogan," he said. "You lost, or something?"

Vogan approached Parker, and offered his hand.

"No—it's not that," he said. "Something rather ghastly has happened and I…. Well, I wanted to see you fellows and have a talk with you. I want all of you to understand things in their proper light, because…. Well, frankly, what's happened doesn't make me shine as a humanitarian."

The other reporters stopped playing cards now and eyed Vogan with interest. Parker pushed a chair over to the wealthy man, using his foot to do so. Rex Parker never overstrained himself.

"Sure, Mr. Vogan," he said affably. "Let's have the dope. It's about a suicide over at your place, isn't it? The news came in a little while ago, but we don't usually bother about small stuff. What's your angle?"

"I'll tell you." Vogan sat down. "My butler—Austen, by name—stole a few things from me. I suspected him, and tonight I set a little trap and caught him red-handed. I ordered him to pack his things and wait for the police. Instead he drank poison. That makes me seen like an inhuman, vengeance-bent rascal. After all, the amount he stole wasn't big enough to bankrupt me by any means.

"It's my desire to get this over to you gentlemen of the press. I'm sorry Austen couldn't face things. I'd have given him that money outright rather than have him kill himself. Perhaps, under ordinary circumstances, I would hardly have bothered to call the police and would simply have thrown him out. But—well, several friends of mine have recently been robbed by their servants—employees who came with forged references. I think Austen's were forged also, though I as yet have not had an opportunity to investigate. A stop had to be put to such depredations sooner or later, so I thought it was high time to take action."

PARKER LIT a cigarette, betraying none of the excitement that teemed under his hat.

"Don't worry, Mr. Vogan," he assured. "We all know you as a fair and square guy. The press isn't out to lambast people—turn them into what they aren't. We believe you. Don't we, boys?"

There was a chorused assent from the others.

"We'll underplay the suicide, Mr. Vogan," Parker went on, "mention your name only as a matter of record, and indicate that your butler took his own life because he was a coward. That's the truth, and that's what we want. You had nothing to do with his death."

Vogan smiled tightly.

"Thanks, gentlemen. It has always been my impression that you fellows would go to all extremes so long as a prominent name was mentioned in connection with a case of this kind. I'm extremely grateful. Perhaps a few boxes of cigars—or a case of Scotch—just to show my appreciation?" He laughed a little. "Ah, I struck home that time, didn't I? Scotch it is—the cigars, too. Most of all, however, you have my admiration and esteem. From now on I'll never deny a member of the press an interview and if I can ever help you in any way, my office is open. Good night, gentlemen, and thanks again."

"Say," Waller of the *Clarion* grunted when the door closed behind Vogan, "he's not a half bad guy at all. I always took him for a stuffed shirt, and anyhow what's he got to worry about? With all this war news, a little thing like the suicide of a crooked butler rates about four lines on Page Seventeen.... Come on, you guys—I bet two bits on this hand. Feed the middle of the table. What the hell—a suicide should bust up a big game like this?"

Rex Parker waited five minutes after Vogan left. Then he sauntered out of the press room and made his way to Sergeant Gleason's office. He walked in, grinned at the bluff, beefy Homicide sergeant and sat down on a corner of his desk.

"What about this butler suicide thing at Phil Vogan's place, Sarge?" he asked.

Gleason shrugged. "I sent Blane up there and he reports it as obvious suicide. Nothing to it, Rex."

"Maybe," Parker said softly, "you're wrong. Listen, Sarge. There have been too many burglaries of that kind lately, and every one of them has had the same finesse—identical methods, too. There are forged references, a careful planning of the crime to take place when there is easily disposed of loot in the house. What if this Austen—Vogan's butler—didn't kill himself, even though everything points to that fact?

"Blane is no whirlwind of a detective, you know. He may have missed something, and I know the way he works. If it looks like suicide—then suicide it is—so far as he is concerned. He'd probably not go far with an investigation under the circumstances he ran across in Vogan's house. Yet, tying up the fact that the butler was a crook, with these numerous thefts by other servants, may mean something—like murder, for instance.

"I think I'll go up there and have a look. Suppose you get in touch with Blane and tell him to leave things just as they are. Assign him to some other case."

Gleason shrugged.

"Why not? Blane reported back. He locked up the room in which the butler died, and said he was going back again in the morning to make a further examination. The case didn't warrant any intensive action on his part and the fingerprint boys were busy on another job at the time. Also we don't like to bother important people like Vogan any more than necessary.... So you're going to have a look, eh? How, Rex? As a reporter, or as the Masked Detective?"

Rex Parker grinned and headed for the door.

"Use your own judgment, Sarge. Maybe I'm wrong, but this looks big to me—bigger than anything Rex Parker might tackle. Suppose some clever crook organizes thieving servants. Imagine what a haul he could make? See you later."

REX PARKER used a taxi to reach his apartment far downtown, in the heart of Greenwich Village. Once home, he locked the door, pulled down the shades, and sat before a triple vanity which had aroused no little amusement when it had been brought in. His fellow tenants had not been able to quite figure out what a confirmed bachelor wanted with a triple mirror.

Rex Parker had a use for it, and did use it more often than could have been guessed. Now he looked himself over for a moment, then he went into a clothes closet. He pulled aside his three spare suits, grasped a hook and tugged at it. A narrow section of the wall came away, opening like a door. Behind this were shelves and racks. They contained clothing he had picked up in different places around the city, principally second-hand stores. And the shelves were covered with various kinds of jars and tubes.

Parker selected what he thought necessary, returned to the bedroom and stripped off his clothing. He sat down before the vanity again and deftly applied grease paint and skin dyes. He was rapidly becoming a master at the art of disguise. Winnie Bligh, with her knowledge of dyes and cosmetics, had taught him most all of what he knew, and he had been studying and experimenting in his spare time until he was becoming adept himself.

As he worked, he had a well confirmed hunch that this wouldn't turn out to be just another ordinary case. It was, to all appearances, a new wrinkle in crime—if someone had organized and was directing a band of servants. While such people were not usually criminally inclined, they were more intelligent than the average rough-and-ready crook.

They could work smoothly, grasp opportunities and not try to make them, as so many cruder types of lawbreakers did. Backed with plenty of money, and with a man of brains to guide them, such an outfit could become a dangerous factor, especially if the leader, or leaders were already resorting to murder, as Rex Parker suspected.

Under his skillful fingers, Parker's even features changed. His face became broader, and he looked older and heavier. His hair turned to a neutral shade, his eyebrows became the same color. His cheeks bulged out slightly—and naturally. Nostrils were closer together, and even the color of his skin had undergone a change until it seemed more florid.

This finished with, he donned a dark suit, thrust an automatic into a hip pocket, one especially constructed to receive it and present no telltale bulge. After a final and satisfied glance, he cleaned up the room, then hurried out of the building.

The Masked Detective now, he took a cab and paid off the driver two blocks from where Vogan lived. He approached the house on foot.

CHAPTER III

MURDER STRIKES FAST

VOGAN'S HOUSE was entirely dark, indicating that the owner was still out for the evening. The Masked Detective walked softly up on the front porch, glanced at the front door lock—and then his hand froze. He bent, looked over one shoulder to make sure he was unobserved and drew a tiny flashlight from his pocket. Spraying the lock with its ray he confirmed his first idea that someone had picked that lock not long before. Someone not too familiar with methods of burglary, for whatever instrument had been used, it had slipped often and scratched the metal.

It was possible that the intruder was still in the house. The Masked Detective turned the lock gently, withdrew his master key, and opened the door a crack. He whipped his gun out, snapped off the safety, and gave the door a gentle shove—enough to open it wide, but not to force it back against the wall.

Nothing happened. He stepped inside, tense and ready for trouble. Not a sound could be heard. He closed the door quietly and, with an occasional flash from his light, walked on crepe-soled shoes toward the staircase. If anyone had sneaked into the house, he was certain it was for one of two reasons—to complete the robbery which Austen had failed to do or, which was more likely, eradicate certain clues which might give away the fact that Austen had been murdered and had not died by his own hand. In that latter case such an intruder would likely be on the top floor, where Vogan's servants lived.

The Masked Detective reached the second floor, located the narrow, steep staircase which led to the top floor and crept up it for about three steps. Then he heard a startled gasp, and a second later a chair came hurtling down the steps at him.

He was unprepared for an assault of this kind and the chair smashed down on his shoulders. He lost his balance and slipped. Before he could get up, a gun banged and the bullet plowed into the floor inches away from his face.

There was only one way to fight this kind of a battle. The Masked Detective's automatic pointed straight up that staircase and he let two quick shots go. He heard someone scramble back from the head of the stairs and knew that he had missed—but that was not surprising for he had deliberately fired wild. The Masked Detective was not a cold-blooded killer.

A moment later there was a terrific clamor and banging. The Masked Detective went up the steps three at a time now. And the first sight that

Unprepared, the chair smashed down on his shoulders.

met his eyes was someone standing in front of a closed door and attempting to smash it with a heavy chair.

The man whirled and heaved the chair in the direction of the stairway. The Masked Detective ducked, and this gave the unknown a slim margin of time. He raced madly down the corridor, turned into a room and slammed the door behind him. A key turned in the lock.

The Masked Detective sped in the same direction. He placed the muzzle of his automatic against the lock and fired once, shattering the mechanism. He kicked the door wide and prepared to attack, but a cool breeze from an open window told a story of its own. The intruder had prepared an emergency exit. There was a rope ladder dangling out the window—a ladder made of silk, even to the rungs. It was light and compact enough to be carried about, and yet strong enough to hold the heaviest man.

There was no sign of the intruder, and no way of guessing his identity. He had uttered no word, and not once had the Masked Detective glimpsed his features.

YET THE Masked Detective was one up on this game because he knew that the man wanted something behind the locked door further down the hall, and he hadn't got it. The Masked Detective sped toward the door. Attempts had been made to pick the lock, but while the burglar's instrument had worked on the front door successfully, this was a cheaper lock with a wide keyhole and no mechanism within reach of the instrument.

The door opened, however, to the expert manipulations of a skeleton key. The Masked Detective stepped into the room of a dead man. This was clearly where Austen had expired. The glass from which he had taken the lethal dose was still on the table, set on top of a hand towel. A small bottle without a label stood beside it and a .25 caliber automatic was on the bed.

The Masked Detective lost no time in going to work. He kept his ears open and his senses alert, though, just in case the intruder returned.

Since he had first undertaken his profession of solving difficult crimes, the Masked Detective had made an art of carrying compact equipment with him. Now one pocket gave forth a kit of fingerprinting equipment. With a tiny bellows, he dusted the glass on the table with a fine powder about the color of pure aluminum. But first of all he noticed that the glass had not yet been dusted by the police.

There were several prints near the rim, indicating that someone had picked up the glass by draping his fingers down around the top of it. Certainly a man intent on drinking a lethal dose of poison wouldn't have picked up the glass that way and tried to drink through his fingers. Those prints had been made by a detective, probably, who merely wanted to sniff of the few drops of solution left in the glass.

The Masked Detective concentrated on the sides of the glass and got no prints at all. He frowned. If suicide was so obvious, why weren't the fingerprints of the victim on the sides of the glass? Unless—suppose he had been forced to take the poison, and the murderer had worn gloves or, which was even more obvious, used the towel on which the glass rested?

The Masked Detective prowled around the room, investigating the bureau and the contents of a clothes closet without finding anything significant. Then he heard the scrape of tires on gravel. A quick look out the window showed him that Vogan was driving into the garage.

The Masked Detective quietly closed the door and went downstairs. Vogan entered a few moments later, turned on the lights, and shivered as though he did not like to enter a house in which a man had died just a few hours before.

He turned into the living room and started for a small built-in bar. Then he stopped suddenly and stared, for he had a visitor. The man sat in one of the most comfortable chairs, with his legs crossed. A black velvet mask was over his eyes, and he was smiling calmly. Vogan's gaze flashed to the man's lap, and he saw the automatic that rested there.

"Who are you?" he gulped. "What do you want?"

"Don't mind the mask or the gun too much," the visitor said. "I'm the Masked Detective, and I've taken the liberty of doing a bit of investigating in your home, Mr. Vogan. I hope you don't mind the intrusion. At that I probably saved you from danger, because someone got here ahead of me—someone with a gun, and he didn't seem to mind using it."

"How do I know you're the Masked Detective?" Vogan demanded. "How can I be sure you're not this—this other intruder you just mentioned? Why do you want to search my home?"

"You'll have to take my word for it," the Masked Detective said quietly. "If I were the intruder, I wouldn't be sitting here this calmly. I'd have taken what I wanted and fled. Or if it so happened I had wanted to kill you, this gun in my lap would have done the deed long ago."

VOGAN NODDED, but his lips twisted a little wryly. "It sounds logical enough," he finally admitted. "I suppose I'll have to take your word for it…. Now will you please explain why you are here? And what you suspect me of having done?"

"You?" The Masked Detective laughed. "You're not suspected of anything, Vogan. I'm here because of what happened in this house today. You see, your butler Austen did not commit suicide. He was—murdered."

"Murdered? Are you sure? Men from Headquarters said it was suicide. I asked them not to muss the place up, and they didn't. It was too obvious that poor Austen had taken his own life. You must be mistaken."

"I'm not," the Masked Detective said firmly. "Take my word for it, Austen was murdered by a sly, ingenious devil! Tell me—just where was Austen when you found him?"

"On the edge of the bed. The glass of poison and a vial of the stuff were on a table near him. The stuff he took must have hit him so quickly he never moved again. Sergeant Blane, the detective who came from Headquarters to take charge, locked the door of Austen's room and asked me not to molest anything there until after an autopsy had been performed."

"It's molested now," the Masked Detective said, and grinned. "Quite a bit, too. I'm afraid Blane won't like it.... How long had Austen worked for you?"

"About three months. I got him from an agency. As I recall, it was the Home Service Company over on Leavenworth Street. Yes, I'm sure it was, because I remember making out the check for the fee. Austen had good recommendations, but I was careless enough not to check up on them. The agency was supposed to do that, so I didn't bother. He was a highly trained butler. I thought I had a find. Then I missed some studs—expensive ones—and then a pair of cuff links vanished. Austen was the only person I wasn't sure of, so I set a little trap for him. In fact, I have a picture of him looting my safe. That's all I can tell you. He was a reticent type, Masked Detective."

"Probably had reason to be," the masked man observed. "Now if I were you, I'd phone Sergeant Blane immediately. Tell him that the glass from which Austen was supposed to have taken his poison bears no fingerprints other than Blane's—where he picked up the glass by the top. I think he'll understand that a man contemplating suicide makes no attempt to hide fingerprints. In fact I shouldn't be at all surprised if Austen realized he was doomed and deliberately lifted the glass with a towel so he wouldn't leave any prints. I say this because from what you have told me there were no signs of a struggle, as there would have been if another person had forced the poison down Austen's throat.

"What I believe is that the intruder I drove away returned because he probably recalled that Austen hadn't left any prints and wanted to destroy that glass in such a way as to arouse no suspicions—like knocking it to the floor and then grinding it to bits as if someone had stepped on it accidentally."

"Yes, of course," Vogan agreed. "If it was murder, I'm much relieved to know that you're working on the case. Sergeant Blane was too ready to take things for granted."

"Did Austen ever have visitors or friends?" the Masked Detective asked.

"Not one so far as I know." Vogan shook his head thoughtfully. "Come to think of it, I noted that the other servants often remarked about his being a lonely man. Yet—yes, I remember now—Austen did mention a brother once. I—"

THE FRONT door buzzer resounded through the house. Instantly the Masked Detective drew back against the wall, edged his way toward the hall, to the front door, and took up a position behind it so that he could leap out if this was an attempt to enter the house by the same man he had encountered, or some friend of his. He signaled Vogan to answer the summons.

Vogan left the room, came through the hall, and opened the door— only to be confronted by a slender, poorly dressed man of about thirty-eight. He had one hand dug deep into his side pocket and there was a scowl on his face.

"Your name Vogan?" he demanded roughly.

"Yes, I'm Vogan. What is it?"

"My name," the stranger said, "is Austen. I'm the brother of your butler. Yeah, the one who died here tonight. You killed him, Vogan! You murdered him because he found out things you didn't want him to know. He wouldn't have taken poison—not him! Not unless somebody forced it through his lips. You killed him and you can't deny it. That's why I'm here—to give you what's coming to you!"

CHAPTER IV

CAPTAIN BLIGH'S ASSIGNMENT

THE MASKED DETECTIVE gave the heavy door a hard shove, but he was a fraction of a second too late in attempting to leap from behind it or slam it shut. Austen's brother had been primed to kill. The trigger of the gun in his pocket had probably been half pulled the moment the door had been opened.

The gun went off, and Vogan took the slug high in the chest. He reeled backward, both hands clapped against the wound.

The assassin wheeled and darted down the steps. The Masked Detective was after him in a flash.

The killer looked over one shoulder, saw this man with a mask and a gun shouting for him to stop, and gave vent to a yelp of alarm. He stopped all right—stopped and turned around to take aim. His gun blasted, but the Masked Detective weaved as he came on, and the slug missed.

The killer tried to get in another shot. A foot kicked up and the gun flew out of the gunman's hand. He emitted another yelp that was cut off abruptly when that same foot flashed again and struck him on the jaw. The Masked Detective was an artist in fighting with the feet. That was his one big specialty, that was his greatest asset when it came to close-in fighting with criminals.

He examined the killer, found him unconscious. But he was more worried about Vogan, who might be alive. The Masked Detective turned back into the house, knelt beside Vogan and gently raised the wounded man's head. Vogan was slipping out fast. Bloody froth was on his lips and his eyes implored the Masked Detective to do something.

"I'll get a doctor," the Masked Detective offered.

"No—use." Vogan's voice was thinly weak. "I'm—I'm done. Why did he want to kill me? Why did he?"

Vogan shuddered and in that last precious moment of life before death could claim him, his mind wandered. He kept repeating again a single phrase over and over.

"The Devil's Stepladder. Devil's Stepladder—Ladder—Devil's...."

Then he was dead!

The Masked Detective laid him down gently, arose and looked out the door. The killer he had left unconscious was gone! The Masked Detective sped out to the porch.

There was a single shot—a shouted imprecation and then a pistol began banging away. When the Masked Detective reached the sidewalk, Austen's brother lay dead—drilled by at least four bullets from a gun that was still smoking in the hand of a uniformed patrolman.

The Masked Detective quickly raised both hands.

"Don't shoot!" he warned. "I'm the Masked Detective. That man you just killed murdered Vogan, who owned this house."

"Keep 'em high!" the patrolman warned. "Until I have a good look at you."

The Masked Detective gave a twist of his wrist and his automatic spiraled to the lawn in front of Vogan's house. "Be quick about it then," he snapped. "You've heard what I look like and I could have shot you a moment ago."

The patrolman jammed his gun against the Masked Detective's middle. One look, and the assured tone of the masked man's voice satisfied him, and he lowered his pistol.

"That guy was crawling along the sidewalk when I came running in answer to them shots I heard a minute ago," the patrolman explained. "As soon as he saw me, he began firing, so I let him have it."

"Worse luck," the Masked Detective groaned. "Not that it's your fault. I'd have done exactly the same thing if I'd been you, but I wanted this man alive. He might have answered a couple of questions—like why he thought Vogan had murdered his brother, and—and something about the Devil's Stepladder."

"The Devil's Stepladder?" The patrolman gaped. "What's that got to do with it?"

THE MASKED DETECTIVE turned back toward the house.

"How I wish I knew," he said, with a sigh. "All I do know is that Vogan, dying, tried to tell me something. He kept saying those words over and over again. Whatever the Devil's Stepladder means, it must have been of paramount importance in Vogan's mind, because he seemed to think of nothing else.... You'd better stay here, Officer. There'll be a crowd in a few moments. I'll go inside and call Headquarters."

After the two bodies had been removed, the Masked Detective sat alone in Vogan's study. This thing had taken a bizarre turn, had got completely out of hand and was more of a mystery than ever.

He was certain that the man who had claimed to be the murdered butler's brother, really was a brother. He hadn't lied. But how in the world had he become obsessed with the idea that Vogan had been responsible for the butler's death, and worked himself up to a pitch where nothing but vengeance predominated in his mind?

There was a chance that the butler had met his brother several times and perhaps had criticized Vogan, displaying an extreme dislike for his employer. Perhaps something had happened to make Vogan issue a threat of some kind. He had been known to have a short temper. Then, when the butler had died, his brother had simply assumed that Vogan had killed him.

If that were the case, then this murder was isolated from the rest of the whole business—that which had to do with a gang of servants who plundered the property of their masters. And Vogan's last words probably were just the ramblings of a dying man. The Devil's Stepladder meant nothing.

All events, from the moment of the arrival of the butler's brother to the time when he died under that patrolman's gun, must be cast aside as having nothing to do with the real case which led up to these events. Yet the Masked Detective was determined to check on the butler's brother, to discover everything possible about him—who his friends were, where he had been staying, what had led him to believe Vogan a murderer.

Or was Vogan really a killer? Had he forced his butler to take that poison and returned to the first floor in time to meet Sergeant Blane? It wouldn't have been hard to trick Blane. He was a good man, but somewhat slow-witted and the type who might be overawed by Vogan's wealth and position.

If Vogan had been involved, then who was the intruder who had come to invade Austen's room of death? Certainly not Vogan, unless he had parked his car nearby, entered his own home like a burglar, and attempted to smash down the door and in that way laid the groundwork for clues which would unerringly point to someone else—even to the extent of providing himself with a silken rope ladder.

That was possible, but the Masked Detective knew Vogan not only by reputation, but on several occasions had been in a position to size up the wealthy man, to form an opinion of him. The man had possessed a temper, true, but would anyone with his money murder a mere butler?

The Masked Detective remembered that Vogan had mentioned taking a picture of Austen robbing the safe. He searched the house and located a dark room rigged upon the second floor. Prints were hung up to dry in the room. A single look proved that Vogan had told the truth. A picture of the butler was among those prints, and the consternation and fear on Austen's face couldn't possibly have been faked. Vogan must have been hurriedly developing those even as Austen was facing death.

THE MASKED DETECTIVE slowly removed his mask. It was merely an outward sign as to his identity and the disguise beneath it was so perfect that even the closest observer would never have recognized this face as that of Rex Parker, crime reporter.

His first step must be to investigate Austen and his brother. Then would come a ferreting out of this league of servants who preyed on their masters. The Masked Detective needed the aid of the police in this, especially concerning the records of the Austen brothers, if they had any. Sergeant Gleason was always willing to cooperate with the Masked Detective.

Winnie's fingers stopped as a gun pressed against her neck.

And somehow the Masked Detective had a feeling that this case would disclose the machinations of a true devil—a disciple of Satan himself.

He left the house, and nodded to the patrolman who stood guard at the entrance. Hastening down the street, he made two phone calls from a drug store not far from Vogan's home. Then he took a taxi downtown, switched to the subway in case he was being followed, and finally approached his own home on foot.

He let himself into the apartment, and heard a chuckle. When he snapped on the lights, he saw two people in the room. One was a girl, about twenty-five, and unusually pretty. She was a tall girl, just about Rex Parker's own height. She had dark eyes and raven black hair, worn rather short. She was smiling, and did not move.

The other occupant of the room was Sergeant Gleason. He jumped up, reaching for his hip pocket. The Masked Detective grinned.

"Relax, Sarge," he drawled. "Even if I don't look as handsome as Rex Parker, I'm still him. Watch and see."

Parker applied cold cream, wiped it off. He rinsed his hair and restored its natural color. Then he removed pieces of cleverly applied putty and two tiny aluminum disks from his nostrils.

"I'll be damn—darned," Gleason muttered. "That's the best job you ever did on that funny face of yours. Well, Winnie Bligh and I got your calls. What the devil happened?"

"The devil is right." Rex Parker patted Winnie's wrist and sat down close beside her. "To be more explicit—the Devil's Stepladder. That's what Vogan was muttering about as he died."

"I know about the murder," Gleason grunted. "The report came in to Police Headquarters before I left. I knew you'd gone there to look over the house, and—well, I was worried. I thought maybe you knocked him off."

Winnie looked up sharply.

"Why, Sergeant Gleason!" she chided. "Don't you know that neither Rex Parker nor the Masked Detective is a killer? It doesn't always require a gun to outwit crooks. Rex, tell us all about it."

Rex Parker did, and had considerable to tell.

"I can't make out what it is all about," he went on, "but it's big. I can almost feel it. There have been a great number of minor robberies in town during the last few weeks, as of course you know, Sarge, but possibly you haven't connected them—though you may have been thinking them over since that hint I threw out to you.

"These robberies have been accomplished through the stealth and craft of servants hired by wealthy families. There have been few complaints, because the victims dislike publicity and their losses were not large enough to warrant direct police action.

"Tonight, Phil Vogan caught his butler in the act of stealing. The butler then apparently killed himself. But I'm sure he was murdered. About an hour ago the brother of this butler appeared, claimed that Vogan had murdered the butler, and then proceeded to kill Vogan. Unfortunately the brother of this butler was shot to death by a patrolman, so it was impossible to question him."

GLEASON TAPPED the arm of his chair for a moment.

"*Hmm*—sounds like something at that, Rex," he admitted. "Since you mentioned it, I have been thinking about how a league made up of servants could make a stupendous haul if they worked together. Those people often have a chance to get at small fortunes.... Well, how can I help you?"

Rex Parker leaned forward.

"The victims do not want publicity, Sarge, and the crooks know it. That's why they don't steal large sums. This is a clear indication that the crooks do not want publicity either. Therefore, one way to stymie them is to dish it out. Suppose I, as Rex Parker, cover this story and write modest articles about it in such a manner that the crooks won't like it, but neither will they suspect we're getting on their trail. It will at least serve to put wealthy families on guard against newly hired servants."

"And then?" Winnie asked hopefully.

Parker smiled at her.

"Don't worry. There's a juicy spot in this for you, too. I'll be too busy to handle many of the details, and there's where you come in, my pet. I've got one special job for you right now."

"I'm ready," Winnie said. "You know, I've had a feeling all along that something was going to pop, so I spent a little more time than usual in the office these last few days, and I've written up a few columns in advance.... Listen, Rex—you won't just start this case and then turn it over to Gleason, will you? You've got to see it through, and you must work hard at it."

Rex Parker grinned and spread his hands in a hopeless gesture. He looked at Sergeant Gleason.

"See, Sarge? Cap'n Bligh is at it again. When I named her after that hell-roaring old rapscallion of a seagoing man driver, I certainly was right. She drives me—on and on and on."

Winnie frowned. "Rex, you know I don't like being called Captain Bligh. But you're just a little bit lazy, and I've always got to keep pushing you around."

Gleason howled. "You're half right and half wrong, Winnie," he said. "As Rex Parker he certainly doesn't go out of his way to overtax himself, but when he becomes the Masked Detective, why he's like a tornado, whirlwind and typhoon combined. Don't worry about him seeing this through. Now Rex, you were saying something about a job for Winnie."

"Yes, Rex," Winnie chimed in. "Let's get going on this before someone else is killed."

Parker seemed to be thinking intently for a moment, then he spoke in a precise voice.

"Your most logical approach is through the William Price Detective Agency," he told her. "They handle a lot of smaller cases for the various insurance companies which would cover wealthy families. There must have been a few claims by some of the victims that the insurance people would put into the hands of the agency for investigation.

"Price isn't exactly a friendly type of man, and sometimes I've wondered if his business is on the level. He recovers jewels, for instance, with astounding speed and thoroughness. He never turns a crook over to the police, so he may be working hand in glove with the thieves. Here's the way you want to handle him, Winnie. You're covering a story—about the several small robberies. You simply want him to confirm some of the ideas you already have. If he throws you out, so be it. We shall have accomplished our purpose in providing proof that there is going to be some publicity. Price probably will broadcast the news as fast as he can."

Winnie was eager to get started.

"I'll see Price right away," she said. "I already know a lot about his agency. Everybody does. His office stays open twenty-four hours a day and the big mope sleeps back of his desk half the time. I'll write a report in case something happens so you and I can't meet, Rex."

"Just a word of warning," Parker cautioned. "Be careful. Two men have been murdered—and I suspect this was accomplished through the machinations of this gang, if one exists, as I believe. Price may be part of it. Watch your step."

CHAPTER V

DANGER SPOT

WINNIE TAXIED to the offices of the William Price Detective Agency and surveyed the building with obvious distaste before she entered. It was an old place and dirty-looking. Faded letters, some half peeled off, indicated haphazardly that Price's offices were on the second floor.

When Winnie reached the offices, a sleepy-eyed hulk of a man was slouched in a chair behind the receptionist's desk. He looked at Winnie as he looked at all female callers. With few exceptions they all wanted the same thing—to have a husband trailed. They didn't expect much in the way of politeness, he always reasoned, so why give it to them?

"I want to see Mr. Price, personally," Winnie said. "It's most important. If he isn't in, I'll come back."

The big man got out of his chair, leered at her, and walked toward a closed door.

"Park, baby," he said huskily, "and I'll see if he's in. Fine time of the night to be wanting help."

A moment later the man came out, left the door open and jerked his thumb at it. Winnie passed through the squeaky gate that separated the offices, marched into the room, and took an instant and vast dislike to the big man seated behind the desk.

William Price was bulky, heavy-jowled, and he had piggish little blue eyes. His hair was sparse and straw-colored—what was left of it. He eyed her closely, grinned, and arose. He shoved a chair forward and closed the office door.

"Well," he said in an insinuating voice, "what can I do for a nice-looking doll like you?"

"Never mind the blarney," Winnie retorted with vigor. "I'm a reporter on the *Comet*. I'm covering a series of recent robberies, mostly in the homes of wealthy people. I know you're supposed to have investigated some of them with reference to insurance damages. There's fifty dollars for what information you can give me. I make the offer because I can tell from your manners you're not above taking it."

Price's face slowly became suffused with the crimson of mounting rage. He half arose, growled a mild oath and then sat down again—hard.

"Listen, sob sister," he rumbled at her, "the kind of work I do is confidential, get it? I don't talk for no papers, and I don't know anything about no robberies. Fifty bucks is chicken feed to me, but don't make any bigger offers because you'd just be wasting your time. So scram, sister, before I forget I'm a gent and toss you out."

"How can you forget something that doesn't exist?" Winnie shot back. "Listen, Mr. Price, I've got an assignment. You could make my job a lot easier, but since you refuse, I'll simply snoop around and get the information I need anyhow. I can see that what you last desire is publicity, but that's exactly what you're going to get, and not the kind you'll enjoy reading. I think these robberies are more important than they seem to be—and I'm going to get at the bottom of them."

She stalked out, slammed the door, and glared at the sloppily clad man behind the receptionist's desk. She wrinkled her nose.

"By the looks of this place, the exterminator man will be around any year now," she flung at him in parting. "You'd better duck when he shows up or there might be a mistake made."

WINNIE MAINTAINED a neat little three-room apartment in a nice section of the city. She proceeded there immediately. Her present mission was finished. She had discovered that Price had something to hide, and she had cast her insinuations that some publicity might develop. Rex Parker hoped that might put the leader of this servant gang he believed to exist on the defensive, and bring him into the open. Now she had to write a complete report about the matter.

She let herself in with her key, turned on the lights—and froze. Winnie Bligh had company. Three of the strangest crooks she had ever laid eyes on. They were all quietly dressed, all soft-spoken, and yet their words held a particular kind of venom. She heard each of them speak, but one particular one seemed to be the chosen spokesman. He was a short, hand-rubbing, greasy-appearing man with a fawning attitude.

"Good evening, Miss Bligh." He actually bowed a bit as he spoke. "I'm sure you will excuse us for breaking into your home this way, but what we have to say is most confidential. In the first place we want to hasten to assure you that we are quite aware that a reporter's salary doesn't buy Duesenberg cars or fur coats—and surely you would not be averse to owning either.

"We have information that you are covering a small, unimportant story concerning a few trivial robberies. Such publicity will not speak well for people who wait on others for a living, so we have come to you with a business proposition. If you will please report that there is no story, will stop making any further investigation, one day next week you will be agreeably surprised to receive an envelope which will contain two thousand dollars."

Winnie looked her surprise, and quickly decided that it might be safer to pretend the offer was interesting.

"Well—two thousand dollars doesn't grow on bushes, gentlemen," she murmured. "I take it you represent some organization of butlers, chauffeurs and house maids? That you're only interested in protecting yourselves? That's reasonable. Make it three thousand and I'll be reasonable, too."

"Very well." The spokesman nodded. "We shall consider it a bargain. Mind you—no stories of any kind. Just report that whoever tipped you to these small, insignificant crimes must have been having a pipe dream. Next Wednesday, say, look for a long envelope in your mail-box. Good night, Miss Bligh, and we are grateful for your cooperation."

All three men bowed and filed out. Winnie closed the door, locked it.

"Well!" she said, half aloud. "It must be big when they raised the ante without an argument. Is this hot stuff!"

She removed her hat, hurried over to a small desk and pulled her portable closer to her. She shoved a piece of paper into the machine and started to write.

> Price Detective Agency denies knowing anything, but the old boy flared up. He, or someone in his office, tipped others and there was a reception committee of three in my apartment when I got there. I was offered two thousand dollars, and then three, to lay off. The men—

Winnie's fingers, poised above the keyboard, stopped suddenly. She blinked, wetted her lips, and then raised both hands shoulder high.

The muzzle of a gun was pressed against the back of her neck.

"VERY SENSIBLE," a voice breathed in her ear. "Now stand up and keep your hands exactly as they are."

Winnie obeyed, then turned around slowly. She was prepared for anything, but the sight of the gunman was a distinct shock.

He wore a bowler hat which was perched at a very precise angle on his head, and he seemed to have no hair. At least none was visible below the hat. His face was long and almost livid white. He had a straight, rather large nose, eyes that were set wide apart, and narrowed now. Only on his lips was an expression of his savage determination. They were thin and tight.

Winnie gulped.

"How did the funeral come off this morning?" she asked.

The man gave vent to a low, nasty laugh.

"Very funny," he said shortly. "But I'm not an undertaker, young lady, and I don't like your implication that I look like one. You will, however, subject yourself to the services of one if you are not careful. You made a bargain a few moments ago, and you did not intend to keep it. That is why I remained here—hidden—to see for myself if you really would go about writing a story."

Without removing his eyes from Winnie the man ripped the sheet of paper out of the typewriter and crumpled it into a ball. He wadded this into his coat pocket.

"I think," he said suavely, "that we will take a short automobile ride. If you retain your wits, you will not be harmed. If you try to get away—you won't. Pick up your hat, put it on. In your bedroom you will find that I have already taken the liberty of packing your bag, presumably for a short, hasty trip. You will get the bag at once."

Winnie shrugged.

"I can't argue with a gun, mister. You hold all four aces right now, and I'm not going to call you."

She headed for the bedroom. As she passed through the door, her left hand darted out and grabbed the back of a chair. She sent this skidding toward the strange gunman. Winnie moved fast in desperate circumstances, and the funereal-looking man was too confident of the threat of his gun.

He tripped over the chair and lost his balance. In a flash Winnie made a dive for him. She grabbed the hand which held the gun and pointed the weapon toward the ceiling.

The strange gunman let go of his weapon, and in the same movement flicked the gun over on top of Winnie's bed. Winnie found that the arm he held in an upward position was coming down, and all her strength could not prevent it.

Winnie's hand was caught in what felt like a vise. She struggled vainly, for her two arms were slowly pinned to her sides. The gunman was smiling coldly. He gave Winnie a terrific shove.

She went flying across the room, hit the wall with a thump, shook the cobwebs out of her brain and turned to meet the attack.

But all she did was turn, for the attack was already there. The cadaverous-faced man's left hand closed around her shoulder, held her at arm's length, while his right hand turned into a great fist.

Winnie saw it coming, but she could not move. The fist hit her flush on the jaw and Winnie passed out, into a dream world filled with tall men dressed in black, and who went around lifting houses from their foundations and ripping up big trees by their roots....

WINNIE AWOKE some time later, to find herself seated between two of the three men who had met her in the apartment and made her an offer to lay off. Neither of them seemed viciously inclined.

"You will kindly refrain from making any commotion," one said. "If you don't, we shall be forced to inflict some rather painful treatment."

He held a blackjack in his lap and made suggestive motions with it. Winnie relaxed, and fought to get back her wits.

There seemed to be no attempt to conceal the route of the car in which she sat. It was heading downtown at leisurely speed, with the third member of the trio who had called on her so unconventionally at the wheel. Winnie saw no signs of the man who looked like an undertaker.

Each of her captors held one of Winnie's wrists in a firm grasp, and she realized that if she tried to escape that blackjack would put a quick end to her efforts. She decided to play docile for the time being.

The car finally pulled up in front of a five-story building. It was well after midnight now. The section, devoted to small manufacturing firms which rented the entire floors of the various old and musty buildings, was quiet and dead appearing. A patrolman sauntered down the street. Winnie's captors whispered a word of warning to her, and the patrolman went on past the car, hardly favoring it with a second glance.

"You will please be good enough to get out," one of the men told Winnie. "Keep in mind the fact that we will kill you if necessary, so no tricks."

Winnie got out, preceded by one of the men, and followed immediately by the one who had displayed a blackjack. The third member of the party had slipped from behind the wheel to run around the car. He was now waiting in case she tried a desperate getaway.

She was taken firmly by both arms and led across the sidewalk to one of the dilapidated old buildings. The fourth floor was fully lighted, the rest of the building dark.

CHAPTER VI

REX PARKER RECOGNIZES A CLUE

ONE OF the men used a key to open the lobby door. There was a rickety old elevator on the ground floor, and Winnie walked into this, guided by her captors.

It toiled up to the third floor, where Winnie was propelled out of it and down a dimly lighted hallway. They stopped her in front of a door with the lettering:

EXCLUSIVE CIGARETTES, INC.

This door was opened with a key.

Winnie found herself in what seemed to be a small cigarette manufacturing plant. Cigarette rolling machines were in evidence, as were bales of tobacco, and a large number of boxes which bore no labels.

"Walk straight ahead, please," Winnie was told. "We are extremely grateful that you did not create a rumpus."

"Thanks," Winnie answered grimly. "At least you give me credit for having a few brains, although I'm a helpless girl. Where's the lug who punches like a mule's kick—with both feet—and doesn't much care who he hits?"

"Oh, him? He'll be here directly, Miss Bligh. Now, over in the corner if you please. I'm sorry that this place is in such miserable state. It's actually filthy, but I suppose one can't very well keep a place like this neat."

Winnie sat down on an old kitchen chair which was pointed out to her. After about ten minutes, she heard someone approaching the room. It was the cadaverous-looking man. He seemed smoother and more sinister than ever. Certainly he did not display any of that enormous strength which he possessed.

In one hand he held Winnie's traveling bag, and he placed this on one of the workbenches. Then he carefully removed his black gloves and walked over to look down at her.

"I hope," he said calmly, "that you will have learned a lesson. I pride myself on being able to handle two or three ordinary men, and a slip of a girl has no chance at all. Now, Miss Bligh, we shall get down to business. We're all busy people and not given to accepting excuses nor delays. I took the liberty of bringing some of your stationery along. You will write exactly what I say. Please move closer to the bench."

Winnie hitched her chair toward the bench. All the while she was aware that the entire building shook, and from the floor above came the steady rumble of heavy machinery. The top of the workbench was littered with fine dust—white stuff. Winnie glanced up at the ceiling.

"That is just plaster," the cadaverous gunman told her. "There is a printing plant upstairs and the machinery doesn't do this building much good. It keeps shaking calcimine down over everything. I detest the place, so please hurry."

Winnie took a proffered pencil, pulled a sheet of her own stationery toward her, and waited.

The long-faced man spoke in terse tones.

"Write this at once," he commanded. "Address the letter to your superior, whoever he may be. Tell him you have a clue—a hot one. That is the customary expression, I believe. Uncouth, if you ask me. However, indicate that this clue is important enough to take you to Sandusky. State that you will write more fully from that point sometime tomorrow."

Winnie shrugged.

"Why not?" she said coolly. "Say, you don't intend sending me to Sandusky, do you?"

"Write as I have ordered," the leader of the men who had captured her snapped. "There will be a letter from Sandusky tomorrow, and you will write it, but you won't go there. Apparently this 'story' you are on will take you to Denver on the day after, and thence around the country. You will write all the letters when I so demand it. They will be forwarded by air to certain friends of mine and properly mailed. This one will be taken to your apartment, where a messenger boy will be sent for and told to deliver it at once. Please hurry."

WINNIE WROTE the letter because there wasn't anything else she could do. Before she laid down the pencil, the leader gave further orders.

"Your last line will indicate that you need about one week in which to complete your investigation," he said, "and your employers are not to worry about you. Write that."

Winnie threw her pencil down.

"I'm a fool to do any more of this!" she exclaimed. "What's the use? When I've written all these letters, you'll just put a bullet through my skull anyhow, so why should I help you?"

The cadaverous man made a quick motion. Instantly both of Winnie's arms were seized, and she was jerked back until her head rested on the back of the chair. A third man slapped a wide piece of adhesive across her mouth and plastered it firmly over her lips.

Then the leader stepped a little closer. Without a change of expression he simply pressed Winnie's nostrils tightly together and spoke in a voice that betrayed none of the sadism that was part of him.

"This is a most unpleasant way to die, my foolish young friend. You cannot breathe, and you will hardly live more than three or four minutes. Blink your eyes rapidly when you make up your mind to obey me."

Winnie tried to squirm, but she could not move a muscle. Her lungs clamored for air. Things began to spin. It was hopeless to fight these men when they had the upper hand this way.

Winnie rapidly blinked her eyes, and the fingers pinching her nose were instantly removed. She drew in a great breath of air. The adhesive was removed also—in a single yank. She picked up the pencil and wrote as directed. Then she signed the letter, shoved it close to the edge of the workbench, and addressed an envelope—one of her own. These men seemed to have forgotten no detail, no matter how trivial.

As she finished the addressing, her elbow hit the letter and it fluttered to the floor. Winnie picked it up again, but took care to grind it gently into the debris so that some of the dirt adhered to it.

She murmured an apology for her carelessness, rapidly folded the letter, put it in the envelope and licked the flap. One of the other men took it in gloved fingers, thrust it into his pocket and went out.

"Thank you," the cadaverous leader said, as if Winnie had performed a great favor of her own free will, "Now, as for your immediate future. This cigarette manufacturing plant happens to be controlled by interests which I also serve. You will be kept here for approximately a week. There is a storeroom at the rear. I'm sorry but we'll have to tie you up—but as comfortably as possible. Two men will guard you, and mark me, they have orders to kill you if there is the slightest show of resistance on your part. Tomorrow I shall return so you may write another letter. Until then—good night, Miss Bligh!"

The odd-looking man adjusted his hat carefully, bowed slightly, and left. Winnie sighed, got up and preceded her two remaining captors into an empty supply room. There was a cot against the wall and she was quickly lashed to it.

"Boy," she groaned, when they had left her there, "will I be stiff if I'm kept like this for a week!"

AT THREE A.M. Rex Parker, haggared-eyed, walked into the police laboratories. He was no stranger here, for even long before he had the faintest idea of becoming the Masked Detective, he had studied all the various methods of tracing clues, examining minute bits of evidence for a lead to a murderer, and this place had held vast interest for him.

"Hello, Rex." The single police expert on night detail looked up from a book on toxicology which he was studying. "You're getting to be a regular owl. What's up?"

Parker forced a smile to his lips.

"Nothing much. I couldn't sleep, so I thought I'd drop down and catch up on my microscope work. You don't mind if I use the facilities of the lab, do you?"

The expert waved a hand.

"Help yourself. You've always given us a swell break in your stories. No reason why we can't let you putter around." He laughed a little.

"Since you've always done it anyhow. Anything you don't understand or can't find, just sing out."

Parker walked over to a bench on which were several microscopes. He took a brown envelope from his pocket and shook from it another envelope—a white one—to the bench. He picked up this with a pair of long forceps, used a fingerprint powder, and shook his head sadly. The envelope had, as he had expected, been handled by many different people.

This letter had come by special messenger to the night editor of the *Comet*. Knowing that Parker not only had an interest in Winnie Bligh, but that he was also supposed to be the confidant of the Masked Detective, he had sent for Parker, and given him the letter.

With no results from the envelope, Parker now dusted the surface of the letter itself which had been handled only by the editor after it had been opened. Two sets of prints developed. One set he knew must be the editor's, but the other were those of a woman. Rex Parker had

Winnie sailed through space and both feet went through the window.

Winnie's fingerprints. He had taken them long ago for just such an emergency.

Two minutes work informed him that she had handled the letter and, more than probably, written it. Certainly the handwriting was hers, but Parker had a wholesome respect for the art of forgery.

"They've got her," he said bitterly. "There can't be a mistake. She's in trouble, and this letter is just a ruse so that the office won't start the police hunting for her."

Sitting down at the long bench he turned the letter over, scanned the back of it carefully, and then thrust a section of the paper beneath a microscope. With the low power he detected tiny bits of calcimine adhering to the paper. He picked up the envelope, carefully dumped a few crumbs of brown substance onto another piece of paper and studied these under the microscope.

"Tobacco," he muttered. "Cigarette tobacco, by the way it's cut. Light-colored, too."

He picked up a piece in his forceps and touched it to the flame of a Bunsen burner. The tobacco gave off a pungent odor.

"Turkish or Egyptian," Parker told himself.

He spent half an hour studying books in the huge library at the rear of the room. All of the volumes he took down from their shelves were concerned with tobacco. He applied several tests and confirmed his original diagnoses. This was Egyptian tobacco of a rather rare type—difficult to obtain since the War had begun. Even in normal times it was used only in making the most expensive types of cigarettes.

"Winnie somehow managed to get that debris on the paper," Parker reasoned. "She meant it for a clue, and it is—after a fashion. Yet how does it happen that dust, probably from a calcimined ceiling or wall, is mixed with the tobacco?"

HIS AGILE mind went over this problem intently. Rex Parker possessed almost miraculous powers of concentration. Gradually he concocted a picture of the circumstances surrounding this tobacco and the calcimine. A small cigarette manufacturing plant in an old building which had calcimined plaster ceilings. Above the shop some kind of a business which entailed the use of machinery, or much traffic across its floor, so that the ceiling dust was shaken down.

Dragging out some remarkably complete city directories, Parker checked all the cigarette manufacturing plants in the city, then compared their addresses with those of other firms listed at the same place. Finally he came upon the firm known as "Exclusive Cigarettes, Incorporated." In the building that housed that firm was a printing establishment, which specialized in heavy job work. Such a plant would use big machinery, and if it were above the cigarette factory, the rumble of which could easily loosen dried calcimine and plaster from the ceiling below. For Parker recalled how even the skyscraper which housed the *Comet* trembled slightly when the presses rolled.

He sped back to his apartment, went immediately to the secret cupboard in his closet, and withdrew several articles necessary for a disguise. He applied these with sure, deft hands until he had created new features radically different from those of Rex Parker, reporter.

Now he looked actually meek—like a man accustomed to being brow-beaten and ordered about. He selected a rather shabby suit, an old shirt that was somewhat frayed, a battered hat, and shoes that needed a shine badly. In moments he stood before his vanity, a man whom no one who knew Rex Parker would have recognized.

CHAPTER VII

SOMETHING IN THE WIND

LEAVING HIS apartment, Rex Parker hurried to a private garage several blocks away. He unlocked the door and drove out a shabby-looking coupé. This car was as deceptive in appearance as the man at the wheel. Both looked decrepit, anything but sturdy, yet there was a vast amount of power beneath the old hood just as there lay power beneath the old suit that covered the Masked Detective's body.

He headed downtown, praying silently that Winnie Bligh was only being held a prisoner, and that she had not tried to battle her way out of an impossible situation and thereby lost her life. Winnie was given to dangerous impetuosity at times.

The Masked Detective parked the car, and from a safe distance studied the building which he had located by a mentally scientific application of clues and wits. The entire place was in darkness.

The Masked Detective was always extremely careful in approaching places like this, where a trap might have been set for him, so now he studied the neighborhood intently. But the Masked Detective was not equipped with X-ray eyes. He could not possibly have detected the man who sat in a darkened room across the street from that building and watched the entrance intently.

As the Masked Detective slipped quietly to the door, this man picked up a telephone and made a brief call. Then he grabbed up an automatic on the floor beside his chair, jammed it into his pocket and fled.

The Masked Detective opened that lobby door in twenty seconds, and he took care to lock it after him in case some inquiring patrolman would find it open and start an exploratory trip through the building. He located the cigarette manufacturing plant and pressed his ear against the door for a second or two. There was no sound inside, and he wondered if he had guessed wrong this time.

Quietly he picked the lock, slipped into the main workroom, and used a tiny flashlight to sweep away the darkness. Then his heart jumped for he heard a muffled voice—Winnie Bligh's voice! It came from the rear, from a room back of the main factory room.

But the Masked Detective did not respond in a headlong rush. He picked his way along to be sure no pitfalls were in his way, that no armed men were lurking, ready to kill.

He reached the door from behind which the voice had come. It was locked, from the outside, and the key was in the lock. That made the Masked Detective hesitate. It was almost too open an invitation. Yet he was sure that Winnie was behind that door and the only method of getting to her was by opening it.

He turned the key softly, and then listened. Finally he tapped on the panels gently.

He heard a startled gasp, and then Winnie's frantic voice.

"Don't come in! Run for it! Run before it's too late!"

But the Masked Detective did not run—especially since it was Winnie who was in danger. He turned the door knob, drew back his foot to kick the door open—and then a holocaust broke loose.

The entire building seemed to shiver and shake as though it rested upon the summit of a volcano ready to spurt into life. A great creaking sound made him look up. The whole ceiling was caving in!

He threw the door wide, used his flash, and saw Winnie lashed to a cot. He also saw that the ceiling in this room was sagging too. A water pipe snapped somewhere, and geysered water across the room. The Masked Detective caught the odor of illuminating gas.

THEN HE gave one great leap across the floor, heading toward one of the sturdy workbenches on the opposite side. He wrenched this away from the wall, pushed it toward Winnie and finally got it above her. The Masked Detective ducked under it also, and hurled himself across Winnie's helpless form.

A second later the full fury of an old, collapsing building rained down on them. One big machine plummeted through the ceiling, hit the floor, and kept right on going.

"Steady!" Winnie heard a cool voice say through the roar of sounds. "We'll get out of this all right!"

"We can't!" Winnie groaned. "They knew you were coming. They had everything set so the whole place could be destroyed. Two men who were guarding me got a phone call. They ran out—but they told me first that I'd better start praying. One of them said all he had to do was yank a lever and the whole place would cave in. They had weakened the supports that hold up a lot of heavy machinery. It will all come down!"

Winnie's words were drowned out in the roar of more breaking timbers and the crash of whole sections of the ceiling. The floor trembled violently, other pieces of heavy debris came plummeting down. A cloud of dust from the plaster choked the nostrils of both, made them cough rackingly and cover their faces.

The sturdy bench covering their bodies was the only thing that saved their lives. It also guarded the flooring under it so that Winnie and the Masked Detective were not hurled below with the rain of tools, machinery and timber.

The Masked Detective drew a knife from his pocket and quickly cut Winnie loose. But they remained huddled under the bench, for there seemed to be nowhere else to go. Most of the floor across the middle of the room had given way, so that there was a yawning abyss about eight feet wide between them and any possible exit from the place.

"We've got to get away from here quickly!" the Masked Detective said hoarsely. "The whole building is getting weaker by the minute, and pretty soon the walls will cave in, too! This was nothing but a fire-trap to start with—a frame structure that should have been condemned years ago. We—"

He stopped short and sniffed.

"Yes, I smell it too," Winnie said, in a strained voice. "Fire! The whole place is full of gas fumes! We'll be blown up or burned to a cinder!"

The Masked Detective wormed his way from beneath the bench and stood on the edge of that gaping hole. In one hand he held the rope with which Winnie had been tied. Then, without a word, he signaled Winnie to grasp one end of the long bench, and they lifted that end high as the Masked Detective gave quiet but hurried instructions.

Working together, in danger of the floor caving in any second, they raised the end of the bench right up through the hole in the ceiling. It cleared the edges by several inches. The Masked Detective motioned Winnie away, gave the bench a hard shove and it careened down. Its further end landed on the still fairly sound flooring across the room and formed a bridge—not too perfect, but usable.

At the Masked Detective's insistence, Winnie sped across it and the Masked Detective followed. They had to force open the partly closed door at the other side, but in a moment they were in the main plant of the cigarette factory.

BUT BY now the fire was really getting started. From upstairs came one crashing detonation after another as the gas that filled a room exploded. The smashing collapse of floors and walls had broken the gas pipes. Possibly some kind of a lead smelting outfit, electrically operated and hot, had been left running in the printing plant. That had been responsible for the fire that flared up instantly, though the killers who had set this trap had not relied on the aid of fire to wipe out their trapped enemies in the cigarette factory rooms.

The crashing in of the floor and ceiling would have accomplished that purpose with anyone but the Masked Detective. But his thinking, his instinctive action, had been too swift for the immediate annihilation of their girl prisoner and himself.

Winnie climbed over a small mountain of debris, skirted the hole in the middle of the floor and turned to help the Masked Detective. She saw that crime fighter edging his way toward several steel filing cabinets. He clung to them, on the very brink of disaster, for the hole in the floor gave him barely enough room to keep his balance.

But he opened those filing cabinets—opened them fast. He plowed the contents and rolled up a whole sheaf of papers which he stuck beneath his belt. Winnie extended a hand which the Masked Detective grabbed, and in one leap he cleared the chasm.

Flames were roaring through the corridor outside the office. With their arms across their faces they started down the steps. A veritable wall of fire stopped them. The blaze had also caught in the lower part of the building, and had spread as fast as though this were dry, waste timberland.

"Upstairs—fast!" the Masked Detective choked and led the way.

There was not much left of the floor on which the printing plant had been located. Most of the machinery and equipment had fallen through the weakened flooring. The corridor, however, was intact, although beginning to burn fiercely.

The Masked Detective checked his rush and stopped near a window. He opened it wide, looked out, and groaned. There was no way to reach the roof—no trap-door so far as he could determine. Apparently when repairs had to be made on the roof, a ladder had been used.

Fire apparatus would be on its way shortly, of course, but it might arrive too late. Another few moments and the already weakened building would be gutted by fire and would collapse entirely.

Looking down into an alley the Masked Detective saw that there was a building about fifteen feet away from him—one that was much more modern, fire-proofed and provided with other improvements. By the light of the flames, the Masked Detective could see that this building was equipped with window washer's hooks which had been firmly planted in the cement.

He still held the rope with which Winnie had been tied. Realization that it might require a desperate effort in order to get Winnie and himself clear had made him hang onto it.

Quickly he ran the rope through his fingers and fashioned a slip-knot. He leaned as far out of the window as possible with Winnie hanging onto his legs, to steady him, and threw the noose. It missed. He tried again, and it still fell short.

WINNIE'S FRANTIC voice reached him.

"The floor is giving way! I can feel it under my feet!"

"Hang onto me!" the Masked Detective shouted back, and threw the rope again.

It caught! He slid back, and motioned to Winnie. "Take a hitch in that rope, jump out and swing over to the other building. You'll land somewhere near the window of the floor below. Kick it in! Climb through and then throw the rope back."

"But what about you?" Winnie protested. "This floor—"

"Get going!" the Masked Detective snapped.

Winnie was well aware that the Masked Detective's orders were not to be denied. She felt strong hands grip her as she climbed out of the window. Then she was given a hard shove. Winnie sailed through space and both her feet went through the window. Her clothes were ripped, her flesh was torn by the glass.

But Winnie had stamina. In a few seconds she had kicked all the glass out and slipped through. She looked around swiftly, discovered a heavy paper weight on a desk and tied it to the rope. Then she gave it a heave. The Masked Detective, apparently balancing himself on the window sill, grabbed it, and without a second's hesitation let himself drop.

Winnie was ready with eager hands to grasp him as he swung to the smashed windows where she waited. She helped the Masked Detective worm his way inside and both of them dropped into chairs, exhausted. From outside, mingled with the sirens of fire trucks, came a rending, ripping roar and one wall of the old building from which they had just escaped came down.

The Masked Detective dug into his pocket, extracted a pack of battered cigarettes and proffered one to Winnie. They lit up, and then both laughed in genuine relief.

"Close, Winnie," the Masked Detective said. "Too close for comfort. But here we are. So now you can tell me—just what happened?"

Winnie told him quickly. The Masked Detective rubbed his chin and eyed the glowing tip of his cigarette a moment as he mulled it over.

"Then we are up against a gang of clever and intelligent people," he concluded. "And it *is* a gang, just as I thought. They're even daring enough to allow themselves to be seen without masks—which shows they are pretty sure of themselves. I doubt they guessed I came to rescue you. What I believe is that they had things arranged to destroy that building if it looked as though there was the slightest chance of its being invaded by police or anyone else. It wouldn't have been hard to weaken the supports, then prop them up again so that these props could be removed in a hurry and let all that heavy machinery fall. That alone was enough to tear the old place apart. But perhaps our friends slipped, in their eagerness to wipe out evidence and enemies. Let's have a look."

The Masked Detective pulled the wad of papers he had salvaged from beneath his belt. He coolly turned on a desk light in the office which they had appropriated, and studied the papers.

"Have a look, Winnie," he invited. "Here are the addresses of many customers of that firm. Now for a little deduction. Suppose you controlled a gang made up, primarily, of household servants. What would be the easiest way to keep in touch with them and never show your hand?"

The masked man looked up at the girl, and answered his own question.

"By sending packages of cigarettes to their masters," he said. "Perhaps the wrapping paper contained a message which would naturally fall into the servants' hands. If our theory is right, Winnie, we may have here a neat little list of places which will be, or have been, made victims of the gang."

"We?" Winnie grimaced. "All I did about this was let myself get caught. And you can bet I didn't stop to look for any evidence when that building started to cave in. All I wanted to do was to put lots of atmosphere between that place and myself."

CHAPTER VIII

GENTEEL SNATCH

JUST AFTER dawn, in Rex Parker's apartment, Winnie and Rex Parker told Sergeant Gleason what had happened. "So it's clear that I was right about this," Parker finished. "There *is* some kind of a league, but just how it operates remains to be discovered. Winnie was told that her letters would be mailed from various parts of the country, which seems to indicate that the league may be nationwide in scale.

"That spells trouble, because whoever heads the outfit isn't going to keep on being satisfied with the small stuff that's been pulled so far. Because they were so willing to kill Winnie and me—when they couldn't possibly have known who I was, either—indicates that whatever their big coup is, it's not far from reaching its culmination."

"Twice they mentioned something about a week being enough to keep me under cover," Winnie broke in eagerly. "Like Rex, I think they may pull the big job then."

"Quite correct," Parker agreed. "Which doesn't give us any too much time. I've studied this list of mailing addresses again. It contains two names of people who have already been robbed. Now, if crooked servants are placed in other homes mentioned in this list, it shouldn't be hard for me to contact the gang. So we'll do that little thing just as soon as we're rested a bit.... Winnie, I'll pick you up at the corner of Clinton and Murdoch Streets at exactly three o'clock this afternoon. We may have to do a little law-breaking, but you won't mind that. A simple job of kidnaping will suffice."

"I'm ready to commit murder," Winnie declared angrily. "So long as those too darned polite crooks are on the receiving end. What I couldn't do to that walking cadaver who bosses them! Or"—she hesitated and frowned—"could I? He threw me around as if I were a two-pound sack of flour. That guy is no sissy, take it from me."

When the Masked Detective had taken his needed rest, and promptly got busy early that afternoon, there was little resemblance between the slow-moving, smiling young man who punched the doorbell at the home of wealthy Bruce Wickham, and the dreaded marauder who wore a black velvet mask and threw fear into the hearts of crooks. Yet they were one and the same. A wooden-faced butler let him in. "Good afternoon, Mr. Parker," he murmured. "Mr. Wickham will see you. He received your phone call. Do you mind waiting a moment while I get him? He's in the gardens."

"Take your time," Rex Parker said affably.

Wickham was on the list of the cigarette company, and a probable victim for the gang, so Parker had selected him for his first investigation. He had phoned for an appointment, indicating that the *Comet* was interested in a polo club which Wickham was sponsoring. But his real reason for coming was to get a good look at the butler or some other likely servant.

Parker picked up a book as he sat down. When the butler turned to leave, the reporter's eyes studied every move the elderly man made. Each motion of his body. His voice and appearance were already firmly affixed in Rex Parker's memory.

Bruce Wickham came in with outstretched hand. He was a middle-aged man and one of the city's biggest insurance executives.

"I'm glad to see you, Mr. Parker. Nice of your paper to take an interest in my project."

Parker was feeling in his pockets, and drew out his cigarette case. It was empty. Wickham picked up a cigarette box and proffered it.

"Try one of mine," he invited. "Have them made especially for me. Exceptionally good stuff, too."

PARKER ACCEPTED one of the cigarettes and glanced at it. This was the type made by Exclusive Cigarette Corporation. The mailing list he had found was the McCoy, all right.

He talked to Wickham for half an hour, mostly about the proposed polo field. When he left, there was no manner of suspicion in the mind of his host that Rex Parker had put in an appearance for a far more specific and important reason than to discuss the building of a sport's field.

At three o'clock, Winnie Bligh was slowly pacing the area around the corner where she was to meet the Masked Detective. She saw a cheap sedan pull up, and a gray-haired man beckoned to her. Winnie held her breath. That might be the Masked Detective, or it might also be one of this strange gang who had recognized her, and now wanted to lead her into another trap.

"I'm at your service, Miss Bligh," the gray-haired man said deferentially. "Perhaps I could get you a Scotch and soda—or do you prefer rye? Or shall I say a nice juicy fire in a building that's caving in?"

"Rex!" Winnie said in a whisper. "What are you supposed to be this time? That's one of the best disguises I've ever seen."

"My name," the Masked Detective said, "is Curtis. Just Curtis, and I'm the butler in Bruce Wickham's house. There is only one hitch to it—the real Curtis doesn't know about the new arrangements yet. Now here is what you do...."

Winnie listened and nodded.

"A genteel snatch," she observed. "That wouldn't be hard, the way you've planned it."

Moments later Winnie rang Bruce Wickham's doorbell and the real Curtis answered.

"I'm from the boss's office," Winnie said. "And here is a letter from him identifying me." She presented a short note which was signed with a remarkable replica of Wickham's signature. "He wants the entire contents of his library desk drawer," she said quickly. "Just take it out and help me cart it to my car. Hurry, will you? Mr. Wickham gets a little annoyed when he's kept waiting. Or perhaps you know that!"

"Of course."

Curtis nodded, hurried to the library. Winnie indicated the drawer and the servant quickly pulled it free. But she gave him no chance to hand the burden to her. She sped out to the car and opened the rear door. Curtis was out of breath and upset about having to do this menial work. He got into the car to set the drawer down, and for one or two seconds the door was closed. Then Curtis came out again—only this Curtis was not out of breath and he did not look annoyed.

Winnie got behind the wheel of the car and drove off.

The Masked Detective, dressed exactly as Curtis had been, looking precisely like the white-haired butler, returned to the house and calmly closed the door. He began an inspection of the place. He caught a maid humming gaily as she dusted the rungs of a chair and he shook a reproving finger at her.

The Masked Detective went upstairs, and easily located Curtis' room on the servants' floor. He closed the door and sat on the edge of the bed.

Everything was working perfectly. He didn't know the names of the other servants, and he didn't know which one of them was on the payroll of the gang. It might even be Curtis himself. He had to find that out quickly, before Bruce Wickham returned home.

ABOUT HALF an hour later the doorbell buzzed. The Masked Detective, in his disguise as Curtis, went to the door. A uniformed messenger boy extended a package, wrapped in brown paper.

"Kindly use the service entrance hereafter," the Masked Detective snapped, for the benefit of the other servants who might be within hearing distance.

He carried the package into the pantry, unwrapped it, and revealed several cartons of cigarettes, all labeled as being especially made by the Exclusive Cigarette Corporation. He rolled up the wrapping paper and dropped it into the waste basket. Within two minutes the chauffeur, whose name the Masked Detective had discovered to be McLeod when another servant had spoken to him, picked up the waste basket and headed for the back door.

"I'll do you hard working people a favor," he said, grinning, "and burn this stuff."

The Masked Detective waved his hand impatiently, as if that were quite agreeable. He maneuvered around the house on an excuse of disposing of the cigarettes, and was able to look out of the window. McLeod had set the waste basket on the ground and was removing the brown paper in which the cigarettes had been wrapped. He stowed this under his jacket, then burned the rest of the contents of the basket.

The Masked Detective smiled grimly. McLeod was the man—the crook planted in Wickham's house. His hunch that messages were sent by means of those cigarette deliveries had turned out to be accurate. However the Exclusive Cigarette Company had not mailed this package, and would never mail another from their old address. Good old Winnie Bligh had taken care of mailing this one, at the Masked Detective's instructions.

The Masked Detective had been suspicious of McLeod from the moment he had seen the chauffeur, after the Masked Detective had taken the place of the real butler. McLeod was a skinny-faced, somber-looking man who hung around the house far more than a chauffeur should.

McLeod came back to the kitchen, then headed for the interior of the house. The Masked Detective walked into Wickham's study and sensed that McLeod was watching him. He looked around furtively, then hurriedly dipped into Wickham's supply of expensive cigars. He stowed these away and then went to his room. He hid the cigars, returned to the first floor, and caught a smirk on McLeod's face. Things were working out all right—as he had planned them.

The Masked Detective had little time in which to work. Whatever this band of servants intended to do would probably reach a head in a matter of only a few days. Therefore he must get busy at once, and if anything was to be discovered here, he must find it.

He returned to Wickham's study, closed the door, and began opening desk drawers and prowling through them. In one he discovered a small jewelry box containing a stick pin, a diamond-studded tie clasp and a platinum watch-band. There was a picture of Wickham on the desk—a portrait of the master of the house in an army uniform of the First World War days. The Masked Detective had turned this so that he could catch a fair reflection of the two windows in the room. He kept watching this reflection, and smiled thinly when he caught a glimpse of McLeod's chauffeur's cap. The man was certainly keeping his eyes on the butler.

The Masked Detective put his apparently stolen jewels into his pocket and then went up to his room again. He concealed the loot in a corner of his bureau drawer. Now all he could do was wait for developments.

CHAPTER IX

NO NEED
FOR MURDER

BEFORE WICKHAM put in an appearance, developments came—two hours later. The Masked Detective was called to the house phone. McLeod was calling from the garage.

"You'd better come out here if you know what's good for you," McLeod said softly. "I was looking in the study window this afternoon. Get what I mean?"

The Masked Detective hung up quickly. He waited a few moments, then went out to the garage. He looked nervous and kept running a finger around his stiff collar. McLeod was seated on the running-board of a limousine, openly sneering at the man he believed to be Curtis.

"I figured you were too damned good to be true," McLeod rasped. "That's why I been watching you, Curtis. I've taken plenty of your orders around here, so now I'll give a couple of my own. I want that stuff you swiped. Oh, don't worry, you'll get a cut out of it."

"But—but I must have it all," the Masked Detective pleaded. "I—I'm in debt. Unless I pay up, they will approach the master. I—I'll lose my job."

"When you got to pay them?" McLeod demanded. "Before tomorrow?"

The Masked Detective shook his head slowly. McLeod got up.

"Okay, Curtis. Now get this. Things are going on that you've never heard about—things that make your little job of snitching the work of a piker. Tonight—at nine o'clock on the dot—come to Eleven-seventy-two Rainer Boulevard. It's an apartment house. Ring the bell to Number Five B and when you get the buzzer, give your name on the lobby phone. Then come up."

"But I don't seem to understand." The Masked Detective was carrying out Curtis' manners perfectly.

"You will," McLeod promised. "And if you don't show up, a couple of cops will be along before midnight to pick you up. Be a smart guy and do as I say. You'll be out of debt in two weeks if you team up with my outfit."

"I'll be there," the Masked Detective declared with pathetic eagerness. "I'd do anything to pay off the men who keep demanding money from me. I feel as though I've misjudged you, McLeod. I'm sorry, if I've ever spoken harshly to you."

McLeod waved a hand, forgiving all in one gesture.

"Forget it, Curtis. Only lay off a little on errands. And say, you might try to dig up the combination to the boss's safe, eh?"

At the prescribed hour, the Masked Detective, sedately dressed in Curtis' clothes, rang the bell at the designated address. He gave his name in a nervous voice over the lobby phone, then he took the self-operating elevator to the fifth floor.

Two men were waiting when he opened the door. Neither of them was the plug-ugly type of crook. They were neatly dressed, clean shaven, and looked intelligent.

"Good evening, Curtis," one said. "You are to follow us, but first of all try not to betray too much surprise at what you shall soon learn. It's all for our mutual benefit, I assure you."

The Masked Detective was escorted into a modest apartment. Four other men were there. Two wore chauffeurs' uniforms, another was a bit rougher, and his hands indicated he might be a gardener.

But the Masked Detective gave them only a passing glance. Sprawled in one of the larger chairs in the room was a man who instantly attracted him. He was somber-appearing and pallid-faced. He answered Winnie Bligh's description of the cadaverous gang leader perfectly.

"SIT DOWN, Curtis," this man said. "My name is Diggs and my profession is similar to your own. McLeod tells me you are in need of cash—even to such an extent that you tried to steal your master's property. Now, don't protest. Excuses mean nothing to me. You've never heard of us, Curtis. We're a new organization built up to take for ourselves some of the wealth our masters flaunt in our faces. Do you follow me?"

"Quite." The Masked Detective licked his lips, still acting nervous.

"Good," the man who called himself Diggs said. "Then we understand one another. Now for a word of explanation. We operate this way—and mind you, a word from you to anyone else of what I say will have serious consequences. Suppose you robbed that pompous master of yours—

Wickham. Suppose things were so arranged that you'd surely be caught if you remained. That's where we come in. You take whatever you like, share it with us on a certain percentage basis and we provide you with another job, a thousand miles from here. We arrange references that cannot be questioned."

"And then," the Masked Detective asked casually, not wishing to betray any eagerness, "I rob my new masters. I really don't like it, Diggs."

Diggs leaned forward and tapped the supposed Curtis on one knee.

"You wouldn't like going to prison either, Curtis, and you will if you refuse to help us," he threatened. "You wouldn't talk about what I've just told you, either, because if that happened—I'm afraid you'd come to a very sudden end. Buck up, man. You've served other people so long you've got no will power of your own…. Will you do it?"

The Masked Detective straightened up and stuck out his chin.

"Yes, I'll do it. I'm sick of watching others live like kings and waiting on them hand and foot. Wickham keeps a lot of cash on hand at certain times. If you'll advance me enough to pay off some nuisance debts, I'll replace what I took today, and bide my time until there is enough in the safe to make it really worthwhile. I know the combination."

Diggs arose and clapped a friendly hand on the Masked Detective's shoulder.

"Fine, Curtis!" he applauded. "And I guarantee you'll never be sorry. I rather think…. Listen—the buzzer in an emergency signal! You two men go down and see just what's up. Hurry!"

Two of the men he indicated sped out of the apartment. They returned in about five minutes and carried between them an unconscious man whose face was covered with blood. Behind them came a pale-faced, hand-wringing man dressed in the clothing of a gardener.

"Mr. Diggs, sir," he whined, "I—I don't know what to say. This—this man is Mr. Gwenn, my employer. I did as you told me. I robbed the house of all the jewelry I could find. I was afraid the police would come before I had a chance to get clear, so I started to bury the loot in the garden. Mr. Gwenn came along—I think he suspected me all the time. He said I'd go to prison, so I—I struck him with the shovel. I couldn't leave him there. He wasn't dead. I didn't know what to do so I brought him here. Nobody saw me."

"You stupid fool!"

Diggs stepped close and struck the trembling gardener a hard backhand blow across the mouth. Then he knelt beside the unconscious man, ripped open his shirt and laid a hand against the region of the heart. He looked up grimly.

"No, he isn't dead, but he's dying. The only thing we can do now is to finish him and make it appear accidental. What car did you use, Makin?"

The half-sick gardener gulped.

"The sedan, sir. The same one the master left in the driveway when he came home."

"That's lucky," Diggs said, as he arose. "We'll carry him out. Makin, you began this and, by heavens, you'll finish it! Put him in the car, take him to some lonesome road. Prop him up somehow and then run over him. Do a good job of it, do you hear? Then remove all traces of the impact from the car, back it up, and park it beside the body. Drive a nail into one tire and scatter tools around so it will look as though he was trying to fix a flat and someone ran him down. I'll provide you with a headlight glass which you will drop on the road as if it had been knocked out of the hit-and-run car."

THE MASKED DETECTIVE stood meekly to one side, an expression of horror on his disguised face. He watched the unconscious man closely. His breathing was rhythmic and strong.

This man was in no danger of dying, yet Diggs wanted to have him killed. Why? Because he might reveal that his gardener was a crook? Hardly, because that would be an obvious fact anyhow.

There was something else—something much bigger. Why wasn't the process of transferring suspected members, of which Diggs had boasted, being used in this case? What was the necessity for murder when it would have been far simpler just to dump the injured man somewhere and send the gardener away to some new job—as had been done with so many others who were apparently caught in the act?

Why did Diggs insist this man was dying?

Several other men came into the apartment, apparently by appointment. All were servants, if their manners were any gauge.

The Masked Detective made his way unnoticed to the door which led into the other room. No matter what happened now, he had to save the life of this unconscious man. Everything else became subordinate to that. There was a fair chance that he might also be able to have this band of crooks rounded up at the same time.

He sidled through the door, hurried in the direction of the exit and a moment later sped down the stairway, disdaining the slow elevator which was still at the floor level.

PARKED A quarter of a mile away was his swift coupé. He stopped in a drug store and made a hasty call to Police Headquarters before he reached the car. By the time he drove back near the apartment house where the crooks had their meeting place, he saw two men supporting their unconscious victim as though he were drunk.

They stowed him into a big car and the Gwenn gardener got behind the wheel.

He pulled away, and the other two men stood near the curb watching him disappear.

The Masked Detective had to hand it to Diggs as a cold-blooded crook who lived up to his precepts in the way he operated. He was having a man killed as coolly as he might have eaten breakfast. He took no personal part in the affair and when it was done, he would have that gardener of Gwenn's in a grasp of iron. Perhaps that was his motive.

CHAPTER X

FUTILE RAID

A S SOON as the two men turned back to the apartment, the Masked Detective went in pursuit of the gardener, who had driven away. He followed the man at a discreet distance and when they started to leave the city limits, he shut off the headlights on his coupé.

The gardener was going far out, and seemed to have a certain spot in mind. It proved to be a paved road which led to a golf course, closed for the season now. He finally stopped the car, got out and opened the rear door.

He dragged the unconscious man to the road, left him there a moment, and fumbled around the side of the road until he found a large rock. He carried this to the unconscious man, propped him up against it and then went back to the car. He opened the door, started to slide behind the wheel, and suddenly found himself looking into the muzzle of an uncompromising automatic. Behind it was a masked man.

"Go back there," the masked man said calmly. "Carry your master to this car and do it carefully. I wouldn't mind shooting you down any more than I would a hyena. Move!"

"But if I—" the gardener protested weakly.

"So far there is against you only a charge of robbery, assault and attempted murder," the masked man said grimly. "That doesn't add up to the electric chair. And I happen to know that what you are now planning to do will strap you in the hot seat. If the information will make you move faster, I'm the Masked Detective."

The gardener's already white face turned a shade more ashen. He bit his lower lip until the blood ran and then he seemed to experience a wave of relief.

"I never wanted to kill him," he said, his voice trembling. "That devil Diggs—you must know about him, too, since you know so much—he made me do it. If I refused, or didn't carry out his orders, he'd kill me. What could I do but obey? You don't know him! He's worse than—than any killer you ever heard of. But what if the master dies?"

"He's in no danger of dying if he gets attention quickly enough," the Masked Detective snapped. "Bring him to the car."

The gardener obeyed willingly. The Masked Detective examined the unconscious man and discovered that his rather long-range diagnosis had been correct. He got into the back seat with the injured man and kept his gun on the gardener as he drove back to town. Just past the outskirts, twin headlights, red in color, indicated that a police car was parked there. At the Masked Detective's orders, the gardener stopped beside the police car.

A powerfully built man got out of the police car and came over. The Masked Detective met him. It was Sergeant Gleason and he eyed the masked man quizzically.

"What happened at the raid?" the Masked Detective asked in a whisper, and in Rex Parker's normal voice.

"Nothing! Not one damned thing. We broke down the door with axes and there wasn't a soul in the place. Had it surrounded, too—or thought we had anyhow. What's it all about?"

"I'm not sure yet," the Masked Detective replied. "Behind the wheel of this car is a prisoner. Charges will be filed later. Meantime hold him, and don't let a word of his arrest leak out. Keep him out of contact with other prisoners—no phone calls, no mail, no visitors for him. I'll explain fully later on. It's rather amazing to learn the raid was fruitless, but it only shows that I'm working against clever men. Thank you, Sergeant, for helping me out."

"No thanks necessary," Gleason answered. "But I wish I knew what you were up to."

GLEASON PUT cuffs on the gardener's wrists and led him to the police car. The Masked Detective climbed behind the wheel of the sedan and drove straight to Gwenn's home. He wheeled the car into the garage, got into the back seat once more, and found Gwenn coming out of his coma. The Masked Detective helped him into a sitting position.

"You'll be all right in a few moments," he said. "Rather nasty blow you got, but not especially serious."

Gwenn turned his face toward the Masked Detective's and his half-closed eyes blinked wide open as he started back weakly.

"Don't worry about the mask," he was quickly told. "I'm the Masked Detective. Your gardener struck you with a shovel. Remember?"

"Yes—yes, I remember," Gwenn said weakly. "He stole some of my property. But—but what happened? If you really are the Masked Detective…. But how can I be sure in my own mind? Maybe you're a colleague of Makin's."

The Masked Detective laughed.

"If I were, you'd be dead, Mr. Gwenn, plastered to the pavement of a road that leads to your country club. Makin, the gardener, is in the hands of the police. Mr. Gwenn, I saved your life, and am happy that I was able to. Sergeant Gleason of Headquarters will verify that fact. But in return I want your help. You are to give an interview to the newspapers as soon as you are able.

"Tell them that your gardener, Makin, is a thief and that he assaulted you. That you woke up in your own car far in the country and Makin seemed to be preparing a method of murder, with you as the victim. Tell the reporters you paid Makin two thousand dollars in cash to save your life, and that you let him get away."

"Of course." Gwenn was sitting up, and feeling a little better. "I believe you. No man with evil intentions could talk as convincingly as you do. I'll do as you ask, even if I don't know what the whole thing is about."

The Masked Detective looked at Gwenn squarely.

"One more thing," he said. "Disregarding the gardener's motive for killing you to protect himself—is there any reason why another person might desire your death?"

"Why no—no, of course not," Gwenn said. "I have no enemies. There is absolutely not a single reason why anyone would want me killed, neither for profit nor for revenge."

The Masked Detective helped Gwenn out of the car. The man was quickly recovering his strength as the Masked Detective led him to the door of the garage.

"Remember about the interview, Mr. Gwenn," he repeated. "It's most important to my plans. And later on you can send out to the golf course road for your car. I'm taking it back there."

Gwenn stuck out his hand.

"Thank you," he said fervently. "I realize that you saved my life, and I'm eternally grateful. I think—"

Gwenn, trying to walk alone, became suddenly weak. He slumped against the door of the garage and swayed drunkenly. The Masked Detective leaped to his side.

"You're not as fit as you think," he said. "I'll help you inside the house. If there are any servants around, I'd rather they didn't see me."

"All out," Gwenn muttered. "I—I guess you will have to help me further. My legs feel like rubber."

THE MASKED DETECTIVE half carried the man into the house. He laid him down on a davenport, poured out a two-ounce drink of brandy and held Gwenn up while he drank it.

"I'd better phone your doctor," he told Gwenn. "Mind giving me his number?"

Gwenn did and the Masked Detective walked over to the desk, sat down and dialed the number. As he delivered the message, his eyes drifted across several papers on the desk. He suppressed a grunt of amazement as he saw a four-inch-square white card, with a matching envelope beside it. The envelope was addressed to Gwenn and the card bore only a few words. They were:

Things going smoothly. Expect splendid results soon.

It was signed:

Devil's Stepladder

The Masked Detective turned quickly toward Gwenn. He hesitated a moment. The Devil's Stepladder, whatever it might be, was a big factor in this case. He could take a chance and ask Gwenn about it, but if it so happened that Gwenn was not exactly as innocent as he appeared to be, the whole thing might be given away.

Gwenn's death, so callously plotted by the man who called himself Diggs, may have been motivated by Diggs' desire to get rid of someone in the know, or someone who might demand a share in the profits of this murder and robbery game. The Masked Detective decided to say nothing yet. So long as he was not suspected, Gwenn would hardly try to get away.

"The doctor will be here soon," the Masked Detective said, after he finished his phone call. "I'll stay close by until he arrives. There is a chance that there may be another attempt on your life, Mr. Gwenn. Perhaps I'd better furnish you with a police guard."

The other nodded.

"Yes—yes, of course." Gwenn tried to sit up. "A splendid idea. If you think my death is desired by someone, as you have suggested, I'll be glad of any kind of a guard."

The Masked Detective turned to the phone again, and guardedly arranged with Sergeant Gleason for protection for Gwenn. And his agile mind was telling him that Gwenn had accepted a guard too readily to be mixed up in the affairs of the gang. Anyone so involved would have protested against policemen near him all the time.

After the Masked Detective had witnessed the arrival of the doctor and two detectives hastily dispatched by Sergeant Gleason, he drove Gwenn's sedan back to where he had left his own speedy coupé parked. He headed back to Wickham's house, left the coupé, and straightened his clothing. The mask was in a hidden pocket, and so was the gun.

He had taken a bold chance in leaving Diggs and his men so abruptly, but he reasoned that Diggs would hardly have had time to miss him before the raiding squad arrived. There had been many other things on Diggs' mind besides his business with "Curtis." Anyhow, now the Masked Detective would have to bluff it out, but he was a past master in that art.

Wickham was home when the Masked Detective entered the house, dressed exactly as Curtis had been, and looking the exact counterpart of the butler. He indicated to Wickham that he was ready to serve him, and then went to his room. Wickham had wanted nothing, so the Masked Detective relaxed for a few moments and pondered his problems.

How had Diggs and his bunch of crooked servants made good their escape? Had they been tipped off somehow? And why—again—had Diggs ordered the murder of Gwenn, been so insistent upon it? What did the Devil's Stepladder mean? The Masked Detective was sure now that Vogan's dying words had not been just random phrases. They meant something that had been paramount in the dying man's mind.

Gwenn, perhaps, knew the secret, and the Masked Detective was determined to approach him soon. First however, he had to establish an alibi for his disappearance from Diggs' gang.

The phone at his small night table rang about fifty minutes later. Instantly he recognized Diggs' cold, calculating voice.

"My dear Curtis," Diggs said, "I'm sorry about that bit of excitement. We had to run for it rather quickly, and I didn't recall seeing you about."

"I'm afraid I didn't bother to indicate just where I was," the Masked Detective answered in Curtis' voice. "I followed the rest of the men, found myself clear of the police and came right on home."

"I thought that must have happened." Diggs' voice dripped honey. "You're a good man, Curtis. It was a close shave, too. We got out the rear exit two jumps ahead of the police. I wish I knew who tipped them off. I also hope this little incident will not make any difference in your affiliations with us."

Diggs' tones changed as he spoke the last sentence. They implied that if the raid had mattered, Curtis might find it healthier to vanish altogether.

"None at all," the Masked Detective replied. "The way you handled the situation proves your ability. I....Just a moment, please. That damned fool Wickham is ringing like mad for me."

"Hurry!" Diggs snapped, "I've something important to tell you."

CHAPTER XI

THE CLEVERER BRAIN

CAREFULLY PLACING the phone on the table, the Masked Detective darted out of the room. He slipped into a bed chamber, closed the door quietly, and then used the phone there. It would have an outside connection, not tied up at all with the line being used by Diggs. There was a miniature switchboard in the kitchen so that two different wires could be used. He got the telephone supervisor.

"There is a call coming in now—on the other line to this house," he said quickly. "It's vitally important that the origin of the call be checked. A police matter."

In two minutes the Masked Detective had what he wanted. Diggs was calling from a telephone listed under the name of Frank Alden, at 629 Beecher Road. He hung up, hurried back to his own room, and spoke to Diggs again.

"He's too confounded weak to mix himself a highball," he grumbled. "The more I see of Wickham, the less I want to keep on being a mere servant. I'm ready for anything, Diggs. Just give your orders and I'll follow them out to the letter."

"Ah—excellent. Listen carefully. There is to be an important meeting of our little group tomorrow evening at nine. I have transferred head-quarters to another address. A small house at the end of Schoonmaker Lane. Be there without fail. Make a plausible excuse to Wickham. Don't arouse his suspicions, whatever you do, and when the proper time comes, you will make him pay for the work he demands out of you. Good night, Curtis, and I'm very glad you are now one of us…. Oh yes—the cash you need. I'll give it to you at our next meeting."

The Masked Detective agreed to that eagerly, hung up and leaned back against the pillow of his bed. So Diggs was calling from the home of Frank Alden. The Masked Detective had heard of that man a few times. He was known to be wealthy, but also an unknown quantity.

No one seemed to know much about his family or antecedents, or where he had come from when he had appeared in the East about four years before. It was only known that he had come from some vague place in the West. Diggs was tied up with him some way—perhaps acting as the front for the gang, with Alden as the real leader who remained behind the scenes. At any rate, Alden promised to be an interesting study.

The Masked Detective waited on Wickham until the master of the house retired. Then the Masked Detective went to bed also, and slept like a log. He arose early, supervised preparations for breakfast and served it, as discreetly and expertly as though he had done this type of thing all his life.

He begged the day off to attend to some private business, and got it promptly. Wickham indicated he would be out until long after dinner anyway. So, shortly after two o'clock that afternoon, Rex Parker was sauntering along the street, nodding to acquaintances and whistling gaily.

He walked to Frank Alden's pretentious home because it was not far from the newspaper office where Parker worked. He was ready for almost any kind of a surprise, but when the door of Alden's house opened, he barely stifled an exclamation of astonishment.

The butler was Diggs! He was dressed in quiet livery and his manners were as smooth as velvet. He took Parker's hat, led him to the library, and pushed a chair forward.

"I shall announce you immediately, sir," he said smoothly. "Mr. Alden is, at the moment, engaged upstairs with his hobby. Painting, you know. He'll be down directly, sir."

PARKER SHRUGGED and picked up a magazine. Perhaps ten minutes went by and then he heard someone descending the steps. A man of medium height, with light brown hair and rather small blue eyes, came into the room. He wore a paint-smeared smock and did not seem particularly delighted at having a guest.

"I'm sorry," he said as he proffered his hand, "but I don't seem to know you, Mr.—ah—Parker. That is the name Diggs told me, isn't it?"

"Rex Parker," the reporter explained. "I'm on the staff of the *Comet*. I—"

"Just a minute," Alden snapped. Are you the Rex Parker who writes all that crime news about the Masked Detective?"

Parker nodded. "That's me."

"Then what do you want?" Alden asked testily. "I'm very busy and have no time for foolish interviews. Nothing I have to say could possibly interest a newspaper or those who might read it."

Alden sat down back of a small desk and the reporter parked himself in his favorite position on one corner of the same desk. He made a sweeping motion with his hand and upset a small vase which contained three roses. Alden let out an annoyed oath, picked up the vase, and Parker hastily mopped up the water with his handkerchief.

"Terrible sorry," he said. "Stupid of me.... Look, Mr. Alden—we're running a series of stories about the hobbies of wealthy men. You're an amateur painter and your views will undoubtedly be of great interest...."

Alden looked up incredulously.

"Do you mean to say that I'm to be bothered with a trivial thing like that? See here, Mr. Parker, I'm not a busy man under ordinary circumstances, but it so happens that I'm painting today, and I have to pay a model by the hour for her work. Also the sunlight happens to be in a perfect position over my skylight and it won't stay there long. I'm sorry, but... I'll show you to the door."

Parker smiled wryly. "I don't blame you. Mr. Alden. You have my promise that I won't bother you again. Lead the way."

Alden opened the front door himself, and slammed it so quickly that Rex Parker jumped after he passed through. He grinned, patted his inside coat pocket, and the vase which reposed there. Alden might miss that vase, but Parker didn't particularly care, for by the time the wealthy, eccentric master of this house could raise any fuss, Rex Parker would have what he wanted.

But where was Diggs, the butler? How did it happen that he did not stay in attendance as all butlers should do? Diggs had gone upstairs to notify Alden, and Parker recalled that about ten minutes had elapsed, and then Alden came down alone. While Alden was around, Diggs had not put in an appearance. Were they one and the same man? Was Diggs both butler and master in this strange house?

Parker toyed with the idea of bringing Sergeant Gleason into the case, and putting the pinch on Diggs. He rejected that idea as being premature. He had enough on Diggs, true, but now Parker was puzzled as to whether or not Diggs was the real operator of this league of crooked servants. His arrest might put a temporary halt to the league's proceedings, but would it stop the gang forever? Parker doubted that, because he was now more than reasonably certain that Diggs was nothing more than a figurehead—unless he were playing a dual rôle.

REX PARKER proceeded straight to Police Headquarters and the laboratories. He brought out Alden's fingerprints on the vase and found them to be perfectly impressed. He classified them expertly and then visited the Bureau of Identification where shortly a record card was laid before him. It carried a picture about ten years old, but it was a picture of Alden without the slightest question. Parker read the report and whistled softly.

Alden, alias Jim Bartlett, it read, had been a business man in a Western city ten years before. His business, during the height of the depression, had gone to the verge of bankruptcy, like that of so many others. There had been a severe fire with arson suspected, but never proved. However, it had been determined that Alden, alias Bartlett, had then filed a petition in bankruptcy and had concealed the greater part of his assets. There had been a spectacular trial and Alden had gone to prison for three to five years.

This was his only known criminal record, but the crime in itself indicated that Alden was not to be trusted, that he would cheat and lie if necessary. There was also the question as to where he had recouped his fortune, to enable him to live as he did now. Alden's assets had been attached after his sentence to prison.

"A man to watch," Parker mused thoughtfully. "And how he'll be watched! And that walking corpse of a servant, too. Maybe that job won't be too hard, either, because by keeping one under surveillance probably both of them can be watched at the same time. Alden has a lot to account for, but the time isn't quite ripe."

Rex Parker had spent but a short time at Police Headquarters and now he headed for home. Turning a corner on his way to the nearest subway station, he caught a glimpse of a short, underfed-looking man. He had seen that same man not many minutes before, after he had left Alden's house.

Parker's eyes narrowed. Was he being trailed? Had Alden sent someone to shadow him, perhaps hoping that through Rex Parker he would be able to locate the Masked Detective?

Parker decided to find out. He turned the next corner and stepped into a doorway quickly. The skinny runt came into view and slowed his eager steps when he was unable to spot his quarry down the street. The little man seemed badly agitated. For a moment it seemed that he could not make up his mind what to do. Then he turned on his heel and disappeared.

Rex Parker stepped out of the doorway, spotted a taxi cruising down the street, and hailed it. He gave orders to be driven to his apartment. As the cab rolled away, the skinny little man popped around the corner, and his jaw fell an inch. Then he darted across the street and ran into a drug store. He used a phone booth for a moment and was mopping sweat off his face when he emerged.

Parker's taxi turned down the avenue on which he lived. Midway between blocks, the driver slammed on his brakes. Two old sedans had side-swiped one another and blocked the whole street while their drivers argued things out. Other traffic piled up behind Parker's cab.

This looked like an accident, but Rex Parker had his suspicions. In the first place the two cars had crashed too perfectly to have been an accident. The fenders and bumpers were wound around one another as if the drivers had deliberately set out to do this very thing.

Parker paid off his driver, got out, and wormed his way between the stalled cars. His apartment was about ten blocks further on. He reached the sidewalk, got around the jammed traffic, and picked up another taxi at a feed line on the next corner.

WHEN HE finally entered his apartment building, he realized that the delay had occupied a good ten minutes. He approached the apartment door cautiously. It was closed. He listened outside for a moment, heard nothing, and tried the knob. The door was locked. He inserted his key, turned it and then as he gave the door a kick open, he ducked back in case there was a gun trap set to greet him, or someone lurked just inside, ready to split his skull open.

Nothing happened. He went inside—and groaned. Something had happened here all right. The place looked as though two cyclones had struck it. Everything was torn apart. He glanced at the closet behind which was located his secret cupboard and the essentials necessary for disguise. The closet had been ransacked, but apparently the hidden compartment had not been located.

Locking himself in the apartment, Parker opened the hidden door and studied his disguise materials intently. Everything seemed as usual. But perhaps the marauders *had* found it, and had taken care not to molest anything.

Parker sat down with a worried frown. Who had sent men to do this job? Alden, or Diggs? Or were they the same person? Perhaps not either one of them for, on the other hand, it was highly possible that someone else had been having him trailed all day.

What mattered most of all was the problem as to whether or not this unknown person or persons knew that Rex Parker was the Masked Detective. Such knowledge, in the wrong hands, could spell a great deal of trouble for Parker.

He looked around the room and his anger began to mount slowly. So far he had been more or less on the defensive. Now he determined to take the other side and challenge these unknown forces.

But first of all he had to keep his appointment with Diggs—as Curtis, the butler in Bruce Wickham's home. That was the first and most important step. If Diggs plotted any serious moves, Parker would then be in a position to thwart him. He might also learn something about this search of Rex Parker's apartment, and about Alden.

CHAPTER XII

DIGGS SHOWS HIS CLAWS

R EX PARKER spent the rest of the afternoon working as crime reporter for the *Comet*. He showed himself at Police Headquarters, had a short, confidential chat with Gleason, telling him of what had happened. Then he visited the newspaper offices and apprised Winnie of the day's events. "The real Curtis is tied up and locked in the old farmhouse as you instructed, Rex," Winnie told him, and smiled. "Old debbil Diggs won't find him."

"You'd better watch your step," he warned. "Diggs is a dangerous guy. If he associates you in anyway with the Masked Detective, there's liable to be some fireworks—and you'll be the one who gets burned."

"Rex," Winnie said firmly, "get those men! Run them down. Give them no peace. Uncover their plot, whatever it is. Expose them for the rotten crooks they are! Do it quickly, before they take action against you."

Parker grinned. "You echo the sentiments that reside in the depths of my heart, Cap'n Bligh. However, I'd like to know what really is in the wind, before I put the clamps on Diggs. If he is just a prince of crime and the kingpin is hiding behind an ambush, we'd gain very little by throwing Diggs into a cell. Business like this has to be cleaned out from the top down. It's a hydra-headed monster. For every head you lop off, two more grow in its place, and it goes right on living and growing.

"It's tough to let Diggs keep on running his end of the business, when I could grab him in a second—but that's the way it is, my sweet…. Well, I've only got the day off from Mr. Bruce Wickham. I must get back so I can show my handsomely disguised face. I'll slip out during the evening again. Boy, this butler's life is something."

The Masked Detective was in Wickman's home two hours before the master of the house put in an appearance. Half an hour before the designated time to keep his rendezvous with Diggs, the Masked Detective left the house without asking Wickham's permission. He reached the address he had been given, studied the lay-out for a moment, then walked onto the porch of the bungalow and rang the doorbell.

Diggs himself let him in. Diggs was smiling, but somehow the Masked Detective did not quite like the look in Diggs' eyes. They were too calculating; too shrewd.

"Please come in, my dear Curtis," Diggs invited suavely. "You are punctual. The others are here, so we shall immediately hold a council of war. Follow me, please."

"I—I'd like to get that money," the Masked Detective said hesitantly. "You know—to pay off those creditors. If they ever go to Mr. Wickham, I won't have a job ten minutes after they leave."

"Of course, of course." Diggs put a friendly hand on the pseudo Curtis' shoulder. "It really doesn't make much difference though, because I have information that your master has removed certain highly valued jewels from his bank and placed them in the house. By this time tomorrow your pockets will be lined with more cash than you've ever hoped to possess, Curtis. What's more, you'll be on your way to a new job."

The Masked Detective walked into a room crowded with men. They were all servants and most of them looked worried and distraught. When Diggs took the floor, one of these men moved forward. His face was pale, but he looked determined to get something off his chest.

"MR. DIGGS, sir," he began, "I've been thinking things over and—well. I don't care about this business. Three months ago you approached me. You know that years ago I served time in a reformatory. You know that should this information reach my employers, I would be discharged immediately. I know it also. No matter where I go, you can prevent me from getting work. I don't know any other line. Now I'm appealing to you as a man and as a—a member of our profession. Lots of others, like me, feel the same way. We want to get out of it."

The expression on Diggs' face sent the speaker cringing and retreating. Diggs followed. He raised one hand and gave the man a cruel slap across the face. The rebel was strangely affected by that blow. It seemed to make a near maniac of him. He gave vent to a yowl of rage, lowered his head and charged forward.

Diggs took a punch to the midriff, but then the battle was over. His two hands clamped down on the rebel's shoulders with such strength that the man winced in agony.

"You've got all of us!" the rebel yowled, despite the ever-increasing pain. "You're blackmailing us into working for you! You made us sign confessions of our guilt to hold over our heads. But you'll pay. You'll—"

He stopped talking at that instant because Diggs let go of one shoulder and slammed him full in the face with a doubled-up fist. The rebel was thrown backward. He stumbled, dropped to his knees, and Diggs moved in with a sardonic grin on his lean face. He kicked the man under the chin.

The Masked Detective heard the sound of bone cracking under the impact. He had to use all his will power to hold himself in check, reminding himself that a much greater cause depended on his not going berserk. But this Diggs was a fiend incarnate. Beneath his smooth, polished manners he concealed a sadistic, cruel nature.

A dangerous foe, this Diggs with the funereal features and the cunning brain of a sly crook. If anything happened so that the Masked Detective fell into his hands, he could expect little compassion.

Diggs walked over to where the rebel lay sprawled out. The man should have been completely unconscious from that last blow, but somehow he was not. He struggled into a sitting position, his hand dipped into his inside coat pocket, and he started to draw a gun.

From just behind the Masked Detective came an explosion. The rebel dropped flat, a bullet through his brain. One of the group calmly blew smoke out of his pistol, then thrust the gun back into a holster. Diggs glared at the stunned men.

"Are there any more members of this group who wish to offer their resignations?" he demanded. "No? I thought not. At the first sign of revolt, you get what this fool received. Remember that I hold documentary evidence against all of you. If you try to betray me, and I don't succeed in closing your mouths, you will suffer with me because when I go into the hands of the police—so do you! Now we shall get down to business, and when the meeting is over, two of you carry this corpse outside. Put it in a car and dump it somewhere. Take care that you do not touch any part of the body to which prints may adhere.

"Now this meeting is formally declared open. I have this to say, and pay attention—all of you. The various people in whose employ you are still trust you. In the course of the next few days there is to be a War relief ball. Your employers, especially the women, will try to outshine one another at that affair. All their jewels will be taken from the bank safe deposit vaults, and for one night they will be at our fingertips. That is the night we act. Your further instructions will follow shortly by the usual means.... And a word of warning. I have reason to believe that the Masked Detective is working against us."

"The Masked Detective!" It was chorused by several voices.

DIGGS SNEERED openly.

"It's amazing how cowardly men can become after they've taken orders for so many years. The Masked Detective means nothing to me except that we shall have to be a bit more careful. Remember that his successes have been against moronic underworld types. He can't fight brains and cunning. The only fearsome thing about him is his reputation.

"Oh, yes—watch out for a man named Rex Parker. He's a reporter, and the confidant of the Masked Detective. The man has been calling on some of our homes recently, but he is an absolute stupid type—no one to be afraid of; just to watch. Now about the instructions. You will receive word soon as to what you must look for—something along the lines of the cigarette wrapping paper we used up to now. It is no longer safe to operate through those channels.

"There is just one more item of business. We have among us a traitor—a fool who submitted to my orders, but kept certain mental reservations, because he thinks he is honest even though he slipped from his high and mighty pedestal recently."

The assembled men looked at one another in amazement. The Masked Detective, in his disguise as Curtis, felt a sudden hollow sensation in the pit of his stomach. It was coming. Diggs had somehow learned he was an impostor. Perhaps he even knew that the man who looked like Curtis was in reality the Masked Detective.

"Curtis"—Diggs' voice contained the knell of doom—"step over here."

The Masked Detective obeyed. He did not even have a gun on him. It was a risky business to be armed when in the presence of this strange league of crooks.

"I don't know what you mean, sir," the fake Curtis remonstrated in a feeble voice.

"Don't you, though?" Diggs sneered. "Yesterday there was a police raid upon our meeting place. You disappeared before that raid took place. I suppose that you became frightened when that fool of a gardener dragged his employer in and I ordered him killed. In the excitement, you slipped out and notified the police. Everyone else was accounted for."

"But I—" the fake Curtis protested weakly.

"Whatever you're trying to say is a lie," Diggs snapped. "Over the phone I indicated that we had fled through a rear exit, and you fell for it by admitting you had taken that same route with the rest of us. But we went over the rooftops and I was the last to go. That's why I'm sure you got away. For a time I thought perhaps you were responsible for the fact that Gwenn still lives, but I'm satisfied that Makin double-crossed us and sold out for a few thousand dollars. Curtis, there is one penalty for dishonesty in our ranks. You saw what happened just now—to that fool lying on the floor. That is my answer to treachery."

The Masked Detective realized that Diggs had no idea that he was doubling for the real Curtis. That gave him some measure of relief, but not much. Diggs intended that he should die. But if the leader of this group started an attack, the Masked Detective was determined to sell his life dearly, to concentrate on Diggs and wipe him out, even though the others exacted the supreme penalty from the Masked Detective himself.

He backed away rapidly. He spoke in a loud voice.

"Yes—yes I did notify the police!" he shouted defiantly. "I did what all of you others have hoped to do. Diggs holds you in the palm of his hand. You can see he has no mercy. Sooner or later he'll treat you as he intends to treat me. Here is your chance! Help me fight him! Help me, and help yourselves at the same time. What good will his precious documents concerning your faults be to him if he's in our hands? Use your brains—be men for once!"

DIGGS YELLED in rage and swept forward. The others moved away quickly, taking no part in the affair. The Masked Detective was stumped for the time being. If he used his feet to overpower Diggs, he would give away the fact that he was not Curtis, would reveal himself as the Masked Detective, possibly, for it was well known what an expert the mysterious Masked Detective was at fighting with his feet. Any kind of superior fighting, in fact, would be a dead give-away that he was not Curtis. For Curtis was, to all appearances, a rather old man and not too strong. Still, the Masked Detective decided to fight Diggs, and to keep in character unless Diggs indicated that he meant to kill quickly.

Diggs seized the supposed Curtis in an agonizing grasp and the Masked Detective struggled weakly and quite feebly.

"The croaking of a desperate man, eh?" Diggs jeered, and shoved the fake Curtis against the wall. "You're such a pure and holy type, Curtis, that I shall arrange things so that when you die there will be the stigma of a murderer upon you. You shall serve me well at the same time. You men there—hold him. He's as weak and shaken as a kitten."

Three men grabbed "Curtis" while Diggs rubbed his hands and sneered.

"We'll get the gems belonging to Curtis' master, and we'll arrange things so it will seem that Curtis himself took the jewels and disposed of them," he promised. "Bring a car around.... Locke, Bryant, Jenkins— come with me into the next room. I'll tell you how to handle this affair."

The three men who followed Diggs were not like the others who remained. The Masked Detective had sized up most of the treacherous servants, and realized these three stood apart. They were far more dangerous and therefore probably in Diggs' confidence.

"You fools—and cowards," the supposed Curtis berated the others who closed in around him as soon as Diggs and his three lieutenants were gone. "You had a chance to act, and you failed."

"Shut up!" one man snapped. "We couldn't help it. Diggs has evidence on all of us. It's hidden somewhere, and he's arranged it so that if he is killed the papers will reach the police. And you don't quite understand things either, Curtis. The three men who followed Diggs are servants— yes—but they are confessed murderers, too. They wouldn't hesitate to kill again, and each one of them carries a gun. You saw what one of them did already. If we had followed your suggestion, they would have shot us down like tenpins. We're sorry for you, but that's as far as we can go."

In five minutes the three killers came out of the other room. Diggs did not appear again, and the Masked Detective wondered why. Perhaps he was off somewhere to establish an alibi, but that fact hardly made the Masked Detective's lot any the easier. Guns were jabbed into his ribs.

"We'll go back to your house now, Mr. Curtis," one of the men growled. "Make a false move and you'll be blown in half. It hurts badly to die of a bullet in the abdomen. Remember that!"

CHAPTER XIII

THE TABLES TURNED

DURING THE short ride to Bruce Wickham's home the guns in the hands of Diggs' three lieutenants were significantly displayed. Apparently this affair was not just a sudden decision on Diggs' part. He knew the house would be empty—the other servants away and Wickham himself out.

They drove boldly into the garage. The Masked Detective was forced out of the car and marched through the rear door of the house, after it was unlocked with the key taken from "Curtis." They led him to the spacious living room and, at a gestured command, he sat down. So did the others.

The man named Jenkins seemed to be in charge. He kept glancing at his wrist watch and growing more impatient by the minute. One crook took up a post near the front door, and watched the street intently.

The Masked Detective remained fully in character as Curtis. He kept rubbing his hands, loosening his collar with a forefinger. Now and then he shivered, but all the while his mind remained calm and he watched for a chance to turn the tables on these men. His life was at stake now. Just what they intended to do was a mystery, but the Masked Detective no longer cared if Diggs discovered the man he took for Curtis was a masquerader.

His two captors, however, remained constantly alert. So did the one at the front door. Guns were held in readiness. The Masked Detective had no chance in the face of those weapons.

Then the phone rang and the jangle of the bell made everyone jump. Jenkins answered it, speaking in a low voice.

"He's leaving in five minutes?" the Masked Detective heard Jenkins say. "That gives us just fifteen to get set. Okay—we'll be ready." Jenkins hung up and arose. "Come on, Curtis," he snapped. "You're going to open the boss's safe. You know the combination, but just in case you want us to think you don't—we know it, too. The chauffeur who works here didn't spend all his time in the garage."

"Then—then you'll have to tell me what it is," the fake Curtis half-blubbered. "I—I'm so nervous I can't think. You're not really going to kill me, are you? I—I'm just a helpless old man. I made a mistake trying to fight Diggs, and I realize that now. You won't kill me, will you?"

"That all depends"—Jenkins jabbed him with his gun—"on how you act. Open the panel that conceals the safe. Hurry—or by hell you'll get it right away."

The Masked Detective knew where the safe was hidden. He had made that one of his first objectives. In a moment the shining surface of the small vault was revealed. Jenkins gave the combination, and "Curtis" opened the safe with fingers that trembled so badly he missed the tumblers twice.

"Now reach in and take out those nice plush boxes," Jenkins ordered. "They contain about sixty thousand dollars worth of fine gems.... That's right, Curtis. Now open the boxes and offer us the gems like a good fellow.... Fine! You might make a good member of the league at that. Now walk over to the corner of the room nearest the front of the house. March—did you hear me?"

The Masked Detective obeyed. He still could not figure out their intentions, and only with effort restrained himself from putting into action a desperate attempt to get clear. Apparently Wickham was on his way home and the phone call had tipped off these three killers to that effect.

The man at the door hoarsely whispered a warning.

"Here he comes! He's stopping in the driveway. Get set. I'm putting out all the lights here. Take care of the others."

INSTANTLY BOTH crooks seized the Masked Detective's wrists and held them firmly. Someone walked up on the front porch. There were voices, and Jenkins rasped a whispered oath.

"Damn it, he's not alone! We'll make use of the fact though, by letting whoever is with him see Curtis. We're all ready."

Every light in the house was darkened. A key rattled in the lock, turned, and the door was opened. Wickham came in first. As he reached for the light switch, the man guarding the door went into action. He used some kind of a weapon that made little noise, but had deadly effect.

It crunched against Wickham's head and he went down with nothing more than a soft moan.

The fake Curtis was shoved forward. Some light streamed through the open door. The Masked Detective had a glimpse of Wickham's guest, a short, stubby little man with shell-rimmed glasses and a look of intense horror on his face. Then the little man wheeled and began running like mad.

"Good!" Jenkins said. "He'll spend five minutes trying to find a policeman."

Jenkins drew a knife from his pocket. He pulled the Masked Detective's arm up and by using pressure on the wrist forced his fist open. He thrust the handle of the knife into it, let go of the wrist and pressed the fingers of the supposed Curtis against the knife handle.

The Masked Detective knew now what Jenkins' clever plans were. Wickham was unconscious on the floor. His guest had seen the face of the man he would swear to be Curtis, the butler. When the police arrived, they would find Wickham dead, with a knife in his heart. The butler would be dead also—apparently a suicide, and his prints alone would be on the knife handle.

It was time for the Masked Detective to drop his pose. As Jenkins forced the knife handle into his palm, the Masked Detective really did seize it. With a savage wrench he tore himself loose from Jenkins' grasp. The crook gave a bleat of alarm and started to raise his gun.

The knife flashed, and the blade sliced through Jenkins' forearm. The gun fell to the floor. The other crook stepped back to aim better. He had started to bring down the gun into position when a foot came up from the darkness. The gun went sailing high, hit the ceiling, then clattered to the polished floor beyond the edges of the rug.

That same foot flashed again. The second crook straightened out, careened backward and fell. He did not move a muscle after that.

The third man, who was in the hallway, had a better chance to act. The darkness prevented him from distinguishing his target well, though. Inside, Jenkins, himself injured by the knife, saw one of his men go down under the attack of this elderly, white-haired butler. For a second he could hardly believe his eyes. Then when he saw that footwork, and because he had a little more intelligence than the average crook, he suddenly realized just how he had been tricked. This man was the Masked Detective! He had heard how that Nemesis of all crooks fought with his feet.

Jenkins decided the healthiest spot for him was somewhere in the wilds of Borneo, and he proceeded to start for some such place. Wheeling, he made a dive for the door—and made a fatal mistake. The crook in the hallway saw a shadowy form hurtling toward him. His gun blasted as rapidly as he could trigger the weapon.

Jenkins stopped as the pellets of lead smashed through his body. He tried to talk, tried to make his fellow crook realize who he was. It did not matter, however, because three seconds later Jenkins was dead.

THE MAN with the gun did not wait to see what happened after that. Outside on the street, Wickham's guest was yelling bloody murder at the top of his lungs. The crook sailed through the door and did not even know that the Masked Detective was coming after him.

On the porch steps, however, the Masked Detective stopped. Wickham's stubby friend, accompanied by two patrolmen, was running toward the house. The patrolmen had their guns ready. The Masked Detective did not want to suffer Jenkins' fate and be killed by his own friends. He promptly elevated his hands.

"Keep 'em there!" one of the patrolmen snapped. "Joe, go inside and see what the devil's happened."

"I can tell you," the Masked Detective said calmly. "Mr. Wickham is lying in the hallway unconscious. One of the men who intended to murder him is in the living room, also out cold. Another crook is dead, shot by a third killer who got away."

Wickham's friend stepped closer and shoved his spectacled face nearer to the Masked Detective's.

"That's the man who attacked Wickham," he declared. "I saw him in the hall. He's the man, all right."

One of the patrolmen came back from inside the house, his face stern and uncompromising.

"Mister," he said, glowering at the Masked Detective, "you certainly didn't lie about what I'd find in there. Keep him under your gun, Joe, while I call for an ambulance, the medical examiner and a morgue wagon. One of those guys is awful dead—four or five slugs right through his chest."

"Just a moment," the Masked Detective put in. "While you're at it, have Sergeant Gleason come down here, too. That's most important, because he knows something about this case."

In fifteen minutes the quiet of Wickham's home was broken by the arrival of all kinds of help. Gleason took charge, glaring at the man he believed to be Curtis.

"Okay," he said to the supposed butler. "You better have a good story. Wickham will come to his senses pretty soon. He'll know what this is all about, so don't lie."

"Why, Sergeant," said the man who looked like Curtis, "I've never lied to you yet. That's why I asked you to come here. I'm the Masked Detective."

Gleason gaped for a moment. Then he quickly cleared the room.

"For the love of Mike, what kind of a mess is this?" he demanded.

The Masked Detective grinned.

"I took the place of Wickham's butler to trap these crooks. I got one of'em—that man lying on the floor over there. They intended to murder Wickham, steal his jewels, and put the blame on me, supposing me to be Wickham's butler. And the dead man has the gems.... Say, just who is the stranger who yelled for the cops?"

Gleason kept shaking his head from side to side.

"I can't figure it. There are three guys here and you got clear. Wickham's friend? Oh, him—his name is Denny. He is some kind of a business consultant. Works for Wickham.... Hey, that egg you kicked in the teeth is coming out of it."

The Masked Detective walked over to the side of the crook, lifted him by one arm and dropped him into a chair. This was Locke, or so he had been called by Diggs before they had led the Masked Detective to what they hoped was his doom. The crook called Bryant had got away.

"WELL"—THE MASKED DETECTIVE straddled another chair as he spoke to Locke—"you look rather surprised to see me still alive. I'll make that surprise better. I'm not Curtis, Wickham's butler. I'm the Masked Detective, and this man at my side is Sergeant Gleason of the Homicide Squad. I might add that homicide includes murder— of which you're guilty—and that they keep an uncomfortable instrument of death in our prisons for rats like you. Would you like to talk? No doubt about it, eh? Good! What do you know about Diggs?"

"Nothing," Locke answered in a surly voice. "He found out something about me. I had to help him or he'd have turned me over to the police. I didn't want to kill anyone. He just wouldn't give me a break."

Sergeant Gleason walked over to the telephone.

"I'm going to send out an alarm for Diggs," he announced. "It's high time that bum was tossed into the clink."

"Wait," the Masked Detective said. "I want him for myself, and I'll be on the way in two minutes. You"—he turned again to the shivering crook—"tell me what Diggs is up to—and tell the truth! Without any delay."

"We—we have plans to take over a lot of money and jewels," Locke said. "Mostly from rich people who hire members of the league as servants. That's all I know. I swear it."

"What does the Devil's Stepladder mean?" the Masked Detective snapped at him.

"The—what?" Locke gaped. "I don't know. Never heard of it before."

The Masked Detective shrugged and turned to Gleason.

"Hold him," he said. "Watch Wickham and his friend Denny, too. I'm going after Diggs."

CHAPTER XIV

THE MAN
WHO FAINTED

SOME ASTOUNDED-LOOKING policemen stood by as the Masked Detective, still disguised as Curtis, hurried out the front door. Gleason shouted commands that he was not to be stopped. The Masked Detective jumped into Wickham's car parked in the driveway. He sent it rolling toward the house where Diggs worked.

One of the three crooks had managed to get away, and he had been scared stiff when he disappeared into the night. There was a chance that he might be so frightened that he would hardly think to warn Diggs. If that was the case, then Diggs was due for an uncomfortable surprise.

The Masked Detective stopped the car in front of Frank Alden's home. He ran up on the porch, quietly took a look through the window of the living room and saw Frank Alden, alias Jim Bartlett, nervously pacing the floor. The Masked Detective extracted a bunch of keys from his pocket, tried four of them without making any noise. The fifth opened the door.

Alden whirled around as he heard a slight cough. He made a motion to head for the desk at the other end of the room, but something told him this white-haired man in the rather disheveled livery of a servant might get there first.

"Good evening, Mr. Alden," the Masked Detective said. "I'm looking for Diggs. You will please help me find him. Notice that I keep one hand in my coat pocket. There's a most efficient gun there and if it went off, you wouldn't like it."

"Diggs is gone!" Alden half shouted. "I don't know where he is."

"Perhaps you do, if you think hard enough. Mr. Alden, the jig is up, as they say in the comic strips. I know you are Jim Bartlett—in fact, I know all about you. We're going to search this house, and then have an informative little talk."

The Masked Detective went through the place from top to bottom. Alden certainly had told the truth. Diggs had cleared out. Back in the living room, Alden sat down wearily.

"I'm not exactly a fool," he said in a tired voice. "That getup doesn't deceive me. You're no servant. Who are you?"

"The Masked Detective," came the quiet reply.

Alden groaned. "I should have known. When that reporter came yesterday and introduced himself, I remembered that he was associated with the Masked Detective. As soon as I missed the vase, I knew what had happened. My fingerprints were finally to be checked against police files. I could have run away, you know, but I'm sick of running away. I served my prison term. I've committed no further crime and—well, I'll confess to one thing. If you had found Diggs here, it would have been as a corpse. I was ready to kill him.

"That man didn't work for me—he ruled me. Somehow he found out about my past, ingratiated himself into my sympathy, and got a job as my servant. Then he put the screws on me. I've paid him thousands of dollars. I've taken his insults, but for the last time. You're not a regular law officer, so I'm not afraid to talk to you. Diggs deserves to die if any man does."

"That," the Masked Detective retorted, "isn't exactly news. Just sit exactly as you are. I'm afraid you won't like this indignity, Mr. Alden, but it's necessary."

THE MASKED DETECTIVE stood over Alden and suddenly reached down, grasped a handful of his hair and tugged. The hair did not come loose. "Sorry," the Masked Detective said. "I did not see you and Diggs at the same time. I thought possibly you might be playing two rôles—that of master and servant."

Alden looked up with a strange smile on his lips.

"Then that's settled anyway."

"Oh, no, it isn't," the Masked Detective countered. "Diggs could have been wearing some kind of a cleverly constructed shield to hide real hair and make him seem bald. You're not out of the woods yet, Alden. Just what did Diggs have on you?"

"The crime I committed, years ago. The crime of which you know, from my fingerprints. I was trying to live it down. I—well, I did conceal assets, more than the authorities ever found out. When I got out of prison, I salvaged some of the hidden cash, took a few plunges into the market and my luck held. I'm rich now. I'll promise to pay whatever debts I accumulated those years back, even though they were legally wiped out by a bankruptcy court. Diggs threatened me with exposure, though, and—"

"And possibly with something that concerned the Devil's Stepladder as well, eh, Alden?"

Alden frowned. "I don't quite understand."

"Then you're no exception," the Masked Detective said. "Nobody else seems to understand either. I really don't know what to do with you, Alden. You paid a certain penalty for a crime. Diggs made you suffer further. You seem to be in earnest about things, so I'll take a chance. What you have told me is confidential—so long as you are willing to cooperate.... Now, about Diggs again. How does it happen that I did not see you together—that, in fact, I've learned you two were never seen together?"

"Because he insisted upon it," Alden declared. "He made me do the damnedest things sometimes. I know how crazy this sounds, but it's the truth."

The Masked Detective walked toward the door.

"If Diggs should come back," he said, "phone the police at once. And be careful of him. He's as poisonous as a cobra and twice as treacherous."

The Masked Detective went back to Wickham's residence. Gleason was there, talking to Wickham whose head was bandaged, and to Denny, the still pop-eyed man whose presence had helped to save the Masked Detective's life.

Wickham looked at the Masked Detective and shook his head doubtfully.

"Do you mean to tell me that I've been giving orders to the Masked Detective?" he asked. "That you aren't Curtis? I swear there's no differ-ence."

"Ah, but there is." The Masked Detective smiled. "If I had been the real Curtis, you'd be on the way to the morgue by now, Mr. Wickham. The real Curtis will be back before morning. Don't be harsh with him. He still isn't aware of what's happened.... Now let's get down to business. The men who were prepared to kill you knew exactly when you left for home. Where were you, Mr. Wickham, and whom did you see just before you left?"

"Denny and I had dinner together," Wickham answered. "At the Century Club. I don't recall seeing anyone else who—"

"I do," Denny chimed in. "That crack on the head made you forget, Wickham. Dwight Gwenn saw us leave. He was sitting in the lobby reading a newspaper."

"I—I don't seem to recall," Wickham said vaguely. "My head still hurts. Perhaps I ought to lie down."

"In just a moment," the Masked Detective said. "One more thing. Did you ever connect the Devil's Stepladder with these happenings, Mr.—"

WICKHAM SAT bolt upright, his eyes wide open with the shock of a complete surprise. His face was flushed, like that of a boy caught in a lie. Then, with a moan, he slumped out of the chair and curled up on the floor.

Denny threw an angry glance at the Masked Detective and bent down to assist his friend. Without looking up he said:

"I don't know what you meant, but with Wickham's condition such as it is, I hardly think you should have shocked him. I've been his business consultant for months, and I know him well. He has never mentioned anything about a Devil's Stepladder to me."

"Save your breath," Sergeant Gleason said, as he helped pick up Wickham and place him on a davenport. "The Masked Detective faded away right after Wickham took his nosedive. Like you, Mr. Denny, I haven't the slightest idea what the Devil's Stepladder is about, but it certainly struck home with Wickham. Better call a doctor. Our brand of first aid doesn't seem to be so good. Something tells me he's going to have a pretty excited patient on his hands when Wickham comes to."

Denny went over to Wickham's desk, ran through an indexed telephone file attached to the base of the phone and found the name of Dr. Gary. He dialed the number, asked if Gary was Wickham's regular medical advisor, and when he received an affirmative answer, requested the doctor to come at once.

Gleason was busy meanwhile. With the aid of one patrolman, he picked up Wickham and carried him to a bedroom upstairs. Then he came down again and sat glumly waiting for the doctor.

"Wickham knows the answer to this business," Denny offered. "I spoke hastily a moment or so ago, I'm afraid. He did mention the Devil's Stepladder to me earlier this evening, but he didn't elaborate on it, and changed the conversation so quickly I was not able to grasp what he was talking about. Why doesn't that doctor hurry?"

Twenty-five minutes later a big car pulled up. It carried marker plates bearing the initials M.D., indicating that they had been issued to a physician. Dr. Gary proved to be a dapper little man who breezed straight upstairs behind a patrolman who offered to lead the way. He returned in five minutes.

"The patient will sleep for a while—very necessary," he said. "If anything further develops, call me at once. There is a concussion of the brain—not serious—but it might bear watching."

"Don't worry, Doc," Gleason grunted. "Wickham happens to be a most important man right now. We'll watch him, all right."

Gleason relaxed, but Denny kept walking around the room nervously. They heard brakes squeal in front of the house. A taxi had pulled up and a glance through a window showed them a man getting out. He was bareheaded and there was blood on his forehead. He ran into the house.

"Where is he? Wickham, I mean!"

"Just who are you and how come that bump on your head?" Gleason snapped. "I was assaulted and robbed! I'm Dr. Gary. I received a call—"

Gleason's eyes popped wide in horror. He gave a shout, raced up the stairs and ran into the room where Wickham lay in bed. A patrolman sat across the room reading a newspaper. Gleason pulled the covers away, took one look and groaned. Denny and Dr. Gary barged in. The doctor made a quick examination.

"Why, he's dead. Look! That spot of blood on his throat! It looks to me as though he were given a hypodermic injection directly into the jugular vein! By a rank amateur at that."

"Fooled!" Gleason groaned. "The killer walked in here, murdered Wickham under our very noses and then calmly walked out again. Mr. Denny—we're a couple of fatheads!"

CHAPTER XV

MURDER AGAIN

MEANWHILE THE Masked Detective, still disguised as Curtis, the butler, returned to Rex Parker's apartment. There the disguise was quickly removed and, concealing all traces of the clothing he had worn, Parker donned a neat dark suit.

Again leaving the apartment, he got a cheap coupé out of a public garage nearby. This car was registered in Rex Parker's name, and he never used it when in the guise of the Masked Detective.

It was time to set the real Curtis free, and Parker headed out of the city to the shack in which the butler was held. He felt particularly cheerful about the way things were going. Whatever the Devil's Stepladder meant, it certainly had knocked Wickham over. He had left Sergeant Gleason in charge at the Wickham house, so Wickham, well guarded now, was safe. As soon as he recovered his wits, Parker meant to make him talk. Perhaps even Curtis knew something.

Driving past the outskirts of town, Parker stopped the car in a clump of trees towering above an old shack. He opened the door of the small building, stepped inside and looked around. Curtis was lying on a cot in the back room. He was apparently asleep. Parker lit a match, applied the flame to the wick of a lantern and, holding this high, he approached Curtis.

"Everything is all right now, Curtis," he said cheerfully. "The Masked Detective sent me to free you and—incidentally—to reward you for the punishment you've had to take. I'll cut those ropes away. Wake up!"

The form on the cot did not stir. Rex Parker felt the first pangs of fear. He grabbed Curtis by the shoulder, turned him on his back—and swore softly. Curtis was dead! He had been stabbed through the throat.

Parker looked around. On a table nearby was the remains of a lunch. Winnie must have returned to the shack with food for Curtis. She had been trailed. Of course, that was it! Some of these crooks knew her. For a moment his heart stopped beating. Had Winnie been taken then? Was she in danger once more?

Parker headed pellmell out of the shack, but he stopped short. Four men were in the front room. Each held a gun trained on him. They were well dressed and bore no resemblance to ordinary thugs. The spokesman had that same damnably polished manner of a servant that Parker had already run into.

"Good evening, Mr. Rex Parker," the man said suavely. "You were unpleasantly surprised a moment ago, I take it. We were sorry to have been forced to kill Curtis, but you see—he might have known too much. Turn around please, and keep your hands high while we search you. It's too bad that your colleague, the Masked Detective, didn't put in an appearance. But perhaps we can remedy that."

Parker was quickly searched. Then his wrists were bound behind his back and they led him to where a big car was parked. He was forced into it and two of the crooks sat on either side of him while the other pair occupied the front seat.

"Listen, you oily heels!" Parker snapped. "What happened to the girl you trailed out here? If she has been harmed, so help me—"

"Please be quiet," one of the men said. "The girl was not molested. We should have taken her prisoner except for the fact that if she had been missed, you would naturally then have notified the Masked Detective to be on guard. We're going to a certain house where you will be held temporarily. While we are on the way, you might be thinking seriously about revealing to us the identity of the Masked Detective. The only way to save your own life is by bringing your friend and mentor into the open. If you refuse, I assure you things will hardly be pleasant—and there is always the girl whom we can get at any time we choose. Reflect carefully, if you please."

REX PARKER did. He was in a bad spot. These four men were not the ordinary type of servant who belonged to Diggs' organization. They were like the three who had plotted Wickham's murder. Ruthless and deadly. In full accord with the plans of their superior and willing to obey him in everything.

Unquestionably they would resort to torture. They would capture Winnie, if necessary, and use her to try and make him talk. Yet what could he say? They wanted the Masked Detective, and they had him, although none of them possessed the remotest idea of that.

The car turned into one of the poorer sections of the city, nosed down an alley, and came to a stop in a courtyard. It was black dark here. Parker was ordered out and led into an old tenement house. They marched him up the stairs to the second floor, unlocked a door, and entered a cheaply furnished rent. Its windows faced the street, but Parker was given no chance to approach them.

He sat down on a davenport that creaked under his weight and emitted a cloud of dust. Lights were turned on. The four men took up positions around the room and maintained strict silence.

After almost an hour had gone by, someone tapped on the door in a signal. One of the men opened it, and Diggs walked in. He was dressed as usual, with that stiff hat set on top of his bald head. Rex stared at him, trying to penetrate the icy surface of this man, trying to find out if he would be disguised. Diggs rubbed his hands together in satisfaction and leered.

"So we have Mr. Parker with us. Excellent! Of course, Mr. Parker will tell us who the Masked Detective is, and how we can reach him."

"I couldn't if I wanted to." Parker growled. "I've never seen the man's face. He always wears a mask whenever we meet."

Diggs smiled confidently.

"I expected that answer. Naturally your knowledge of his identity would be a weak spot in his armor of anonymity, so I believe you, Mr. Parker. However, you do know how to bring him into the open. His only contact with the world is through you. Therefore why not save yourself a great deal of pain and trouble by telling us just how this is done?"

"Why should I," Parker countered, "when you'll probably murder me the moment my information is out?"

"Ah, but death is sweet compared to prolonged agony, Mr. Parker. I promise that the moment we have contacted the Masked Detective to our complete satisfaction you will be released. You are only a small particle so far as I am concerned. By the time you get back to your paper, we shall have accomplished our purpose. Unfortunately the Masked Detective may know too much of our plans and already have a way to stop us. Therefore we must first eliminate him and then we can carry through our plans to our satisfaction. You will be a prisoner for perhaps three days only."

"Nothing doing," Parker snapped. "I'm dumb."

Diggs smirked, and rubbed his hands some more. He turned to one of the crooks.

"Take the car and go at once to the offices of the *Comet*. Park at a convenient place. I shall phone Miss Winnie Bligh and inform her that Rex Parker needs her at once. She will come through the door immediately, and when she does—shoot her down."

"Hey—hey wait!" Parker yelled as the crook started for the exit. "You can't do that! She doesn't even know what this is all about."

"Well?" Diggs asked smoothly. "Will you contact the Masked Detective then? It's your last chance."

Parker nodded glumly.

"All right, I'll do it. It takes time though. I have to advertise for him—in the *Comet*. My agreement with him is simply to expose those he works against. I'm not supposed to die for his sake, or let a girl be killed to shield him. He can take care of himself, I guess. Hand me some paper. I'll write the ad. Insert it in the first morning edition of the *Comet*. He'll answer right away—by the time the third edition hits the streets."

HIS HANDS were unbound, but two guns drilled into his ribs. He was furnished with paper and a fountain pen. He looked up at Diggs.

"Where do you want to meet him?" he asked.

Diggs was showing his elation.

"Shall we say, near the monument to a dog—the leader of a dog-sled team which carried serum to sick people in the far north. It's in one of the darkest portions of the public park. An ideal spot. Yes, that's the place,"

Parker wrote slowly while Diggs bent over his shoulder to watch him:

> Felix: Imperative you come home. Mother very sick. Family has moved, but meet me at ten tonight. I'll be waiting in Central Park near monument to Alaskan husky dog. Will take you home. Acknowledge. R.P.

Diggs rapidly drew on a pair of gloves, picked up the note and read it again. He looked down at Parker.

"Of course this note contains no element of trickery? Because if it does, the girl will be the first to suffer."

"There's no trick," Parker groaned. "Don't you think I know when I'm licked? Bring me the morning editions when they appear. I'll spot the Masked Detective's answer."

Diggs signaled with one hand and Parker was quickly tied up again. Diggs left immediately and the four guards took up shifts of two each while the other pair slept. Parker dozed, too, forcing himself to get rest. He would need to be alert and ready when things happened.

In the morning, one of the men shook him awake. Several editions of the *Comet* were placed on a table along with some lukewarm food. He studied the papers while he ate. He was unbound, to feed himself, but all four crooks hovered close by.

"Sometimes," Parker explained, "they insert small personal ads like the one the Masked Detective would use, almost any place in the paper. Here—look! This is the answer!"

It was a single line of type that read:

> Meet you as requested. Felix.

"Get in touch with Diggs right away," one of the crooks told another. "He'll want to know about this."

Parker picked up the paper.

"Say, you fellows don't mind if I read, do you?" he drawled. "It's kind of tough sitting here with nothing to do."

"Help yourself," he was told. "Just be careful, that's all."

Parker walked over to the davenport, sat down, and crossed his legs. He read the front page without knowing a word that flashed before his eyes. The crooks paid little attention to him as he slowly turned the pages.

In the center of the paper, sandwiched between a doctor's column and a mess of kitchen hints, was Winnie Bligh's daily column on advice to the lovelorn. As Parker read it, his face betrayed none of the excitement that surged within him. There was a letter, presumably from someone who had sought Winnie's advice and was now acknowledging the worth of it. It read:

Dear Miss Bligh:

Things turned out just as you predicted. Love overcomes all obstacles. My parents refused to allow me to see the boy I love even though I am of age. They kept me a veritable prisoner in my own home. Taking your hint to contact him I managed to smuggle a letter out. Whenever my cruel stepfather was away from the house, I managed to paste a round piece of newspaper in the middle of the upper window pane. He saw it and knew it was safe to come and see me. He brought a lawyer one night and I signed papers which finally effected my release. Can you imagine how simple it all was—just a round piece of newspaper stuck in the window? Thousands of people saw it, but only one knew what it meant.

THERE WAS more in the same vein, but Parker did not bother to read it. He turned to the sport pages, and finally flung the newspaper on the davenport beside him. Glancing at the windows fronting the street, he saw that the shades were the heavy, opaque kind.

The crook who had been sent to call Diggs came back.

"He'll be here in a little while to formulate the final plans," he announced. "This is the beginning of the end for the Masked Detective. I always said he was vulnerable, that he would have a weak spot. This reporter was it. There couldn't possibly have been any tricks pulled. We know the Masked Detective will be at the rendezvous and then—"

Diggs arrived in about an hour. He nodded to Parker and on his steely features was a triumphant smile.

"Tie his hands again," he ordered. "Never mind his feet. He can't walk anywhere except around the room. Then come into the next room with me. There is no use letting him know our intentions."

"But perhaps he might—" One of the crooks seemed doubtful.

Diggs waved a hand.

"What can he do? He knows very well that if he breaks a window to attract attention, or starts screaming for help, we will kill him instantly and also take good care of that girl friend of his."

CHAPTER XVI

DEATH LISTENS IN

PARKER'S HANDS were tied again and in a moment he was alone in the room. There was no time to lose. Rex managed to get enough play with his bound hands to reach the newspaper and tear a rough circle out of one page. He got up, tiptoed quietly to the table. The dish of oatmeal which they had given him was still there. It had dried out to a sticky mass. Parker forced the middle of the round chunk of paper into it.

Then he went to the window. Now came the most difficult part of his work—to reach the upper sash so that his signal would not be seen by Diggs or his men.

He hooked a chair with his foot, pulled it as quietly as possible to the window and clambered up on it. If he should be caught now, everything was lost. From the next room he could hear Diggs' voice purring smoothly as the cadaverous leader laid his plans for murder....

When Diggs and the men came back, Rex Parker was lying on the davenport. The newspaper was wadded into a mass at the foot of the davenport and he was methodically kicking it to pieces with his feet. Diggs stood there looking down at him for a moment. He seemed undecided what to do. Then he gave a snort.

"Good-by, Mr. Parker," he said. "I am sure you have resorted to no tricks and therefore you shall be repaid in kindness." Diggs turned to one of his men. "Wait about half an hour after I leave—then the knife. Quickly, so there will be no pain. That is his reward. He worked closely with the Masked Detective and he would have been the first to gloat over our failure, so he must be considered an enemy."

Diggs turned on his heel and stalked away. Parker was watching him narrowly, noting how he always seemed to drag his feet along, making scraping sounds with them. Then Diggs was gone.

One of the crooks glanced at his watch and, unable to resist an impulse to show his power, drew a knife. He pressed a button and the blade slid out of the handle with a snap. Rex Parker shuddered and turned his face toward the back of the davenport.

He counted the seconds methodically, like a man in a death cell waiting for that inevitable moment. It was almost time.

Then firm hands gripped Parker's shoulder and turned him around until he looked up into the face of the killer. The man seized Parker by the collar, yanked the button away, and pulled open the neck of the shirt. The knife started down. Parker—with arms tied, helpless now in every respect, since the first act of the men left guarding him after Diggs had gone had been to tie his feet also—looked death full in the face during that ghastly moment.

Then a gun roared. Again and again the explosions reverberated through the house. A woman cried out in horror. The man with the knife jerked with each blast of the gun. The knife he held slowly slipped out of his hand, fell across Parker's chest. The would-be killer followed, draping himself on top of his intended victim, pinning him down.

Only for a second, though. With a mighty heave Parker hurled the corpse off him—and then went suddenly limp. Sergeant Gleason, a smoking gun in his fist, was threatening the only other member of the murder quartette who still stood on his feet.

Winnie Bligh elbowed a path through several uniformed patrolmen and rushed straight toward Rex Parker. She saw that he was tied and tugged at the knots, crying for help in an exasperated voice. When Parker was finally free and his arms were about her, she sighed in contentment. She had eyes neither for the staring cops nor the dead and wounded crooks. Nothing else mattered but that Rex Parker was saved.

"I GOT your note—the ad," she whispered. "I knew it meant you were in trouble. Oh, Rex, every policeman in the city—every detective, radio car, every mailman, sidewalk inspector, even firemen—they were all looking for a window which had a piece of newspaper pasted to it. I was so afraid you wouldn't read my column or understand it—or that they wouldn't let you see it."

"Neatly done." He grinned down at her. "Worked, too, although not a second too soon. Naturally, Diggs will know better than to keep the rendezvous in the park now. Winnie—I've got to find Wickham. He's in danger. They killed poor Curtis. Some of the rats must have followed you here when you delivered food to him. They killed him because they were afraid he knew too much of their plans. Wickham must know even more. He's in danger!"

"Hold it, Rex." Gleason approached and spoke in a low voice. "Wickham is dead, too. I'll explain later—when we've cleaned out this place."

"What of Gwenn?" Parker asked. "Are you sure he's all right?"

"I saw him about an hour ago, and I doubled the guard around his house," Gleason said. "Don't worry about him."

Two of the crooks were dead, another badly wounded, and the fourth so terrified that he could make nothing but squealing sounds. Parker took this man by the arm, led him into the next room and plopped him into a chair. He closed the door and eyed the man with hatred shining in his eyes.

"Get a grip on yourself," he warned. "You're going to answer some questions. And don't forget—you stood by while your pal was getting set to slit my throat. I wouldn't mind whacking your ears off. In fact, I'd enjoy it. Now—where does Diggs hole up, when he isn't working for Alden?"

"I don't know," the crook whined. "They never told me much of anything. All I know is that there is going to be a big job pulled sometime tomorrow night. Diggs has men and women planted in five hundred places all over the country. They'll strike at the same time. Diggs was afraid the Masked Detective was wise and that's why he wanted to wipe him out. But I haven't anything against the Masked Detective—or against you either. I couldn't help what they made me do."

"Funny how all of you have the same sob story," Parker ground out. "Diggs blackmailed you into helping him is all any of you can say. Didn't it ever occur to you that he'd only lead you into deeper and more serious crime? Why didn't you go to the police with the story and take your chances, rather than turn into an abettor of murder?" His eyes narrowed thoughtfully. "So the big job comes tomorrow night, eh? What'll you bet it won't come off? Maybe Diggs will take care of the Devil's Stepladder matter at the same time, eh?"

The man just stared for a moment.

"I guess I didn't hear you right, sir. I thought you said something about a stepladder, and the devil."

"Skip it," Parker snapped. "Get up and walk ahead of me. If you think of anything else you might like to talk about, have the turnkey phone and I'll come over."

WHEN EVERYONE but Sergeant Gleason and Winnie were gone, Rex Parker began a careful search of the premises.

"I don't expect to find much," he told them. "I think they happened on this tenement and just moved in…. Say, that was a clever scheme by which Wickham was killed. Shows that Diggs is nobody's fool."

"When I lay eyes on that guy that killed Wickham," Gleason promised, "I'll shoot first and ask questions later on. The boldness of that bum—or his mob. Denny and I were in the house, there were at least four patrolmen on deck—and that damn fake doctor just walked in with a professional air, murdered Wickham under the eyes of one of my men, and then coolly marched out again! That was done so well I think it must have been the ringleader of the mob himself who did it. Maybe Diggs, in a disguise…. Say, how do we stop that job from being pulled tomorrow night, Rex? We don't know what homes are controlled by crooked servants."

"I'll take care of that angle," Parker said, "by printing a front-page yarn and putting it on the nationwide press releases. I'll warn everyone with servants of whose integrity they aren't positive, not to bring home any valuables from the bank."

"But that's just staving it off," Gleason argued. "They'll pick another day later on and go through with it."

"Not when I'm finished," Parker promised grimly. "See you later, Sarge—and watch Gwenn. I'll see him later, as the Masked Detective. Gwenn is our one and only hope now."

There was nothing in the tenement that might furnish a single lead, as Rex Parker had prophesied. He was soon through with his search and heading for Winnie's car which was waiting on the street. He slid into the front seat beside her and she drove off for the *Comet* Building.

"We know about Diggs' plans anyhow, so far as the robberies are concerned," Parker said thoughtfully, "but darned if I can figure out this Devil's Stepladder that seems to be mixed up in the business. I'm sure Wickham would have told me if he'd lived. I'm not so sure about Gwenn."

"But Rex," Winnie argued, "what is Diggs' main theme in this affair? Remember that he has probably one of the largest, most intelligent and dangerous gangs in the history of crime at his fingertips. If he could pull something like he plans for tomorrow night, the profits would run into the millions. Perhaps the affair of the Devil's Stepladder is just a wrong steer meant to throw dust into your eyes and confuse the main issue—which is plain robbery."

"No, Winnie. Vogan was murdered because he knew too much. Wickham, and his butler, too, knew the same thing, whatever it is. That's why they were killed. It's my opinion that Diggs has either another identity or that he works for some as yet unknown person. Probably it all started with this league of crooked servants, but this other thing concerned with the Devil's Stepladder appeared, and Diggs is merely taking advantage of it.

"No question but that a great deal of money is involved. If we could only figure out what it means! The name of a book, a place, just a password—it could refer to anything. Well, disregarding those things for the moment—I won't forget what you did for me, Winnie."

"Tut," she said, "and tut. It merely evens things up a bit.... Here we are, Rex. Put everything you've got into that yarn. Give the facts so strongly that there will be no doubts in the minds of the people who are liable to be affected by Diggs' plans. You can do it."

"Okay—" he started to say.

"Captain Bligh," Winnie finished for him with a smile. "Rex, watch out for Diggs. He may go actually berserk when he learns you got away."

PARKER HURRIED to his typewriter, thrust a sheet of paper into the machine and pounded out a yarn. It gave all details about the plans of the league he had uncovered. It warned everyone to beware, especially of servants recently hired.

He wrote the story as though the Masked Detective had dictated most of it to him. After the yarn was dispatched to the desk, he leaned back and stared at the ceiling. It was his move now, once more. Gwenn seemed to be the pawn. If he refused to talk, then action must be taken through other sources.

Parker thought of William Price, the private detective with that unerring ability to unearth stolen jewels with such remarkable speed. Winnie's visit to him had resulted in swift action, indicating that Price had a toehold, at least, in the case. Price, therefore, became pawn Number Two.

Alden, alias Jim Bartlett, had either told all he knew or at least all he would admit knowing. Alden was still something of an unknown quantity.

Even Denny, Wickham's friend, cropped up in Rex Parker's mind. He remembered that Denny had spoken of seeing Gwenn at the club just before he and Wickham had left for home. Then there was that mysterious phone call received by the crooks who were setting a trap for Wickham. It indicated that they were to swing into action because Wickham was on his way.

Gwenn could have been responsible for that. Diggs might have been lurking around, too—or employees of the club might fall into the ranks of Diggs' forces.

CHAPTER XVII

DETECTIVE'S DOUBLE

GOING DIRECTLY home, Parker mixed himself a highball and fell asleep in an easy chair without touching the drink. When he awoke, it was getting dark. He pulled down all the window shades, made sure the door was locked, then brought out his disguise equipment.

He referred to a picture constantly as he created new features over his own, and nodded in satisfaction at the result. When all was finished, he shoved an automatic into a hip pocket, stowed his mask away, and slipped out of the apartment.

Half an hour later he was inside Dwight Gwenn's home, and even the squad of police posted around the house were not aware of it. Gwenn was in his study, bent over a desk while he studied various documents before him. He looked up, sensing the presence of a visitor, then arose with such a start that his chair tipped over.

Gwenn saw a man with a black mask over his eyes. Before his brain could function properly and indicate that this man of whom he had heard so much had in all probability come as a friend, Gwenn exhibited some of the terror stored up within him.

"I'm not here to harm you," Masked Detective said. "There is no need for fear. There are things you might throw light upon, however. That's why I'm here."

Gwenn picked up his chair, put it back on its four legs, and sat down. There was something in his still terrified eyes that showed he almost sensed what was coining. The Masked Detective came to the point promptly.

"When I brought you into the house after your gardener attempted to murder you," he said, "I noticed something on your desk, when I went to telephone—an envelope addressed to you and a matching card which said something about the Devil's Stepladder."

Gwenn flushed. He answered so rapidly that the Masked Detective got a half-formed impression that the speech had been mentally rehearsed a dozen times for just such a contingency.

"That card? Oh, yes. I remember it well. Came that same day, but I'm darned if I know what it's all about. Someone must have made a mistake. I don't know a thing about any Devil's Stepladder."

"But Vogan knew about it," the Masked Detective said quietly, "and Vogan was murdered. Wickham knew about it, and he is very dead. His servant, Curtis, apparently had learned something about it also—and his body is at the morgue. An attempt was made upon your life—and I don't mean the accidental one when you were assaulted because you happened to catch your gardener burying loot he'd stolen from you. During your unconsciousness you took quite a trip—as you know. What you don't know, probably, is that a man named Diggs ordered your death—deliberately. Diggs also had those others killed. You've got to talk, Gwenn. It may mean your own life if you don't. Once the information is in other hands, there will be no reason why you should be murdered. You'll protect yourself by talking."

"I can't," Gwenn said suddenly, and then flushed deeply again. "I mean it's impossible to talk about something I know nothing at all about. Maybe I could learn something though. I know a lot of Vogan's friends—Wickham's too. Give me a little time. I'll do all I can."

The Masked Detective got up.

"Mr. Gwenn." he said calmly, "you're a fool. Either that, or a knave of the first water. If I were sure of the latter, I'd pound the information out of you. I'm not. The fact that you were slated as a victim seems to repudiate any suspicion of guilt on your part. The thing couldn't possibly have been framed. Therefore I'll leave you. Think it over. Call Sergeant Gleason if you change your mind."

GWENN SLUMPED deep in his chair and his eyes centered on the surface of his desk. He heard one of the French windows close softly. The Masked Detective was gone.

Gwenn sprang to the window and peered out. He could see no one in the gloom. He pulled the curtains across the window, closed the door of the room, and sat down back of his desk again. He opened the drawer, took out a small red leather notebook and thumbed the pages hurriedly. Then he picked up the telephone.

Gwenn was calling long distance and there was some trouble before he got his party.

"Mr. Clive," he said. "Get me Mr. Clive—quickly."

The voice that came back to him was a trifle unsteady.

"This is Mr. Clive's niece. He—he's dead. He was—mur-murdered this afternoon."

The phone fell out of Gwenn's hand, rattled on the desk top, then dropped off the edge and hung by its cord. It was a full ten or fifteen seconds before Dwight Gwenn got his wits back. He dialed a local call next, and had some difficulty, because his finger shook so badly it became hard to use the dial.

"Mr. Denny?" he asked in a hoarse whisper, and then relaxed. "It is you! Thank God for that! Listen. Denny, I just called Clive. He's dead—murdered! I—I was afraid you'd be dead, too. I—I've got a feeling I'm next. Listen! The Masked Detective was just here. He knows about the Devil's Stepladder. He demanded that I talk, but I didn't. I bluffed my way out—successfully too, I think. But we've got to tell someone. They'll get all of us next. Bloom and Woods and Zaret. We can't afford to keep this matter a secret any longer. I'm afraid, and not ashamed to admit it either."

"So am I," Denny answered. "Clive isn't the only victim. Zaret got it, too—in San Domingo. His chauffeur robbed him and slit his throat. Bloom is all right so far, though. I talked to him twenty minutes ago and warned him. Woods is on a hunting trip and beyond contact. We can't do anything without the consent of all concerned, but I'll say this—we'll give Woods until tomorrow. If he doesn't get back to his lodge, I'll get in touch with Bloom again. We three will use our own judgment."

Gwenn was so nervous and afraid that he merely nodded at the phone as though his image were being transmitted over the wire. He heard Denny hang up, but Gwenn just sat there, frozen in terror. Then he heard another significant click. A second phone had just been cradled.

"Someone was listening!" Gwenn screamed wildly. "Someone heard me talk. Help! Police, out there! Police! Someone must be in the house."

A uniformed sergeant barged in. He was followed by two officers. At Gwenn's insistence that someone was in the house who should not be there, they rapidly searched the entire place, especially rooms in which there were telephones. As they came downstairs again, the sergeant spoke softly.

"This guy is getting to be a psychopathic case. From now on two of us stay right by his side. And keep your eyes peeled, boys. He may be nuts, but you never can tell. If somebody plants a hunk of lead in his hide, we'll be on the carpet—but good."

WILLIAM PRICE, private detective of shady reputation, had his office door locked and bolted. A desk lamp glowed and cast its ray upon several neat piles of gleaming jewels. Price had a jeweler's eye-piece screwed to his eye and studied the gems one by one, clucking his tongue in gratification when a particularly valuable stone passed under his inspection.

Those of the gems which were well known, and therefore hard to dispose of at good profits, would go back to their owners, and still Price would be making money. The insurance companies would pay a substantial reward. Price rubbed his fat jowls and grinned in great glee.

The phone buzzed and he answered it. Impatience and annoyance were in his voice. Both vanished as soon as he recognized the voice on the other end of the wire.

"Yes, Mr. Diggs," he said, his tone fawning. "What can I do for you?"

"I've got more—do you understand what I mean?" came the voice over the wire, and Price murmured that he did. "It's risky to meet you in the usual manner any longer. The Masked Detective seems to be everywhere and the police are getting suspicious. In exactly ten minutes I shall be somewhere near the loading platform of the Apex Oil Company's warehouse. I shall expect to see you there."

"I'm practically on my way," Price said.

He hung up, hastily swept the gems into sacks and put them in his safe. He spun the combination, grabbed his hat, and streaked through the outer office. A dirty-looking, skinny-faced man who sat at the reception desk was startled by Price's energy.

"Be back pretty quick!" Price called over his shoulder. "Big doings, pal."

Price didn't bother to use his car. The Apex Oil Company was no more than four or five blocks away. He reached the alley quickly, slowed down and looked around vigilantly. Certain that he was not under observation, he slipped into the alley and picked his way through the darkness.

He spotted the loading platform, saw rows of steel oil drums slacked high around it, and approached eagerly. He knew that Diggs had some kind of a big job in mind. Maybe he had already pulled it off and this time....

Price mentally licked his chops.

He saw a dark figure move out from behind the oil drums and Price started forward to meet the man. He did—but met only one part of the stranger's anatomy. His fist. It clipped Price squarely on the jaw, rocked his head back, and as he passed out a vague impression was in his stupefied brain that this eerie figure wore a mask of some kind. Then the same fist hammered out of Price's head all ability to think.

The Masked Detective smiled grimly, lifted Price by his shoulders and dragged him over to a small brick tool house. He had already picked the padlock. Price was shoved in, the door was closed, and the lock clicked.

The Masked Detective removed the mask and if there had been anyone to witness this strange bit of action, that person would have been even more astounded. Because when the mask was removed it looked as though Private Detective Price had just assaulted himself.

The Masked Detective's features were an exact duplicate of Price's. His clothing matched that of the private detective, even to the iron hat which Price was never without, an eccentricity he shared with his criminal friend, Diggs.

IN THIS amazingly accurate disguise, the Masked Detective hurried back to Price's office. As he swept through the door, just as Price would have barged in, he saw the skinny little guy in the outer office. Instantly the Masked Detective recognized him. Here was the man who had shadowed him from Alden's home, and from whom he thought he had slipped away only to run into a traffic jam—which had been no accident, but had delayed Rex Parker while someone searched his apartment. So Price had been behind that. Perhaps Alden, too.

"You ain't been gone long, Boss," this skinny runt squeaked.

"Nope," the Masked Detective growled, went into Price's private office, and slammed the door.

He opened drawers and investigated their contents without finding anything significant, then turned his attention to a big, old-fashioned safe in the corner. He examined this and groaned. The Masked Detective was no burglar. Safes were safes, and without a good substantial load of nitro he was as helpless as the next man against them. Then he had an idea.

"Hey!" he bellowed, and the sawed-off mug popped in fast. "You been monkeying with the safe?" the Masked Detective roared in Price's voice.

"Me? Gosh no, Boss! I didn't even get up while you was gone. The safe looks okay to me."

"Sure," the Masked Detective said with heavy sarcasm. "It looks swell, only I can't open it. The numbers don't work. Listen—is there somebody around here who can open these boxes? I thought I knew a guy—"

"Sure, Boss. Just down the street a ways. He's a whiz at it too. I often thought I'd ask him how would he like to do a little job on the Q.T., but—"

"What do you think I'm runnin'?" the Masked Detective barked. "This is supposed to be a detective agency. You beat it down and bring that guy up here—fast!"

The runt disappeared like magic. The Masked Detective grinned and proceeded to investigate the outer office, paying especial attention to the filing cabinets. They were filled with duplicate letters, some ten years old, and few of a more recent vintage. But one thing the Masked Detective discovered. Price certainly didn't bother with many of the cases a regular agency handles.

His panting messenger came back in fifteen minutes followed by a bulky man who carried a heavy kit of tools. The Masked Detective indicated the safe with a jerk of his thumb.

"It's stuck. Open her up."

"What's the combination?" the safe expert asked as he knelt beside the safe.

The Masked Detective swung around in Price's swivel chair and glowered at him.

"Think I'm spilling dope like that to a guy I never saw before?"

The expert's face turned a dull red.

"Brother," he said grimly, "I've been opening safes for a long time around here, and nobody ever made a crack like that to me. It'll cost you just fifty bucks to get this can open—and in advance."

The Masked Detective looked properly squelched. He drew money from his pocket, counted off fifty dollars, and then pretended to be working on some papers. The expert had the safe open in twenty-five minutes.

"Next time," he advised as he gathered his instruments, "just turn the dial a little more carefully. She wasn't stuck at all—so far as I could see."

CHAPTER XVIII

THE SECRET IS OUT

QUICKLY THE Masked Detective closed and locked the office door, as soon as the safe expert had left. He grinned broadly. There were more ways of opening a safe than blowing it up or trying such foolishness as grinding down the skin on the fingertips to try and feel the tumblers. Fifty dollars was a cheap fee.

First of all he took out the sacks of gems. The Masked Detective had studied up on the descriptions of the jewels taken in several servant robberies, and some of these gems were clearly that loot. This connected Price closely with the case.

With this loot tucked in his pockets, the Masked Detective turned to several fireproof steel boxes. He pried them open, and inside he discovered a number of unsealed envelopes. Each one carried evidence against someone—a butler, a housemaid, a chauffeur, or gardener. A card was attached to each file, giving a full description of the servant, his or her name, employment record, and facts concerning adaptability for crooked work.

Many envelopes also contained signed confessions. There were photostats of arrest warrants, showing convictions of some. Photographs of others, some of which were evidence enough to convict.

"Diggs boasted of these," the Masked Detective grunted, "and Price has them in his safe. That ties Price to Diggs' coat tails but he can't be Diggs because I imitated Diggs' voice to trap Price and of course he wouldn't have fallen for it if he was the real Diggs. He wears the same kind of bowler hat, of course, but—"

Price would be coming out of his punch-induced coma by now, the Marked Detective reflected, and would be setting up a terrific clamor. The masked man had to be away from this office when Price came back. Hurriedly, he bundled up the documents, found a good-sized briefcase in the supply closet and thrust them into it. He closed the safe, shoved the briefcase under his arm and walked into the outer office.

"Be away for a couple of days," he told the runt. "Anybody comes, tell 'em I'm on a big case."

As the Masked Detective walked swiftly up the street, he heard a police whistle shrill from behind the Apex Oil Company's building. Price had been found. The man who had been Price for a time hailed a taxi and was driven blocks away before he changed cabs.

Safely in his own apartment he studied the papers again. What they contained was the work of many months. Diggs, or whoever controlled him, had built up an empire of crime. Here was material for hundreds of potential robberies.

Each case history indicated where that particular servant worked at the present time. Some of the records indicated that Diggs' victims had been honest for many years until he caught up with them. These were marked as dangerous, and not trustworthy on big jobs.

By comparison of many files, Rex Parker discovered how the servants were shifted around from one job to another, and provided with falsified references. It was a crime ring beyond comparison.

What, then, did the Devil's Stepladder have to do with the affair? The net results of robberies pulled by this unwilling gang of crooks would provide huge sums of money. Still Diggs was not satisfied. Why? Because whatever it was that was known as the Devil's Stepladder offered something even bigger and more profitable? If so, it must run into millions.

THE PRICE disguise removed, Rex Parker made a paper-wrapped bundle of the documents, but had to get rid of Price's briefcase in which he had brought home his find. He carried the briefcase into the hall, opened the incinerator slot. A roar told him that the building engineer was burning rubbish. He let the briefcase slide down into the blaze.

Half an hour later he was in Sergeant Gleason's office. He shoved the bundle of incriminating documents at the Homicide detective.

"Pick up Private Detective Price and hold him on suspicion," he said. "He's been fencing some of Diggs' loot—and he kept Diggs' papers for him. In that bundle you will find evidence against a large number of servants now employed in various homes of the wealthy all over the country. They comprise Diggs' mob.

"Some of them are unwilling victims who slipped once, paid the penalty, and deserve a break. You can straighten out the good from the bad, and let the cops have a field day. Those employed locally are the prospective thieves who would have struck tomorrow night, if my article had not warned their masters. Now you can pick them up."

"Of all the breaks!" Gleason gloated. "Say, this just about washes up Diggs and his mob. His whole racket has gone up the flue."

"Sure," Parker agreed. "But we still have to land Diggs and that won't be easy. He's got something else up his sleeve—even bigger than this servant gang business. I think it all began with his league of servants, but then Diggs discovered this Devil's Stepladder business and got set to put that through to a finish. He can still do it. We've only half licked that gent. Mind if I use your wash-room a minute?"

Rex Parker, as Parker, did not come back from that wash-room. The man who did was dressed in the same clothes, but his face had changed. Parker had become the Masked Detective again, using a quickly applied and effective disguise.

"I'm going visiting," he told Gleason. "The Masked Detective is accepted in a lot more places than Rex Parker would be. See you later. And those papers I gave you came from the Masked Detective. Understand?"

The Masked Detective left Police Headquarters, stopped at a drug store and used the phone book to check the residential address of a certain banker. Ideas were floating through the Masked Detective's brain. First of all Vogan, Wickham, and Gwenn were all involved, and there was some mighty reason why Gwenn refused to talk even when his life was endangered.

Diggs, with his empire of intimidated servants, could have netted himself large sums of money, represented by the loot he planned to acquire. Yet, despite this, Diggs seemed to have something else in mind. It must involve millions, and the victims of his murderous attacks certainly must be providing the motive.

Through his investigations, the Masked Detective had quietly determined that Vogan, Wickham, and Gwenn all banked with the same big financial institution. Perhaps the answer to the Devil's Stepladder mystery lay in the mind of a bank official, especially if negotiations of any kind were already under way.

The Masked Detective taxied to the home of the banker whose address he had found, and eyed the suave butler who admitted him suspiciously. The servant might be one of Diggs' cohorts.

The banker himself, he quickly discovered, was a democratic type and easily accessible.

"I WANT information," he was told by this quiet-eyed stranger. "It may mean the lives of certain men. I am the Masked Detective. If you wish confirmation of my identity, you have only to phone Sergeant Gleason at Police Headquarters."

The banker waved his hand.

"That isn't necessary. I haven't been a banker forty years for nothing. I can size up men rather well. And I believe you. What can I do to help?"

"Mr. Vogan and Mr. Wickham were murdered, as you know," the Masked Detective said. "I have reason to believe there is a gigantic plot behind their deaths. I believe that Mr. Gwenn is also in danger. All of these men handle their financial affairs through your bank. It's my fervent hope that you can tell me something of their recent activities, especially if they involve a great deal of money."

The banker whistled.

"I don't know how you stumbled upon this matter, or if you are merely guessing. But you've hit the nail on the head. Those three men you mentioned, with five others, are engaged in one of the biggest scale deals ever handled through my institution. Considering only private deals, of course. Let's see—there is a Mr. Zaret—Woods—Clive—Bloom, and Denny involved."

"Denny?" The Masked Detective seemed surprised. "You mean a rather plump man with shell-rimmed glasses and a fat face?"

"Yes, that description fits him. Now here is the gist of their plans. Of course I tell you this in the strictest of confidence, and except for the fact that you assure me men's lives are endangered—and I know that two are already dead—I would hardly reveal what I know. Those men, all of them, are engaged in the building of a huge tin smelting plant somewhere out of the city.

"You see, this country smelts no tin. It imports large quantities from the Dutch East Indies and from England, which still maintains its smelting plants despite the War. Recently, attempts have been made to set up plants of this kind in the United States, but for sundry reasons—most of them involving red tape—little has been accomplished.

"As a patriotic gesture, this group of men have decided to invest their own capital in a gigantic enterprise. Each man has set aside assets that run into the millions. They maintain individual accounts, share the costs, and pay off from these accounts."

The Masked Detective frowned.

"That hamstrings the whole affair. These private accounts are controlled only by the individuals. One of their number, say, who might conceivably be killing off his associates to get for himself the entire plant, couldn't possibly gain access to those large sums, could he?"

"Never," the banker affirmed. "With Vogan's and Wickham's deaths, those sums automatically became a part of their estates, and they were out of the game. The plant is only half completed, and no single member of the group has assets enough to finish the job. I cannot see how any man of that group could hope to profit by the murder of his associates."

"Neither do I," the Masked Detective said. "It's more puzzling than ever. But, anyway, you have my gratitude for your help. It's cleared up the greatest part of this mystery. There is, of course, no necessity for my telling you this conversation has been in the strictest privacy. Oh, yes, one more thing. Are you certain a man named Frank Alden isn't a member of this clique?"

"Alden? No! He banks with us, but he has no connection whatsoever with the organization."

THE MASKED DETECTIVE walked slowly up the street. So a vast patriotic project lay behind all this. Were spies possibly involved? Was the murder of these men actually a clever piece of sabotage? The United States needed tin smelting plants badly.

With the source of supply threatened in the Dutch East Indies and that which came from England in considerable doubt, the United States was forced to get its precious metal from Bolivia.

To make use of any of the South American ore, tin smelting plants had to be set up. Congressional committees had been wrangling over the affair for months with nothing definite as yet decided upon.

One thing the Masked Detective did know—sawed-off, spectacled Mr. Denny was going to have to think fast for an explanation as to why he denied any knowledge of the Devil's Stepladder.

The Masked Detective hailed a taxi and was driven to Denny's home.

CHAPTER XIX

SHOTGUN WELCOME

NO LIGHTS were gleaming in the Denny home, a two-story, single family house in a quiet part of the city. The Masked Detective prowled around the place for a few moments and made sure Denny, and his family—if he had any—were not at home. Apparently the man maintained no staff of servants.

The Masked Detective walked up on the porch, selected a comfortable chair and sat down to wait. It was quiet here and he needed time to think. The case had suddenly grown by leaps and bounds into something with possible international complications. The servant racket was finished, exploded to the high heavens, but Diggs was still loose to carry on his work against these men who were building their vast project.

Diggs puzzled the Masked Detective. Sometimes he was certain the man was in disguise—an extremely clever job, too. If that was not true, then Diggs had a master who issued the orders to kill. Perhaps Diggs had organized his servant league and operated it successfully. The real brains behind the tin smelting business may have contacted him with a favorable proposition, and Diggs had then proceeded to handle both crooked enterprises.

A car rolled down the street, slowed up, and the Masked Detective tensed. The car turned into the driveway, stopped, and Denny got out. As he approached the porch, he was adjusting his glasses. The Masked

Detective saw him take keys from his pocket and head for the front door.

"Good evening, Mr. Denny," the Masked Detective said.

Denny spun around, and one hand darted toward his hip pocket. He peered through the darkness at this tall man whose eyes were covered with a black domino.

"The Masked Detective!" he said hoarsely. "I—I think I know why you're here and believe me, I'm glad of it. I had some rather horrible news a short time ago and I'm afraid, frankly, that I may be the next man to die. I want to talk to you. You're the only person with ability enough to help me."

"That's why I came," the Masked Detective said. "Shall we go inside?"

Denny nodded and stepped up to the door. The Masked Detective stood directly behind him, towering over the much shorter man. Denny got the key in the lock, twisted it, and started to push the door open.

The Masked Detective gave a sharp cry. His right hand swept out and sent Denny spinning. At the same time he went into a nosedive. There was a terrific roar. Flame and death hurtled through the door. If the Masked Detective had been standing, that charge would have torn him apart.

Denny, flat on his stomach, looked up with a ludicrous expression of awe on his face.

"Wh-what happened?" he chattered.

The Masked Detective held a gun in his hand as he moved through the doorway.

"You can come in now," he told Denny. "It's safe. Somebody planned to welcome us with a shotgun charge. Have a look. It's hooked up so that when the door was opened more than a few inches, the trigger went off. It's one of the most diabolical traps I've ever seen."

The Masked Detective carefully dismantled the gun, taking precautions against smearing any possible fingerprints. A radio car howled up and two patrolmen who had been on nearby beats puffed into the house. The Masked Detective identified himself, and Denny backed him up.

"There is no use looking for the killer," the Masked Detective said. "He set his death machine and got away long ago. However, you might take this apparatus to Headquarters and have it checked for fingerprints."

WHEN THE police had gone, Denny and the Masked Detective sat down in the living room. Denny was highly agitated and seemed more determined than ever to talk.

"I've underestimated you," he blurted. "I thought your reputation was built on sand and that when you encountered really clever crooks, you'd be as helpless as the police. I'm sorry now.

"Here is the real background to this business. Several men, including myself, are engaged in building a large tin smelting plant at a place called the Devil's Stepladder. Some sort of a formation of rocks in the valley gave it that name years ago, but like most things, the name only sticks around that particular region and is rarely heard of elsewhere. We took the name for a sort of password as our method of maintaining secrecy. Letters, phone calls and messages which included those two words positively identified the information as authentic. We've been afraid of spies—saboteurs.

"Vogan was a member. So was Wickham. I lied when I denied any knowledge of the Devil's Stepladder. I thought Vogan had been killed in a manner that proved his death had nothing to do with our project. Then Wickham was killed, and I was not so sure. Now two others have died. A Mr. Clive and a Mr. Zaret—both out West. They were murdered by thieving servants."

"I happen to know you are telling the truth," the Masked Detective said quietly. "By keeping this information from me so long you have possibly sacrificed the lives of two men. However, you were in no position to judge the consequences, so we'll skip it.

"The killer seems to be bent on exterminating all of the people involved in this plant at the Devil's Stepladder. Just why, we can't be sure. We can only guess that foreign powers wish this country to be without a supply of tin which is so important in the manufacture of armaments. The killer must realize that the destruction of this one plant won't keep others from being built—but it does mean delay, and that's probably all he desires at the moment.

"There is no doubt but that the killer knows the location of the plant because he seems to know everything else concerning it. He may decide to balk your efforts by destroying the place. We must prevent that."

Denny wiped his glasses and squinted at the Masked Detective.

"We shall," he said firmly. "I'll arrange at once for a guard around the job, with orders to shoot to kill if any prowler appears. You know, I'm greatly relieved to get this off my chest. We pledged one another never to reveal the secret, but when murder horns in, pledges are off. Gwenn will back up my statements, and I'll inform him that you know all the details."

Denny offered his hand as the Masked Detective walked out on the porch. He stood watching as the figure of this dreaded manhunter merged with the darkness. Denny put his glasses back on, entered the house and double-locked the door.

The Masked Detective phoned Headquarters after he reached the business section of the city. Sergeant Gleason was excited when he answered.

"Winnie's been trying to get in touch with you!" he exclaimed. "Alden phoned your office and wants you to contact the Masked Detective. Says it's vitally important."

"I'll go right up there," the Masked Detective said. "Have you located our good friend Private Detective Price yet?"

"He's flown the coop. There's an alarm out for him and we're watching railroad stations and airports in case the punk shows up. Don't worry. With that mug of his he'll never get clear. You sure you don't want some help?"

"I may need it soon," the Masked Detective answered. "And fast. Mind sticking around, just in case? Thanks, Sarge. This business is clearing up. I'll have the answer to it all before morning, I hope."

HE HUNG up and stayed in the phone booth a moment while he tried to figure out just what Frank Alden, alias Jim Bartlett, wanted. Then he returned to the vicinity of his own apartment, got the dilapidated old coupé out of its garage, and drove directly to Alden's house.

The place was lit up from top to bottom. The Masked Detective drew on the domino which served as his mark of identification, then hurried up on the porch and rang the bell. A burglar chain rattled, a key turned, and the door was opened halfway. The Masked Detective started back with amazement and shock.

Diggs stood in the doorway, as cool as ever. A .45 caliber automatic was in his fist and murder in his eyes. Just inside the door stood two of Diggs' trusted men. They also held guns.

"Do come in," Diggs invited blandly. "I've been wanting to meet you face to face for some time."

The Masked Detective, standing on the threshold, did not move. He was trapped this time. Three guns menaced him and Diggs was primed for the kill. So this was what Alden wanted to see him about! The Masked Detective smiled wryly.

"Seems as though you've got the drop on me, Diggs," he said. "Of course I'll come in."

The Masked Detective's left hand was flat against the partially opened door. Suddenly he gave that door a terrific shove. Diggs' pair of gunmen were directly in line. True to their colors—vivid yellow—they had shielded themselves behind the door to a certain extent. The heavy door hit them simultaneously. Their guns went off, but the bullets only plowed into the thick oak of the door.

At the same instant the Masked Detective lunged forward, ducking low. Diggs pulled trigger, but missed by a fraction of an inch. Then the Masked Detective butted him full in the stomach. Diggs flew backward and lost his balance completely. He went down, but he was far from out. His hand still clutched the gun, and he tried to bring it to bear.

The Masked Detective's right foot shot out. It clipped Diggs under the chin and snapped his teeth together with a sharp click. The Masked Detective flung himself upon the man. He seized the gun hand of the killer, twisted it, and encountered terrific resistance. The Masked Detective drove one knee into the killer's midriff which elicited a grunt of pain, and followed this up with a slashing right to the face.

Diggs' nose flattened and stayed that way. Then one of the pair of gunmen leaped into the battle. The Masked Detective threw himself to the left, and avoided that slashing blow with a gun barrel. He reached out, grabbed the man by one ankle and heaved. The gunman toppled over, his pistol spraying the ceiling with lead.

But the second man was closing in, seeking for an opening through which he could perforate the Masked Detective and not hit Diggs by accident. The Masked Detective gave Diggs a shove floorward, crouched, and lunged. The gunman brought his weapon to bear, but suddenly found that his target was only an inch away from his own body.

The Masked Detective straightened up when he was exactly at the feet of the gunman. The killer gave a shriek of dismay and tried to back up. A fist breezed past his nose and he dodged to the left—straight into the path of a terrific right uppercut. The man was lifted from the floor by the force of that blow. When he landed, it was not on his feet.

The Masked Detective spun quickly around, ready to dive upon Diggs. But the chief crook was gone. The only way he could have escaped was up the stairs to the second floor or through a rear exit. His gun lay in a corner where it had fallen during the mêlée. The Masked Detective started up the stairs, then stopped.

Frank Alden came along the balcony, clinging to the railing with one hand, and massaging his jaw with the other. His eyes were partially glazed, but he saw the mask and was alert.

"I—I'm sorry I brought you into this—mess," he said slowly. "Diggs came back."

"And he went up those stairs," the Masked Detective said grimly. "What happened to your jaw?"

"Diggs—he struck me. I've been half unconscious, trying to drag myself to a telephone."

The Masked Detective's eyes narrowed behind the mask. He had punished Diggs with a blow to the jaw, and Alden's jaw was swelling rapidly. Could he have been Diggs after all, have raced upstairs and made a lightning change out of his disguise?

The Masked Detective searched the house. Diggs was gone all right.

CHAPTER XX

BOMBS FOR DESTRUCTION

HURRYING BACK downstairs, the Masked Detective tied up the two gunmen who were still unconscious. Then he faced Alden.

"You wanted to see me," he snapped. "It turned out to be a neat trap and you'd better have a pretty good reason for getting me out here."

"I have." Alden dug into his pocket. "I was throwing out Diggs' things a little while ago. There was an old suit and I searched the pockets. I found a key. It's marked with the name of the Sheridan Apartments and has a number on it also. I thought—perhaps...."

The Masked Detective took the key and examined it. He thrust it into his pocket.

"I may be making a serious mistake," he told Alden, "but I'm going to trust you. To relieve your mind I'll add that Diggs no longer has any documentary evidence against your past. I turned all the facts over to the police and if you haven't been lying, they will destroy that evidence and keep the matter strictly confidential. Diggs probably came back here to get this key—or sent his men to do the job. They overheard you phoning and took advantage of the situation. That's how I look at it. Which places you pretty much in the clear, Alden."

"Thank heaven for that," Alden declared fervently. "I've repaid all of those creditors I cheated those years ago. I didn't have to, because the law was on my side as a bankrupt, but I paid off anyway. I realize it still looks bad for me. I'm about Diggs' build and I could have fixed my face to resemble his, I suppose. I swear I didn't! Diggs is as much my enemy as he is yours."

The Masked Detective nodded at the other.

"I'll have police sent out for these men," he said. "If they make any trouble before the police arrive, bat them on the chin. Good luck—Frank Alden."

The Masked Detective ran out to where his car was parked. He peeled off the mask and drove to the business district. There he soon located the Sheridan apartments, and fifteen minutes after he left Alden's house he was inserting the key into the lock of a door of a fifth floor apartment. He opened it cautiously and kept a gun in his hand. The Masked Detective was not a killer, but the influence of a gun meant a great deal sometimes. And if he was in another jam, he might shoot in self defense. Diggs was a ruthless, crafty killer who did not deserve a break.

There was no one in the place. It was a luxuriously fitted apartment. The furniture was expensive and modern. There were several rumpled newspapers at the foot of a big easy chair. He picked them up. They were all turned to the pages outlining a story of Private Detective Price's treachery. On a table beside the chair, an ash tray was filled with the butts of cheap, strong cigars—the kind Price was never without.

Price had been here then, hiding out from the police. Why had he left such a secure spot when he must realize every policeman in the city was on the lookout for him?

The Masked Detective walked into a bedroom, and noted that none of the usual articles to be found on a dressing table were on this one. The drawers were empty, too. Someone had been sleeping on the bed— on top of the silken spread. There were dirty shoe marks to indicate that the sleeper had not bothered to undress. Price, probably.

THE MASKED DETECTIVE opened a closet door. Two suits hanging on the rack, both of them the somber sort of clothing worn by Diggs. He saw a pair of queer-looking shoes on the floor, picked them up, and grunted in satisfaction. With trouser cuffs to cover their tops, they looked like ordinary shoes, but they had been built up to lend the illusion of height.

Diggs *had* worn a disguise then. He was the real leader of this gang—the arch killer and thief. But who was he? Alden? And had the Masked Detective made a bad error in letting the man go? No—Alden was out. Unless he wore similar shoes he was approximately the same height as Diggs.

Gwenn, probably? The man had acted suspiciously, and he needed about this amount of added height to resemble Diggs. Denny? Then how come that murder trap set at his home? Or possibly Price was the ringleader, posing both as a hireling, and as the real head of the mob.

The Masked Detective prowled further in the various rooms. One, at the rear of the apartment, was closed and securely locked. The Masked Detective listened for a moment, heard no sound, and attacked the door with his shoulder.

That was quicker than using keys by a trial and error method.

He burst through the flimsy panels in less than two minutes. He found the light switch, turned it on—and grew pale.

This room looked something like a hobby room. There was a bench against one wall and on it were several items which made the Masked Detective's blood run cold. Someone had been engaged in the dangerous task of creating bombs. Extra-high-powered explosives were there, packing, fuses and fairly large steel shells. When crammed with the exploding chemicals they would have the ability to blast away even a large building.

The Masked Detective raced back into the living room and picked up the telephone. He dialed Police Headquarters and asked for Sergeant Gleason.

"Send out to Alden's house and have a pair of Diggs' high-hat thugs picked up," he said quickly. "Don't bother Alden. Then, Sarge, after you give those orders, I've got a very special task for you. Listen closely...."

The Masked Detective spoke hurriedly for a few moments, hung up, and darted out of the apartment. Disdaining the slow elevator, he went down the stairs four at a time, swept through the lobby, whipping off his mask before anyone spotted him. He piled into his car and sent it rolling toward Denny's house.

He breathed relief when he saw that the place was lighted up. He banged on the door and pressed the bell alternately. Denny opened up after he had peeked through a small side window.

"What's wrong?" Denny gasped. "Is—is someone else dead?"

"Not yet," the Masked Detective panted. "Unless we hurry, there probably will be though. Listen, Denny, this is no time for explanations. You've got to guide me to this Devil's Stepladder region and the tin smelting plant you and your associates are building down there."

"But I don't understand!" Denny cried. "The place is forty miles from here. It's late, and—"

"If you don't get started, it will be too late," the Masked Detective snapped. "Diggs and his mob are getting ready to wreck the place somehow, and the only way we can stop them is with speed. I've got a car out front. You get your hat and coat."

"Yes—yes, of course," Denny said. "But Gwenn ought to know about this, too. After all—"

"I tried to contact him, but he isn't home," the Masked Detective said. "None of the police guard thrown around his house saw him leave. I've got an idea he's already on the way, and if he happens to be mixed up with Diggs…. Well, use your own imagination. I'll explain further on the way. Will you hurry?"

Denny grabbed his hat and coat, slammed the front door, and ran alongside the Masked Detective to the ancient-looking coupé waiting at the curb.

"Never mind if this bus looks like a crate," the Masked Detective said. "You'll be surprised when you step on the gas. Take the wheel and give her all the speed you can. I'll sit beside you."

"But it's your car," Denny protested.

"Bother whose car it is! Can't you realize we're losing time? You've got to drive, because Diggs may realize we'll start for the smelting plant. He may have us under observation right now, and try to stop us. I can't drive and shoot at the same time. Get going!"

DENNY GASPED and got behind the wheel. The Masked Detective ran around the back of the coupé and piled in beside Denny. He drew his automatic and placed it carefully in his lap, finger on the trigger, safety off.

"Let them try and stop us now," the Masked Detective said stonily. "If we're lucky, we may nab Diggs. Certainly we'll nail some of his men."

Denny slid into first gear, pushed his foot on the accelerator, and things happened to make him cry out in astonishment. The old jalopy's motor purred like a kitten and picked up with the speed of a racing car. Denny had to hang onto the wheel with both hands.

The car was weighted down, somehow, and held the road despite its terrific speed. The Masked Detective kept yelling for more and more miles an hour. Denny gulped and glanced down at the gun in the Masked Detective's lap.

"I wish you'd point that thing in another direction."

"Sorry. I didn't realize."

The Masked Detective changed the direction of the gun slightly, but his hand remained tight around the butt. They left the city limits and the funny old car really showed her stuff. She streaked along the highway at a dizzy speed which kept Denny on edge, yet every time he tried to let up on the gas, the Masked Detective shouted for more and more speed.

They covered the forty miles in two minutes less than the mileage. The difference would have been greater except for the city traffic which Denny was forced to negotiate at a slower rate. Ahead of them in the darkness, a high structure finally loomed up. To the left was a towering cliff.

"There's a rock formation on the cliff," Denny explained. "Looks like a stepladder and leads straight down. Natives named it, because it looks like it's a passage for the devil to climb in and out of hell by.... There's the plant. Two sections are practically completed. The main building is over on your right."

"Pull up—quickly," the Masked Detective ordered. "Douse the lights. We may run into company, so be ready. Got a gun on you?"

"N-no! I—I've been carrying one, but you came so abruptly and I was so confused. I forgot to take one."

"Tough luck. Now here is what we do. I think a private detective named Price got here ahead of us and has either set the stage or is engaged in his rotten work now. There may be a trap, so watch yourself. Stay slightly ahead of me so I can protect you with my gun. If you lag behind, the crooks might land one on your skull and I wouldn't know the difference. If you see anything, speak very quietly. We'll head for that north building."

But—but if they think we're coming, there may be a trap!" protested Denny. "They'll have us if we go inside."

"They'll have us if we don't," the Masked Detective said sternly. "Move along! Every minute gives those devils that much more time to finish their job. Don't worry. If anyone appears, I'll shoot faster than you ever saw a gun discharged. You've got to come along, because I don't know my way around. That door—does it lead into the building?"

"Y-yes," Denny gulped. "But there are no lights, no electricity inside the building yet. Haven't reached the wiring stage. It's dark. We won't be able to see anybody if men are there."

"Leave that to me," the Masked Detective said grimly. "Through the door now—and watch out that you don't stumble against something and warn them. They'll probably be near the middle of the building. Don't forget—this is your one and only chance to save the investment you and the others have put into this business so far. It's no time to turn yellow!"

CHAPTER XXI

IMAGE OF DOOM

FEARFULLY DENNY sidled through the doorway. He and the Masked Detective passed along some kind of engineer's quarters, strewn with blueprints and drafting tables. Denny stopped suddenly—so suddenly that the Masked Detective bumped against him.

"I think I hear something." Denny breathed. "They *are* here! You don't know how many. We're trapped!"

"You mean they're trapped," the Masked Detective countered. "I've got nine slugs in this gun, the safety is off, and there are more clips in my pocket. Remember about the safety—don't stop so abruptly again or I'm liable to send a bullet through you by accident. Get going, Denny. We've got them now."

Denny walked as though he was treading on T.N.T. His breathing came with almost explosive violence. Once he brushed against a loose piece of board and gave a low, startled cry of fear. The Masked Detective asked for utter silence, and they stood there, in the inky darkness, listening. The sounds they had heard upon first entering the building were gone now.

"Th-this way," Denny panted. "It leads right into the middle of the building. But I—I think we ought to get out of here before it's too late."

"Nonsense!" snapped the Masked Detective in a whisper. "Carry on. They'll show themselves soon, and then—fireworks."

Denny shivered violently and took another half dozen steps. Then, with a suddenness that froze both men into inactivity, two flashlights sprayed the darkness away and centered on them. Two guns were thrust forward, plainly visible in the light.

"Look!" someone said in a harsh voice. "The Masked Detective and a pal! Drop that rod, wise guy! We'll blast you down in half a second."

"Stumped!" the Masked Detective groaned.

He let go of his gun, and it fell to the dirt floor. There was a sudden rush behind them. Two burlap bags descended over their shoulders and were drawn tight with a cord. Ropes curled about their legs. One of their captors yanked them, and the Masked Detective and Denny tumbled to the ground. They were firmly trussed. Denny was shrieking crazily, his words muffled and inaudible beneath the burlap sack. Someone kicked him sharply.

"But what a haul!" a man's voice gloated. "We nailed the Masked Detective and one of his stooges just like that. Go get Price. I dunno whether to park a few slugs in these two guys or let him take care of 'em."

There was silence for a few moments. Then the same voice spoke again as footsteps approached and stopped.

"Yeah, I'm sure it's the Masked Detective. I tell you I saw the mask. Listen, Price, I got eyes, ain't I, and the flash was right on the two of 'em. The other guy was with the Masked Detective so that makes him his pal, don't it? What'll we do with 'em?"

"Leave them here," an authoritative voice ordered. "They'll get what's coming to them all right."

For a few moments they could hear swiftly retreating footsteps, then a complete and vast silence held sway. The Masked Detective inched himself over until he struck Denny. By their voices, they managed to estimate one another's location.

"Looks like we're in for it," the Masked Detective said.

"We've got to get out of here!" came Denny's muffled yell. "See if you can get at the ropes around my arms!"

"Impossible! This burlap sack reaches down below my hands. I'm stuck, Denny. Unless help comes, we're licked. Those mugs will return in a few minutes, and—well, use your imagination."

DENNY BEGAN shrieking after a couple of minutes went by, though the shrieks did not carry far through the burlap. The man was half crazy from terror.

"We've got to get away!" he yelled. "The place will be blown up! There are bombs planted all around. Price put them there! They'll go off any minute and we'll be buried in the ruins of the building. Help me—you've got to help me!"

Someone reached down and lifted Denny to his feet. A knife slit the ropes restraining his arms. The burlap sack was removed and Denny found himself encircled by a ring of flashlights and men. Towering above him was the Masked Detective.

"Bombs, eh?" the Masked Detective said in deadly seriousness. "Except for Price and his boys, nobody except Diggs knew about the bombs. Which means you are Diggs, Denny. I've known it for some hours now, but you furnished the indisputable proof. Price and his men were captured before we got here. The fellows who attacked us were detectives, led by Sergeant Gleason who gave a pretty good imitation of Price's voice. You couldn't take it. When you thought those bombs were ready to go off, you lost your head. By that admission you convict yourself, Denny, even if I had nothing else to go by."

Denny's eyes were wide and round. He brushed away the shell-rimmed glasses that had somehow stayed on his nose. Like a caged animal, he turned his head, looking for a loophole in the cordon of men. There was none.

"Which of you is Sergeant Gleason?" he demanded, and Gleason stepped into view. "This man may or may not be the Masked Detective," he accused. "I accompanied him here in good faith. He told me about the bombs—that's why I was so afraid. His knowledge of them convicts him rather than me. I demand that his mask be removed. If Diggs happens to be in our midst, you'll find him beneath that mask."

"Aw, nuts," Sergeant Gleason growled. "I know what I'm doing. Why don't you stop faking, Denny?"

"Let me convince him," the Masked Detective said calmly. "He is Diggs, all right. He started a league of crooks drawn from the ranks of servants. He first got evidence enough to make them lose their jobs if their employers heard of it. Then, under his guidance, they pulled other jobs, and from then on they were in his power. Unless they obeyed him, they knew it would mean prison—or probably death at his hands.

"But Denny—or Diggs—kept on building his strange empire, adding to his legions as fast as possible. All the time he kept growing richer, too, from the proceeds of the hauls turned over to him. Price fenced the stuff that couldn't be recognized, turned the other goods back to insurance companies for a fat fee. Gradually Denny's league grew more powerful.

"Somehow, certain agents of tin smelting companies abroad heard of him. I imagine they got their knowledge through one of Denny's servant-crooks. They came to him, put up an attractive proposition. Denny was to use his servant gang to murder certain people, all involved in the building of this tin smelting plant. Those foreign interests couldn't afford to have any domestic competition.

"Denny, to gain the confidence of his victims, joined their forces by throwing some of his dishonestly earned money into the enterprise. He had nothing to lose because the alien forces backing him would make good his loss several times over. Denny—or Diggs, as you will—knew that by using his huge servant gang to kill off the other members of the Devil's Stepladder enterprise, there would be no suspicion upon himself. The deaths of the members would look like the work of a gang of thieves, some of whom were caught in the act, and who murdered to get clear. It eliminated any suspicion of Denny."

THE ACCUSED Denny glared at the Masked Detective, but each statement made by the crime fighter created highlights of fear in his eyes. The fear of a man exposed.

"He began with Vogan," the Masked Detective went on. "Austen, Vogan's butler, was to be framed, but Vogan caught him before the stage was set. Austen was killed because he knew too much. Then Austen's brother, also a member of Denny's league, was told that Vogan had committed the murder, was egged on to take revenge. He did, and one of the owners of this tin smelting project was dead.

"Then came Wickham, but things went wrong there, too, because I happened to be on the scene. So Wickham was murdered at the first opportunity Denny found. It came when Wickham lay unconscious and Sergeant Gleason asked Denny to get a doctor. Denny did—but when Gleason helped to carry Wickham upstairs, Denny called one of his men and gave him instructions to waylay the doctor, take his place, and poison Wickham. This was done with finesse, I'll admit. But Denny was the only suspect who could have given out the information that Wickham was helpless. With his doctor on the way, the stage was set.

"Denny tried to confuse the issue after that assault on Wickham. In the first place Denny came along purposely, because his men who thought they had Wickham's butler in their hands were preparing to frame Wickham's murder on the butler. Only the butler happened to be me. Denny returned with Wickham so that he could pretend to witness the crime and get the police. The evidence against Curtis would have been perfect then.

"Denny came into the house, heard Wickham slugged and ran out. When he returned with the police, he instantly accused the man who looked like Curtis—yet he hadn't seen Curtis there. He just believed he was there.

"Then, after I had identified myself, Denny indicated that Gwenn had been at the club when he and Wickham left. That would alibi Denny, and put the blame for the phone call which had warned Denny's men, upon Gwenn. But at that time Gwenn was home with the strongest alibi possible. There was a police guard around his house. Denny didn't know that."

"I guess that'll strap your Denny-Diggs in the chair," Gleason grunted.

"And this will help to pull the straps tighter," the Masked Detective went on. "Gwenn gave the whole thing away. He made a phone call to Denny, and I was still in Gwenn's house listening in. I learned from

Gwenn that there were other murders—out West—that had been pulled off with considerable skill, and apparently were not connected in any way with those in the East. I went to see a certain banker for information. His servant was in Denny's—or Diggs'—pay. He called Denny, and when I showed up at Denny's house later, Denny instantly made a clean breast of everything—or apparently he did.

"First of all though, he set a neat little trap, having a pretty good idea that I would show up at his house after leaving the banker. A shotgun was fixed so that it would go off when the door of his house was opened. But it had been very carefully aimed. Denny would naturally stoop a little to insert the key and, being small anyway, he had the shotgun arranged so the charge would go over his head and straight through mine.

"He tried to pin the blame on Frank Alden, because Alden was a borderline fugitive from justice. I really believed that Alden and Diggs were the same person until Denny started to show his teeth."

GLEASON SNAPPED handcuffs around Denny's wrists. He sent the man spinning into the arms of two detectives.

"Well, that's that," he said. "You busted up one sweet racket, Masked Detective, and…. Hey, where *is* the Masked Detective?"

No one seemed to know. They streamed out into the open. A car had just stopped at the scene and two people jumped out. One was Winnie Bligh and the other was Rex Parker. No one suspected that Rex Parker had simply popped into the waiting car, removed his disguise and mask and then met the police.

"Sarge!" Parker cried. "Are we too late? The Masked Detective told me to get down here. Winnie and I came as fast as we could!"

"Got a camera?" Gleason asked. Rex Parker darted back to the car and came back with one. Gleason shoved Denny forward.

"Help yourself to a picture of a killer, Rex," he invited. "I'll give you the whole story later. As usual, the Masked Detective blew out of here about the time you turned that corner up there and—as usual—he leaves the credit for this pinch to me. You can reach the guy, I'm told. Tell him thanks, for me."

Winnie's right hand found Parker's and held it tightly.

"And for me, too," she whispered. "Only I'll never forgive you. Why wasn't I in on this finish?"

Rex Parker led her back to their car.

"There's still time to make that Chinese place you like, for some chow mein before it closes up," he told her. "We'll deliver the picture of Denny in the toils of the law and fill up, huh?"

"After you write the story," Winnie said. "Rex, you're not going to take a chance on being beaten on your own story after—after all this, are you?"

He grinned down at her.

"Okay, Cap'n Bligh. Only the story was written hours ago. It just needs an ending tacked on. Let's go!"

www.ingramcontent.com/pod-product-compliance
Lightning Source LLC
Chambersburg PA
CBHW032235010726
47494CB00002B/510